**"The right man could handle
any woman,"
Phil thought. "Even Laura..."**

Her face glowed as she looked up at him.

Phil lightly placed the tips of his fingers at the hollow
of her throat, then let them glide down...

He lay upon his side now and breathed in her musky
woman scent while his lips followed where his fingers
had led.

They delayed climax for as long as they could, bringing each other to the edge and then drawing back.

Then neither one could hold out any longer, falling
into a raging sea of passion, drawn under to still and
quiet depths...

BITTER HARVEST

Morton J. Golding

A JOVE BOOK

BITTER HARVEST

A Jove Book/published by arrangement with
the author

PRINTING HISTORY
Jove edition/July 1983

ISBN: 0-515-05520-4

Jove books are published by The Berkley Publishing Group,
200 Madison Avenue, New York, N.Y. 10016. The words
"A JOVE BOOK" and the "J" with sunburst are trademarks
belonging to Jove Publications, Inc.

PRINTED IN THE UNITED STATES OF AMERICA

For H. M., who did not lose faith

And, as always, for Pat

Part One

1

Philip Aronson III woke up that morning with a blinding head-ache and a painful erection.

Though it was only a few months since Phil had turned seventeen, he was feeling like a sick old man. He was not even sure if he had the strength and coordination to climb out of bed and walk to the bathroom to urinate.

He knew what the problem was—all that booze he'd con-sumed at Lew Bocca's party. He nearly retched as he thought of the bootleg stuff and promised himself not to touch another drop of alcohol until Prohibition was repealed.

He breathed deeply to try and settle his stomach, then fo-cused his eyes on the stridently ticking clock which stood atop the dresser. Eleven-thirty. Eleven-thirty A.M. on the first of January, 1933.

So, Happy New Year.

But what exactly had happened at Lew's New Year's Eve party? Phil's memory of it was jumbled and confused. It was like what raw, unedited newsreel footage must be, he thought, with some portions standing out in sharp detail while others were so blurred and misted-over there was no making them out at all.

The most frustrating part had to do with Rita Crane. He had a clear recollection of taking the dark-haired, well-stacked Rita into the bedroom and giggling boozily with her over the con-dition of the bed which was already so crowded with writhing couples that there wasn't any room for them.

"To hell with the bed," said voluptuous Rita, and they tum-bled together to the soft bedroom carpet where Phil unbuttoned her blouse and pulled down her slip and bra. He was kissing her heavy breasts and reaching between her thighs when *some-thing* happened to interrupt them.

Something? What something? He had no idea. That was where the film went out of focus. He could not remember anything—not even if he'd managed to score.

He tried it from a different angle. Perhaps if he could re-collect what happened afterward, he could work backward. But it was no use. He knew he must have made it home and into his bed but he couldn't remember doing so.

Phil cursed—silently, but viciously. The situation stank.

One of the best things about sex, Phil believed, was the prestige it could bring him with other guys his age—the ones he knew in school and from the neighborhood. Most of *them* thought it was a big deal if they could touch a girl's breasts or place a hand on her crotch. Total victory was having a girl help them masturbate.

Lew Bocca, who was almost five years older than Phil, liked to sneer at those guys. He called them "punks" and "jerk-offs."

"The only thing they know to do with their cocks," he would say, "is to hold them in their hands."

Lew didn't feel that way about Phil—whom he had taken under his wing two years before after seeing him in a street fight with a far heavier and older rival. He thought of Phil as a younger version of himself—a hustler, a guy who liked to win.

Not scoring with Rita—or not being able to remember if he had or hadn't—was like letting Lew down!

If it weren't for Lew, he never would have had a chance with her. Rita was not a girl, but a woman; a divorced woman of twenty-one who had a real job and an apartment she shared with two other females. She would never have bothered with Phil if she hadn't met him at the party (he was the only one from high school there). And she would have had nothing to do with him if Lew had tipped her off to his actual age.

Lew was a great guy, Phil thought gratefully. A-number-one. All you had to do was look at him to see he had the world by the balls. Phil felt proud to be his buddy.

And Lew wanted to do even more for Phil than he had. He had spoken to his uncle—Al Bocca—and wanted Phil to work for their outfit as a runner on weekends, holidays, and after school.

As tempting as that offer was, Phil had not yet accepted it. If his parents found out there would be hell to pay. And he wasn't sure he could carry it off without their knowing.

Phil blamed his father for the problem. The old man never approved of his friendship with Lew. The Boccas were gangsters, he said, and should be locked up in jail. Whenever Phil tried to defend them, his father lost his temper all over again.

In a way, Phil supposed the Boccas really were gangsters. They were bookmakers (what Lew wanted him to do was to pick up and deliver gambling money), and they also handled bootleg liquor.

But so what? Every adult Phil knew had a bootlegger. And he had a strong feeling that most of them gambled. Certainly his own father did both. As Lew himself once pointed out, he and his Uncle Al performed necessary services.

His own old man was too much of a hypocrite to understand that!

The trouble was, his father had kept on ranting and raving until he'd convinced his mother, too. That was what stopped Phil from taking the risk and accepting the deal. If his father had gotten too nasty, he told himself, he could have moved out of the apartment—maybe moved in with Lew. . . .

But he didn't want to hurt his mother.

Christ, though. Getting a job with the Boccas and earning his own money would be a lot better than staying in school or working in his father's clothing store the way he had last summer.

Phil sighed. The thought of what his mother might say always managed to weaken him. If it weren't for that, he would have told the old man off long before this.

Phil swore softly as his need to urinate grew more imperative. Like it or not, he was going to have to leave his bed. He sat upright before he realized he was naked.

At least the room was warm. Perhaps too warm, in fact. Bob—his kid brother with whom he shared the bedroom—must have shut the windows when he got up. Steam heat hissed from the clanking radiators.

Phil forced his legs over the side of the bed and rose to his feet. Though stockily built and on the short side, he was well-muscled and had more body hair than most of his friends.

He walked to the closet and got into his pajamas, slippers, and bathrobe. He closed the front of the robe carefully in order to hide his stiff organ and left the bedroom.

When Phil had finished his bathroom rituals and entered the kitchen, he found his parents sitting at the table drinking coffee from their "everyday" cups.

The kitchen was glaringly white. The floor was of white linoleum tile, and the table and straight-back wooden chairs were painted the same color.

It had been his father's idea. He wanted to make it easy to tell if the maid who normally came in six days a week (she had Christmas Day and New Year's Day off) had properly cleaned the kitchen dirt and grease.

"Happy New Year," Phil said, smiling at his father and kissing his mother tenderly on the cheek. He was determined to sound and act cheerful today. Maybe even *be* cheerful.

"Happy New Year," his father grunted.

His mother said the same words, but sounded more as if she really meant them.

She was still beautiful, Phil thought, despite her years. She was a tall, striking, full-bosomed woman with shiny black hair, green eyes, and a soft olive complexion. She looked as though she might have Levantine blood in her; as a matter of fact, her paternal grandparents had come to America from the Middle East. They were descended from Sephardic Jews who had escaped to the more tolerant Levant, following the anti-Semitic Spanish massacres of 1391.

When Phil was a little boy, his mother had entertained him with family stories that her grandmother had told her. She'd made them sound like fairy tales, and he liked to pretend that there was something magical about her as well. He would make believe that she was a noble lady—a queen, perhaps—who was living in disguise. As soon as the time was right, she would take Phil and his baby brother (their sister had not yet been born) to her proper country in the sky.

It made sense to Phil who even then could sense the disparity between his parents. Why else would she have married his father—that short, overweight, forever complaining man whose own ancestors came from some unpronounceable place near Russia—if it were not to save his brother and himself.

Now, of course, he could no longer believe in such fairy tales. He was sure that his mother had wed for the simple reason that she'd been as poor as she was beautiful and Philip Aronson, Jr., was the only son of the founder and owner of the fine men's custom tailoring shop where her own father was then employed as a fitter.

But his father was speaking to him now. Complaining.

It seemed that Phil hadn't carried out his promise to phone

6

home from the party last night and wish his parents a happy New Year.

"I'm sorry, Papa," he said with a forced smile. "I must have forgotten."

"How could you forget to call your parents on New Year's Eve?" his father asked incredulously.

"I'm sorry," Phil said once more. "I know I said I'd call. I guess I just didn't think of it."

If Phil had hoped that his admission would take the wind out of his father's sails, he was sadly mistaken.

"That's your trouble," the older Aronson said. "You never think. It's a good thing I'm not like you. You know where we'd be then? Not in this fancy apartment, I can tell you. We'd be out on the street. Standing in bread lines. Selling apples..."

Phil's father now launched into an all too familiar litany of how he had saved his family from ruin by staying out of the stock market during the boom years of the late 1920's when most everyone else was getting in. It was one of his father's favorite examples of how important it was to always use your brains.

"My wealthy customers used to laugh at me," his father said as he had so many times before. "'Come on in, Aronson,' they used to say. 'Get your feet wet. The water's fine.'"

Mr. Aronson paused dramatically as he always did at this point.

"You know where they are now?" he asked rhetorically. "Bankrupt, many of them. Busted. Men from fine old families, customers of Aronson and Co. for twenty-five years and more, not able to pay for a shirt they ordered."

Mr. Aronson shook his head sadly.

"While me?" he went on. "I still have the business my father left me. My family is well fed. I can pay my bills. And why? Because I had the foresight to put my money in the bank instead of gambling in the stock market trying to make an easy buck."

He stopped talking to look hard at his son.

Phil attacked the plate of eggs his mother set before him. He knew what his father wanted now—for him to say that he understood the lesson and would profit by it. He was concentrating on the eggs to avoid saying that.

It wasn't that he disagreed with his father's theory about using his brains. He agreed very much, in fact, and had to give the old man credit for having been shrewd when it counted.

7

He didn't like being forced to say so, however. It was too much like bowing down and kissing ass.

"So, do you understand how important it is to *think?*" Phil's father said at last.

"Yes, Papa."

The elder Aronson felt frustrated. It was nothing he could put his finger on, but his son was not reacting—never seemed to react— the way he was supposed to. What was wrong with him?

Mr. Aronson decided to assert himself with what he knew would be a sore subject.

"One way for a boy to use his brains," he said as Phil continued to eat, "is to choose the right friends for himself. You should select the sort of friends today who can be of use to you later on. Am I right?"

"Yes," Phil said. He nodded agreeably—even though he knew what was coming next.

"That Lew Bocca," said his father right on schedule. "The one whose party you went to last night. You think *he's* the sort of friend who will do you good in the future?"

"I think so, Papa."

"You think so?" Mr. Aronson shook his head in disgust. "That's because you're not using your brains. How could he be good for you? He's mixed up with gangsters. I've heard too many things about him and that uncle of his. And wasn't his father killed in some gang war?"

"It was an accident," Phil protested. "The taxi he was riding in was hit by a truck."

"So?" Phil's father smiled knowingly. "Who arranged for that truck to hit the taxi?"

Phil was silent.

"And his uncle," Mr. Aronson pressed. "He's a bootleg-ger . . . a gambler."

Phil knew that he had to change the subject and grabbed wildly at the first idea that entered his mind:

"Lew told me they might drop in at the store."

"What? . . . They? . . ."

"Last night. At the party. Lew Bocca said that he and his uncle might come into the store and see about having some suits made."

"Isn't that wonderful, darling," Phil's mother interjected. She was clearly upset at the way the conversation was going.

"We'll see," her husband grunted. "First let them come to the store and we'll see how wonderful."

"But if they do come," Phil said slyly, "my knowing Lew would do us good."

"We'll see," his father repeated. He gave his son a look of baffled anger, then stood up from the table and announced that he was going into the bedroom to rest.

His wife stared after him for a moment or two before turning to her son.

"You shouldn't aggravate your father like that. He's a good man. We're lucky to have him."

Phil tried not to show that he was bothered by her remark, but it spoiled his small victory. Why did his mother always have to take the old man's side? Didn't she realize how much he—Phil—loved her?

"When your grandfather died," she went on, "all the workers were worried about the store. What would happen to it? they wondered. But your father took hold and made it bigger and better than ever.

"They all said what a good job he did. My parents, too, who never really approved of your father even while they were urging me to marry him. They were socialists, you know, as well as atheists. But I told you all that—how they broke my grandmother's heart. Even *they* had to admit what a fine job your papa did.

"'Sophie,' I remember my father saying before he died, 'if any boss could be called good, then your Philip is such a boss!'"

"Yes, Mama," Phil responded. He had heard this story before, too.

"And later—when this awful Depression began—I didn't know what would happen to us. But thanks to your father, we've been saved from the worst of it.

"And the only thing he wants is for his children to be successful and happy. You, your sister, your brother. You're the ones he plans and schemes for."

"I know, Mama." Phil smiled. He didn't want to argue with her.

"And there's something else, darling. I didn't want to say anything before, but I'm not so happy about your choice of friends, myself."

Phil was stung. This was something he hadn't expected.

"You mean Lew? Just because his uncle?..."

9

"It's not just his uncle. There's something about him that . . . I don't know. . . . Anyway, he's too old for you."

"He's only a few years older than I am," Phil protested.

"At your age, a few years is a long time. He's a man already. I don't know what he sees in you, unless . . ."

She broke off, then added: "Tell me, darling: Is he trying to involve you in something illegal? Use you in some way?"

"Mama! . . . Please. You're getting as bad as Papa."

"Am I?" She shrugged with exaggerated contriteness. "We can't help it. That's the way parents are. We worry about our babies."

Phil had to laugh. He stood up and kissed her on the forehead.

"I wish you wouldn't upset yourself," he said. "I'll be all right. Really."

His mother smiled and kissed him back.

Phil went into his bedroom and began to dress.

The remarks about Lew had upset him. He couldn't be angry at his mother, of course. She was a woman and couldn't be expected to understand about guys. But he *was* mad at his father. Why couldn't the old man stay out of his affairs and just leave him alone?

He had evened the score a bit, though, when he'd told his father that Lew was going to drop into the store and bring his Uncle Al.

Phil chuckled at the memory. It would really be something if Lew would really do that. He would love to see his father's face if the two Boccas really did come into the store and start examining the merchandise. The old man would have to eat crow then. And he—Phil—would be a hero.

Maybe he should speak to Lew about it.

Phil pulled a heavy sweater over his head, ran a comb through his hair one final time, and put on an extra dab of brilliantine. He was looking pretty sharp, he thought. A real dude.

When his mother saw him, though, she worried if he would be warm enough. "Shouldn't you have on a jacket, too?"

"It's not that cold out."

"I don't know . . . I heard the weather report on the radio. The man said it was in the teens."

Phil kissed his mother reassuringly and turned toward the front door. He wanted to leave the apartment before his father came out again to take up his time with more nagging.

He was starting to reach for the knob when the door swung open and a small, dark-haired girl ran into the foyer. Her head was held low and if Phil hadn't caught her firmly by her shoulders, she would have butted him in the stomach.

She tried to twist out of his grip. "Le' me go, you big . . . you're hurting me!"

"So take it easy, then. Who do you think you are? Tuffy Leemans? Maybe you should try out for the New York Giants football team."

"Stop teasing your sister," Sophie Aronson said automatically. Then she took a closer look at her nine-year-old daughter and gasped.

"Naomi . . . what happened to your face? It's all bruised. And your skirt is torn!"

Phil noticed the beginnings of a mouse under his sister's left eye. He snorted. "Nommie's been fighting again," he said with a laugh. He thought his sister was funny as hell—especially when she grew all serious and angry the way she was now. That was when he most loved to tease her. The trouble was she was so damned spoiled she couldn't take it.

But Sophie was talking sadly to her now.

"Naomi," she said. "Your language. And fighting. I don't know what I'm going to do with you."

"But he started it, Mama. It was Tommy Benson and he called me a bad name."

"Tommy? You mean you fought with a boy?" Sophie's eyes widened in shock.

"Better watch out, Nommie." Phil grinned. "You're going to get hurt."

"Hurt? Phooey. I chased him home with a bloody nose. And I told you not to call me Nommie, you! . . ."

"Stop shrieking!" Sophie cried in exasperation. "You're giving me a headache."

The girl's face was contorted with rage. Her eyes—the same green eyes as her mother's—blazed.

Phil wondered why she was so angry. She couldn't take any teasing at all. If she weren't so damned spoiled, she'd know that he was only fooling. That he really loved her.

Mr. Aronson stormed into the room.

"What's going on here?" he demanded as he pulled his bathrobe snugly about him. "Can't a man have some peace and quiet in his own home?"

11

"It's him!" Naomi said, pointing a finger at Phil and speaking up before either of the others had a chance to. "He's been picking on me!"

"What are you doing that for?" Mr. Aronson snarled.

"I'm not," said Phil. But the statement sounded weak even to himself.

He felt his stomach twist as he held in his anger. Why was his father always jumping on him? He'd only been teasing the little brat. Just kidding around with her.

"Please, Philip," Sophie said, distracting her husband's attention from her son. "I want to speak to you about Naomi. She's been fighting again. And this time with a boy."

"With a boy?" the elder Aronson repeated.

He gazed down at his youngest child, who met his glance without fear. She looked like her mother—not only the same eyes but the same skintone, the same hair. But her personality—her fierce temper and mercurial moods—were pure Aronson.

Phil, who was studying both of them, grew more outraged as he realized his father was trying to hide a smile. She was going to get away with it, he thought.

"Well, Sophie," he heard his father temporize, "she's still very young."

But Phil's mother remained firm: "Not that young. She's far too old to keep behaving like a tomboy."

"You're right darling," Mr. Aronson said.

He turned to his daughter. "You heard your mother?"

"Yes, Papa."

"And from now on, you'll try to act like a well-brought-up young lady who'll make me proud of her."

"Yes, Papa. I truly will. I promise."

"So, Sophie," he said to his wife. "She promises to do better."

"I hope she will," Mrs. Aronson said softly.

It was wrong, Phil thought resentfully. Why should she get away with this? Not be punished at all?

Not only wasn't it fair (he and Bob had always been punished for fighting when they were nine—and they were boys and supposed to fight!), but it made Naomi think she could get away with anything—that she could bloody a boy's nose one minute, then bat her eyes like a cute little girl in order to get out of trouble. There were rules, damn it! And Naomi was going to get herself in trouble if she kept breaking them.

If he had a daughter some day, he thought vengefully, she would be brought up right!

"I'm going outside," he announced.

"So," said his father. "Goodbye."

"You're sure you'll be warm?" his mother asked.

"Absolutely, Mama."

Out of the corner of his eye, he could see Naomi surreptitiously sticking out her tongue at him. He saw responding to it as beneath his dignity.

2

John, the uniformed elevator man, greeted Phil by name as he stepped into the dark, wood-paneled interior of the metal cage.

"I just brought your sister up a little while ago," John went on. "That kid is really something, you know."

Phil grunted. He was in no mood to discuss his kid sister. She was a brat, he thought, and she'd stay a brat until his old man decided to put his foot down with her. The trouble was that she had a great knack for getting around people.

John shut the outer door, then pulled the inside gate shut with a clatter.

"You must be proud of her," he said as he threw the control lever to the down position. "There're a lot of boys her age hang around this building. But that little Naomi, she's tougher'n any of them."

"Yeah," said Phil.

He left the elevator as soon as John opened the doors and strode through the ornately furnished lobby to the outer vestibule. Sam, the doorman, was standing at his accustomed station just inside the building entrance.

He was wearing his heavy winter overcoat of deep maroon with gold epaulets and braid. The four rows of brass buttons down the front of the coat were highly polished—so much so that they looked as if they could shine in the dark. Sam was proud of his uniform, which was much more gaudily elaborate than the one John had to wear, and he kept it looking immaculate.

As Phil entered the vestibule, Sam wished him a good afternoon and nodded his head.

The greeting was a compromise. Sam had a ritualized set of gestures and salutations with which he greeted people according to age and position. If Phil had been a few years older, Sam would have touched the visor of his cap and called him sir. A few years before, Sam had saluted him by pretending to throw a punch to his head.

"I just saw your sister," Sam said now. "She's a great kid."

"Yeah, I guess she is. But have you seen any of the guys around?"

"None of your gang, if that's what you mean. Just a few of the younger kids."

"Yeah . . . well. Maybe I'll find someone down by the Drive. Be seeing you, Sam."

It was cold out despite the nearly cloudless sky. As Phil crossed West End Avenue and approached Riverside Drive, it began to feel colder still. He was almost sorry that he hadn't taken his mother's advice and dressed warmer.

As he reached the corner, three green double-decker buses belonging to the Fifth Avenue Coach Company rumbled by along the Drive. The scene reminded him of the old New York joke:

Question: "Why are buses like wolves?"

Answer: "Because they like to travel in packs."

Only these buses looked more like a pack of ungainly elephants.

Phil ran across the road without waiting for the light to change and walked along the narrow strip of parkland between Riverside Drive and the railway tracks of the New York Central. He had read in his favorite tabloid, the *Daily Mirror*, that Parks Commissioner Robert Moses planned to cover over those tracks, extend the park to the northern tip of Manhattan and build a scenic highway (partly on landfill) which would join up with the West Side Highway at Seventy-second Street.

Although every New York newspaper had endorsed the plan, Moses was having a rough time obtaining the money he would need to carry it out. In the meantime, there was enough open space near Phil's block to have a game of touch football.

Which was happening now.

The players were all younger boys, and Phil was about to turn away when he realized that his brother Bob was among them.

Phil edged closer and saw Bob jump into the air in order to grab a poorly thrown pass. As he continued to watch, Bob made a sliding, twisting run through the opposing team.

Phil felt like cheering. He was proud of Bob who, though not as strong and muscular as he himself had been at fourteen, was quicker and more graceful.

Bob came to a halt, laughed, and turned around. When he noticed Phil, he handed the ball to a friend and ran over.

"Hey," he said. "What's up?"

"Hey, kiddo. That was one hell of a catch you made. And a damn good run, too."

Bob flushed with pleasure. "It wasn't that much."

"Hell it wasn't." Phil punched his brother lightly on the arm.

"Did you see Naomi yet?" Bob asked, turning the discussion away from himself.

"Yeah."

"Did she tell you how she gave that cruddy Benson kid a bloody nose?"

"Yeah, how do you know about it?"

"I saw the whole thing. It happened a couple of blocks away from here. The Benson kid was calling her names."

"What sort of names?" Phil asked sharply. Naomi was his sister, after all.

"I don't know. Nothing rough, though. Just kid stuff. But when he wouldn't let up, Naomi started punching."

"Why didn't you stop it?"

"I would've," Bob said with a grin, "if she hadn't been winning."

"Christ." Phil looked disgusted. "You're as bad as the old man. Neither one of you gives a damn if she acts like a girl or not!"

"That—that's not true," Bob stammered. It always upset him to argue with his older brother. Even when he knew that he—Bob—was in the right.

"And anyway," Bob added. "What's the big deal? She's only nine years old. Some boy tried to—to bully her, and she punched him out. What's wrong with that, for crap's sake? It's what you used to tell me to do."

"Because you're a boy," Phil drawled with exaggerated

15

patience. "Can't you tell the difference yet between a guy and a dame?"

"Shit, Phil..."

"Dames don't go around punching guys. Not unless they want to take a chance on getting hurt bad."

"But—but Naomi's not a dame yet. She's still a little kid."

"But she's going to be a dame, ain't she? So she's got to start learning to act like one. Like when I was a little kid, I had to learn to fight. So I could take care of myself the way I can today. Know what I mean?"

"Yeah..."

"Same with you, right?"

"Sure, but—"

"So Nommie's got to learn how to take care of herself the way a dame does!"

"What—what way is that?" Bob demanded.

"Jesus. I don't know. But what she *shouldn't* have done was to get into a goddamn fight!"

"Would you have wanted her to run off crying to you or me?"

"That would've been better than what she did."

"Even though she didn't need our help? She—she handled the whole thing pretty good by herself."

"Shit." Phil shook his head angrily. "You haven't heard a fucking work I've said. Well, let me tell you this: If little Nommie turns into a goddamn tramp in a few more years, you'll know why!"

"Because she won a fistfight?" Bob asked, disbelievingly. "When she was nine years old?"

"Because she's so fucking spoiled she thinks she can do what she wants!" Phil hissed. *"I'm* the only one in the family who doesn't spoil her. And for that she hates me and says I pick on her."

Bob regarded his brother for a moment or two, then lowered his eyes. "I don't think she really hates you."

"No? Well, she sure doesn't like me. The one she loves is the old man. That's because he spoils her worse than all the rest of you put together!"

"Yeah, well..." Bob shrugged. "Even if he does, he's the boss."

"Maybe you're right," Phil said after he had swallowed back a bitter retort. "Anyway, I guess you want to get back to your game."

Phil watched the game for a while longer and saw his brother make another fine run.

Bob was quite a kid, he thought. Quite an athlete. If he wanted to—and decided to work seriously at it—he could probably make the first-string football team of his high school in a couple of years.

Except that Bob wouldn't want to. With the exception of boxing—which was his favorite—he wasn't that involved with any sport. And even boxing wasn't as important to him as his books and his studies.

They were very different, Phil and Bob Aronson. So different, in fact, that people were often surprised that they got along so well.

But Bob looked up to his brother and learned the ways of the street from him. To him, at least, Phil was a very special person.

It was perhaps the fact that his brother admired him which enabled Phil in turn to admire the more scholarly Bob. He enjoyed the fact that Bob always came home with top grades in school. And when his father taunted him for doing poorly himself, Phil would grow angry at his father rather than jealous of Bob.

Phil waved goodbye to his brother and crossed Riverside Drive once more. He was still looking for someone of his own crowd to kill time with.

He had walked another block when he heard his name being called. It was Harry Engels, a tall, sandy-haired youth who had been in Phil's high-school class until fairly recently when he had to leave school to work in his father's stationery store.

Harry and Phil were not exactly friends. Phil thought of Harry as a boring sap who liked to whine a lot. He usually avoided him if he could.

On the other hand, they were certainly not enemies. And since Phil was in the mood for company, he gave Harry a friendly smile and asked him how he was doing.

"Pretty good," Harry replied. "The old man didn't open up the store today, so I got to take off."

"Great," Phil told him.

"Yeah. On most Sundays, the old fart makes me keep working. He says we close down on Saturdays and that's enough. But since today's not only Sunday, but New Year's Day as well, he decided to give us both a break. Next week, though, it'll be back to normal."

"Stop complaining," Phil said. "At least you're making some dough. I'm still stuck in school."

"Yeah, I'm making some dough," Harry shot back bitterly. "The only thing is, my father makes me give back most of it to pay for my room and board. How's that for bullshit?"

"Maybe he can't afford to keep you," Phil suggested.

"That's what he says. Blames it all on the frigging Depression. But I think he's just cheap."

Phil shrugged. "What did you do last night?" he asked. "Were you at a party?"

"Yeah," Harry said. "I went to Manny Eisler's."

"Did you take anyone?"

"Sue Ann Langer. Know her?"

"A tall blond? With a cute butt?"

"That's the girl." Harry smirked.

"I've seen her around at school," Phil said. "But tell me— was it any good?"

"Was what any good?" Harry winked lasciviously. "The party? Or Sue Ann?"

"Sue Ann, of course."

"Besmirching a lady's name, eh?" Harry growled in comic outrage. He aimed a playful left to Phil's stomach and a right to his jaw.

Phil blocked the punches and feinted a kick to Harry's crotch.

"Hey, buddy, don't do that," Harry said, clutching himself in mock horror. "Sue Ann'd never forgive you."

"Oh, yeah?" Phil grinned. "Maybe she'd thank me."

"Not Sue Ann! She *loves* what I got."

Phil decided to be charitable and keep his doubts to himself.

"Do you know if the Greek's is open today?" he asked Harry.

"Yeah. At least they told me yesterday they'd be open."

"As long as there's nothing doing around here then, I think I'll walk up to Broadway and have an egg cream. Want to come along?"

Harry said he would and the two started walking along a side street.

"What did *you* do last night?" Harry asked. "I thought maybe you'd be at Manny's."

"Naw. I was at Lew Bocca's place."

"No kidding." Harry was clearly impressed. "What's Bocca like? I mean really."

"What's he like? He's a real great guy."

Harry nodded seriously and waited for details. When none came, he gave into temptation and pressed: "He knows a lot of gangsters, doesn't he?"

Phil saw quickly that Harry realized he was out of line. He decided to try staring him down without speaking at all, and was only mildly surprised at how well it worked.

It all had to do with power, Phil thought. In the hierarchy of neighborhood males, Phil's toughness and street smarts placed him on a higher level than the softer Harry. But Lew, with his aura of real violence and danger, was higher still. And now that Phil was known to be Lew's friend, he shared somewhat in that aura.

"I—I'm sorry," Harry was saying. "I know I shouldn't ask that kind of . . ."

"Forget it," Phil said flatly.

"Ah . . . who did you take to Bocca's?" Harry asked, trying to start Phil thinking of other matters.

"I didn't take anyone. I met someone there."

"Uh . . . who?"

"An older dame. Really built. You wouldn't know her."

And with that statement, Phil scored a second victory over Harry. Not only had he been a guest at Lew Bocca's New Year's Eve party, he had picked up a woman there. That did place him on a hero's pedestal.

The only thing that Phil regretted was that his triumph had come so cheaply. It would have felt much better if he'd had to struggle for it.

3

The Greek's was a small, undistinguished shop on Broadway in the low Eighties which specialized in ice cream, sodas, sandwiches, and coffee. The store's owner, John Klagos, had christened it the Golden Eagle Restaurant and Ice Cream Emporium. To its neighborhood customers it was known simply as "the Greek's."

As Phil and Harry sipped their egg creams at the counter, Harry mentioned that there was a good movie at the local RKO.

Phil didn't want to know what the film was. He already knew that he didn't want to see it. Or at least not with Harry, who was already beginning to get on his nerves.

Harry was really trying to move in on him, he thought resentfully. The guy was not just a meathead but a leech as well. He should have run like hell when he heard Harry call his name.

And yet, he realized in a burst of self-honesty, he had welcomed Harry's company before in order to have someone he could impress. Was it fair to turn on him because he was so damned impressed that he was acting like an ass-kisser?

Fair, schmair, Phil thought to himself. Harry was still getting on his nerves.

He deliberately ignored him, swiveling slightly on his stool in order to look out of the store's front window.

Outside, the wide and semi-fashionable avenue which was Broadway between Columbus Circle and Harlem was filling up with holiday life. Young married couples paraded in their winter finery, wearing what new clothes they had and hoping no one would notice a too shiny overcoat or a worn muff or a pair of scuffed shoes. Little girls not yet involved with fashion played hopscotch in the winter sun and scooted out of the way of baby carriages. Little boys flexed undeveloped muscles and tried to wrestle other little boys to the sidewalk. Elderly folk threaded their way through the bustling throng in order to head for the well-weathered benches which the city had placed on the paved tongues of Broadway's grassy center islands.

As Phil looked on, a streetcar wobbled and clanked its way along a track that had been embedded in the asphalt roadway. The car braked at the trolley stop and several people got off. One of them was Rita Crane—the girl he had met at Lew's New Year's party.

He dropped some coins on the counter and told Harry that he had to leave. There was someone outside he wanted to see.

"Uh . . . who?" asked Harry.

Phil winked at him, slid off the stool, and ran out the front door shouting Rita's name.

She was still at the streetcar stop, waiting for the light to change. She waved at Phil, then crossed over to join him at the corner.

"What are you doing here?" she asked, laughing.

"Waiting for you to show up."

Rita giggled. "Fool."

Phil tucked her arm under his. "That was some fandango last night," he said, wondering if he was going to find out what had happened between them.

"Mmnnn. Didn't you just love it?"

Rita's voice was as childlike as those of the little girls who were playing near them on the street. But there was nothing childlike about the body his arm was pressing against.

"Yeah," he said. "The party was great."

"And isn't this a lovely day."

"It sure is," Phil told her. He would have liked to return to the subject of last night, but didn't know how to go about it.

"Do you live near here?" he asked.

"On Columbus Avenue."

"I'll walk you home."

They started walking uptown, then turned east along a side street.

Still trying to make conversation, Phil asked Rita where she had been today.

"To see my ex-mother-in-law. She's in the hospital."

"Your ex-mother-in-law?" Phil echoed in surprise.

Rita giggled squeakily. "Isn't it a scream? No one can believe we're on such good terms. But she was always very sweet to me. It was Ray who was the s.o.b."

"Ray's your husband?"

"My former husband," Rita said emphatically.

"Sorry," Phil said. "But what'd he do that was so bad? I know it's none of my business, but—"

"That's all right. I don't mind talking about it. Not any more, that is."

She paused for a moment and then went on: "I guess it was the Crash that did it. Everything was fine before that. He worked on Wall Street and I had my job in the department store—you know, behind a counter. But then Wall Street went blooey and Ray lost his job while I kept working.

"I guess he got jealous of me—know what I mean? The longer he stayed out of work, the nastier his temper got. It was awful. He even began hitting me."

"That's terrible," Phil said. "I can't imagine anyone doing a thing like that."

He was lying of course. He could imagine it quite easily. Though he did feel that any guy who slapped his girl around was pretty much of an asshole. Especially if he didn't have a better reason than Ray seemed to have.

But Rita was still speaking: "One night it was worse than ever. He really hurt me bad that night. Bruised me . . ."

"That was when you left him?"

"The next day. I just didn't come home from work. I left my clothes there and everything. I even had to buy a new toothbrush until it was safe to go get my things."

"He didn't try to make you stay?"

"I think he would've. But his mother was with me. She was on my side, see."

Phil wondered if his own mother would ever take a girl's side against him. He didn't think so. No matter what he had done.

"No wonder you went to visit her in the hospital," he said.

"She's real sweet. My own folks don't even know I exist."

"Yeah," Phil said vaguely. "Parents are weird sometimes."

They had reached Columbus Avenue now and were crossing under the elevated railway structure that kept it in eternal shadow. A train rumbled over their heads and Phil ducked involuntarily.

Rita noticed. "Loud, isn't it," she said with a smile.

"Yeah," Phil grunted. He was glad he didn't live on Columbus. He had read somewhere that the "el" used lighter trains than did the subway and ran them at slower speeds. But even so, their noise and vibration made them rough to live next to.

"I understand they may tear the el down in a few years," he said. "Once they get that subway all dug on Central Park West."

"Yeah?" Rita sounded skeptical. "Where'd you hear that?"

"I don't know. Some guy mentioned it." It was actually his father.

"Well, I'll believe that when I see it," Rita told him.

They paused then as Rita indicated the entrance to her tenement building.

Phil surveyed the doorway, which was sandwiched between a shabby hardware store and an empty establishment with a TO LET sign tacked to its boarded-up window. On the sidewalk directly under the window, an unshaven derelict was fast asleep

22

with a horse blanket wrapped around his body.

"I wonder about the nag he stole that thing from," Phil said, pointing to the blanket. "He must be freezing his rear off, huh?"

Rita first giggled, then made a face. "There are always one or two winos sleeping there. It's really disgusting."

"Yeah," said Phil. "But listen—why don't I come up to your place for a few minutes. We can talk more there."

Rita frowned. "Well . . . I don't know. Both my roommates are away and I don't want you to get the wrong impression. I mean, lots of guys think when a girl's been divorced, it's anything goes."

"Gosh, Rita, I don't think anything like that."

"Don't you?" She studied him for a moment. "Well, maybe you don't. You *were* sweet last night when I said I didn't want to go any further. Some fellows would've gotten mad, but you understood how I felt."

So that's what had happened last night: Nothing! He had understood how she felt.

Phil was briefly furious at himself. Then he grinned mentally. If having been sweet last night would get him into Rita's place today, it had been worth it.

"What do you say?" he asked, allowing the grin to show. "Are you going to trust me to come up?"

"Well . . . for just a few minutes, then."

Phil followed the girl into a dingy hallway and up several flights of stairs which became successively more ill-lit and grungier.

"A great place for a murder," he remarked as he followed Rita up the third dreary flight.

Rita halted briefly to catch her breath.

"That's what Kay likes to say," she puffed.

"Kay?"

"One of my . . . roommates. She likes to try and scare me."

"What does Kay think about climbing stairs?" he asked as Rita started going up again.

"That it's . . . good for the figure. Me, I'm always pooped . . . when I get to the top."

They started to climb still another flight and Phil realized they were going to the fifth and final floor of the old building.

Rita unlocked a door at the end of this last hallway and gestured for Phil to enter.

The room he entered was so bright that he had to blink his

eyes. Sunlight was streaming through a skylight, and when Rita raised the frayed window shades, the living room was bathed in even more light.

He took off his sweater while she hung up her gray cloth coat and put away her deep-crowned blue hat. He tried to keep his "sweet" image and not stare too obviously at her. But the way her breasts stood out under her tight cotton blouse made that difficult.

"Isn't it bright and cheery in here?" Rita said. "And we're high enough above the el so that the noise isn't so impossible."

As Phil nodded politely, a train rumbled by under the window. It was still pretty bad, he thought.

"Why don't you sit down?" Rita said, smoothing the cover which had been arranged over the sofa.

"Thanks."

He assumed that underneath the cover the sofa's cushions were as worn as the rug and the single armchair. The room was clean, however, and an effort had been made to keep it neat.

"Would you like a drink?" Rita asked. "Lew brought me the bottle. He said it's the real stuff—made in Canada."

"That would be great," Phil said, dismissing the New Year's resolution he had made in bed that morning.

Rita left the room briefly and returned with a bottle. She got a pair of glasses from the kitchen, and poured some amber liquid into them.

"What do you want in it?" Rita asked.

"Nothing," Phil replied bravely.

"Me too," Rita giggled.

Phil took a sip. It was raw and fiery—much more likely to have been made in some secret bootlegger's still in the U.S. than openly in Canada.

"Good," he gasped as he tried to keep from screwing up his face.

Rita was spluttering also: "Yes . . . it is."

They set their glasses down.

"What sort of work do you do for Lew?" Rita asked.

It took Phil a moment to digest the question. When he did, he promptly forgave Lew for passing the rotgut whiskey to Rita. He must also have conned the girl with a story that Phil was working for him instead of going to high school. He wondered how old Lew had said he was.

"I do lots of things for Lew," he said, knowing that he must not give the game away now.

"Like what?"

"Maybe you'd better ask him," Phil said.

Rita went on the defensive: "Oh . . . I—I don't want you to think I'm being nosy."

"Forget it," Phil said.

He grinned amiably and raised his glass in a toast. It was a gesture he had once seen William Powell make in a film.

He took another sip—a smaller one this time—and was able to handle it a bit better than he had the first.

He watched Rita surreptitiously as she also took a second drink. Hers, he was pleased to see, was at least as large as her first.

"Here's to us," Phil said.

He placed an arm about Rita's shoulder and allowed his hand to drop until it brushed lightly against her full bosom. His hand moved gently until it was cupping her through her blouse and slip and bra. She let the hand stay where it was for several seconds before bringing her own hand up to push it away.

"Hey there," she said pertly. "And I thought I could trust you."

"You can," Phil said, "a little. Would you really want a guy you could trust a lot?"

"Oh, you," Rita giggled. She took another sip of her drink.

Phil kissed her as soon as she lowered her glass. Her lips were still half parted and his tongue slipped between them to explore her mouth.

"Rat," Rita sighed when Phil moved back again. But there was very little real accusation in her voice. She was breathing heavily now and her face was flushed.

"When will your roommates be back?" Phil asked.

"Roo—roommates?" Rita stammered, as though she needed to make an effort to recall what the word meant. "Sometime tonight . . . late, I think. They went to Albany. One of them has folks there. She asked me to come too, but I had to stay."

"Three cheers for your ex-mother-in-law," Phil said.

Rita giggled again and Phil kissed her more vehemently than he had before. Her mouth opened of its own accord and their tongues met. He pressed his chest against hers until she sank back under him on the couch.

25

She squirmed suddenly. "You're hurting me!"

"Sorry." Phil cradled her head in his hands and kissed her gently over her face and forehead. He let her head rest against his shoulder and began to unbutton her white cotton blouse.

"Don't rip anything," she said as he reached inside.

"I won't," Phil heard himself say. He had one hand under her skirt while the other was inside the top of her slip where it was trying to shoehorn its way between breast and brassiere.

"Ow, that hurts," Rita complained in a harsh change of mood. "And you *are* going to tear my clothes."

Phil tried not to show his annoyance. He was feeling the softness of her breast now, and the softness of her thighs. He wanted her to stop complaining and cooperate.

"Please," Rita said sharply, and tried to pull away.

Phil cursed inwardly and withdrew his hands. "Sorry. . . . Let's go to your bedroom."

"No, I don't think . . ."

"Come on," Phil said. He rose to his feet and lifted her up with him. He kissed her again and pulled her to him. His erection was large and throbbing against her belly. "It'll be nicer there."

"I don't know. . . . I have to think . . ."

But though Rita struggled to get away, Phil was sure her heart was not in the fight. He held her tightly until he felt her body relax and her thigh press meaningfully into his crotch.

"All right." She sighed in surrender. "But you really are a rat."

She brought him into the smaller of the two bedrooms. The larger, she explained was shared by her apartment-mates. She herself preferred privacy to space.

"It's a nice room," Phil said vaguely.

"Is it?" Rita's grin was sharp and challenging. It seemed odd to Phil, but now that she had taken him into the bedroom there was something stronger and more definite about her. It was as if the very intimacy of where they were had given her more confidence and strength, a certain toughness even.

"I bet if you closed your eyes," she said, "you couldn't tell me what the room looks like. Go ahead. I dare you: close your eyes and describe it."

"You win," Phil said uneasily. "I could describe you, though. I mean, I've only got eyes for you."

"Liar." The girl laughed happily. "You don't have eyes for

me at all. What you have for me is standing up below your belt."

Phil wasn't used to that sort of language from a girl. He was as much taken aback by it as he was titillated. It was almost as though she were challenging him to take on the aggressive masculine role.

"And what do you have for me?" he countered.

"If you haven't learned that by now, big boy, it's too late for me to teach you."

"Don't worry your sweet head about that," Phil said. He sat next to her on the bed and began to slide his hand along her smooth inner thigh. "I know damn well what you have."

"Do you?" Her tiny, high-pitched voice was even higher and smaller now. "What?"

He touched the cotton crotch of her panties, then went under the crotch in order to reach her pudenda.

"Right there," he said. "The gates of Paradise . . ."

"Bastard," she breathed. Then, as his fingers continued to manipulate her: "My God, that feels good . . ."

She reached for the great bulge at the front of Phil's trousers. "This feels like it's gonna explode."

"Keep holding it like that . . . it just might."

Rita let go of him and giggled dreamily. "Let's get rid of all these dumb clothes."

Phil released her and got off the bed, turning his back to undress. He was not sure why he turned his back—perhaps because the act of undressing was so clumsy and strangely vulnerable.

He had removed his shirt and undershirt when he cursed suddenly and stopped.

"What's wrong?" Rita asked.

"I forgot to bring . . . you know . . . protection."

"Protection? Oh, you mean a rubber."

"Yeah."

"It doesn't matter. I have a diaphragm."

Phil stepped out of his trousers and turned to glance at her. She was really something. He'd never known a girl who had her own diaphragm before. That was the great thing, he thought smugly, about going with a woman who used to be married.

Rita had removed her slip and was sitting on the bed to unhook her stockings from her garter-belt. She smiled at Phil, enjoying his presence. "Undo my bra, will you, honey?"

27

"Sure."

Phil knelt behind her, still wearing his underwear. He undid the bra clasps and slipped the straps over her shoulders. He reached around to give her heavy breasts a gentle squeeze. They felt soft in his hands.

"Careful . . . don't hurt me."

"I won't," Phil said, giving her breasts another squeeze.

He dropped his undershorts, slid his hand to her belly to grip her crotch and pressed himself triumphantly against her rear.

"My God you feel strong," the girl said.

And he was strong. He knew it and felt it in every part of him. He was the master. . . .

He used his finger again and felt the girl squirm with pleasure.

"Get my diaphragm," she moaned. "From that drawer . . ."

Though resenting the interruption, Phil did what he was asked. On the way back to the bed he saw the admiring way she kept staring at his nude body and was no longer resentful.

Rita removed the diaphragm from its case and inserted it with quick, practiced motions.

He felt a twinge of jealousy as he wondered how many other men had seen those motions.

He cut the thought off. He was here now!

"Am I your girl from now on?" Rita was asking.

"Sure, baby."

He parted Rita's thighs and knelt between them. Moist and undefended, she was no longer a challenge.

He entered her and thrust deeply. His penis was a weapon which gave him dominion over her: the ultimate weapon in the war between men and women.

Rita had been almost too easy to conquer, though. Other women could be more difficult. Yet even now—even while mounting furiously towards climax with Rita—he was looking forward to meeting those others and conquering them as well.

Nor would his challenge be confined to sex, he thought, as the power of sex engulfed him. He would challenge anyone— male or female—on any grounds!

He was a winner: A driving, pounding, ever thrusting winner.

Now and always, a winner!

Now! . . .

4

Young Phil Aronson—caught up in his visions of sex and power—could not have cared less about the bank in which his father kept his money. It was enough that the old man did have money in the bank, and that some day he—Phil was sure— would have more.

If Mr. Aronson had bothered to learn about his son's attitude, he would have considered it one more proof that Phil was not a serious person. For there was no more serious choice a man could make in these days of the Great Depression than the selection of a bank. The choice of the wrong one could mean utter financial ruin when—as all too often happened— it had to shut its doors for good and did not have the money to repay its depositors.

This was happening at a staggering rate. In the comparatively short period of time since the stock market crash of 1929, more than one-fourth of all the banks in the country had collapsed. And neither size nor location was any guarantee against failure. This was shown in 1930, when one of the largest and most important banks in New York City went into bankruptcy.

The Bank of the United States boasted more than four hundred thousand depositors and had $200 million in assets. Its very size added to the illusion of safety, and its list of stockholders included a wide spectrum of cautious and conservative investors.

No one has ever counted the number of people who lost all or part of their money when The Bank of the United States went under. But among them were a fair proportion of widows whose late husbands had forced them to swear never to sell their shares in what was considered to be one of the safest stocks in the nation.

Phil's father took that failure as an object lesson. Not only did he refuse to purchase any stock at all, no matter how safe it was reputed to be, but shortly after the collapse became public knowledge, he removed his money from another large and well-known bank with which he had been doing business for years.

Mr. Aronson's new bank was the venerable Greystock Bank and Trust Company, a small but highly prestigious bank with an aristocratic past.

The Greystock had been founded in the year 1801 by a wealthy associate of Alexander Hamilton. Since that time, it had been controlled by the Anglo-Saxon elite of the financial community. It did not accept just anyone as a client. In order to be permitted to deal with the best, one had to have a certain standing oneself.

Mr. Aronson understood that he would not have been welcome at the Greystock before the stock market collapse and the start of the Great Depression. The mere fact that he was Jewish—albeit not a religious Jew—would have seen to that. But when many of its distinguished Anglo-Saxon customers began to lose their fortunes, the bank found that it could no longer afford to make distinctions on the basis of race or background.

Until the start of 1933, Phil's father could not have been happier with his new banking relationship. It had brought him not just safety, he believed, but business prestige as well. His suppliers treated him with new respect when they learned that the Greystock Bank and Trust Company considered him a good credit risk.

Then, in mid-January of 1933, some nasty rumors about the bank began to surface.

The word was that certain high officials of the Greystock were milking it for funds. Poorly secured loans were supposed to have been made to bank officers, board members, and their friends. Some of those same people—or so it was said—were transferring large sums of money to secret accounts in European banks.

The rumors were hard to pin down, and no one had much luck in finding out who it was that started them. But they did persist.

Mr. Aronson refused to panic at these stories. But since it would have been irresponsible of him not to investigate further, he did telephone his account executive, who invited him to lunch at one of the private dining rooms in the bank's Wall Street office.

Like most everything else about the Greystock, the small dining room Mr. Aronson was shown to was subdued and quietly elegant. The oak-paneled walls were darkly stained, the carpet tasteful, and the framed oil portraits were of such famous past Americans as Samuel Adams, DeWitt Clinton, Andrew Carnegie, and John Jacob Astor.

Thomas Leyland, Mr. Aronson's account executive, was the sort of man born to grace such a room. A distinguished and handsome fifty-two, he had been hired by the Greystock upon his graduation from Princeton University and had remained with the bank ever since. As he himself liked to say, he was firmly in the Greystock mold.

After they finished a fine steak luncheon ("It's a shame there's no wine," Leyland said with a chuckle, "perhaps the bank should have its own bootlegger.") Mr. Aronson related some of the stories he had heard.

Leyland listened earnestly and offered his customer a Havana cigar to go with the coffee.

"I've heard those rumors too," he said after they had lit their cigars. "And I don't blame you for being upset by them. I'd be upset myself if I didn't know the facts."

"The facts?"

"That there's not a word of truth in them. The Greystock today is as sound as—" He interrupted himself. "I was about to say as sound as a dollar, but considering the state of the nation these days it's probably a good deal sounder."

When Leyland chuckled again, Mr. Aronson joined in the laughter. He was beginning to feel more than a little embarrassed.

"You make me feel bad about bringing the subject up," he said. "I should've known that the Greystock..."

"No, sir," Leyland contradicted firmly. "You did the right thing. It was only natural for you to worry that where there was smoke there might be fire. And how else were you to get at the truth except by coming here and asking questions?"

"Well, yes," Mr. Aronson confessed. "That's what I was thinking when I phoned you."

"I appreciate your frankness," Leyland replied. "Let me be equally frank with you. The bank has been investigating the source of those lies. And, while we have no proof yet, we're morally certain that they were started as part of a deliberate communist attack on the American banking system."

"But...I don't understand...."

"I'll explain in a moment. But first, are you aware that President-elect Roosevelt plans to close every bank in the country when he takes office on March 4th?"

"I've read newspaper speculation."

"Well, that speculation hasn't gone far enough," Leyland said grimly. "I have it from an unimpeachable source: *All* banks—sound and unsound—will be forced to shut down for several days. When they're allowed to reopen again, the country will have been taken off the gold standard and the government will be offering loans of *paper* money to any bank that is in trouble."

"Maybe that's what has to be done," Mr. Aronson said. "I don't know. But the country can't afford many more bank failures."

"But what if the cure proves to be worse than the disease?" the banker challenged. "I personally believe that America will rue the day it turns away from a gold standard. Gold means sound currency. And no country can survive without sound currency. Look what happened to Germany ten years ago. A terrible inflation like the Germans had is even worse than a depression."

"You're right. . . . You're right. . . ."

"And as far as the bank failures are concerned," Leyland continued, "it may well turn out to be a good thing for some of the weaker institutions to fall by the wayside. Of course it troubles me to see banks fail—to see depositors lose their savings—but we have to recognize the fact that society as a whole may benefit when the weak are permitted to die and the strong survive."

"I understand," Mr. Aronson said eagerly. "It's like in my own business. My own store survived, while others which were not so strong . . ."

"Precisely." The banker nodded with satisfaction.

"And that's what's happening now? To the banks?"

"And will not continue to happen. Roosevelt and his advisers will not have the moral courage to allow it."

Mr. Aronson felt a glow of self-righteousness at having voted for the reelection of President Hoover.

"But what has all that got to do with the rumors about the Greystock?" he asked. "Didn't you tell me the communists were involved?"

"I'm coming to that: I'm sure you realize that the communists have links with some of Roosevelt's closest advisers."

"Yes . . . yes . . ."

"So it should come as no surprise for you to learn that they know what the President has in mind for the banks. But the communists don't think he plans to go far enough."

"What do you mean?"

"They'd like to see the federal government take over the banks entirely. When the Roosevelt bank holiday is ended, and the banks open their doors again, it would be under government ownerhsip!"

"But that—that's crazy."

"To *us* it's crazy. But the Reds would like to turn America into another Russia where the state controls everything and everybody. Taking over the banks would be a step on that road."

"But do you really think that could happen? Here?..."

"The communists would certainly like it to happen," Leyland said. "And while Roosevelt himself is not a communist, there is reason to believe that certain of his advisers are under Red control. It may well be that the rumors concerning the Greystock were started with the connivance of those advisers."

"My God!... But why the Greystock?"

"Perhaps because we have a reputaion for integrity and probity which is out of all proportion to our size. If enough people believe those vicious stories and start a run on the bank..."

"God forbid!" Mr. Aronson interjected.

"Yes. But if that did happen, can't you imagine what some of the president's more radical advisers would be saying—that if a distinguished old bank like the Greystock has proved to be unsound, no bank in the country can be safe."

"And you think that would convince him to take over the entire system?"

"I don't know whether it could convince him," Leyland said dourly. "But it would surely make him think about it most seriously. And when you consider the fact that the president-elect is known to have leftist tendencies..."

"Yes," Mr. Aronson said. "It would be terrible. Terrible..." He hesitated briefly. "Let me ask you a question, Mr. Leyland. Would you have any objections to my repeating this discussion to certain people I know? I think it's important that businessmen especially should understand the real dangers today."

"You're right, Mr. Aronson. That is important." The banker paused. "But can you repeat only the gist of our conversation and not mention my name?"

"Yes. Of course."

"Then go ahead, sir. And God bless you. You are a·true gentleman."

Mr. Aronson fairly beamed with pleasure.

It was exactly nine days later that the *New York Sun* scooped its afternoon rivals in reporting the failure of the Greystock Bank and Trust Company.

Though the *Sun* attempted to get statements from the entire executive staff, its writers could only reach one-fourth of them. The rest could not be reached for several more days; then it was discovered they were in mid-ocean aboard the French liner *Ile de France*. Among those passengers was Mr. Thomas Leyland, his wife, and his teen-aged daughters.

5

During the month of January, Phil began to spend more and more time away from home. He was hardly there at all on weekends, and during the school week he'd usually arrive late for dinner.

He told his parents that he was doing extra work for one of his classes and had to spend a great deal of time in the public library. That was a lie, of course. Phil didn't want his parents to find out that he was actually working for Lew Bocca's Uncle Al.

It was Lew who offered him the job on the day after Phil's encounter with Rita Crane.

"There's nothing to it," Lew told him as they walked together toward the Greek's. "My uncle wanted to know if I knew a younger guy who was quick on the uptake and could be trusted. I told him you were the man."

Phil glowed at the compliment. "What do I have to do?"

"Like I say, practically nothing. Uncle Al'll give you some envelopes to deliver. The only thing is, the names and addresses on them will be in code."

"Which I'll have to learn," Phil said. "No sweat."

"Now there'll be a number code on the backs of the envelopes. The numbers there will correspond to different sums of money. What you'll do is take the envelopes to the right addresses and either pick up or deliver the money. You'll get twenty cents for each pick-up or delivery you make. Got it?"

"Hey, no shit! Twenty cents each?" Phil whistled softly. That would add up to a great deal of money at a time when even a little money was hard to come by.

"What's wrong?" Lew teased. "You think my Uncle Al's some kind of cheap screw?"

"Hell, no."

"One thing, though." Lew's eyes grew hard. "I promised my uncle that you're an honest guy. Don't screw me up. It's not just that you'll embarrass me. Uncle Al gets mad when someone tries to doublecross him. Play it straight and he'll treat you swell. But try to pull a fast one on him and he'll chop your balls off."

"Hey, Lew." Phil protested. "Listen. If you don't trust me, forget the whole thing. Don't you think I appreciate what you're doing?"

For a moment, Phil was worried that he'd gotten out of line. But Lew liked a guy who stood up for himself.

"You're okay," Lew said, punching him lightly on the shoulder. "It's going to work out fine."

Phil grinned and hid his relief.

"I'll tell you something, though," Lew said. "Quit that asshole school of yours and come in with us full time, and it'll work out even better."

"I can't do that. I already told you. My old man wouldn't let me. He wants me to go on to college and then come into the store with him."

"Is that what you want to do?"

Phil shrugged, then paused for a moment and stared down at the clean sidewalk. "Maybe I would tell him to go to hell if it weren't for my mother. It would hurt her bad if she thought I was into something like bookmaking. Something that wasn't one hundred percent legal."

"Who said anything about bookmaking?" Lew demanded.

Phil stared at his friend. What else could it be with all that business of codes (to fool the police of course or at least disguise the evidence) and the pickup and delivery of money.

"Sorry," he said. "I thought your uncle asked for someone quick on the uptake. He must've said slow."

Lew laughed; then his face turned serious. "Just don't be too quick. Sometimes you get into situations when it's better not to know too much."

Phil nodded.

"But as far as your mother is concerned, I guess you're right," Lew went on. "You never want to hurt her unless you absolutely have to. I lost my own mother when I was a little kid, you know."

"Yes," Phil said. He did know.

They were at the Greek's now and stepped inside to sit at a booth.

As they waited for John Klagos to bring their order of coffee and Danish pastries, Phil looked out of the front window. The scene was less festive than it had been on the previous day and people were no longer wearing their holiday clothes.

"About that money your uncle's going to be giving me," he said suddenly. "Would you be willing to keep most of it safe for me?"

Lew frowned. "I don't get it."

"I'd rather my folks didn't know I had it," Phil explained. "And there's no place at home where I could keep it hidden."

"Right." Lew nodded. "I'll keep your dough nice and safe for you. Whenever you need some to spend on the dames, just come to your 'Uncle Lew.'"

"Check."

"And speaking of dames," Lew said as John Klagos brought over their pastries and coffee. "What do you think of Rita Crane?"

"She's real good stuff," Phil replied with a comfortable grin.

"You got in, huh?" Lew said.

Phil kept grinning.

"She didn't tell you about her... ah... problem?"

"What problem?"

"I don't know. But I hear most of the guys've been staying away from her since she started seeing that special doctor of hers."

Phil's grin was turning sour. "Special doctor?"

"Yeah. He specializes in V.D."

"Oh, my God," Phil moaned. "You're conning me, right? Damn it, you are conning me. There's nothing wrong with Rita. Nothing at all!"

"Isn't there?" Lew responded slyly.

"Son of a bitch," Phil said softly. "You had me going for a minute. You really did."

As Lew broke into laughter, the embarrassed smile on Phil's face began to relax. He was not angry at Lew. In a strange way he was flattered. Though Lew had played a trick on him, it was the sort of trick he believed a man would play on an equal.

Phil began working for the Boccas after school on the following day.

He liked the job. It was a kick to carry gambling money past an unsuspecting cop. It was great to have enough dough to play the big shot with a girl. But what he enjoyed most of all was meeting different types of people, taking their measure, and seeing the various ways in which they lived.

For though Phil's activities were confined to the same general area, within that area the contrasts were sharp. There were gorgeously decorated buildings, for instance, as well as shabby walk-ups which were far less inviting than Rita Crane's place on Columbus Avenue.

It did not take long, however, for Phil to decide that for all their dissimilarities, these people had one thing in common—they all felt that they could beat the system, that they could gamble against the odds and win. Which meant, Phil felt, that they were suckers.

In the long run, at least, the odds could not be beaten. As long as a bookmaker keeps his books in balance he simply has to win, while the ordinary gambler—no matter how clever he thinks he is—has to lose. Which was why Phil always carried more money to the Boccas from losers than he carried from the Boccas to winners.

"You can't beat the numbers," Lew Bocca told Phil, repeating a favorite saying of his Uncle Al. "What you got to do is make the numbers work for you."

Which was just what Phil planned to do.

He was coming more and more to feel that there were two types of people in the world: those like Lew and his uncle who had the brains and the moxie to figure out the system and use it; and the others who ended up paying off the first type. Phil knew which he wanted to be.

6

Phil Aronson's life turned a somersault on the evening of February 16, 1933.

He had come home even later than usual that Thursday and, as he entered the lobby of his apartment building, was trying to think of a new excuse. He had pushed the "working late at the library" routine about as far as it would go, and felt that it was time for him to come up with something different. He was so preoccupied, in fact, that he did not notice the curious glances that John, the elevator man, was giving him.

As he got off the elevator and walked down the hall to his front door, he heard his father's voice. The old man was yelling about something. Him probably, Phil thought. His thoughtlessness at returning home so late. He prepared himself to receive a tirade as soon as he stepped into the apartment.

But his father hardly noticed him come in. While Phil went into his own room to toss his overcoat onto his bed, the elder Aronson continued to hold forth in the living room.

When Phil joined his family he became even more puzzled. His father had taken off his tie and suit jacket, his vest was unbuttoned, and Phil could see his wide suspenders. His mother was holding her forehead. Naomi was sitting next to Bob on the sofa and clutching at his arm.

It took Phil several moments to understand that his father was complaining about the Greystock Bank and the people who ran it. They had fooled him, he moaned. They had lied to him and cheated him. Men with the highest reputations had turned into common thieves.

Phil could hardly believe it. He might have resented his father for favoring Naomi. He might have felt that he put him down for not doing well in school and that he did not give him credit for what he did do. But he'd always respected the old man's brains. He had thought that his father knew what the world was all about and had the guts to make it work for him.

It was with a feeling of having been betrayed that Phil realized his father was not what he'd thought. Far from having figured out the system, he had actually trusted it. And now he was complaining that it was stacked against him, that it was dishonest.

Christ, Phil thought. Only suckers didn't know that!

"I was sitting right next to that *momzer* Leyland," he was telling his wife now. "We were as close as—as I am to you. And you know what he said . . . dressed in his black banker's suit and his stiff banker's collar? Do you know what he looked me in the eye and said?"

"What, my darling?"

"That the bank was sounder than the dollar! That's what he said. That the Greystock Bank and Trust Company was sounder than the U.S. dollar!"

Phil was listening more closely now. His anger at his father grew unreasonably. The old man was supposed to win, not lose; con, not be conned.

"What happened?" he asked in a carefully neutral voice. "Did the bank go under?"

His father glared furiously at him. Had he sensed the undertone of reproof? Or was he just mad at having been interrupted?

"Did it go under?" the older man mimicked resentfully. "Did it go under?" He wiped his mouth with a handkerchief. "Yes. It went under. And perhaps if my genius son who spends so much time in libraries would read a paper once in a while, he'd know what was going on in the world."

Now his father was taking it out on him. And why? Because he didn't have the guts to stand up to the bankers.

Phil did not have to think of what he should say in order to take revenge. "But you used to say the Greystock was so safe."

His father's face grew dark and choleric. "What are you trying? . . . To make me angry? . . . Don't you understand what has happened, you . . . you! . . ."

As the elder Aronson lapsed into a fit of coughing, his wife took his hand and kissed it. "Please, dearest. This excitement isn't good for you."

She turned sadly to Phil. "What kind of son are you? How can you taunt your father like this?"

"I wasn't trying to taunt him," Phil said. "I was just trying to understand."

"That's enough," Sophie Aronson said sternly. She didn't believe him.

Phil might have said something more. But his mother regarded him with her lovely green eyes until he lowered his.

"You know something, Sophie," Phil's father said. "I think the boy is actually glad about what happened."

"How could he be glad? . . ."

"Because he's spiteful, that's how. He's spiteful and he doesn't realize what it will mean."

He turned to his son: "Do you realize what this will mean? To all of us?"

Phil felt a new surge of resentment. Of course he realized. He wasn't a moron. There were some things he realized better than the old man. And if his father would talk to him about it —discuss it with him as if he were a real person—he could maybe even help.

But no. He was supposed to be Phil the jerk—the dumb son who didn't know anything. Well, he wasn't the one who'd made an asshole of himself!

"Well?" His father pressed. "Do you know what it'll mean?"

"That we're in trouble," Phil said. "That when the bank went under it took a lot of our money with it."

"Not just a lot," his father said in a breaking voice. "Everything. We've lost everything. . . ."

Phil's eyes darted away from his sobbing father to the others. His mother was weeping silently. His sister was fighting back the tears. Only Bob was forcing himself to be stoic.

"I've lost the store," the old man chanted. "The fine business your grandfather founded and I planned to pass on to you and your brother and your sister's husband. . . . I lost it. . . ."

Phil looked back at him again. Only now was he starting to comprehend the full extent of what had happened. How could the old man have let them do that to him?

"Isn't there anything that still can be done?" he asked. "A loan to tide the store over?"

"A loan?" his father repeated scornfully. "That's how much you know. We're too much in debt already. And the money to make the payments went down with the Greystock Bank."

"But who do you owe money to?" Phil asked. He was determined not to be silenced. At least not yet. "The Greystock?"

"Mainly," his father said defensively. "I have an interest payment due next week. I don't have the money to meet it."

"But if you owe them money," Phil said, "and they owe you money, wouldn't it all even out? I mean, how can they demand their money from the store if they already have it?"

"That seems to make sense," Sophie Aronson murmured, glancing at her son with new respect.

"It would make sense," Mr. Aronson replied darkly, "if they hadn't sold my notes."

"Sold your notes?" Sophie said. "I don't understand. What does that mean, darling?"

"The agreements I signed to pay back the loans. They sold them at a discount to a few private investors."

"So now you owe them?"

Mr. Aronson nodded.

"Maybe they'll do a deal," Phil suggested. "Give you some more time to pay."

Mr. Aronson gave his son a vicious look which was all the more vicious because he was so angry at himself. "Don't you think I tried? Don't you think I got in touch with them as soon as I learned about the bank and phoned some people to find out where my notes were?"

"And they wouldn't agree to hold off for a while?" Phil asked.

"Why should they? There are four all told and all four have interests in other men's stores. The reason they bought the notes in the first place was to use them to drive me out of business. That's what they're going to do—drive me out of business."

He glared at Phil once more. "And so Mr. Wise Guy with your bright ideas. Have you got any more suggestions?"

Phil didn't reply.

"So I'm ruined," his father moaned. "But what do those *gonifs* at the bank care? Sure they sold the notes—it left more money for them to steal when they left the country. They don't care."

And what in hell ever made you think they would? Phil wanted to shout. *No big shot cares about the guy he fucks. If he did, he wouldn't be a big shot!*

But Phil kept his mouth shut as his mother began to weep again, and Naomi released Bob's arm to run to her father.

"It'll be all right, Papa," she said. "You'll see. I could sell flowers. I've seen lots of little girls selling flowers."

Philip Aronson patted her on the head. "You're a good girl. Too good . . . I don't deserve . . ."

"Phil and I can quit school," Bob announced. "We're both old enough to work."

"No, you mustn't," Sophie pleaded. "Don't let them, Philip. Please..."

But her husband was too lost in his own thoughts to hear her.

Phil stared at his father. He supposed he should sympathize with the old man, and in a way he did. But more than that he was angry; and more than angry he was embarrassed.

For the old man had been a sucker. There was no getting around that. And though Phil knew that there were a great many suckers in this world—he visited suckers every day doing the business of the Boccas—he didn't want his father to be among them.

Even worse than this, however, was listening to his father whine and complain about what had happened to him.

It was bad enough for his father to have been suckered, but now he should at least be making plans to get even. Maybe he should go to Europe to try and get his dough back—or at least make those bastards sorry they'd taken it!

Phil had no idea how that could be done, of course. But he did believe that if someone like Lew Bocca's Uncle Al had been in his father's position, he would have managed it. Not that Lew's uncle would ever be in his father's position...

His father moaned again and muttered inaudibly.

All right, Phil thought. He did have to feel sorry for him. But not nearly as sorry as he had to feel for the rest of the family. They had had faith in him—and had been betrayed by that faith.

As Phil thought about the family—his kid brother, his mother, his little sister—he grew angrier still. The old man had demanded that they not only respect him, but that they treat him like some sort of king!

And for the most part they had done it.

Even he himself, Phil realized with indignation. He might not have liked it—he might have thought about rebelling—but he still said yes sir and no sir (yes your majesty; no your majesty) to the old man.

But that was all finished now. Whatever magic his father had once possessed, he possessed it no longer. The old man was finished. And unless someone else in the family did something fast, they would all be finished with him.

But who could do something?

Not his mother. She had been taken care of and protected all her life. It was too much to ask her to take command now. She was still not sure what had happened; she still thought her husband might be brought back to life.

And surely not Bob or Naomi. Though one day Bob, at least, might be stronger than any of them, it was too early and he was too young. He had to finish school—and so did Naomi.

So who else was left? Just him. Phil Aronson. The new, uncrowned king of the family.

King? Him? The thought suddenly struck Phil as funny, and it was all he could do to keep from laughing out loud.

But king or not, damn it, he could at least be a man—a seventeen-year-old man who was going to see to it that his brother and sister remained in school and that no one in the family had to starve. Including his father.

Starting tomorrow, he decided, he was going to work full time. Even as it was, he was making money. And if he could convince Lew and his uncle to take him on full time, he could earn a lot more. Maybe he couldn't keep them in this apartment, and maybe they wouldn't be eating as well as they did now, but they wouldn't have to beg from soup kitchens or sleep on subway trains in order to keep warm during cold winter nights.

He told the others how it was going to be.

They stared at him, not sure whether they should believe him or not.

"I mean it," he said. "Starting tomorrow, I'm not a school boy. I'm a working man."

"You?" his father said with a trace of his old sarcasm. "You're going to support the family?"

"Some one has to," Phil shot back.

"Please," Sophie Aronson said, falling back naturally into her accustomed role of peacemaker between husband and son. "I'm positive your father will have no difficulty in finding a good job. He's very well respected in the industry."

"Everyone respects me," Mr. Aronson said weakly. "I'll just have to take my time . . . find the right position. . . ."

"Sure," Phil said, shrugging off both his mother's statement and his father's response. "And in the meantime, I'll see we don't starve."

"Me too," Bob put in. "I'll get a job too."

"Oh no you won't, buddy." Phil spoke firmly. "You're staying in school."

"But—"

"No buts, kid. The way my grades are, I probably shouldn't be in school anyway. But you're different. You're the bright one of the family and have a chance to make something of yourself. I'm not going to let you throw it away.

"And Nommie." He grinned at his sister. "You're going to stay in school too. Maybe you're not as bright as Bob, but you can still wait a few years before you start selling flowers."

"Don't call me Nommie," the girl pleaded from her father's side.

Sophie Aronson ignored that by-play and regarded her two younger children with tears in her eyes.

"Listen to your brother," she said. "Please . . ."

Mr. Aronson, meanwhile, was glaring balefully at Phil.

"Tell me something," he said. "You say you're leaving school. What sort of a job do you think you can get these days without an education?"

"I don't know yet," Phil said. He was not going to mention the Boccas. That would have been difficult enough to do if he were alone with his father. But with his mother there—and his sister and brother as well—it was impossible.

"I'll get something."

"What kind of something?" his father pressed, pushing ahead like a ferret on the scent. "Mature men with college educations and years of practical experience are starving in the streets. What do you think you can do?"

"Maybe those mature men like to sit around on their duffs feeling sorry for themselves," Phil retorted viciously. "Maybe they'd rather wait for the 'right position' than get a job!"

Mr. Aronson opened his mouth and then shut it again. A slow flush suffused his face. A vein in his temple throbbed visibly.

Naomi wrapped her arms about her father's knees and glared hotly at her older brother.

It was Bob who acted on instinct to relieve the tension and bring the others back to the everyday.

"Phil," he said, winking at his brother and making a comic face. "About that work you're going for. I'll bet you've got something up your sleeve."

Phil had to laugh. "Maybe one or two ideas."

He got up from his chair and stretched.

"I think I'll go outside," he said.

"But what about dinner?" his mother asked. She looked at the eight-day clock on the mantel—her husband's pride and joy. "Goodness. It's so late already. I'll heat up something in the oven."

"Not for me, thanks," Phil said. "I'll get a bite at the Greek's."

Sophie pursed her lips and looked unhappy. She didn't chide Phil, though, or say anything in disapproval.

7

It wasn't until he was inside the elevator that Phil realized just how hungry he was. He really needed that bite he said he was going to get at the Greek's.

Despite everything he was feeling good. Despite the gnawing in his belly, and despite his vividly growing awareness of the frightening nature of his family's problems, he was still feeling good.

He fairly pranced out of the elevator and left the building without noticing the building crew. If the elevator man—not John, but the man on duty in the evenings—gave him a peculiar look, he did not recognize it. Nor did he notice anything the doorman said or did.

It was only some time later that he realized that he had been regarded strangely—and not just on his departure from the building, but when he'd come in earlier. Some improbable grapevine must have picked up the news of what had happened to his family even before he himself had learned of it.

Phil stepped out into the crisp night air and walked slowly along the dimly lit side street. He was in a deep reverie about what had just taken place.

How had he ever found the balls, he wondered, to have said what he said? He had challenged his old man in front of the entire family—and he'd gotten away with it. That was the amazing thing. He had actually gotten away with it!

Only now, he reminded himself soberly, he had to do what he said he was going to do. He had to work his ass off in order to bring in enough dough to support the family. That's what he had promised. And unless he wanted to be shown up as just another young punk with a big mouth, he was going to have to make good.

One thing he was sure of. If he didn't do it, no one else would.

He felt deep in his bones that his father would not—could not—recover from the blow he had just received. The shock of it had left him a broken man. And there was nothing, Phil believed—not all the king's horses; not all the king's men—which would put his father back together again.

He still hadn't reached Broadway when he noticed that three shadowy figures were approaching him from the opposite direction. They were too shrouded in darkness for him to tell anything about them—except that they were male and looked vaguely menacing.

Moments later he passed them and saw that they were just drunk and happy. No problem. Not that there ever was much of a problem. New York remained a comparatively safe city with streets that were well-patrolled by neighborhood cops. There was crime of course—a good deal of it—but most of the crime in New York was carried out by professional criminals who tried to avoid killing their victims and landing in the electric chair.

In the slums, of course, life was held a good deal cheaper than it was in the more middle-class areas. But even slum-dwellers were careful about whom they harmed. Wealthy people could tour the Bowery in safety, for example, and white couples could spend a perfectly safe evening in Harlem at such nightclubs as the Cotton Club—which featured black entertainers though no black customers were allowed inside the door. If the inhabitants of Harlem or the Bowery had any complaints about all this, they kept those complaints to themselves.

As Phil walked along the street in his own neighborhood, the worst he could expect was to meet an angry drunk who might invite a fistfight or an unwashed panhandler begging for money.

He was eating a steak sandwich at a table in one of the rear booths of the Greek's when Jake Karpas came in. He stopped at the counter for a moment, then noticed that Phil was there.

"Hey," Jake said. "Long time no see. Mind if I sit with you?"

Phil shrugged. The reason he hadn't seen Jake in some time

was that he'd had no desire to. On the other hand, he didn't dislike him that much either.

"What's the story?" Jake asked.

"No story," said Phil. He was not about to tell Jake Karpas what had happened to his old man. "What's with you?"

Jake waited for John Klagos to bring his coffee and club sandwich and set it down on the table. Then he leaned over confidentially. "Like to try some real good booze?"

Phil laughed. "Shit. I hear your stuff is enough to put a man in the hospital."

"Oh, hey, don't say that." Jake's sallow face grew even pastier. "I know I had a bad connection before. But not now. This is real Scotch whisky."

Phil stared silently at him while he took a mouthful of food.

"I mean it," Jake said. "Want to know how I found my new connection?"

Phil still didn't say anything.

"I'll tell you," Jake insisted. "Through Lew Bocca. No shit." Jake paused. When there was still no reply, he added: "Look, why don't you try a single fifth. I'll give it to you at the price I had to pay. If you don't like it, no hard feelings. If you do, you can get more but you'll have to pay the regular price which is still pretty damn cheap. What d'you say?"

"Why're you doing me such a favor?" Phil asked.

"'Cause I like you, man. You're a friend."

Phil grinned. "Are you sure it's not because you got yourself stuck with a whole load of hootch that might not be worth so much once Prohibition ends?"

Jake stiffened. "Look. Do you want it or don't you?"

"Where do you keep the stuff?"

"At my place." Jake was grinning again. He figured the sale was made. "You know. Around the corner."

"And what are you asking?"

"Just like I say. You can have a fifth for what I had to pay for it myself." Jake named a figure.

"Don't try to crap me, buddy. You never paid that much in your life."

The two argued for a while, then came to an agreement. Though Phil was certain that Jake was still going to make a profit on the deal, it would not be as big a profit as the one he'd tried to con him out of at first.

"But this booze," Phil warned. "It'd better be good."

"It is . . . I swear. Honest to God Scotch whisky."

"Yeah, sure. But if that Scotch turns out to be rotgut instead, I'm coming after you. Just remember that."

The grin remained on Jake's face, but it turned somewhat sick. As a free-lance with no real protection, he was used to harsh treatment from dissatisfied customers. And he knew Phil meant what he said.

The two paid for their food, then went to Jake's place where Phil purchased the whiskey.

The problem now, he thought when he left Jake, was to find a girl to help him drink it. He was still feeling happy about himself, and wanted someone to share that feeling with him.

Rita Crane, he thought. She lived nearby. And though in the past week or so he had smugly wondered if he was not outgrowing Rita, he had to admit that she was not only well-stacked but a damn good lay.

He dialed her number from a pay booth on the corner of Columbus Avenue. The phone was answered by Kay Lentz, one of Rita's roommates, who informed him that she wasn't there.

Phil was irrationally angry. "Is she coming back soon?"

"I don't know," Kay said. "I doubt it."

Phil's sense of outrage grew. She had to be with some other guy.

"You want to leave a message for her?" Kay asked.

"No, I don't think so. I'm only calling because I just bought a fifth of what's supposed to be Scotch whiskey, and I wondered if she wanted to help me find out if it's real."

"I know she would," Kay said with one of her husky laughs. "She'll be sorry she's out."

Phil thought quickly. Kay had never impressed him as his type. She was too thin and flat-chested. Too boyish looking, even. But still and all . . .

"Hold on a minute," he said. "How would you like to help me test that booze?"

Kay hesitated only imperceptibly. "Why not?"

Whatever enthusiasm Phil had managed to work up over Kay was sharply reduced when she opened the door and he saw that roommate number three—a dowdy looking blond named Sidel Lunderheit—was also in the apartment.

Phil cursed silently. He'd assumed that he and Kay would

be by themselves. The girls had that sort of arrangement. When one of them had a guest, the others got out of the way. But maybe this was too short a notice.

"Come on in," Kay said. She was a tall girl with a wide mouth and freckled cheeks. She wore her brown hair short with simple bangs. "I'll hang up your coat."

Phil handed the overcoat to her and removed the liquor bottle from a brown paper bag. "Would you like me to fix the drinks now?"

"Just two. Sidel has to leave. Isn't that right, dear?"

Sidel looked sullen. "Yeah. I guess it is."

Phil waited for the short, dumpy blond to put on her coat and leave the apartment. Then he took the bottle into the kitchen.

"What's her problem?" he asked.

"She's mad because I tossed her out." Kay grinned. "She said that you're Rita's property and it's not right to leave us alone. But if you want to know the real reason, it's that it's too cold out and she didn't have a place she wanted to go to."

Phil poured the drinks. "I prefer the first reason."

"You would," said Kay.

They returned to the living room and sat side by side on the badly sprung sofa while they sipped at their drinks.

"This is good liquor," Kay said.

Phil had to agree. Jake had not lied to him.

Kay took another sip. "I was just wondering," she said.

"About what?"

"If everything Rita said about you is true."

"What did she say?"

Kay shook her head. "Maybe I'll tell you some day. If we get to know each other better."

Phil looked at her. Despite the boyish figure, there was something very sexy about that wide mouth. He removed her glass from her hand and set it down so he could kiss her on the lips.

"Do we know each other better now?" he asked.

"Maybe a little better," Kay drawled.

There was a note of mockery in her voice which made Phil feel as if he'd been flicked by a whip. Who did the bitch think she was?

"I'll tell you one thing Rita said," Kay went on in her husky drawl. "You have one hell of a wicked temper."

Phil narrowed his eyes. "Maybe you'd better be careful, then."

"Does that mean little Kay should be afraid of the big mean man?"

It was the sort of provocative challenge that Phil knew how to respond to in only one way. He grabbed the girl and pulled her against him, crushing her mouth with his own and tightening his arms about her body.

Kay tried to pull away from him but he wouldn't let her. His aim was not to hurt her so much as to overwhelm her with his own power and strength. The fact that she was being hurt in the process was almost coincidental.

She did not see it that way. She twisted her head slightly and bit him sharply on the lower lip.

Phil's reaction was automatic. He released her with a curse and backhanded her lightly across her face.

"Bastard!" she said, touching her face where he had hit it, then lunging for his eyes.

But if her temper was as fierce as his, her strength was no match for him. He grabbed her wrists, forcing the claws of her hands away from his face. She tried to escape from the couch altogether in order to launch some new attack, but Phil shouldered her back against the cushions.

"Want to quit?" he asked. "Be a good girl?"

That phrase only incensed her further. She twisted around and tried to use her knee.

He sensed the threat to his crotch almost before it came and blocked it with his muscular thigh. Furiously offended that she would attack him there, he released a hand so he could slap her once more across the face.

But the woman-scent of her, the feel of her supple body against his, the very violence of their struggle were working to arouse Phil now. He tore open the top of Kay's blouse and reached inside her slip to find her bra. He forced the cups away from her small breasts while his other hand went under her skirt to pull down her briefs.

Kay clawed at his face and throat. She ripped his shirt open to get at his chest. She undid his belt and the fly of his trousers to reach roughly inside his shorts.

But though they both thought they were still fighting, it had become a very different kind of fight. Neither of them now wished to maim or wound or cripple.

Phil's fingers were inside her, stroking and caressing her clitoris.

Kay had pulled his trousers and undershorts down around

his ankles. She kissed his penis and balls, then turned her head so she could speak.

"You are a real bastard," she said. "But at least a well-hung one. That's what Rita said about you—if you still give a damn."

Phil didn't. He didn't give a damn about anything unconnected to this present moment when he was rock-hard and enormous and felt as if he were going to explode.

"To hell with Rita," he said.

He yanked her briefs all the way over her shoes, then pushed her head back on the stained cushions and knelt between her legs. He guided himself into her and thrust home as deeply as he could.

Kay gave a shuddering cry—first of pain at the size and fury of him, then of pleasure. Her arms went around his neck and her nails dug passionately into his skin.

Phil thrust again. He was using all his masculine power. Once again his penis was the weapon that enabled him to conquer.

And he deserved to conquer, damn it! Had he not faced down his father? Had he not taken command of his family? He was a man—and he was proving that he was a man!

He thrust into Kay again and again, until—triumphant— he exploded inside her.

Part Two

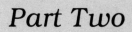

8

Al Bocca ran his operation from an office in a brownstone building located east of Broadway in the mid-Eighties. The name on the office door was Southwood Investment Corporation. Some seven years earlier, Al's late brother—Lew Bocca's father—had taken over that corporation as payment on a bad debt.

On the late afternoon of the day following the collapse of the Greystock Bank, Phil Aronson delivered his normal quota of cash-filled envelopes to the Southwood office. Phil himself was not feeling very normal. His emotions were swinging wildly from joy to terror, from hope to despair. No sooner did he set the envelopes down than Al Bocca motioned him to wait. He would speak to Phil as soon as he got off the telephone.

The fact that it had been Phil who'd asked for the meeting did not seem to matter now. Nor did the fact that Lew Bocca had been so encouraging this morning. For now was make or break time—and it was all up to him. If he could convince Al Bocca to employ him full time to do the same sort of work he'd been doing on a part-time basis, he could earn enough money to prove to everyone—especially himself!—that he really was the man of his family. If he couldn't convince him, he'd have to crawl home with his tail between his legs.

Phil did not even like to think about the third alternative—that his request might not merely be turned down but regarded as presumtuous and insolent. In which case he might not be able to crawl home.

So he tried to compose himself as he sat quietly in the corner of the room. He kept sneaking covert glances at the man on the telephone and heard him issue gentle suggestions which were, in fact, the most imperative of orders.

Al Bocca was a slender, fine-boned man with a full head of white hair and a trim, white mustache. His speech was courteous and his manners aristocratic. He was not a man to be taken lightly. While his toughness was of a more subtle character than that of the younger, more muscular men he called his assistants, it was also more dangerous. As his nephew Lew once put it, when Al Bocca looked at someone with those cold gray eyes of his, the guy felt like finding a hole in the floor to crawl into.

Al said goodbye to the person he'd been talking to, hung up the telephone, and smiled sweetly at Phil.

"I'm sorry I was so long," he said. "Come over here. Please. Sit by me."

Phil crossed over to take the indicated chair at the side of the desk. "Thank you. . . ."

"My nephew told me what happened to your father. It was a terrible thing."

"Yes." Phil wondered at the note of genuine sympathy he heard in Al Bocca's voice.

"I don't know what this world's coming to," Bocca said. "When a man can't trust an old established bank like the Greystock what can he trust?"

He turned to the two assistants who were in the office with him. Both were short, squat men with suspicious bulges under their jackets.

"Did you boys hear about that? The Greystock Bank going under while most of its officers disappeared from the country?"

"No, Al. I didn't know that. It sure is lousy, though."

"Yeah. A real shame."

Al Bocca's gaze swung back to Phil. "Lew tells me you want to take over the support of your family."

"Yes, Mr. Bocca."

"Call me Al, Phil. Men who are my friends call me Al."

Phil appeared puzzled.

"A few days ago you were a boy," the white-haired man explained. "But now you are taking on a man's responsibility. And when a boy takes on a man's responsibility, he becomes a man. Do you understand me, Phil?"

Understand him? Phil could hardly believe it. It was as if Al Bocca had been taking the thoughts from his own mind.

"Yes," he said. "I understand."

The door opened then and Lew Bocca walked in. He waved generally at Phil and his uncle's two men. Then he said a more formal hello to his uncle.

"I'm glad you got here," the older man said. "Your friend

and I were just about to discuss the possibility of his working for us full time. You said that was what he wanted to do, correct?"

"Yes, Uncle Al."

"What do you say, Phil? Is that true?"

"Yes . . . ah . . . Al."

"Very well. As I explained to you, you're a man now. You have a right to decide certain things for yourself. But remember: Once a man commits himself, he stands committed. He can no longer make a boy's excuse that he is sorry. Or that he didn't know what he was doing." Al smiled. "Do you *capish,* my friend?"

Phil said quickly that he did. Perhaps a little too quickly.

"Good," said Al Bocca. "You'll be a soldier in my army. For a month or two you can work with Sal and Billy here, in order to learn the ropes. Then you can help Lew. Is that all right with you?"

It was not all right. Far from it. He did not want to train to become a gunman, a hood, an enforcer. Yet what could he say? How could he turn down the offer without insulting the man who had made it?

Phil decided to temporize. "What sort of work would I do?"

Al Bocca frowned. And when he spoke, his voice was just as courteous as it had been, but far more dangerous. "You tell me: what sort of work do you think you would do? You know the nature of this organization. You know what we are—what we do. Or has anyone tried to fool you about that?"

As the pause that followed lengthened, Phil knew he had to reply. "No—no, sir. No one tried to fool me."

"Call me Al. Please. I like you, Phil. I'm just trying to understand you."

"Yes . . . Al."

"You see, Phil, if you were a stupid person that would be one thing. But we both know that you're not stupid. So why do you ask a question to which you must already know the answer?"

The very stillness in the room was frightening. Sal and Billy were staring at Phil with gimlet eyes. Even Lew's eyes had taken on the icy hardness of his uncle's.

Once again he knew he had to come up with an answer. But what?

"I don't know," he heard himself say. Then. "I'm sorry. . . ."

"Perhaps you don't wish to become more closely involved

57

with us," Al Bocca went on. "I'm a reasonable man. I can understand that. It isn't everyone who has the stomach to put certain pressures, say, on a man who does not choose to honor his legitimate gambling debts. Nor is it everybody who could face the necessity of taking drastic measures to eliminate an especially unpleasant business rival.

"I repeat, Phil. I can understand this." Al Bocca smiled angelically. "All men are not made the same way," he went on. "And only God can judge between them—decide who is stronger, who is wiser, who more of a coward. Me, I do not claim to be God. All I can say is go your way and do what you think is right."

Al paused to consider the different faces in the room. As he did so, the silence grew louder.

"But what I cannot understand," he continued almost sadly, "is why you have wasted my time today. You indicated to my nephew that you would like to work full time for me. He spoke to me about it and I made time for you. What went wrong?"

He turned to Lew. "Perhaps you misunderstood your friend," he suggested gently.

"I'm sure I didn't, Uncle Al," Lew replied earnestly. "I would never have brought the subject up unless I was sure."

"That's what I thought," his uncle replied.

"And so, Phil. I'll ask again: what went wrong?"

A pulse was pounding heavily in Phil's throat. His armpits were drenched, but his throat was dry. Whatever he said now had to be the right thing. Had to be.

"I thought . . ." he began weakly, "I could keep doing what I've been doing . . . only full time."

Al Bocca seemed to consider this carefully. He frowned in thought. "Why?" he asked.

"Why?" Phil repeated.

Al Bocca laughed softly. "Look at it this way: We offer you a chance to make some real money—not just pennies like you've been picking up. We show you a way for you to rise in the world. You turn it down. What I want to know is why."

All right, Phil thought. Stalling time was over. He had to come out with something; and that something had better be good.

At the same time though, he couldn't tell the truth—or at least not all of it. He couldn't say that being a gunman or a muscleman for the Boccas was just plain stupid in his opinion, that it was no way to beat the system. He couldn't say that the

Sals and Billys of this world were odds-on favorites to wind up dead or in jail or both, and that the Boccas themselves stood a good chance of following them. He couldn't remind them of the "accident" in which Lew's parents died and say that he— Phil Aronson—had no desire to take such risks or become involved with such things and that, if he worked with them, it would be at one step removed from certain knowledge and responsibility.

But he did have to say something.

"My mother..." he told them. "She thinks I'm something special. It might kill her if she learned I was involved in what she felt was wrong."

"Who would tell her?" Lew Bocca wanted to know.

"I said if she found out." Phil's tone was slightly defensive. Was Lew against him too?

"Phil has a point," Al Bocca told his nephew quietly. "I think it's fine that a young man can still worry about hurting his mother's feelings. There should be more of that in the world, today. It would make it a better place."

He turned to his men: "Don't you think so, boys?"

"Yes, Al."

"You're right, Al."

Phil was drawing a deep breath of relief when he realized that he was being premature. Al Bocca was not yet done.

"But still and all," he was saying, "I have a strong feeling that there is something else. That your concern for your mother's feelings is not the whole story. Am I right, Phil?"

Phil could not speak. Those cold gray eyes Lew warned him about were drilling into him now. It was as though they were trying to invade his brain in order to get at the information stored there.

"It's not that you think you are too good for us, is it?" Al Bocca asked.

There was an uneasy rumble from Billy and Sal.

"No," Phil said. "I swear..."

"I didn't think so," Al Bocca mused. "But there *is* something else."

He smiled suddenly; his whole face lighting up. "Is it that you feel you are not truly suited to work with us? That you want to be our good friend, but not our colleague and associate?"

"Uh...something like that." Phil was again astonished at his questioner's ability to read his mind.

"That's all right," Al Bocca said soothingly. "I understand. Perhaps your wants can be made to fit in with our purposes."

He stopped for a moment.

"Phil, I can always find men who know how to squeeze triggers or show off their muscles. But young men with brains are much harder to find. And perhaps they have to be handled differently to help them reach their potential.

"What do you think, Lew?"

"I don't know, Uncle Al. Maybe you're right."

"I know I'm right," Al Bocca said with a firm nod of his head. "And your friend here does have brains. I've said that to you before, haven't I, Lew? That Phil Aronson has brains."

"Yes, Uncle Al. You have."

"And he wants to make his success in the business world; the so-called legitimate world. Not here. Not with us. But in the legitimate world of the Greystock Bank and Trust Company."

He swung around suddenly to confront Phil.

"Only you want to play the part of the Greystock," he said. "Not the part of your father. True?"

"Uh . . . yes. If I can." How could the man see through him this way? How could he know?

"You can, Phil," Al Bocca assured him. "All it takes is four things: Brains, balls, friends, and money. You already have the brains and— you wouldn't have walked in here today if you didn't have the balls. That leaves friends and money. We'll be your friends and we'll put you in the way of making a little more money. Perhaps later on—when we get to know you better—we will help you make a lot more money."

"Gee, thanks. I—"

"Don't thank me now. Maybe later you'll have the chance."

"Later?"

"Listen," Al Bocca said. "And try to understand. Right now we are taking a very small risk with you. We're allowing you to keep picking up and delivering our money. As time goes on, you may want to build a customer list of your own. If so, we'll help you lay off the bets—for a percentage, of course."

"Of course," Phil said. This was what he had hoped for, but was nervous to ask about.

"And all the while," Al Bocca continued, "you can be working at another job. Just to prove to your mother—and the world—that you are not connected with anything bad."

Phil nodded eagerly. It was just what he wanted.

"As for the future . . . well, like I say, we'll see what happens. Right?"

"Yes. Great!"

"But remember one thing, *mio figliòccio*." Al Bocca's tone had turned deadly serious. "Nothing is for nothing. Sooner or later a day will come when you'll be expected to repay loyalty with loyalty."

"I know that."

After all, he was thinking, what could they ask for? Al himself had admitted that he was not a suitable killer or muscleman. They wouldn't ask him to become involved in that. And Phil was certainly not stupid enough to try to cheat them out of money.

"I'll always be grateful," he said. "Really."

"All right, then," Al Bocca said. "That's enough of that. Now tell me if you have any ideas on what your other job should be. The one you'll be working at for your mother's sake."

It was the second time Al had used that same sarcasm. Once again Phil chose to ignore it.

"Maybe I should be a delivery man," he said.

Lew looked puzzled, but his uncle laughed in appreciation. "I see you have given this some thought," he said. "And you're probably right. That would be the kind of job which would let you roam around the city. The thing is, you don't want to work for a boss who would keep too close a check on your travels."

"Say, Al . . ." It was Billy speaking.

"Yeah?"

"I think I know a place. It's on Amsterdam—right near where I live."

"What about it?" Al asked.

"It's not doing too good, see. It's owned by an old coot named Lubbuck who sells some meat and vegetables, but mainly canned goods. He doesn't have anyone to help him at all, now. Why don't we talk to him and get him to hire Phil. He's the sort of old fart who doesn't know what's going on around him."

"Sounds like a good boss." Al grinned. "What do you say, Phil?"

"I don't know," Phil admitted. "But I'd rather you didn't talk to him."

"Why not?"

"I'd rather speak to him myself. See if I can't work out some kind of deal."

Al Bocca nodded slowly. "you want to do this on your own, do you? Okay. That's fine. But if you do need some help..."

"I'll come to you," Phil said.

9

Phil obtained his job with Adolph Lubbuck's Superior Food Market by progressively reducing his salary demands until he was finally agreeing to work for nothing. Not a very impressive way to start out in the business world, he told himself.

And yet, from his own point of view, the store made a perfect headquarters. The job would give him all the mobility and freedom of action he wanted; and while he personally found old Mr. Lubbuck a good deal more shrewd than Billy had, the old man would be getting too much value from Phil to check up on him closely.

From the moment he stepped into the store, with its cracked walls, scarred counter, and uneven floorboards, he felt sure that Mr. Lubbuck had no money. The place had a dingy, unwashed look—the sort of shop where he himself would have been reluctant to purchase food.

The store owner did not attempt to hide his plight.

"My fine young man," he said. "You seem intelligent. Look around. Does this look like a successful, flourishing market to you? The sort of store that could afford an assistant? A man to make deliveries?

"Once it was," he went on without waiting for Phil to reply. "This was the finest food store in the whole neighborhood. We dealt with only the finest people who could afford to pay the highest prices.

"But now? Now?...Now I'm lucky to stay in business."

"But supposing I could bring in more customers?" Phil said. "More money?"

"If you could do that? If you could do that?" Mr. Lubbuck sighed deeply. "What that would do would be to delay the inevitable.

"Listen to me: Even if a miracle happened and business improved, I'd still have to go bankrupt within a few months. I only hope that I can save a little something from the wreckage so that my wife and I don't get thrown out of our home and end up with all our possessions on the sidewalk."

Mr. Lubbuck smashed his fist against his beefy palm.

"That's the sort of shape *I'm* in," he concluded bitterly. "That's the sort of man you asked for a job!"

The man reminded Phil of his father. Not only had he gone to fat like his father, but he was also sure the world had beaten him.

Phil could not do anything about his father, of course. The way the two of them grated against each other, the old man wouldn't listen to him if he tried. But maybe—just maybe— he could do something about Lubbuck while also helping himself.

The idea intrigued him.

"Mr. Lubbuck," he said with a quiet forcefulness. He was trying to communicate a confidence he didn't really feel. "Please. Let me put it this way: I really do believe there's a chance of not only saving you from bankruptcy, but of bringing this store back to what you told me it once was—the finest food market in the whole neighborhood.

"Now I won't lie to you. I can't guarantee anything. But I honestly feel there's a very good chance."

"You believe?" Mr. Lubbuck studied Phil carefully as though trying to decide whether he was in full control of his faculties. "And who are you? A young man . . ."

Phil waited patiently. He saw no sense in trying to reply or explain himself.

"And how would you expect me to even pay you?" Mr. Lubbuck asked, stroking his great jowls. "I know. You're not asking for very much. But the way things are, I couldn't pay you even that."

"All right," Phil said. He had known for some time that it was going to reach this point, and he wasn't particularly bothered by it. "Let me have a piece of the store instead of a salary. That way the place will have to start showing a profit before I get any money at all."

"A piece of the store? . . ." Mr. Lubbuck turned the idea around in his mind. "How big a piece would you want?"

Phil shrugged. How big a piece could he get? He had his

fish all but hooked now. He didn't want to frighten him off by appearing too greedy.

"I think a one-third interest would be fair," he said. "I am taking a big risk. You said before that you were heading for bankruptcy. My share won't be worth anything unless I can help you avoid it."

Mr. Lubbuck nodded reluctantly.

"Or maybe it would be wiser for you to give up the store, after all," Phil went on, hoping that his intuition wasn't playing him false. "Do you have any adult children who would invite you to live with them?"

"Only a married daughter," Mr. Lubbuck growled. He was dismissing the idea as brusquely as Phil had hoped he would. "She has children to take care of plus a husband who's a real *momzer*. I'll live on the sidewalk forever before going there!"

"So why not give me a chance to show what I can do?" Phil pressed.

"And how would you live in the meantime?" Mr. Lubbuck wanted to know. "Until all those great profits you're expecting the store to make start to come in?"

Phil had to suppress a grin. The old man, he thought, must be wondering if he was planning to steal the store's stock and fixtures and then run away.

"I have some money put away," he said blandly. "And I expect to make some more through tips."

It was obvious that Mr. Lubbuck did not believe that this was the whole story. Still, Phil thought, it was all the story he was going to get.

It did not really matter to him how much Mr. Lubbuck believed. What mattered was that he find the entire deal too sweet to ask embarrassing questions.

"Would you take a twenty-percent interest in the store?" Mr. Lubbuck asked suddenly. "A third is too much for a place I put my whole life into."

"Even if the place itself won't exist much longer?"

Mr. Lubbuck made a face. "I talk too much. I should learn to keep my big mouth shut. But even so . . ."

"How about a fourth, then? That's as little as I could possibly take."

"So? . . . All right. A fourth it is. You're a hard man for one so young."

Phil just grinned.

10

When Phil told his family about Lubbuck's Superior Food Market, the reaction he received was a mixed one: his mother was proud, his brother enthusiastic, his sister bored, and his father dubious.

"Why would he want to make you his partner?" the elder Aronson wanted to know. "It doesn't make sense. What do you know about retail food business?"

Phil felt indignant. Lubbuck had more faith in him than is own father!

"Maybe we should just thank God that he did it," Sophie Aronson put in gently.

But her suggestion only added to her husband's disgruntlement. "How much is he paying you?" he asked his son.

"Enough," Phil said flatly. Telling the old man anything like the truth would have invited still more questions he didn't want to answer.

"How much is enough?"

"Enough to keep us going," Phil said nastily. "How much are you bringing home now?"

"Please, darling." Sophie Aronson placed a calming hand on her son's cheek. "You know your father is busy liquidating the business. He hasn't had time to look around for anything else."

"Yeah . . . okay."

"You think it's been easy for me?" his father demanded.

"Of course he doesn't think it's easy, Philip," Sophie said soothingly. "How could he?"

But her husband ignored her.

"You do think it's easy!" he said accusingly to Phil. "God forbid you have to look on the ruin of everything you tried to build up. You'll see how easy it is!"

Phil grunted something noncommittal. He had already won the big battle with his father, he told himself. There was no reason to restage it now.

He turned to his mother. "Have you heard about any new apartments yet?"

"There's one thing: Mrs. Sadie Goldstein—you remember her?—told me that her cousin lives in a very nice building in Washington Heights. According to Sadie, several of the better apartments there have just become vacant. They're supposed to be quite reasonable. . . .

"On the other hand," she went on reflectively, "Washington Heights is a pretty long distance from where we've always lived. It's very nice, of course, but I hoped we could stay a little closer to this neighborhood."

"Yes," Phil agreed. "Especially since I'll be working around here."

"That's true," his mother said. "I wasn't even thinking about the food market."

Phil smiled. He did not mention the Southwood Investment Corporation, which was also located in the same general area.

"But Mama," he said. "We are going to have to do something soon. We can't afford to stay on here very much longer."

"Don't worry. We'll find a place. I'll keep asking—"

She was interrupted by an angry moan from her husband. "How can this be?"

"Philip? . . ."

"How can my wife and son be making the decisions in my own home? Like I'm not even here. Like all my experience doesn't count."

"But, darling, somebody has to decide."

"And I'm not capable? All these years I was capable of making decisions and now I'm not?"

"We didn't mean . . ."

Sophie placed a hand over her mouth. Her eyes grew moist. "Tell us what you think, Philip. We want your advice. Really."

"No," Mr. Aronson said. "No, you don't. You couldn't give a damn what I think. You'd rather have a seventeen-year old boy . . ."

"Jesus Christ!" Phil said in disgust.

"I know what you both are thinking," the elder Aronson complained. "I'm no good. Just a failure . . ."

"Please," his wife begged. "Don't do this."

But Mr. Aronson lurched up out of his chair.

"Where are you going, Philip?"

"To my room. Where else? To my bed."

Naomi, who had been growing more and more upset, rushed

66

to her father and caught him about the waist. "I want to go with you," she begged.

"Of course, my darling. Of course..."

Phil glared after them. His thoughts were savage. Neither one of them appreciated what he was trying to do. They would both be happy if he fell on his ass!

Bob could understand his brother's indignation.

"Don't worry about them," he said quietly. "Papa feels helpless right now and that makes him mad. You know? And Naomi's just a little kid who can't bear to see him that way. They'll get over it, though—if you're not too hard on them."

Phil stared in wonder at his younger brother. "There are times when you really surprise me," he said.

"Where did you learn so much about people, Bob?" their mother asked. She was even more astonished at the insight than her elder son.

"I don't know so much, Mama," Bob muttered. He was embarrassed and wanted to change the subject.

"Listen, Phil," he said. "I have an idea for Sunday."

"What's that?"

"You know how you said the store could do with some painting and cleaning up? I'll bet the two of us could do a lot of it if we went there on Sunday."

"Hey, that'd be great! Thanks."

"I'll help, too," their mother offered.

"You, Mama?"

"Of course, me. What do you think?" She was smiling now, grateful to concentrate on something other than the family's troubles. "I've been cleaning and polishing things since before either one of you was born."

Mr. Lubbuck—who'd been warned by Phil not to mention the details of their arrangement to either his mother or his brother—joined the three Aronsons at the store that Sunday. And by the time they were through with it, the place looked bright and cheerful. Metal shone and sparkled, the floor was scrubbed and waxed, the walls and ceiling were freshly painted.

"I never thought it could look so good," Mr. Lubbuck said happily. "Now all we need are some new customers."

"You're having trouble getting customers?" Sophie asked.

"No, Mama." Phil shot a meaningful look at Mr. Lubbuck. "We have plenty of customers. But we could always do with more. Isn't that right?"

"Of course," Mr. Lubbuck said. "We can use as many customers as we can get."

"And we'll get them," said Phil. "When they see how great the place looks, they'll just have to come in. Right, Mama?"

"I hope so," said Sophie.

Phil knew what his mother was thinking: she was remembering her husband's confidence and what had happened to his fine store just a short time ago.

"Don't worry, Mama," he said. "Everyone has to eat. We'll stay away from crooked banks and pull in the customers like crazy."

"He's right," Bob said confidently. "You'll see. Phil's always right about things like this."

11

If Phil turned out to be right about pulling in new customers, it was not merely because of the store's improved appearance. Far more important than that were the efforts he was making to get people to try the place.

Whenever Phil was doing something else, he was also thinking of the store. And when he saw a chance to promote its interests, he would always seize upon it.

"Mr. Leghorn," he might say when phoning a man to tell him that the horse he'd picked came in a winner. "Congratulations. You've won thirty-six dollars today. Maybe you'll want to throw a party tonight and need some fancy groceries. I can deliver them to you when I bring over the money."

He rarely received a flat rejection. A person who had just won money was usually in too generous a mood for that. More often he was told to "speak to the wife. It's the little woman who does all the shopping around here."

But that was all right, too.

"Sure, Mr. Leghorn," Phil would reply. "I'd like to do that. But say—would it be all right to use your name? If I could tell her you said it was okay to call . . ."

"Well . . . uh . . . I guess so. If you want."

With that sort of entrée, Phil could almost always convince the lady to try the store at least once. And while not everyone who sampled the market became a regular customer, enough of them did to make a real difference in the market's financial condition.

Mr. Lubbuck was delighted. "You told me you'd save me from bankruptcy," he admitted gratefully. "And it looks as if you're right. But how did you do it? I don't understand how you're getting all these customers."

"Does it really matter?" Phil wondered.

Mr. Lubbuck considered that briefly, then shook his massive head. "No. No, my young friend, it doesn't matter. Whatever it is you're doing, just keep on doing it."

At the same time, Phil was using the store to help him enlarge the customer list for his bookmaking enterprise. That housewife whose husband had given Phil permission to contact her about using the market, might eventually confess the desire to place a small bet on a horse.

"Would my husband have to know about it?" she might ask plaintively.

"Not at all, Mrs. Leghorn. Not at all. Anything you wanted to bet would be strictly between us."

Phil also became the bookmaker of a number of servants, several of whom had a passion for gambling. It wasn't rare for cooks or butlers to spend more than three-fourths of their salaries on gambling.

By the time Phil's eighteenth birthday had come and gone, both his businesses were starting to be profitable. His bookmaking activities were bringing in most of the money, of course. But the food market was doing well enough to give him a small but steady income.

By now, too, he had removed his family from their former apartment. They were living not very far away, however, as Sophie had found a less expensive though pleasant flat just off Amsterdam Avenue in the mid-Nineties.

Although Phil's father had liquidated his former business, he had not yet begun to look for a job. He was going to, he promised, just as soon as he began to feel a little better. Right now, he was simply too sick.

Phil wondered about the sickness. It was true that his father looked bad, appeared weak, and spent most of his time lying in bed. But no doctor they could find was able to put a name to his mysterious ailment.

His mother, on the other hand, wanted to find a job.

"But Mama," Phil protested when she told him. "What could you do? You've never worked in your life."

"Don't be so sure what I've done in my life," said Sophie. "As a matter of fact I worked in the store for almost a year before your father and I were married."

"But lately, Mama?. . . . What could you do now?"

"I certainly know how to clean. If nothing else, I could be a cleaning woman."

This made Phil angry. Even the thought of his mother doing that sort of work was an insult. He was not knocking himself out every day so she could do that.

"But I want to help," his mother persisted.

"You can help best the way you always have, by making a home."

"So? I'll make a home, too."

"But you don't need to work, Mama. I'm bringing in enough for us." Phil smiled. "We can even afford to have our own cleaning woman once a week to help you out."

"Let me tell you something," Sophie replied earnestly. "All these years I stayed home and attended to the house while your father went out and supported us. I'm not saying a word against that. It was the way your father wanted it. But now *I* want to bring home some money too—even if it's only a little bit. I think it would do me good."

Phil sighed. "Okay, Mama," he said reluctantly. "But you're not going to be a cleaning woman."

"So, I'll have to find something else."

And to Phil's surprise, she did. The husband of her friend, Lotte Abel, was a furrier who was looking for a reliable woman to work part time in his office, answering the phone and taking messages. He was delighted to hire Sophie Aronson.

Phil's younger brother also wanted to contribute to the family's upkeep.

"I'm not a baby any more," he told Phil. "I'll be fifteen by the end of September. Lots of guys my age are working. How do you think it makes me feel to see you and Mama go to work while I have to stay in school."

"But listen, buddy," Phil replied. "You don't have all that much further to go. The way you've been able to skip grades, you'll graduate in a couple of years. Don't fuck it all up now."

"But now's when I should be working. Helping you. Christ, if Mama can find something . . ."

"What Mama found has nothing to do with it," Phil said. "We're talking about you. And you have a chance to make yourself into something that none of us could hope for. Become an accountant, maybe. Or a lawyer. Then you could really contribute something. Right?"

But though Bob nodded his head as if in agreement, Phil recognized the stubborn look in his eyes. He couldn't chain the kid to his school desk. If he wanted to keep him at his books, he was going to have to make some sort of compromise.

"Listen," Phil said. "When does school break for summer vacation? Next week? The week after?"

"The week after."

"Great. So I'll make a deal with you. You can work with me this summer if you'll swear not to give me any crap about not going back to school in the fall. Okay?"

"Well . . ." Bob wavered.

"Come on." Phil grinned. "Don't be a brat. We'll have fun this summer. You'll be a big help to me. And then you can go back to your real job. What do you say? Can I have your word?"

"Yeah, I guess so. Yeah."

"Give me your hand on it then," Phil said.

When Naomi learned that Bob would be working at the store, she wanted to work with him. But here Phil was able to put his foot down.

"This isn't play, Nommie," he said. "It's going to be real hard work. And I can't afford to have my kid sister messing things up."

"I won't mess things up," Naomi promised earnestly. "I swear. I want to work hard."

Bob, who had been watching the by-play, poked Phil in the arm. "Why don't you give her a chance?"

The intensity on his sister's face almost made Phil give in. But how could he? It would be hard enough to have Bob in the store and not give away anything about his secret book-making business. He'd never be able to do it with nosy Nommie around.

"Sorry, Nommie. It won't work out. Maybe you can keep Papa company."

"All right," Naomi sniffed. She was obviously close to tears. "I will . . . *but don't call me Nommie!*"

Phil's social life, these days, was restricted to Kay. Despite her boyish build and the deceptive look of innocence in her wide brown eyes, the girl was entremely talented in bed. Her imagination, for one thing, was much more highly developed than that of the voluptuous Rita. She loved to experiment, and when she was in the mood, she would try anything.

She was also insatiable. A truly serious bout with Kay could leave Phil feeling as limp and used up as an old dishrag. This might not have been bad if he didn't have to get up early to go to work the next morning. But he nearly always did.

He made the mistake of complaining to Kay about this one night, and she teased him unmercifully.

"Poor baby. Did itsy-bitsy Kay knock her great big man out cold?"

Infuriated, Phil decided to show the anger he actually felt. He made a fist.

"The great big man'll cold-cock itsy-bitsy Kay if she doesn't watch her goddamn mouth!"

"He wouldn't do that," Kay laughed. "Or the next time he wants some nookie he'll have to make love to his great big hand."

So Kay was not only sexy, she could be mischievous and feisty as well. A good deal more mischievous and feisty than Phil had bargained for.

Another problem with seeing Kay was that she was still sharing the walk-up with Rita and Sidell. For while Rita herself didn't seem to mind the fact that he'd changed his allegiance, the very fact of running into her at the apartment was embarrassing to him.

That didn't happen very often, however, as Rita and Sidell continued to honor their old agreement about being away whenever Kay entertained.

In a way, this was what bothered Phil. It annoyed him that Rita was so casual about the situation. Even if she hadn't really liked him (and he *knew* she must have liked him), she should have had the decency to fight for what was once hers.

Phil found the whole episode—or lack of an episode— vaguely insulting. It would have been far better for his ego if Rita had challenged feisty Kay to a cat-fight over him.

But she hadn't. And he went on seeing Kay.

12

By mid-July, the weather in the city had turned almost unbearably hot and clammy. Those who could afford it had already made their escape to summer homes in the mountains or along the shore. Until this year, the Aronsons would have been among them.

Phil's family used to rent a house in one of the small resort towns north of Asbury Park on the New Jersey shore. They would join a beach club, giving Phil a chance to swim in the rugged surf or flirt with the girls who sat around the salt water pool and displayed their bathing-suited figures.

Most weekdays, Phil's father would leave them in order to commute to the store. He went to New York by train and, when Phil was younger, his mother would take him to watch his returning train come in.

Since the spur line to the shore was not electrified, the trains were detached from their electric engines some time after leaving Pennsylvania Station and were furnished with steam locomotives to pull them the rest of the way. The engines were on the small side and puffed and gasped asthmatically as they started up. Phil enjoyed watching them and, as late as last year, would wander over to the railroad track in order to do so.

But that was last year. *This* year the only trains he watched were subways and elevated trains. The only wandering he did was through the streets of the sweltering city.

The hot spell grew worse and worse. Mr. Lubbuck's market was close and airless, while the slow-moving electric ceiling fan was a good deal less than adequate. There were times in the store that Phil thought he might literally suffocate.

But it was even more difficult for him to keep making his food deliveries and attend to his gambling business. The best customers—both his own and Lubbuck's Superior Food Market's—were out of the city for the season. Those who were forced to stay behind had become cranky and tight-fisted under the double blows of the Depression and the cruel summer weather.

It was more than discouraging for Phil. It was enervating. There didn't seem to be any use in it. He was working harder and harder and earning less and less.

He felt like giving up. He actually might have, he admitted to himself later, if it were not for his brother, whose basic good nature helped Phil to keep events in perspective. It was Bob, working alongside him in the store, who kept reminding him that the summer weather would have to break eventually, that winter would have to come, and with it complaints about the cold.

By now, Phil's mother had settled into her part-time job at the furrier's.

Her attitude toward this work surprised Phil. He had met her boss, Leonard Abel, and knew him as a short, stout man with a small head and a nasty disposition. Though Abel could be unctuously obsequious to his customers, he behaved to his cutters, fitters, and other workers in the same manner that he did to his wife, Lotte—like a petty tyrant.

Phil expected that his mother would stay in her job for no more that a week or two. But she showed no signs of wanting to quit. On the contrary, she not only got along with Leonard Abel, but even managed to change his attitudes toward the other workers.

Despite the fact that Phil realized his mother enjoyed what she did, he found himself having flashes of resentment about it. The fact that she was working at all seemed somehow to diminish his own accomplishments. It was as if he wasn't needed quite as much as he thought he should be.

He tried his best to hide these feelings. Every so often, however, they slipped out. She really didn't have to work, he might say. It seemed silly for her to have to leave the house every morning at eight-thirty and not get back until two P.M. when there was no need.

"Do you have any complaint about the way the apartment is run?" his mother responded once.

"Of course not. I'm just worried about you. Your health."

"My health has never been better. But I think you're more worried about your own pride than you are about my health.

I can understand that. Your father used to have too much pride, also."

"I wish he had a little of it left," Phil grumbled, thinking that if his father still went out to work, his mother wouldn't have to. For, though the elder Aronson protested about doing a woman's job, he did make the beds in the morning, prepared breakfast, and tidied up so that his wife could leave.

"Your father is a sick man," Sophie Aronson said. "And it is his pride that suffers most of all."

One thing which helped make the new arrangements possible was the fact that the Aronsons' present quarters were so much smaller than their former ones. They had fewer rooms, now, with smaller areas to clean. And with most of their finer furniture having been sold to pay debts, what was left did not have to be taken care of quite so carefully.

On the other hand, they did find their new apartment cramped. Instead of a real dining room, for example, they now had to make do with a dining alcove adjoining the living room. Nor was the kitchen large enough for the family to eat in comfortably, now. And since there were only two regular bedrooms, Naomi was shunted into a tiny room off the kitchen which at the turn of the century had been a maid's room.

Phil could not blame Naomi for resenting this arrangement. He didn't like putting his kid sister in a small, dark cubicle without proper ventilation. But what else could he have done? They could not afford a larger apartment; and at least Naomi had a room of her own and didn't have to share one with her two older brothers.

But that did not stop Naomi from spending her days in a sullen angry mood—especially where her brother Phil was concerned.

Phil himself was resentful. She seemed to blame him for everything that went wrong.

At least Bob wasn't that way, he thought gratefully. Bob didn't even complain about the fact that his tips were smaller than he'd thought they'd be and Phil couldn't pay him any money at all for the work he did in the store.

The problem with his sister, Phil thought, was that she didn't know how fortunate she really was!

"Maybe we ought to show her," he suggested to Bob while they were working together in the market. "We could walk her through Central Park, take her to that 'Hooverville' in the dry reservoir and let her see how some families have to live."

"Take it easy, Phil," Bob responded mildly. "She's only a kid."

"Shit! Even a kid ought to show a little gratitude."

"What do you want her to do?" Bob laughed. "Kiss your ass three times a day?"

Phil laughed too. If it were anyone else he might have gotten angry.

"She might try smiling once in a while," he said. "What in hell is she so mad about? Okay, we all know she doesn't live in a palace. But whatever she does have is because of me!"

"Maybe that's the trouble," Bob suggested.

"What does *that* mean?"

"I'm not sure." Bob grinned and shrugged. "But you are kind of taking over Papa's job," he said. "You know—you're the one who brings in the money now and tells the rest of us what to do."

"Hey, wait a minute," Phil interjected. "If you're trying to say that I run around giving orders like some goddamn Mussolini or something..."

"Hell, no. Jesus. Someone has to take over, Phil. And since Papa doesn't want the job any more, you're elected. But Naomi really loves Papa. You know?"

"Yeah? So?"

"So Naomi knows how unhappy Papa is. How hurt. She spends most of the day with him, after all, and she's not blind or deaf."

"Does she think what happened to him is my fault, too? Jesus H. Christ!" Phil was angry. "I didn't bust his bank or wreck his business. And I'm not making him stay home in bed now. I wish he'd go out and find a job!"

"Sure, I know that," Bob said. "And Mom does. But Papa's feeling sorry for himself and Naomi's just a mixed-up kid who doesn't know what she thinks."

"You'll get no argument from me there, kid brother."

"Yeah, but Papa'll get over it. And Naomi—well, she's a nice kid. Maybe if you were a little nicer to her..."

"How do you mean?"

"Well, like this, maybe. You know her birthday's coming up next week?"

Phil shrugged. He had forgotten.

"Why don't we take her downtown to see a movie," Bob

went on doggedly. "She'd like that. It'd be a birthday treat."

"Okay," Phil said. "What the hell. Maybe it'll make the little creep easier to live with."

13

The day was a disaster.

It started out pleasantly enough with Naomi appearing to be genuinely happy to be taken downtown by her brothers. Since it was her birthday, they allowed her to select the film. She picked a musical, *Flying Down to Rio*, staring Dolores Del Rio.

Phil's mood began to turn sour as he sat through the movie. The plot angered him. It was too stupid, just the kind of thing his sister might like. One scene even had a group of girls prancing about on the wing of an airplane!

What Naomi liked best was a dance sequence, "The Carioca," which was danced by a new team. Naomi, who carefully studied every movie magazine she managed to get her hands on, claimed that Fred Astaire and Ginger Rogers had never danced together in films before. Bob liked them too, and even Phil had to admit that Astaire was athletic while Rogers was gorgeous. But dance exhibitions bored him. Personally, he would have preferred a good Cagney gangster film or a Marx Brothers comedy such as *Duck Soup*, which he'd been wanting to see anyway.

After the movie they took Naomi for an ice cream soda.

"Would you like to do anything else?" Phil asked her. "We're not far from Rockefeller Center."

"Let's go there and see the RCA Building," Bob suggested. "That's supposed to be really something. Seventy stories tall."

"The Empire State Building is a hundred and two stories," Naomi said disdainfully.

"Jesus Christ, Nommie," Phil said. "So what?"

"You've already seen the Empire State Building," Bob reminded her gently. "And the RCA Building is where all the radio shows'll be coming from."

"You mean like Jack Benny?"

"Well . . ." Bob shrugged. Actually, he had no idea where Jack Benny did his radio show.

"I thought Uncle Don was more your style, Nommie," Phil put in, naming the host of a well-known program for very young children. "Isn't that right?"

"You! . . ." Naomi spluttered. Outraged as she was by this assault on her ten-year-old dignity, she could not think of a word vile enough to fit her eldest brother.

"Don't call me Nommie!" she said at last.

"Okay, Nommie."

"You . . . damn! . . ."

"Now, now," Phil laughed. "Little girls aren't supposed to use such language."

Bob could see that Naomi was close to tears. He placed a protective arm about her shoulder.

"Leave her alone, will you, Phil," he said. "I thought we were going to show her a good time today. It's her birthday, remember?"

"Some birthday," Naomi sniffed. "First he says mean things about my movie. Then he has to call me by that name!"

"I'm sorry," said Phil who was starting to feel ashamed of himself. "Naomi, I really am sorry."

Naomi sniffed again and gave him a look, as though trying to judge if he really meant it.

Bob gave her shoulder a gentle squeeze.

"Did you hear what he called you?" he asked. "He called you Naomi. I guess that proves he's serious."

Despite herself, Naomi had to grin. "I guess so," she said.

They walked east toward Radio City. They were about a block away when they realized that there were a great number of other people there too. Crowds seemed to be milling about in front of the RCA Building.

"What the hell's going on?" Phil wondered.

"I don't know," Bob replied. He peered down the street. "Some of them are carrying signs, though."

"And there are policemen on horses," Naomi said.

Bob gave his sister a quick glance and then turned to his brother. "Maybe we ought to get her out of here," he said.

78

"No, don't take me home." Naomi's eyes were bright. "I want to see what's happening."

Phil was silent for a moment. He knew that his brother was probably right. The mixture of crowd and police could always turn dangerous. The area was not a safe one for Naomi on her tenth birthday.

But like Naomi, he was curious. They could always run away at the first sign of trouble.

"Let's just get a little closer," he suggested. "We'll take her back in a few minutes."

Bob nodded reluctantly, and the trio drew closer to the private street that bordered the entrance to the building.

They could hear the shouts, now, and read some of the signs.

"Down with Rockefeller!" the crowd was chanting. *"Up with Rivera!"*

The placards read: "ROCKEFELLER IS A PHILISTINE; ROCKE-FELLER THE FASCIST; ROCKEFELLER, DESTROYER OF ART."

"What in hell is going on?" he asked.

Bob was studying the signs. "I think I know," he said. "It's about some paintings. Murals."

"Huh?"

"I overheard a couple of teachers talking about it in school," Bob said.

"What are you talking about?" Phil asked impatiently.

"One of the Rockefellers—Nelson, I think it was—hired a guy to paint a group of murals in the lobby of the RCA Building. But when the guy was finished, the Rockefeller family thought what he did was too communistic. According to those teachers, the whole idea of the murals was to show how much lousier it is ɔ live in a capitalist society than it is in a place like Russia. There's even supposed to be a picture of Lenin showing him as the leader of all the workers!"

"Yeah? No kidding?"

"So what the Rockefellers did," Bob said in conclusion, "was to have the murals covered over with blank canvas."

"And that's what all *this* is about?" Phil pointed incredu-lously at the mounting furor in front of them. "Covering up some pictures?"

"Well, the guy who did the murals is a famous artist. From Mexico, I think. And a lot of people are afraid that the Rocke-fellers won't be satisfied with covering the work over. They think they plan to destroy the murals altogether."

"So why the hell shouldn't they?" Phil demanded angrily. "It's their building, isn't it? Why should they let some god-damned Mexican Bolshie paint propaganda inside the lobby?"

"But it's not fair!" Naomi broke in passionately.

Her outburst startled both her brothers. They stared at her.

"What the hell do *you* know about it?" Phil asked.

Bob's tone was more gentle. "Why isn't it fair?"

"Because it's not . . . I mean especially if he's a really great artist." Naomi shook her head violently, as though trying to unravel knots in her tongue. "It's just not fair to destroy beautiful paintings."

"Even if you own the paintings?" Bob wondered softly. "And even if you don't agree that they're so beautiful?"

"But you could be wrong," Naomi said earnestly. "They might be beautiful even so. And if they were, think of all the people who might want to see them. You'd be stealing their chance from them."

Bob smiled at her. He was moved by her vision.

"Oh my God," Phil moaned. He glared at his brother. "Don't encourage her!"

"But she could be right," Bob said.

"Hey, wait a minute," Phil protested. "Let's be serious. Are you saying that someone could walk into my place, say, and paint whatever he wants to? That just because he's an artist I don't have the right to stop him?"

"No, of course not."

"What's the difference? This Mexican guy wanted to use Rockefeller's wall to paint communist propaganda. What's the difference between that and going into Mr. Lubbuck's store and painting a mural about the dangers of canned food?"

"Look, the Rockefellers asked him to paint the mural. They knew that one of the themes was going to be the rise of labor."

"You mean the Rockefellers knew they were getting a Bolshie mural?" Phil asked in disbelief.

"I guess they didn't think it was going to be as radical as it was," Bob muttered.

"Oh. And did they pay this man?"

"Sure, I guess he got paid. He wouldn't do the work for nothing."

"That settles it," Phil pronounced. "When you pay someone to do a job, you have a right to think that he'll do it the way you want him to."

"But an artist—"

"An artist." Phil pronounced the word scornfully. "Artists paint pictures on applesauce cans. Do you think he should have the right to paint some kid dropping dead from a poisoned apple?"

Bob shook his head. Phil realized this was something on which they would never agree.

"Diego Rivera!" Naomi cried suddenly.

"Huh?"

"That name. It's on the placard there. He must be the person who painted the murals."

"Yeah, probably . . ."

But Phil wasn't thinking about that. He had begun to realize that they had been walking dangerously close to the mob of chanting demonstrators and to the police who were there to control them.

There was a great horde of police. More of them than of the demonstrators themselves, more, certainly, than Phil had originally thought. Some of them were on foot, some were on horseback. All of them seemed to be losing their patience under the taunts of the crowd.

Phil and Bob exchanged glances.

"Let's get out of here," Bob said.

"My thought, exactly."

But Naomi didn't want to leave.

Phil could not understand why. Nor could he comprehend the peculiar smile on her face. It was almost as if she were enjoying the scene—or if not enjoying it, then experiencing it on an entirely different level than either himself or Bob.

"Come on." Phil was exasperated. "Damn it, Nommie, do I have to pick you up and carry you like a baby?"

It was the wrong thing for him to have said. "You . . . you wouldn't dare!" Naomi hissed and shot away from him like a small projectile.

But Bob had half expected this. He grabbed his sister's arm and held it firmly.

"We don't want to see you hurt," he said calmly.

By now, though, they had reached the line of police who were guarding the sidewalk by the building entrance.

"Come on," Phil repeated urgently. He captured Naomi's other arm and gave it a tug.

"That hurts."

"Then let's go," he said. But even as he started to lead the way there was a disturbance on the other side of the police line.

Phil paused, despite himself. He saw a girl who could not have been much more than eighteen. She was bareheaded and wearing a plain blue dress of thin cotton.

"What is the matter with us?" she was crying over the clamor of the crowd. "Are we all cowards? Have we no courage at all?"

Gradually, the clamor ceased as people began shushing each other in order to hear what she was saying.

"Our comrade, the great Diego Rivera, has created a mural for all the working, toiling, striving sweating suffering people of the world. But where is that people's masterpiece? Tell me," she pleaded in a voice dripping with sarcasm. "Has anyone seen it?"

There were mutters, then cries, then roars from the crowd. The girl waited a magic moment before raising her hand and going on:

"You know where it is: It is being held hostage by the despisers of the people. They have hidden it from us. They are keeping it away from our sight. It is OURS! It was created for US! But THEY won't let us see it!

"And we're letting them get away with it!"

Again there were mutters and growls and shouts. The word, "No," was heard and the phrase, "We won't!"

"What shall we do about it?" the girl was demanding now. "What shall we DO? Shall we liberate them? Liberate the Rivera murals?"

"YES!" replied the crowd which was now speaking with one voice. "LIBERATE THEM. LIBERATE THE MURALS!..."

And Phil was half compelled to join the crowd himself. To submerge his own voice and mind and individuality and become a cell of that giant creature which had been called into being by the girl in the blue cotton dress.

It was not only her beauty which made it so hard for him to resist her call. (And she was very beautiful—with breeze-blown, honey-blond hair, an oval face, and compelling eyes that seemed to pierce deeply into the soul of every man, woman, and child on that street.) Nor was it only that startlingly clear voice of hers which could inspire one moment, and then flick painfully like some verbal whip.

82

This girl in her blue cotton dress seemed to embody the spirit of the age in which they lived: poverty, depression, failure. Ironically enough, it was an age of hope as well. In America at least, it was a decade in which the common man was perceived to be coming into his own.

If the country was teetering on the brink of anarchy and ruin, that was seen to be the fault, not of the people, but of those who had been running the country—the bosses, the bankers, the industrialists, the big shots. The ordinary people were perceived as having an instinctive goodness and wisdom which would eventually save the nation and make it greater than ever.

"The people, yes," wrote Carl Sandburg, the poet of the Depression—and thus gave voice to what was felt by millions.

While Sandburg himself was from Illinois, nowhere was his faith in the little man more deeply shared than in New York City. For New York was not only the city of Wall Street—the city of great banks and businesses and high finance—it was also a place of new, radical ideas; a feisty, labor-oriented, melting-pot of a town. Its colorful and pugnacious half-Italian, half-Jewish mayor—Fiorello LaGuardia, the Little Flower—was an Episcopalian who first married a Catholic and then a Lutheran girl of German descent. He was the very personification of a New York melting-pot type of common man who had made good and was taking over the reins of power.

In the New York of the thirties, the *Zeitgeist* was one of brashness and impudence, one which crowed gloatingly that the old had failed and must make way for the new; that the day of the big shot was past and that the future was with the ordinary people.

The precise *form* that that future would take was still being argued over, however. Some of those who rallied in front of Radio City, for example, were committed New Dealers who were satisfied that the nation could be saved through combining private enterprise with Roosevelt's brand of government control and federally encouraged trade-unionism. Others were sure that Stalin's Russia represented the wave of the future and that to accept anything else for America was to sell out the working classes. There were those whose beliefs fell somewhere between those two. There were Trotskyites and old-style "Wobblies", a nick-name for members of the Industrial Workers of the World and new-style Social Democrats.

But at this moment in time they were all one, formed into a unit by the girl in the thin blue dress. At her urging they were ready to challenge the police in the name of the people, to free the murals which had been painted by the people's poet and to defy the young Rockefeller heir who would end up destroying those murals so that the people would never have a chance to see them or be influenced by their political views.

The urge to become a part of that noisy, driven throng was almost too great for Philip Aronson to resist. Almost.

For he did not—could not—give in to it. In the first place, he had his sister with him. He couldn't just leave Naomi with Bob in order to make the quixotic gesture of trying—probably in vain—to liberate a bunch of murals he had never heard of until just a short while ago.

And secondly, no matter what his feelings were telling him, there was a cynically pragmatic part of Phil which made him realize that his own self-interests were very much in conflict with the girl in blue's emotional call to arms.

For Phil himself had his own struggle to attend to. It was a personal struggle, not a mass movement. And it was for him and his family, not for the common man. Phil's entire goal, as a matter of fact, was to make himself into an uncommon man.

So Phil turned his back on the spirit of his times and ignored the cries of "LIBERATE THE RIVERA MURALS!" He started to forcefully shepherd his brother and sister away from where the crowd was trying to break through the police line that was guarding the entrance of the building.

The Aronsons had hardly begun their escape when chaos struck.

A fresh troup of mounted policemen rode in from Fiftieth Street to charge the rear of the crowd. The only noise that was heard was the sound of their horses' hooves striking against the pavement. They themselves did not curse, nor did their horses snort or whinny. The crowd did not even know it was being attacked until the nightsticks began to swing.

And then there *was* noise: Screams and howls and curses which turned gradually to moans and whimpers as the people of the crowd realized how thoroughly they had been defeated.

For within moments the crowd was no longer a crowd—a mass of people with a mind and will separate and beyond their individual minds and wills. It was breaking up, now, into precisely those individual components. Where there had been a crowd—a mob—there was now a group of frightened people, all of whom were trying desperately to flee in terror.

The most horrifying part was that they were not able to flee. Mounted police were behind them. More cops were in front. Wherever they turned there were cops—all of them swinging their nightsticks, punching with their fists, kicking and stomping with their feet.

Briefly—very briefly—the girl could still be heard as she cried brokenly for her defeated army.

Phil was standing half in a daze. What had happened had taken place so swiftly that it was all but impossible to digest.

He felt a hand on his shoulder and turned swiftly. Where he had expected to see a cop, he saw his brother instead.

"Bob? . . . Are you all right?"

"Yeah. You?"

"Fine. . . . Where's Nommie?"

"Jesus!" Bob turned white with sudden panic. "I thought she was with you!"

"What in hell made you think that?" Phil demanded furiously. "You're the one who had hold of her when the action started."

Bob was stung. "Only one arm," he retorted. "You were holding on to the other."

"You're right," Phil conceded. "But when she jerked away from me I thought you had her."

"Me too," Bob said, "When she pulled away from me, I figured you were taking her back to the apartment. Then I—I must have been distracted. You know, by that girl—all those cops."

Phil nodded. "Let's start looking for her. She can't be too far from here."

14

The street in front of the lobby entrance to Radio City Hall was practically deserted now that the former protestors had been marched a block away to be loaded into paddy wagons parked on Forty-ninth Street. A couple of slow-moving sanitation workers were breaking up the placards and arranging the debris in neat stacks. Several ambulances, their sirens wailing piercingly, began pulling away from around the corner.

It was this last sound which caused Bob to shiver in the heavy heat.

"Christ," he said. "I hope she isn't hurt."

"Why should she be?" Phil snapped angrily. "Who'd want to hurt a little kid?"

Bob did not bother to reply. The answer was too obvious and too frightening to verbalize.

Phil approached a large, beefy policeman in his early thirties. He gave the officer his sister's name and description.

The cop was sympathetic. It was a rotten shame, he said. He had brothers and sisters and children of his own, so he knew just how Phil and Bob must feel. But he hadn't noticed any little girls among the crowd. If he had, he would have kept her with him until it was time for him to return to the station house.

They questioned other policemen. But they couldn't find one who recalled seeing Naomi.

"So what do we do now?" Bob asked. He did not even try to hide his growing fear.

"I'll tell you what," Phil said. "We'll walk up to Fifth Avenue and then separate. You can go a block south; I'll go north. We'll circle west to Sixth Avenue, then meet back here."

"Okay."

They did what Phil suggested. But they had no success.

"Maybe we'd better start calling some hospitals," Bob said. "And the local precincts."

"Which hospitals?" Phil asked cynically. "There are a hell of a lot of them in Manhattan alone."

"Well, at least the nearby ones."

"All right," Phil said after a moment or two. "We'll make another circle—wider this time. If that doesn't work we can go to a drugstore, get some nickels and start calling."

Naomi was in no local hospital nor trapped in a police station.

They separated once more and made a still wider circle. They did it again. And again. It was twilight by now and, as the day became dimmer, so did their hopes.

"What are we going to tell Mama and Papa?" Bob asked when it became clear that they could do no more and that they were going to have to turn homeward in defeat.

"I don't know," Phil responded. With his brother so near tears, he was trying desperately to keep his own emotions under control. "I'll try to think of something."

But when they reached home, Naomi was already there.

All of Phil's concern over the girl—his fears over what might have happened to her and his sense of guilt about letting her out of his sight turned instantly into black rage.

He cursed viciously and raised his fist.

Bob caught Phil's arm from the rear while Sophie grabbed her daughter and hugged her protectively to her breast.

"What are you doing?" she shrieked. "Phil!"

"He's crazy!" Phil's father said. "I always knew there was something wrong with the boy. He's crazy!"

Phil took a deep breath. He struggled against his fury with every ounce of strength he had.

"Jesus Christ..." he muttered.

"Still with the swearing?" his father said. "And in front of your mother?"

But Phil was paying no attention to him. He glared at Naomi who was still finding shelter in her mother's arms.

"Do you know what you put us through, you...you little?....Well, do you?"

Naomi opened her mouth and then shut it again—as much from her own stubbornness as from fear.

"Will you tell me why you left us?" Phil demanded. "All right, maybe you hate me. But why did you run away from Bob?"

"I didn't," Naomi said.

"She should ask why you and Bob let go of her!" Their father interjected. "God knows why you two took her to that dangerous demonstration. But if you did, you should at least have kept an eye on her!"

This was too much for Phil. "Papa!" he shouted. "Shut the hell up!"

The room grew horribly still. Phil might have challenged his father before, but he had never spoken to him in that overbearing manner. He would not have done so now, indeed, were he not so incensed—first at what Naomi had done and then at his father's reaction to it.

The older man could not speak. His mouth trembled and tears came into his eyes as he rushed impotently from the room.

Naomi made as though to follow her father, but Sophie kept her where she was.

"Are you satisfied, Phil?" she asked coolly, as she caressed and soothed her daughter.

"Why did he blame me?" Phil demanded. "Does he know that she ran away? Do you? Bob and I went half nuts trying to find her!"

"I spoke to her about what she did," Sophie said quietly. "So did her father."

"I didn't run away," Naomi insisted.

"When did you get home?" Phil asked.

"She got home a little less than an hour and a half ago," Sophie put in. "Your father and I knew you'd be worried about her. We kept hoping you'd phone."

"We didn't want to upset you," Phil explained.

Bob went over to where Sophie was cradling Naomi. He spoke his sister's name and touched her gently on the shoulder.

Naomi jumped slightly. Her eyes darted nervously around the room.

"What's wrong?" Bob asked.

"She's still frightened," Sophie explained. "She had a bad experience this afternoon."

"It's not that," Naomi said half defiantly. "That didn't frighten me."

"So why did you jump when Bob spoke to you?" her mother asked. She was amused despite herself.

"It's him." Naomi pointed directly at Phil. "He doesn't like me."

Phil's stomach gave a sickening lurch. Was she really serious? Did she truly believe that?

"Of course he likes you?" Sophie said. "Why else would he have been so upset when he couldn't find you today?"

"Because he got mad when he thought I ran away from him. He still thinks I ran away. He won't listen . . . even now. . . ."

Phil sighed deeply and felt his eyes grow embarrassingly moist.

"I'm sorry," he said. "No kidding. But you're wrong about my not liking you. I love you, little sister. I really do."

Naomi looked directly at him for several moments. She did not say a word.

"Tell me what did happen," Phil said finally. "I'll listen. I promise."

Naomi seemed to consider this. She nodded her agreement.

"Remember when you let go of my hand?" she said. "And then Bob did? That's when you were both looking at Laura."

"Who?" Phil asked.

"Laura Vaile. She was the girl who was calling for everyone to break into the lobby and free those murals."

"But how do you know her name?"

"I'm getting to that," Naomi said resentfully. "You promised to listen!"

"Sorry . . . go ahead."

"When I saw her get hit by that policeman on a horse, I tried to call to you—either of you." There were tears in Naomi's voice now. "When you didn't answer I looked for you, but you were somewhere in the crowd. Then suddenly, Laura was there . . . right near me . . . crawling over to the gutter . . . and her head was bleeding . . ."

Naomi paused to sob and catch her breath.

"What did you do?" Bob asked gently.

"What was I supposed to do? I—I tried to help. I couldn't find you anywhere . . . and her head . . ."

Naomi shut her eyes tightly. She grimaced.

Sophie leaned over and kissed the top of her daughter's head.

"Her head was awful," Naomi continued. "Her hair was all matted and everything, and she acted kind of dopey when I knelt down to help her."

"Didn't the cops bother you?" Bob asked.

"No." Naomi shrugged. "Maybe they didn't notice us. Laura had crawled a little ways by then, and maybe they were too busy arresting other people to bother with us. . . ."

"Yeah," Phil said. "Maybe."

"Anyway," Naomi went on, "I helped her to a drugstore about a block away, and the druggist put a dressing on her head. That's when she told me her name."

Phil nodded. He should have been the one to have taken the girl for first aid. He was feeling jealous that it had actually been his sister as well as shame for that feeling of jealousy.

"And then you came home?" he asked.

"Yes."

"It's been a tough afternoon for you, hasn't it?"

There was sympathy in Phil's glance and for a curious instant the two shared a rare moment of closeness. But then the instant was over and Phil was transformed back into the slightly disdainful older brother.

"Maybe you'd better get to bed," he suggested.

"Yes, darling," said Sophie. "You've had a big day."

Naomi left the room quietly.

"She must really be tired." Phil grinned. "She didn't even try to put up a fight."

Sophie smiled. "I've saved some food for you, boys. You can have some nice, cold chicken."

"Hey," Bob said. "That's great!"

But Phil was shaking his head. "I may have to go out for a while. First let me make a phone call."

What he was going to do was start calling women. He would try Kay first, but if she were not available he would try others.

Tonight he had to make out. He *needed* to!

He needed a soft, warm female body to thrust into, to prove his manhood with. He needed a place to bury the unspoken shame of losing his sister, of acting like a fool, of not being on hand to rescue an unknown girl named Laura Vaile.

15

The crisp fall weather everyone was waiting for followed fast on the heels of the Jewish holidays.

People were happier now. The autumn tang in the air told them that Thanksgiving was approaching. Christmas would not be far behind. Anyone who had any money at all was in a mood to spend some of it, and Phil's business started to pick up again.

These days, all he had to do was hint that the fifth race at a certain track, for example, might hold a few interesting surprises and a bet would be placed. If he suggested that a dinner would be better if the cut of meat were superior a purchase would be made.

Though he did miss Bob's company at the store, he also recognized that his brother's schooling was far too important to interrupt. In fact it was Phil who insisted that Bob keep his promise and return to school when the summer vacation ended.

Bob himself would have been happier to keep on working.

"It would be a fucking waste!" Phil said furiously. It was a Sunday and they had walked over to Central Park. Last year they might have been having a discussion like this seated at the old, scarred table. But it had been too large for their new kitchen.

"I thought we had a deal. I was going to bring in the dough and you were going to stay in school and work your butt off to get into a good college. True?"

"Yeah, but—I'm fifteen, now. I'm not a kid any more."

"Let's have none of that crap, buddy. You're going to be a professional man—a lawyer, banker . . . like that. One of these days, you and I are going to be together against the whole goddamn world. And when that day comes, I want you trained and ready and sharp as a knife!"

Bob grinned. "Okay."

"Bet your ass," Phil said, punching his brother lightly on the shoulder.

"But, Phil, listen. What about part time? After school, say, and on weekends?"

"No. I already told you I want you to break your ass. How're you going to do that if you work part time?"

Then Bob brought up what he'd apparently really been thinking about. "What about my helping you collect bets?"

Phil looked shocked. He had not expected anything like this. "What put that into your head?"

"I just thought you might need some help."

Phil frowned at his brother. He had a sense that something did not add up. The two of them had never seriously discussed the gambling operation (although Phil realized that Bob had to have at least some idea about it; he was not Mr. Lubbock who did not *want* to know). What made him bring it up now when he'd had all summer to ask questions?

"I don't need any help," Phil said carefully. "But if I did, I wouldn't use you."

"Why not? I'm your brother. Don't you trust me?"

"Jesus," Phil said in disgust. "You're as bad as Nommie. 'Don't you trust me?' What in hell does that mean?"

"Then why won't you let me work for you?"

"I already told you: school."

"I could do both. It wouldn't take that much time."

Phil sighed. "All right, then. The reason I won't let you get involved is that I don't want you mixed up in it. It's no damn good for you."

"But you're mixed up in it."

"Yeah, and that's my problem," Phil snapped. "I want one of us to stay clean."

"Shit," Bob said. "All I want to do is make a little money by picking up and delivering. Like you used to."

Something seemed to click inside Phil's brain. He knew now what had been bothering him.

"Wait a minute," he said slowly. "How do you know what I used to do? We never talked about that."

Bob lowered his eyes.

"Did Lew Bocca put you up to this?" Phil demanded. He was becoming angrier. "Did he suggest that you talk to me and then tell you what to say?"

"Well . . . maybe. But it was something I would've thought of, anyway."

"Bullshit!" Phil growled. He glared at his brother, who would not meet his eyes.

"I'm going to see that son-of-a-bitch Bocca," he added. "And when I do, I'm going to—"

"Hey, he didn't mean any harm," Bob broke in earnestly. "He was only trying to do good for the both of us. He said I could help make your business grow. If it didn't grow, he said, it would probably die. All things have to grow or die."

Phil was not impressed. "I heard his uncle tell *him* that one time."

"That doesn't make it less true," Bob said stubbornly. "Just because he heard it from his uncle."

"What did Lew tell you?" Phil asked. "Exactly."

"I don't know. I just happened to run into him one day and we got to talking. He asked if I liked going to school full time, or would I rather pick up some extra dough."

"And you said you'd like the dough?"

"Yeah . . . something like that."

"Did he tell you how easy it was? With no real risk? Did he say it was just a matter of dragging a briefcase around town?"

Bob grunted.

"Christ," Phil said.

"I don't know what you're so mad about," Bob said resentfully. He was starting to become angry himself. "Lew was only trying to help."

"Sure he was. He was trying to help his uncle."

"But he said—"

"Don't be a jerk, Bob. The Boccas have been pushing me to enlarge for some time. They figure I could be bringing in more dough. And the easiest way to start me in is to get you in the act."

"Yeah, but . . . we'd get more dough too, wouldn't we?"

"Not enough more to make it worth my while to risk your future," Phil said flatly. "And, no matter what Lew told you, the risks are pretty goddamn high."

"Are they?" Bob countered.

"Ask Jake Karpas. Did you hear he'd been picked up by the cops the other day for running hootch?"

"Running hootch?" Bob repeated incredulously. "I thought the police had stopped pulling anyone in for bootlegging now that Repeal is so close to ratification."

"They have stopped. Unless the word goes out to teach someone a lesson."

"Who'd want to bother with Jake?"

"Not Jake," Phil said. "He was working for a new boss who'd stepped on a few too many toes. Jake was picked up by a couple of friendly cops and hauled before a certain judge who put him away for a couple of months. When he gets out he'll be lucky if he's still wearing his balls. That'd really teach his boss a lesson!"

"Jesus!" Bob said.

"Yeah." Phil grinned tightly. "This can be a very rough business. Just when you think you're among friends, you can find yourself right in the middle of a gang war."

"Yet you stay in it."

"Right now I have no choice," Phil conceded. "We need the money. But I've got a few ideas in the back of my head and I'm going to get out as soon as I can."

16

Phil knew a lot more about what had happened to Jake Karpas than he had told his brother.

One thing he knew was that it was Al Bocca who had put Jake behind bars and then passed the word to have him worked over in jail. Jake—stupid as always—had switched his allegiance to a Jersey City organization which was trying to invade a section of Bocca territory in Manhattan. The Boccas decided to make an example of him.

Phil could not blame Al and Lew for wanting to protect what was theirs. Nor could he feel much sympathy for Jake—if a guy behaved like an asshole, he'd be treated like one. What bothered him was the decision of the Jersey City gang to move in. There was more and more of that going on lately.

Phil thought that the increasing violence in the underworld was caused by the approach of Repeal. For with the end of Prohibition, the different gangs would be dividing a far smaller pie.

There would still be money—and legal money at that—to be made from the importation and sale of liquor, but the days of making enormous profits from the sale of terrible gin and whiskey were over.

During Prohibition, most gang wars began because somebody got greedy and wanted more than his fair share. Now they started because people wanted to keep making what they already made and tried to expand their income with other rackets such as drugs, gambling, and prostitution. When they did they bumped up against other racketeers with the same thing in mind.

Phil guessed the Jersey organization had tried to elbow its way into Bocca territory, not to take over the declining liquor business—that was only a feint—but to challenge Lew and Al for their bookmaking business. And he knew the Boccas were going to expand their activities in prostitution.

• • •

Lew asked Phil to run a string of call girls for himself and his uncle.

"It'll be a snap," he said. "Have I ever steered you wrong? Uncle Al and I'll supply the broads—strictly high class stuff, by the way; we'll even have our own doctor on the payroll to make sure they don't get dosed up. We'll start you out with ten of them—that'll be nine plus a sort of captain to keep the others in line.

"All you'll have to do is keep *her* in line." Lew laughed lasciviously. "Get what I mean?"

Phil nodded.

"So what's wrong?" Lew asked. He was bothered by his friend's lack of enthusiasm.

"I don't know . . . doesn't Oscar the Wolf run whores in this area?"

"So what?" Lew was being elaborately casual. "It's a free country. If Oscar says something to you, just send him to us. We'll talk to him."

Sure, Phil thought. And after the talking died down there'd be a war. With himself and his girls directly in the line of fire. This was something he did not need—to risk his ass for the honor of being a pimp!

"What about it?" Lew pressed. "Shit. I thought you'd jump at this. Make a lot of extra loot and have all the free nookie you want? Wow!"

"That's true," Phil said slowly. "But on the other hand . . ."

"On the other hand, what? Don't tell me you're peeing in your pants about Oscar. I told you we'd protect you, didn't I? Or don't you think we can?"

Phil knew that he could not admit to having any doubts about that. The Boccas would not only think him a coward, which was bad enough, but an ungrateful one. Al and Lew had helped him when he needed help. Now they were asking him to do something. He'd better have a pretty good reason if he wanted to say no and make it stick.

"It's the goddamn broads," he said at last.

"What do you mean? Don't you like broads any more? Don't tell me my old buddy's decided to be a fairy?"

"Oh, yeth," Phil said, pronouncing the word with a horribly exaggerated lisp. "Thure . . ."

The two friends laughed together. Phil felt secure enough,

95

now, to use his knowledge of Lew's suspicious attitudes towards women.

"The thing about whores," Phil said, "is that they're like all dames. Great for a roll in the hay, of course, but you can't really trust them. It doesn't matter what you do for them—some guy comes along with a big wad of dough and it's bye-bye, Daddy!"

"Or even a big cock," Lew said with a grin. "Which is why we'll have one of the girls act as captain. She'll be cut in for a small piece of the action in order to keep the rest of them in line."

"And if she decides to shaft us?"

"What is the matter? Don't you think you could slap her down?"

Phil flushed. "Hey, look. I'm not trying to get out of anything. I know what your uncle's done for me, and if he wants me in this deal then I'm in. I just think running whores is a loser's game. Like he says about drugs—it's more trouble than it's worth."

Phil hoped this last statement might have some effect. Lew's uncle had always been against entering the drug racket. Not because it was immoral—he didn't care how people went to hell with themselves, he used to say, as long as they paid him to let them do it. But that was the problem: he didn't think that drug addicts would pay him enough to justify the risk.

Al Bocca had a theory that drugs would never be employed by more than a tiny minority of what he liked to call "real" Americans. Who would be the users? Mainly nonwhites and oddballs. The Chinese, for example, would continue to use opium; Negroes would go for "happy dust," such as cocaine or heroin; while crazy jazz musicians—both black and white—would continue to puff on marijuana cigarettes.

"I don't think that Uncle Al would agree that running whores is the same as dealing drugs," Lew said doubtfully. "But I'll do my best to explain how you feel."

"Thanks," Phil replied. He meant it. He knew Lew would put his objections in the best light possible.

"Like I say," he went on. "If your uncle really needs me in this deal . . . ."

"It's not what my uncle needs," Lew told him. "He thought it would be a good idea if you were in. And he also thought you'd be grateful for the chance."

Phil lowered his eyes. He hoped that this refusal wouldn't come back to haunt him.

As it turned out, Sal Terragano—one of the men Phil had met the first time he'd visited the offices of Southwood Investment Corporation—took over a string of prostitutes under the same arrangement that had been offered to Phil. Sal not only made a great deal of money this way, but he was comparatively safe since Al had come to some sort of an arrangement with Oscar the Wolf.

Lew Bocca liked to rub in the lesson of Sal's success and talked about it to his friend whenever he could find an excuse.

"Did you hear that Sal added four new broads to his stable?" he asked Phil one night when they were having a drink. "Real lookers, too."

"Yeah," said Phil. "I heard."

"It could have been you making all that dough. Next time maybe you'll listen to me."

Phil nodded.

"I guess that was one of the dumbest things you ever did, huh? Turning down that deal?"

"I guess maybe it was," Phil replied.

He didn't really believe it, though. What he did believe was that he'd made an especially wise decision when he'd turned the offer down. For the more he became involved with new illegal activities, the harder it would be for him to eventually leave the rackets. And the hope of some day being able to leave the rackets was always part of his secret dreams.

17

Phil liked to tell himself that he'd never had a real choice. Once his father had come apart at the seams, he was forced to grab at any chance. He had become a bookmaker—gotten into the rackets—because he could find no other way to earn enough money for himself and his family.

He still had no choice. He still needed money for himself and his family. But concern about his family was now urging him to search for an alternative. Remaining in the rackets, he was beginning to recognize, would not be fair to his family.

He felt this way for a number of reasons. In the first place, he didn't enjoy placing them all at risk—and they were at risk simply because they were his family.

Phil was living in a violent world. His enemies in that world, Al and Lew Bocca's enemies, would not hesitate to punish him by going after his mother, his father, his sister, or his brother.

He lived with the fear that this might actually happen some-day. He didn't talk about it. His brother, for instance, was never to find out the true reason for Phil's terror when their sister suddenly vanished on her birthday.

But as much as he feared for their safety, he also worried about how they might be affected by the mere knowledge of his activities.

His father, Phil believed, would take satisfaction from the fact that his eldest son had turned out to be a criminal. He would talk about it to anyone who would listen, and say that he always knew that the boy had bad blood (received from his wife's side of the family). The old man would go on and on about it, never giving him a moment's peace. Eventually, Phil would lose his temper and God alone knew what might happen next!

His mother would react in a far different manner, though the final results would be as devastating. She would be silently sad, he felt, keeping her deepest thoughts to herself. But it would do such terrible things to her that he didn't know if she would ever recover. It could be a final blow that might destroy her will to live.

And his brother?

And his sister?

Though Bob knew some of the facts already, he did not know them all. If he had any idea of just how connected his brother really was, for example, he might insist on joining him in the rackets in order to share his load of guilt. This was something that Phil would not allow.

He made up his mind to discuss that problem with Lew and Al Bocca. Al was the one he had to convince, he realized. He did not know what he would do if he wasn't able to convince him.

As the discussion proceeded, Phil could see that Lew Bocca

was almost as nervous as he was. Lew's uncle listened courteously, however, until Phil had finished speaking.

"Let me get this straight," he said then. "You don't want Bob to get into the business or to know the extent of your own involvement. Is that it?"

"Yes."

"I can understand that." Al Bocca stroked the ends of his fine, white mustache. "You want him to stay clean so he will have a good future. Maybe he'll be a judge, someday, or a congressman. You don't want anyone to be able to get a handle on him, right?"

"Yes," Phil repeated.

He turned to his nephew and to the assistant known as Billy. "That's a nice thing, don't you think? Family feeling."

They both agreed that it was.

"But nice things must sometimes be paid for," Al went on, returning his gaze to Phil. "When Lew suggested that Bob work with you it was because we both felt that he could help you return more money in these hard times. True?"

"Yes, but—"

"But you felt that you didn't want him in the business. You have just explained that." Al Bocca smiled sweetly. "I told you that I understood."

Phil nodded. He had no idea how this conversation was going to turn out. He could only hope—and not argue.

"And then a short while ago," Al Bocca continued mildly, "Lew made another suggestion. He wanted you to take on some girls. But you said that you didn't like to deal with whores, that you couldn't trust them and they made you nervous. Again an understandable sentiment.

"Or don't you think so?" he asked the two others in the room.

"I think it is, Uncle Al."

"Very understandable."

"But still and all, Phil," Al said sadly, "I can't get around one thing: you have cost us money."

"You mean . . . not just with my brother? But also because I didn't take on the girls?"

Al nodded.

"But I thought Sal was bringing in the same money I would have."

"Sal's been very cooperative," Al said gently. "And he hasn't lost by the arrangement. But you and Sal have different contacts, don't you? You know different people. You would find different customers. If you were running girls as well as Sal, we might not be receiving twice the amount we receive from him alone, but we would surely be taking in more.

"Wouldn't you say so?" he asked Lew and Billy.

"Yes, Uncle Al. We certainly would."

"Yes, Al. You're right."

"You see?" Al said to Phil.

"But, Al, I—I didn't know you wanted both of us to take on girls. I thought it was one or the other."

Al Bocca smiled sweetly. "There's a great deal you don't know, Phil. You are a very intelligent young man, but there is a great deal you don't know."

Phil did not reply. Though he still didn't believe that Al would have had the two of them running prostitutes, he was not about to argue.

"Let me say this to you, my friend," Al continued earnestly. "I know in my heart that you are a sincere person. You turned down my offers for honorable reasons. Your honesty is proved by the fact that you refused the extra money not just for us, but for yourself as well.

"But your decision does cost us money. And so I will have to ask you a question: how do you plan to make that money up?"

Al Bocca studied Phil with the steady, stern gaze of a zoological researcher waiting curiously to find out whether or not his experimental animal would come through the test.

Phil realized that he not only had to answer correctly, but must be firm and confident as well. That was also part of the test: how he stood up to such questions.

"I'll hire some more people," Phil said. Good, sharp, aggressive, young people. I'll have them bring in more customers . . . increase my gross."

"Do you really think you can gross more?" Al asked sharply.

"I'm sure I can."

"All right, then." Al Bocca's warm smile was back on his face. "That's all I want to hear. Just do what you say and your brother's in the clear.

"Lew, stay away from Bob Aronson. He's off-limits to all of us."

"Yes, Uncle Al."

Phil felt as if an enormous weight had been lifted from his shoulders. Then Al spoke again:

"There is one thing more," he said. "Bob may not realize this, but you had better. He's going to owe us."

Phil showed his confusion. His brother was going to be kept clean, wasn't he?

"He's going to owe us," Al repeated, "because you owe us, and he owes you."

Phil nodded glumly. He saw the logic. It was inescapable. If it were not for Lew and Al Bocca, Phil and his whole family might be living in a Hooverville. So all of them owed.

"Look, Al," he said. "What can he do for you? He's just a kid."

"Sure he is. Now. But you're saying he can make something of himself. Become a big shot. What I'm saying is, if he does, I may call some I.O.U.s in from you and have you call in some from him. *Capish?*"

"Yes," said Phil.

But all that would come—if it came at all—in the future. For the moment, Bob's safety was assured.

As for Naomi, he had already made up his mind as to the direction he wanted her life to take. She was going to grow up to marry a young man from a wealthy family who would give her servants and all the other advantages of wealth. She would be the kind of matron, in other words, that their mother had deserved to be.

He was not going to permit anything to destroy that dream. By the time his sister reached her teens, he swore to himself, he would be all done with bookmaking.

So he was determined to leave the rackets. But how? That was the question he still had no answers for.

He could not simply walk away. Not only did he need the money, but Al Bocca was not the sort of man to mildly accept what he might think of as disloyalty. They'd probably object to his leaving in any event.

Phil could see only one way to get out of the rackets without incurring the wrath of Al and Lew Bocca. And that was to arrange matters in such a way that they'd benefit more through his leaving than they would if he stayed. If he could find some legitimate, well-paying enterprise, for instance, it might actually pay the Boccas to invest in it as silent partners. Then, eventually, if the business turned out to be successful enough, he would try to buy them out.

He did not ask himself why—if the business was all that successful—Al and Lew would permit themselves to be bought out. For as crucial as that question might be to the future, he could not afford to think about it now. Too much thought could crack his nerve and make a slim chance even slimmer.

He would need all the cool judgement he could muster to come up with a business idea that would fill the bill. He had no notion of what it would be now. He would simply have to go on looking and racking his brains.

In the meantime, however, he could not afford to forget that desperate promise he had made to Al. A promise which was proving even harder to keep than he'd suspected.

Competition among bookmakers was becoming ever more fierce as more and more people entered the field in order to try and recoup some of the income they had lost when Prohibition came to an end. And while Phil's rivals didn't send hoods after either him or the young men he'd recruited in accordance with his promise to Al Bocca (doing that would have meant starting a war with Al himself), they did go all-out in other ways. They wooed clients with easy credit—far too easy for those hard times. They supplied tickets to the latest musical hit by Rogers and Hart or Cole Porter. And if the client was male and wanted a beautiful girl to take with him, they might supply her, too. They did everything they could, in other words, to steal some other bookie's customer while keeping their own customers happy and content to stay where they were.

Phil knew that this was a losing game. The tactics were too expensive and risky not to backfire in the long run. It meant adding to overhead at the same time you were taking markers from people who might not make them good. (If the deadbeat was faking, of course, there were a variety of techniques to make him pay his IOUs. Phil himself—though he didn't like doing it—had occasionally used the services of a muscular "debt collecter" recommended by the Boccas. But if someone was really flat broke, all the muscle in the world couldn't make him disgorge what he didn't have.)

But even though the tactics would fail eventually, they were causing Phil problems. He had assured Al he would increase his take and bring in more money. So far—though he did manage to hold his own—the maneuvers of his competition were preventing him from doing what he promised. And that wasn't good.

102

Nor did Phil want to fight fire with fire. He did ease up somewhat on credit, and was happy to do the occasional favor for a special customer. But it would be crazy, he felt, to go the same distance as his rivals.

What Phil wanted were more regular customers. Not the one-shot wise guys who jumped from bookie to bookie depending on the latest deal, but steady clients who were loyal to *him*.

All of which sounded great. But what could he do about it?

He was never sure how he happened to hit upon the idea of going after college students. But the more he thought about it, the better the idea seemed.

He knew that people his own age—whether they were in college or not—liked to bet as much as their elders did. But college men and women had more money to do something about it. Even scholarship students, or those who attended one of the free municipal colleges such as C.C.N.Y., usually had some money in their background. And those who way was paid through private universities like N.Y.U. or Columbia were extremely well-off in Depression terms.

Best of all, Phil believed that most college students wouldn't trust the average bookie, whom they'd think of as middle-aged, seedy, and decidedly unintellectual.

Well, Phil might not be an intellectual, but at least he was their own age. And a few of his part-time assistants were actually attending college in the city. They were the ones Phil first asked to approach the campuses.

He thought that most of his collegiate customers would come from the fraternity and sorority crowds, since they were the ones with more money to spend. But as he soon found out, they were also the ones with the least need for his services. For the most part, it seemed, they preferred to do their betting with one another.

Independent students, on the other hand—especially those associated with the active campus left—did become his customers. The majority of them could not afford to take part in all-night poker sessions of the sort that went on in fraternity houses. Some were afraid they'd be called frivolous if they were caught gambling openly with fellow students. If they did like to bet, therefore, it was better for them to use the services of a discreet and honest bookie who was willing to accept small wagers.

Which was how Phil and his crew gradually became bookmakers to members of a good many of the city's left-wing youth organizations. They started with those on the college campuses. Then, using the contacts they had made, they expanded to take in off-campus organizations as well.

By the end of January, 1934, the income from Phil's business had grown to a point that satisfied Al Bocca. Nothing more was said about Phil's refusal to handle prostitutes or to bring his brother into the rackets with him.

This made Phil happy, of course. But even more, he was personally pleased with himself. He was starting to feel like an important man with a whole group of people working under him.

And though several of his new group did not work out, most of them did all he expected and more. A few even proved so trustworthy that he had them take over most of the contacts with the left-wingers—thus allowing him to spend more of his own time catering to his original middle-aged and middle-class customers who still brought in most of the money.

During this period, Phil's biggest problem was to find time to pay proper attention to the food store. He solved it by giving a couple of his assistants a bit more cash if they'd help him out there as well.

If Mr. Lubbuck was bothered by the subcontracting, he didn't show it. He had learned by now that it was usually more profitable not to check too closely on Phil's decisions and activities.

18

That April, one of Phil's protégés informed him that members of a group known as Young Americans for Social Democracy had won almost eight hundred dollars by betting on a long shot who won a race held in New Orleans.

Phil reacted with a puzzled frown. "I just don't get it, Sid. That nag didn't figure to win. And you say they all pooled their money?"

"Those who had some, yeah."

Phil shook his head from side to side. "I just don't get it," he said again.

"Do you think maybe the race was fixed?" Sid Frankel asked. He was seventeen, ferret-faced, and avid for information. He was a good worker, but there were times—this was one of them—when he got on Phil's nerves.

"How the hell would I know? If it was, though, no one up here was in on it."

Phil paused, thoughtfully. "You know something: I think I'm going to deliver that dough to them myself. Maybe I can nose around and get some sort of line on what happened."

"You're going to deliver?.... Hey, shit! I mean, it's my ..."

Sid's protest came to a stammering halt as Phil used the glare he had picked up from Al Bocca.

But though his eyes remained cold and hard, he couldn't really blame Sid for being resentful. The Y.A.S.D. had been Sid's account from the beginning. Sid had told Phil about the group and then solicited it for business. He—Phil—had never even visited Y.A.S.D. headquarters.

On the other hand, it was Phil's operation.

"You took the bet, sure," he rasped now. "You want to put up the dough to pay them off?"

Sid flushed deeply, as if he didn't blame Phil for putting him in his place. "Hey, I'm sorry. I didn't mean.... Did you take much of a bath?"

Phil shook his head. "No bath at all. My associates helped me lay off a hunk."

"That's good," Sid said ingratiatingly. "I mean, I do know it's your dough...."

"Forget it, kid," Phil said.

It was not only his commitment to his older customers which had led Phil to allow Sid Frankel to be his exclusive contact with the Y.A.S.D. There were at least two other reasons. One was that the group's Sixteenth Street headquarters was inconveniently far from Phil's own base of operations. But more important was the fact that he was becoming bored with facing large groups of left-wingers.

Taken one or two at a time, Phil found most leftists to be bright, articulate, and fun to be with. And since their sources of information were so different than his, he felt he could learn a great deal from them.

Phil himself was reading more widely now. Though he still enjoyed his favorite newspaper, the *Mirror*, and continued to devour its sportswriters and Broadway columnists, he also looked into the famous Pearson and Allen political column, "Washington Merry-Go-Round," which appeared in the same paper. He looked at other papers, too, such as the more serious *Herald Tribune* and the extravagant afternoon *Journal*. He was also taking Al Bocca's advice and starting to read a couple of magazines: *Time* and *Reader's Digest*.

Phil liked to compare what he had read in one of his more orthodox publications with what a radical might tell him. But by talking and arguing, he was once in a while able to feel that he understood what was really happening.

A large number of Reds was something else again. They rarely *discussed* anything at all. To an outsider like himself, they pontificated upon an already agreed upon line. And when he did overhear them arguing amongst themselves, it sounded like church or synagogue members arguing points of doctrine.

The thing that he resented most, though, was being treated as either an enemy of the cause or a potential convert to it. Since Phil had no wish to be either, he avoided large groups of committed leftists whenever he could.

As he walked along Sixteenth Street toward the entrance of the Y.A.S.D. headquarters, he wondered if he was making a mistake going there at all. And when he stepped inside the group's rundown, officially condemned building, he was sure that he had.

He had come there dressed in the suit he always wore nowadays when he worked. The members he saw—who were either standing around or sitting on bare, wooden chairs—were garbed with defiant casualness, as though they wanted to prove to the world that they had nothing to do with the bourgeoisie. The men had on torn shirts and frayed slacks or overalls, while the women were arrayed in cheap cotton dresses.

The place had a nasty odor. It was not simply musty, Phil had a feeling that the sanitary arrangements were nonexistant. It would be a horribly stifling place to visit in the heat of summer, he believed. And even now, with wide-open windows letting in crisp spring air and sunlight, he was not happy about being there.

He looked around to try to find someone to help him. Everyone seemed to be in animated conversation with somebody else and Phil had a difficult time calling attention to himself. He finally tapped a seated man on the shoulder.

The man interrupted his conversation and got to his feet. He was a tall, muscular youth with close-cropped, straw-colored hair, and blue eyes which grew cold and suspicious as they examined Phil and the way he was dressed.

Phil attempted a friendly smile as he asked for the man he'd been advised to see. "Pardon me. Do you know where I can find Ken Darwell?"

The man with straw-colored hair did not change expression. "Who wants him?" he asked.

"Tell him Phil. Phil Aronson."

The other still hesitated.

Though he was delivering money now, Phil had collected it often enough to realize what the problem was: nobody here knew him. Before this they had always dealt with Sid, and the man he was talking to hadn't even recognized Phil's name. He probably thought that Phil wanted to see the group's treasurer in order to take money away instead of handing it over.

"Why don't you tell Ken I'm here," Phil suggested with another smile. "You might even find that he's anxious to see me."

The man grunted something and walked off. When he returned in another minute or two his sullen expression had been replaced by a welcoming grin.

Such was the power of money, Phil thought cynically. It could change attitudes even here in Bolshie land.

"I'll take you back to the offices," the man with the straw-colored hair was saying. "But why didn't you tell me what you wanted to see Ken for? I would've taken you to him at once."

"I didn't know who you were either," Phil explained. "As a matter of fact, I still don't know your name."

"It's Karl Grannet. But you know something, you were right not to shoot off your mouth before. I never thought about that."

"In my business it pays not to," Phil said rather smugly.

Karl Grannet led Phil through a moldy ill-lighted corridor and into an office that featured a makeshift desk which had been put together by placing a sheet of plywood over three sawhorses.

Phil felt himself recoil. He was getting disgusted with the determinedly shoddy character of the entire place. It was almost as if they were flaunting their poverty, he thought.

He wished that the money he was going to hand them would pay for decoration. Fat chance!

Still smiling to himself over the notion, he turned to greet Ken Darwell, who was in deep conversation with a girl.

"Hi," Ken said, breaking off his discussion. "This is our vice-president, Laura Vaile."

Phil nodded at her. She had honey-blond hair and a lovely oval face which was vaguely familiar.

Had he met this girl before? He couldn't remember.

"Why didn't Sid bring the money this time?" Ken wanted to know.

Phil studied the treasurer. He was tall and extrememly thin, with a headful of black, curly hair. He was wearing thick horn-rimmed glasses and had a prominent Adam's apple which bobbed disconcertingly when he talked.

"What difference does it make?" Phil asked him. He lifted the briefcase onto the plywood "desk" and patted it. "Here's the loot. Why don't you count it to see if it's all there."

"I guess it doesn't really make a difference," Ken conceded. He fiddled with the latch of the briefcase. "We were just curious."

"*I* think it might make a difference," Laura interjected forcefully.

Phil was startled. He shot the girl a questioning look.

"You're Sid's boss, aren't you?" she demanded caustically.

"You know I am," Phil said. He admired the outline of her full breasts as they pushed against the bosom of her dress.

"And he was the one who let us place the bet where we won all that money," she went on. "What did you do? Fire him?"

"Good God! Is that what you think?"

"Well, you did lose a lot of money on it."

Phil smiled and shook his head. He was beginning to enjoy this. "I didn't lose a cent," he said blandly. "*You* won; but *I* didn't lose."

Laura's eyes flashed. There was little doubt in Phil's mind that she disliked him on principle; and no doubt at all that she disliked being teased by him.

"Explain that," she said.

"It's how a bookmaker works: he doesn't gamble himself— not if he wants to keep in business he doesn't. He leaves that to his customers, while he keeps his own books in balance by hedging and laying off bets.

"You want to know what I did when Sid told me about this bet and how much you people stood to win?" he went on rhetorically. "I arranged to lay off half of it with other bookies. Then I hedged the other half by accepting more bets than I usually would on certain other horses in the race."

The girl frowned as if she didn't know whether or not to believe Phil. She looked to the group's treasurer for advice. "Is that how it works?"

"It could...." Ken's Adam's apple seemed to bobble even harder with his effort at thought. "I don't know all that much about it, but it could work that way. I guess the odds on a race have to be set so that the bookmaker gets a percentage."

"You've got it," Phil said. "There are always two sets of odds—one for each side of whatever you bet on—and the bookie gets his in the middle. Where there are two contestants, like in a prizefight, it works this way: let's say the fight's called even money; then no matter which man you want, you've got to give me six to five.

"Now, all that works out fine when roughly the same amount of dough is bet on each fighter," Phil went on. "But if someone wants to place a really heavy bet on one guy or the other, it could throw my books out of balance. And that would leave me with just three choices: number one, I don't accept the bet. Number two, I change the odds—which I can't do, incidentally, if all the other bookies are offering even money. Or, number three, I lay off part of the bet with somebody else."

"And that's where the hedge comes in," Ken said. He was fascinated now, despite Laura's looks of disapproval.

"Exactly," Phil said. "The hedge is how I protect myself."

Ken nodded. "But a horse race is more complicated, isn't it? I mean, in the one we bet on there were eight horses."

"Right. And you could have made three different bets on each horse—win, place, and show. But the principle's the same."

"As far as I can see," Laura interjected contemptuously, "the main principle seems to be that the bookie always wins."

"He doesn't win," Phil shot back angrily. "How can you win if you don't bet? A bookie performs a service. For doing that, he's paid a percentage of whatever is bet."

"And you're very well paid, aren't you?"

Phil's anger was growing. He knew he was being placed on the defensive and he didn't like it.

"Why in hell shouldn't I be well paid?"

"Why? Perhaps because this is a time when real workers are starving and farmers are having their land stolen by banks and sold out from under them. It's a time when fathers are forced to feed their families with stolen hunks of stale bread, and infants starve when their mother's breasts run dry for lack of proper food.

"Can you blame me for resenting the fact that a *bookmaker* is well paid?"

There was a familiar echo in her voice that got to Phil. His answer sounded lame to his own ears: "*You* don't seem to mind making use of my services."

"It wasn't you," Laura corrected. "It was Sid. When we knew we were going to place such a big bet we wanted to deal with someone we had dealt with before. Someone we could trust."

"As much as you could trust any bookie, you mean?" Phil asked sarcastically.

When nobody bothered to answer him, he went on: "What surprises me is that you wanted to place such a large bet. I mean, how could socially conscious people like you risk your money that way?"

It was Ken Darwell who stopped counting the winnings long enough to answer: "We knew that horse was going to win."

"Knew?"

Laura exchanged glances with Karl Grannet. Apparently Ken had said more than he should.

"One of the stable boys was a member here before he went to New Orleans," Karl decided to explain. "We got a letter from him, last week, advising us to put together as much dough as we possibly could and bet it on that horse in that race."

"Are you saying the whole thing was fixed?"

"How the hell should I know? Nobody went into details."

Phil nodded. "But anyway, you took his advice. You bet the way he said to."

"Right."

"And you won. And you surely won't mind spending the winnings." Phil grinned wolfishly. "You know something? If you people don't watch out, you're all going to turn into bloated plutocrats."

"That money is going to Michigan," Laura announced in a low voice which was filled with fury. "To the Landking strikers."

Phil was taken back by her vehemence. "You mean the people who're holding that sit-down strike?"

"I mean the men and women who are occupying a factory in order to protect their jobs and earn a decent wage," the girl said angrily. "I've just come back from there. I saw first hand what the police and the National Guard and Landking's own hired goons were trying to do. I saw them train their guns on women who were bringing food to their men who had occupied the buildings. And I saw them shoot . . ."

Laura's voice broke. She sobbed briefly. Then she straightened up and went on.

"This money is going *there*," she said. "It's going to help buy food for women and children, yes. But it's also going to help smash the union busters!"

Phil was focusing all his attention on Laura. Her tone of voice, her figure, the way she tossed her head as she delivered her militant call to arms, all told him who she was.

"You!" he cried suddenly. "You were in that demonstration outside Radio City last summer. The one who called out to save some murals. You gave a speech."

Laura looked surprised. "Don't tell me you were there, too."

"Only by accident," Phil admitted. "But I did listen to you talk. Then I saw you get knocked down by the police."

Laura nodded. She touched the side of her head, as though the memory had brought back some of the physical pain.

"You were helped by an eleven-year-old girl that day, right?"

"Yes, but . . . how did you know that?"

"She's my sister," Phil said.

19

Laura frowned at Phil. Then, very slowly, her face was transformed by a tentative smile of comprehension. To see those changes come over her made it almost worthwhile to have a kid sister.

"Naomi Aronson," Phil said with a grin. "Remember?"

"Naomi, yes. I didn't get her last name. I think that the cops scrambled my brains when they got me in the head."

Phil nodded sympathetically and looked into her eyes. They were large and violet-colored.

"She took me to a drugstore, you know. A pharmacist fixed me up and didn't question me—though he must have known that the cops were looking to hold anyone who was in that demonstration. Afterward—when I was feeling a little less groggy—I turned to speak to your sister. I wanted to thank her, ask her where she lived. But she'd already disappeared."

"Yeah, she's good at that," Phil said with a laugh. "Disappearing, I mean. She was with my brother and me when she disappeared to go over to you. We had no idea where she was."

"She did get home all right?" Laura asked.

"Oh, yeah. She was fine. Naomi's a streetwise little kid."

"But what about you?" he went on. "From what Naomi said, you were in pretty bad shape."

"I was. As a matter of fact, I still have a scar from that day."

Laura raised a honey blonde curl to let Phil see a vertical line which marred the skin of her temple.

"Bastards," Phil said softly.

"Not really," Laura said. "The police, the National Guard, the private strikebreakers are tame dogs who howl and bite at their masters' bidding. Their masters are the dangerous ones; they are the ones to call bastards!"

"I don't know about that," Karl Grannet put in. "I'd call some cops bastards. They're the ones who enjoy what they do."

"How do you mean, they enjoy it?" Phil asked.

"You'll find out for yourself," Karl told him. "If they ever decide to stomp on you."

"You're right about that," Ken Darwell said. "The cops who take pleasure in it scare me silly."

But Laura still defended her point. "They wouldn't be that way if their masters didn't train them to enjoy brutalizing people. In a just society, they would be educated to protect people instead. Since there would be no classes and very little private property, their masters would *be* the people."

Though Phil could enjoy arguing politics with another man, he rarely did so with a beautiful girl—especially one he had just met. At best, he thought, that would be a time-wasting digression; at worst, it could ruin whatever prospects of romance there were by turning her actively hostile.

In this case, however, a devil got into him and he heard himself ask about the sort of just society she had in mind.

"Like the one they have in Russia?" he asked.

"No," she replied. "Not like that at all."

"To hell with the Soviet Union!" Karl Grannet cried cheerfully.

"We're Marxists," Ken Darwell explained pedantically. "Not Stalinists."

"Basically," said Laura, "we're Trotskyites."

Phil had only the vaguest idea of what those names meant. He did know that Trotsky had been kicked out of Russia by Stalin, and that his followers there had been shot or sent to prison. He had heard that the two Russian leaders had preached different doctrines, but he had no idea as to what the difference was.

"Oh," he said.

Laura grinned impishly. "I think our friend here doesn't know what we're talking about."

"As a matter of fact I don't."

"It doesn't matter," the girl said, her face growing serious. "The whole point is that there's never been a just society. Anywhere. We're working to bring one about."

"Good luck," Phil replied.

Karl snorted. "I don't think he believes it can be done."

"But that's terrible," Laura said. "That's just the sort of pessimism which keeps the ruling class in power. If people believe that things can't be changed, they will never work to change them."

Personally, Phil didn't want things to change. He merely wanted to be a member of the ruling class. But he knew he could not say that.

"You may be right," he told her. "Me, I'm just a bookie."

"Are you telling me that bookies can't think? Or that you yourself simply don't want to?"

Phil noticed that the two others in the room were looking perturbed. It was as though they sensed that something curious was going on between Laura and himself, but were not sure what it was.

It was Phil who first realized the significance of what was happening. Though he was not too clever at political or economic theory, he did understand the chemical reaction between the sexes.

"I'll tell you what," he suggested to the girl. "I'll make a deal with you. If you'll teach me about how you're going to change the world, I'll teach you about bookmaking and other capitalist sins."

Phil's challenge seemed to make Laura feel ill at ease, as if this were all happening too quickly for her.

"Don't tell me you're nervous I'll convert you," he laughed.

"Don't be ridiculous."

"Well, then. Let me take you outside and buy you some coffee. We can have our first mutual lesson in the neutral atmosphere of Nedick's."

"Hey wait a minute, Laura," Karl objected as the girl agreed to go with Phil. "I have to talk with you about something."

"Yeah, me too," Ken said urgently. "I've got to go over some things with you, too. We never settled on how we're going to use this loot once we get it to Michigan. Is it going to the families of the strikers? Or are we going to give it to the Union to use as they see fit?"

"Won't that be up to the membership?" Laura countered. "And Jack, of course, once he gets back."

She was referring, Phil realized, to Jack Schank, president of Y.A.S.D. Sid had told him that Jack Schank was out of town; possibly in Michigan.

"Sure, I know that," Ken said in response to Laura. "But don't you think we should have some ideas ready for Jack and the membership?"

"I say let's give everything to the Union!" Karl put in fiercely. "Then they can buy some guns of their own."

"I don't know," Laura said. She started to leave. "But why don't we talk about it later? After I get back."

Ken frowned. "You won't be gone very long, then?"

"I don't see any reason why I should be," Laura replied.

The girl led Phil into the corridor, then turned in the opposite direction from which he had come.

"We'll make our escape through the rear door," she said with a little chuckle of amusement. "If we went back through the meeting room, we might never get away."

"Your friends seem to think a great deal of you," Phil said as he followed her out of the building.

"Yes," Laura replied seriously. "There are times when I wish they'd think a little less. A girl can feel smothered."

"Well, they're probably worried about your consorting with the enemy."

Laura let out a little snort of laughter.

"If they are," she said, "it's only because I'm female. They'd never get so upset about a guy—no matter who he decided to consort with."

Phil glanced curiously at her. He didn't know how to take Laura. At one moment she seemed usual enough—lively, flirtatious, but with a tough, practical core—your average American girl. Then, in the next instant, she'd transform herself into a fiery radical—another Rosa Luxemburg who wanted to drown the system in its own blood.

Looking about him, he could not help but reflect that this was the perfect neighborhood for someone like Laura. At first glance, it looked like any other mainly white New York neighborhood, though perhaps a little seedier than most. But beneath the surface it was very special; it was the home of a radicalism which seemed to infuse the very air.

As Phil and Laura walked, they were less than two blocks north of Union Square, New York's bastion of left-wing causes. It was there that, less than seven years before, some of the most violent demonstrations against the Boston executions of the anarchists Sacco and Venzetti had taken place. And on every day of the week, one could hear speeches there denouncing the bosses, the system, the politicians. Laura herself had climbed onto soap boxes in Union Square in the past, and she would do so in the future.

But now she was smiling at Phil, an average American girl again.

"Where are we having our coffee?" she asked.

"I thought we'd find a Nedick's or something. Do you have a special place you'd like to go?"

"I share an apartment a couple of blocks from here. I could make you some coffee there if you'd like."

There it was again, Phil thought. The flirt showed herself then—but there appeared to be an intonation behind the flirt.

Or maybe he was kidding himself. She might be—probably was—simply asking him up for some coffee and talk. Man to man, as it were.

On the other hand, he would surely love to have it turn out to be more than that. With that long-legged stride of hers, those swaying hips and great breasts, she looked sensuous as hell—

just the sort of girl it would be marvelous to take to bed.

They had stopped walking now and she was regarding him with a strange little smile.

"I hope you're not turning down my offer of coffee," she said.

"Good God, no," Phil said.

"I was just thinking about what you were saying before," he told her as they started to walk toward her apartment. "About the men in your outfit. You know, you can't really blame them for wanting to protect you. You're one of the Y.A.S.D.'s most valuable assets."

"Oh? And what do you mean by that?"

"Your speeches for one thing. Remember, I was there that day outside Radio City."

"That day . . ." Laura repeated slowly. "That was the first time I ever did anything like that."

Phil didn't know whether to believe her or not. She'd been too effective, he thought, to have been completely unpracticed.

"You mean you'd never spoken to a group of people before?"

"During meetings of the Y.A.S.D. I did. But never outside. The guys wouldn't let me. I was like a mascot to them, I guess, and they didn't want me to get hurt."

"But afterward? You kept making speeches?"

"They didn't want me to. Not after they saw what the cops did."

As she spoke those words, Laura brushed her temple lightly with her fingertips. It was an unconscious salute to the pain that had been inflicted upon her. And as he observed it, Phil felt a poignant stab so sharp it was itself physically painful.

But the girl was still talking.

"After that," she said, "I wouldn't listen to anyone. I knew I could control an audience—make them listen to what I have to say."

"And it's not just ego," she went on as though Phil had interrupted and challenged her. "Though I admit that talking to people and moving them does make me feel good. But the main thing is the Y.A.S.D. The reactionaries own the press, the radio networks, the movies. The only way we have to put *our* principles across is through effective speakers. We can't afford to waste one—even if the particular one I'm thinking of happens to be me."

Phil laughed. "No wonder they made you vice-president."

"It was the other women in the group who saw to that for me. They nagged at the men until they had to agree."

"Really." Phil was impressed. He had never believed that females either could or would combine to help one of their own; especially not a good-looking girl.

"Before that," Laura continued, "the most a woman member of the Y.A.S.D. could hope for was to be appointed secretary. And then she had to know shorthand."

Phil laughed again. "But you made it—you're vice-president."

"Yes. With the guys still feeling that they have to take special care of me. Sometimes I think that our men believe in equal treatment for everybody—except females."

"Maybe that's because they're all leftists," Phil teased. "We right-wingers, on the other hand, believe in giving our women complete equality."

"Balls!" Laura replied succinctly. Then, as if to make extra certain that he understood her feelings: "Bullshit!"

Phil reddened at her language. He opened his mouth to say something about it, then decided not to. He didn't know what he could say.

Laura giggled suddenly. "See what I mean? It really upsets you when a girl uses bad language. If I were a man you wouldn't even have noticed it. Right?"

"Well, I—"

"Admit it. If a fellow had said what I just did it wouldn't have bothered you at all."

"All right," Phil spluttered. "Maybe so. There are certain words I don't expect to hear from a girl. But, damn it, there is a difference between the sexes!"

"Oh? Did you just notice that?"

"Very funny. But you've got to admit that men are stronger than women. And a lot less vulnerable."

"You mean physically stronger? Physically less vulnerable?"

"Yes," Phil said impatiently. "We're not talking about morals, are we?"

"All right. Men are physically stronger. But I've seen too many of them injured by strikebreakers and the police to believe that they're so much less vulnerable than women."

"At least they're less likely to get raped!" Phil shot back without thinking.

"That one again," Laura said scornfully. "I should have

known. Whenever I back a man into a corner on this subject, and he doesn't know anything else to say, he'll invariably threaten me with the possibility of rape."

"But it's true," Phil said defensively. He was uncomfortable with his own argument, but did not know how to drop it without making himself seem more foolish. "Rapes do happen."

"So do hit-and-run pedestrian deaths. Would you want me to lock myself in a room for fear of automobiles driven by drunk drivers?"

"No. I'd just want you to look both ways when you cross the street."

"In other words, to take proper precautions?" There was the barest hint of mischief in Laura's eyes.

"Exactly," Phil replied.

"Never invite a strange man to come up to my place for coffee, for instance?"

"That would depend on the strange man," said Phil, who was not taken off guard at all. "If he's a decent sort of strange man—the sort of strange man one can obviously trust—then go ahead, invite him."

Laura burst into laughter. "I gather you yourself are the trustworthy type."

"Damn right I am."

"I'm so glad," Laura cooed as she linked her arm with Phil's. "I live just around that corner, you see, and I would've hated to have walked all this way for nothing."

"That would've been a shame," Phil said seriously.

20

Laura lived in a building that made the one in which Kay and her roommates lived seem almost modern. It was an abandoned factory that was the property of a now bankrupt manufacturer of women's undergarments. When the building was abandoned, several of the women members of the Y.A.S.D. made an apartment out of what had been a small suite of offices.

"What about water?" Phil asked as the girl led him past a NO TRESPASSING sign and opened a creaky door that looked as if it were about to fall off its hinges. "And electric power. Wasn't everything shut off when the company went out of business?"

"Of course it was. But some of the guys helped us splice into water and power lines. Now we've got as much as we need—and we don't have to pay for it."

"Pretty good," Phil said.

"Of course we don't have hot water," Laura conceded. "But we can use the stove to heat water for washing."

"The stove?" Phil repeated as they waited for their eyes to adjust to the feeble light emitted by a single twenty-five watt light bulb in the ceiling of the lower hall. "Does that mean you have a gas line here, too?"

"Unfortunately, no. Our stove is really a double electric burner. We just call it a stove."

She took his hand then, and guided him toward the stairs. "Careful when we start climbing up," she warned. "The paint is beginning to peel from the plaster walls and some of the steps are in pretty bad shape."

"You mean I could get my suit ruined and my head cracked all on the same flight of stairs?"

The girl laughed. "That's the way it is."

"In that case I'll be careful. But tell me," he went on curiously. "As long as you're not paying for your electricity, why don't you put in some stronger lighting?"

"Because we don't always want better lighting in the downstairs hall or stairways. There are times when people don't want to be seen by the cops. They can hide here and sneak in and out."

"Aren't you making it easy for thugs, though?"

"You're always worrying about rapists and thugs," Laura said. She sounded amused. "Well, we have a great many friends in this neighborhood. I'd hate to see what would happen to someone who tried to get funny."

Phil grunted noncommittally. He thought that Laura was being terribly naïve, but knew that it would be naïve of *him* to say so.

A sudden glare of artificial light attacked his eyes as Laura led him into what had once been a reception area. The only memento left from those days was a printed notice pasted to the wall near a glass partition. The notice instructed all visitors to please be seated and wait for the receptionist to help them. It was signed Undermode Fashion, Inc.

Phil followed Laura past the partition and into the former typing pool room. A man and woman were inside, seated at a card table and listening to a recording of Hoagy Carmichael singing "Lazy River," backed by a band which included the Dorsey Brothers, Benny Goodman, and Gene Krupa among others. The music was coming through an antiquated, wind-up phonograph and sounded scratched and tinny.

The man in particular seemed enthralled by the music. He was ugly, with several missing teeth, a flattened nose, and a patch over his left eye. His right eye was sharp and clear, however, and there was an almost beatific expression on his face as he swayed slightly to the jazz sound.

No one said anything until the song came to an end. Then the woman, who had an attractive face but was too pudgily overweight for Phil's taste, sighed. "That was really great. . . ."

"Yeah," the man replied in a harsh, rasping voice. "It's only too bad that the record's so scratched, the machine so old, and the needle so worn."

He turned toward Phil as if he had just noticed him. "You wouldn't happen to have any of those on you, would you? I'd really prefer an electric phonograph, of course. But even a decent steel needle to stick into this hunk of tin would do."

Phil couldn't make up his mind if the man were kidding or not, but decided to assume he was.

"Sorry." Phil grinned.

"Sure. Forget it." The man held out his hand. "I'm Jed Symmonds, by the way. And the one wearing a skirt is Glenda Krakaur."

"Pleased to meet you. Phil Aronson."

"Are you planning to join our little group?" Jed asked. Phil wondered how old he was. His scars and injuries made him look to be in his forties, but Phil would not have been surprised to learn that he was a good deal younger than that.

"He isn't yet," Laura interjected. "But I may be able to save him from capitalism in spite of himself."

"That'd be a little difficult wouldn't it?" Jed asked. He studied Phil carefully, taking in the double-breasted, dark gray suit, the well-shined shoes, the cleanly shaven face and polished nails. "He looks like the system's been treating him pretty well."

Phil was annoyed. He didn't like to be patronized. Fortunately, Glenda entered the conversation before he had time to reply.

"Don't be so prejudiced," she said. "Some of our best recruits, these days, come from the middle and upper classes. It's a matter of guilt."

Jesus! Phil thought. Thinking him a member of the middle or upper classes. Well, maybe he was!

"And do you feel guilty?" Jed asked, ironically.

"Not a bit of it," Phil said evenly, thinking that at least that was the whole truth.

"What do you do?" There was a certain contempt in Jed's tone. "Go to college?"

"He's a bookmaker," Laura said.

"Oh, yeah? That's worse than going to college. Bookmakers are a pretty right-wing crew."

"What makes you say that?" Phil asked Jed.

"Because it's true. You people are all individualists, aren't you? You get a great big kick out of taking risks and haven't yet found out that the only way to stand up to the bastards who rule this country is to combine with other members of the exploited class."

While Phil did not understand Jed's logic, Glenda seemed entranced.

"How do you know so much about bookies?" she wondered. "Did you ever work as one?"

"I worked *for* one once," Jed replied.

"But Phil told me that bookies don't really gamble." Laura sounded puzzled. "They let their customers take the risks and keep their own books in balance. Isn't that right, Phil?"

"Yes, it is."

"Yeah, well there may be something in that," Jed said. "A bookie does have to keep his books in balance, of course. That's why the English call them turf accountants. But I wasn't really talking about the kind of risk a gambler takes."

"Weren't you?" Phil questioned.

"No, I meant . . . suppose a customer doesn't pay off. Or if you get the big boys mad so they won't let you hedge your bets when you have to. Or if you get clobbered over the head when you're carrying a lot of dough. That kind of risk."

"You don't believe in taking risks?" Phil asked.

Jed let out a single sharp, explosive burst of laughter. "Hell, one look at what they've done to my face'll tell you better than that. Sure I'll take risks. Bigger risks than you'd ever dream of taking! But I won't take them for personal gain. If I did that I'd be no better than John Dillinger. No, the only time I take risks is when I'm standing shoulder to shoulder with other workers who are risking their own hides for the same cause!"

Phil could not help wondering if everyone in the Y.A.S.D. was caught up in making speeches.

"I see," he said.

"Do you?"

Laura, meanwhile, was measuring some coffee into a pot.

"How many want some?" she asked.

"We'll take one cup with you," Jed told her. "Then we've got to go to Bayside to look over the territory of tomorrow's demonstration."

"What sort of demonstration is that?" Phil asked while Laura went into the small washroom in order to pour water into the pot.

"It's against the East Side Boating Club," Jed explained. "They bought some land there with the idea of making a yacht harbor complete with clubhouse and swimming pool."

"So?" Phil said.

"So we want to stop them. The rich have too damn many places where they can keep their yachts, tan their bodies, and stuff themselves with caviar. It's the common man who needs a free park where he can go with his family on a Sunday afternoon!"

"Oh, so you want to put a park there."

"We have it all planned out," said Glenda. Her plump face fairly glowed with enthusiasm. "It'll have an olympic size pool for adults, a kiddie pool, a playground, lots of benches for old people—everything."

"But who's going to put up the money to build it."

"The city, naturally. The Parks Department. Commissioner Robert Moses."

"And what about that yacht club? Don't they already own the land?"

"So what?" Jed said scornfully. "The city can simply condemn the land. It's done all the time. The 'right of eminent domain,' it's called. It's the way the government gets the land on which they can place a park or a highway or put up a building."

Phil nodded thoughtfully. "And you think you can get New York City to do that here?"

"*Maybe* we can," Glenda said. "It's worth a try, isn't it?"

"You see, Moses loves to spit in the eyes of those snobs who run yacht clubs," Jed said. "And he also loves to pose as the friend of the little man. So we figure that if we make enough noise in our demonstration, Moses'll say 'yeah, I like the publicity of being the hero. I'll make those people a park!'"

"And since we'll be the ones who got Moses to do it," Glenda explained, "we'll be heroes, too. People'll see that the Y.A.S.D. really fights for their rights."

Laura strained the now finished coffee into chipped and stained mugs. She placed them on the card table along with sugar, milk, and some spoons the girls had copped from a nearby Automat.

She looked at Phil who was seated thoughtfully at the table. "What's wrong? Don't you agree with them?"

"I'm not sure," Phil said slowly as he readjusted his weight in the straight-back chair. "For one thing, I wonder if you're all being very practical. . . ."

"What in hell does that mean?" Jed Symmonds growled.

Phil, who did not trust Jed's temper, watched the other man carefully.

"I could be wrong," he said, "but from everything I've heard about Robert Moses, he's not the kind of man who enjoys sharing credit with anyone. Especially not with a group who could be attacked in the press as being too Red. If you make *too* much noise tomorrow it's liable to have the opposite effect from the one you want: it could drive Moses and the Parks Department into having nothing to do with either you or your park!"

"Gee . . ." Glenda said unhappily. "Do you think he could be right, Jed?"

"How in hell do *I* know? But suppose he is? Wouldn't *that* do us some good, too?"

"Huh?"

"Let's say the city does walk away from this deal. As long as we keep screaming about that park, it'll look like we're the only ones who care about the interests of the people. Moses, we can say, sold out to the millionaires at the yacht club."

Phil could not help the grin that slowly spread across his face. It was a con game. He loved it. It would serve the suckers right.

Glenda, however, was not pleased.

"Isn't that being a bit dishonest?" she asked Jed.

"What it is is tactics," Jed explained. "And anyway, we'll

be telling the people the absolute truth. None of those big shots who run things—Moses or anyone else—really gives a damn about the little man. You agree with that, don't you?"

"Yes, sure..."

"And we do care about him. We want to help. But the only way to do that is to change the system. Anything else—new schools, parks, make-work welfare—is just tossing him a bone to keep him quiet. So if losing this park will help convince people that the system has to be changed, it's goddamned worth it!"

Phil was enthralled with Jed's logic. He wondered if the man actually believed what he was saying. Maybe he did.

"Do you agree with that?" he asked Laura.

"I suppose so," she said. Then, more defiantly: "Yes. Yes, I do."

"But you don't?" Jed snarled. It was almost as though he were issuing a challenge to fight.

Phil decided to try diplomacy. "Like you say, it's a matter of tactics."

"Yeah. But do you agree with them?"

"Do I agree with those tactics?" Phil said, stalling. "I'm not sure what you mean. Do you want to know if I think your goal justifies their use? Or if I feel that using those tactics is a practical way to help you reach your goal?"

"Jesus Christ," Jed said. "What kind of crap are you trying to give me?"

"Crap?" Phil repeated. He was starting to get angry.

"Because if you are, Bookie, you'd better stop right now. I can take a certain amount of verbal horseshit from my comrades. But not from a goddamn bookie!"

Phil sensed that there was going to be a fight. He had thought there was a chance of that from the moment he'd met the man. But now he was certain. Unless someone interfered, he and Jed would soon be mixing it up.

He moved his chair slightly back from the table. At Jed's first move he was going to sucker-punch him.

Then he felt Laura's hand on his knee.

"Glenda," she said. "Didn't you tell me that you and Jed were going over to Queens? To prepare for tomorrow?"

"You're right. Jed?"

Jed got out of his chair slowly, as though he were making up his mind. Then—also very slowly—he let Glenda guide him toward the entrance door.

"I won't forget you," he told Phil as he followed Glenda from the anteroom.

As for Phil, he didn't say a word until the door was completely shut again. Then he turned to Laura.

"What kind of nut is that guy?" he asked.

Laura stared hard at him. "You bastard."

"Huh?" Phil did not understand. He had been feeling proud of himself for keeping his temper. The very last thing he'd expected was for Laura to turn on him. "What the hell? *I* didn't insult *him*, did I?"

"No? Then what did you do? Or did you think Jed was so stupid that he wouldn't realize he was being mocked."

"All right." Phil's temper was rising rapidly and he didn't really care if it showed. "When I realized what a goddamn hypocrite he was, I didn't do a good enough job of hiding my disgust. Do you want me to say I'm sorry for that?"

"You call Jed Symmonds a hypocrite?" The girl gasped in disbelief.

"Of course he's a hypocrite. What else would you call someone who talks about new parks and playgrounds when he doesn't care squat about them? What he cares about is power. And how's he going to get that power? Through the good old Y.A.S.D.!"

"You bastard," Laura said again. "What could someone like you know about Jed? He's proved his loyalty to the cause—to the people—in a hundred ways. He's twenty-nine, but looks ten or fifteen years older. He had his left eye put out by strikebreakers when he was helping textile workers organize in the South. His nose was broken by a cop's nightstick. You have no right to call a man like that a hypocrite!"

"Excuse me, then," Phil said, his voice dripping with ugly sarcasm. "He's a genuine hero of the coming revolution."

Laura drew her hand back and slapped Phil across his face.

"Don't sneer!" she hissed. "Don't you ever sneer at us again."

Phil's head jerked back from the stinging force of the blow. She was strong—much stronger than Phil would have expected—and he had been taken completely off guard.

"I should've let him beat you up before," she was saying. "I should've let him hurt you."

"Now you're kidding yourself," Phil countered scornfully. "Hurt me? A one-eyed man with half his teeth missing. What would he've done? Slapped my face like you did?"

Laura snarled in fury. She came at him like a jungle cat, making claws of her nails and trying to shred his skin. He caught her wrists and forced her hands away from his face, holding her that way so that she could not hurt him.

She aimed a knee at his groin then, but he moved slightly and took the attack on his muscular outer thigh.

"Take it easy," he demanded, hardly able to believe the fury of her onslaught.

"Bastard," she kept saying. "Son-of-a-bitch. Bastard."

He spun around and tried to leave, but she clawed at the back of his neck and his collar. He turned back, half knocking her down as he did so, then picked her up in his arms and carried her—still cursing and trying to fight—into one of the rear rooms.

He was going to leave her there—toss her bodily onto a cot and run like hell for the front door. But even as she fell, Laura grabbed hold of his tie—pulling it tight and choking him.

He rammed an elbow back, freeing himself by knocking some of the wind out of her. He flung himself on top of her, pinning her body with his own while he clamped his fingers once more around her wrists.

"Had enough? Goddamn it, are you going to be good now? Have you had enough?"

"Bastard!" She half croaked the word as she struggled to gulp in air. "Bastard!"

She tried to knee him, to bring her nails into play, but Phil's fingers were like manacles about her wrists and his muscular thighs kept her legs flat against the mattress. She twisted and writhed futilely until her legs began to part and Phil's knees slipped between them. His crotch pressed into the tender flesh of her lower belly now, and the erotic feel of her aroused his penis.

He tried to ignore it. He truly did. But as soon as he became harder and stronger, it became impossible to ignore.

His desire spread out from his groin and took command of him. His mouth found hers and his tongue probed between her lips. He wanted to conquer her and force her to surrender, but to conquer with his penis not his fists.

Nor did she wish to injure him now. She met his tongue not with teeth but with her own tongue. And when he released her wrists to reach avidly between her thighs, her hands went just as avidly to his belt and the fly of his trousers.

126

Passion had taken control of them both. A passion so strong, so overwhelming, that it made their earlier rage against each other seem pale and weak by comparison.

He reached inside the bodice of her dress, inside her slip and bra. He pulled the hem of her skirt and her slip up to her hips and slid her briefs down past her knees. He placed his hand on her vulva and found that she was already soaking wet.

She had his trousers and shorts down now. She gripped the shaft of his great, throbbing penis.

"Fuck me!" she said. "Come on, you bastard, fuck me!"

He pushed all the way into her, as though he were trying to tickle her throat with his cock.

Once. Twice. And then he came.

21

They lay exhausted on the cot. Unmoving. Side by side.

It took Phil a few moments to realize that he still had his shirt and tie on, and that his trousers and undershorts were around his ankles. He reached down and slowly drew them up.

He looked at Laura. She had already pulled her slip and skirt down, though her briefs lay on the floor.

She opened her eyes to his gaze and smiled.

"I've never done anything like that before," she said, marveling. "First to get that angry and then so aroused . . . my God . . ."

"Why were you so angry at me?"

"I don't know." Laura paused, then corrected herself: "Yes, I do. You reminded me of some other men I knew, in Philadelphia."

"Is that your home town?"

"Yes. My father had a Cadillac agency there. Still does for all I know."

She swung her legs over the side of the cot and rose gingerly to her feet.

"I'm going to wash myself off," she said. "Want to join me?"

"Thanks."

Laura went to a shelf and took down two towels and two wash cloths. All four were marked with the logo of an exclusive hotel.

"Some of our members work at a commercial laundry," she explained. "They bring us all the towels and cloths we need. All we have to do is give them back when we're through."

"That sounds like a fair deal," Phil responded.

He went to the outer room with her and collected two large pots which he filled with water. He brought them back inside where she had already plugged in the electric burner.

"One pot's for washing," she said. "The other's for rinsing. Just don't let them get too hot."

"I won't. But what happens if someone comes in while we're washing?"

"Isn't it a little late to think of modesty?"

"Yeah, I guess it is. But I had my mind on other things before."

Laura grinned. "You'll find a sign in the corner. You can hang it outside the door if you're worried."

Phil picked up the sign, which read PLEASE KNOCK BEFORE ENTERING, and hung it on the outer door handle. As he reentered the room and shut the door behind him he saw that Laura was stepping out of her dress.

He began to laugh.

"What's so funny?" Laura demanded combatively. "Me?"

"No, me. I just realized that you were the first girl I'd ever made love to without knowing what she looked like in the altogether after we were done."

"Oh?" Laura placed her dress on the cot and removed her slip. "And how many girls have you made love to?"

"One or two maybe."

She smiled at Phil as he took off his shirt and undershirt and stepped out of his trousers.

"I was afraid you had a large stable of ladies," she said. "Then you'd have been disappointed in me."

"Good God," Phil said as she reached behind herself to unfasten her brassiere. "I don't think so."

Her breasts were magnificent, full, round, and very firm. Her long, sensuous nipples were puckered and erect.

Phil stepped forward and took her breasts in his hands. He leaned over and kissed them, curling his lips around her nipples and stroking them with his tongue.

128

She shuddered with pleasure and looked down to where his penis was shoving through his shorts.

"You're growing up again," she said. "Becoming the great big man I know and love."

Phil dropped his shorts altogether and pulled down her briefs to reveal Laura's flat belly and thick, brown pubic bush.

He stroked the tight curls that guarded the front of her cleft. "Maybe we'd better postpone washing up."

"Maybe we'd better."

Suddenly both pots began to boil. Phil cursed his frustration and made a move toward the electric burners.

"Let *me* do that." Laura placed a hand on his stomach and then reached down to touch his penis. "I wouldn't want this to get bumped."

Phil snorted, but he remained where he was while Laura pulled the switch. He was fascinated at the way her rear moved when she walked. It swayed fluidly, as though with a separate, practiced motion of its own. A work of art, he thought.

He caught her as she came back, placing his hands under her buttocks and lifting her up. She gasped at first, then giggled happily.

Glorying in his own strength, Phil lifted her higher. Her nipples were above his eyes, now, and he could see those unbelievably tender undercurves where her breasts joined her body. Still higher she went, so that his tongue could explore the hidden swirls of her navel, caress the firm, taut skin of her belly, shampoo the mat of pubic hair.

She grabbed his head to help support herself and whooped for joy. "You are crazy! An A-number-one nut!"

But Phil was not through yet. With one final effort, he lifted her even higher and held her closer so that his tongue could reach the entrance to her cleft.

Laura screamed with pleasure again. "This is too much! I never...ever!..."

Phil felt his arms start to give way, now. He staggered to the cot and lowered the girl onto it.

Her face glowed as she looked up at him. He was breathing hard and the matted hair on his chest glistened wetly with perspiration.

She touched his well-muscled thigh and saw his penis grow yet more rigid.

Phil sat down beside her. He lightly placed the tips of his fingers at the hollow of her throat, then let them glide down her center—between her breasts, past her nvael, over the gentle swell of her lower belly to the top of her pubic bush. He reached down to cup her pudenda and worked his fingers between her nether lips.

He lay upon his side now and breathed in her musky woman scent while his lips followed where his fingers had led. His tongue emerged to find her clitoris—the female phallus, the penis in miniature—and caressed it into hardness.

And her mouth had found his groin. She was kissing his scrotum, his penis, the glans at the head of his penis.

They delayed climax for as long as they could, bringing each other to the edge and then drawing back. Then neither one of them could hold out any longer.

It was like falling into a raging sea of passion which tossed them, swirled them, swung them, and finally drew them under to still and quiet depths.

They came back to themselves slowly. It was hard for Phil to believe the sexual heights they had just attained. The memory of that glory was already fading. It was like a black-and-white photograph of a blazing sunset.

"That was something," Phil said. "Really something."

"Yeah." Laura grinned lazily. "As long as you can keep doing me like that, I don't really mind if you're a bastard."

"Jesus," Phil said after a moment. "Let's not fight again. At least give me time to get my strength back first."

Laura giggled. "Tell me when you're ready."

"It'll be a long, long time."

He propped himself up on one elbow and looked at her.

"Seriously," he said. "You never did explain why you got so mad at me before. Except that it had something to do with men you used to know in Philadelphia."

"My father, mainly," Laura said. "Did I mention that he had a Cadillac agency?"

Phil nodded.

"Well, he and Mom were always sucking up to people who had money. You know," she said sardonically, "the famous Philadelphia Main Liners."

"Yeah?"

"I remember when I was thirteen," Laura continued, "my folks had a big party for all the millionaires they could get to come. I was supposed to be mother's little helper: wear a sweet dress, smile sweetly at the guests, and help serve. Which I did until some fat slob pinched my ass while I was handing out the hors d'oeuvres."

"What did you do?"

"I pushed my plate of deviled eggs right in his face."

"Hey . . . terrific!"

"I'm glad you think so," Laura said wryly. "My father sure didn't. All he had on his mind was that this particular slob was good for a new Cadillac every two years.

"That's when I first decided to leave home," Laura added. "When I realized that he thought like that."

"When did you actually do it?"

"Two years later. In twenty-eight."

Phil did some arithmetic in his mind. She was older than she looked.

"And have you seen your family since?" Phil asked.

"Only twice. Neither time was a success."

Phil nodded. "But what I don't understand," he said, "is why you're comparing me to your father. I don't sell Cadillacs and I don't have a daughter. But if some rich son-of-a-bitch tried to pinch my kid sister's ass, I'd cold-cock him!"

Laura giggled. "Maybe you would."

She ran her fingers through the hair on his chest and kissed him lightly on the cheek.

"I think it was what you were saying before," she went on reflectively. "When you called Jed a hypocrite. My father used to say that *all* leftists were hypocrites. Offer them enough dough and they'd all turn into Red-baiters."

"I don't really believe that," Phil replied. "Though I do think that you people have different standards for yourselves than for everyone else. You're quick to condemn Mussolini in Italy, for example and Hitler in Germany. You scream bloody murder about injustice here at home. But how many of you complain when Comrade Stalin decides to have a few hundred thousand people knocked off in Russia?"

"*We* complain!" Laura sat up indignantly. "I told you we're Trotskyites."

"Okay. So you're Trotskyites and you do complain. But isn't that because your man lost? What would you say if Trotsky was in Stalin's position?"

"He isn't," Laura said patiently. "And even if he were, he'd never behave like a Stalin."

"Yeah? Well, what was he like when he was Lenin's fair-haired boy? What did he do with people who disagreed with him then? Allow them to publish odes in praise of capitalism in the local press?"

"No need to be sarcastic," Laura said. "I realize that many socialist states don't have the complete freedom of speech I would like them to have. But they have to defend the integrity of their own revolutions. That's basic, wouldn't you think?"

Phil snorted. "What *I* think is that when you people want to do something—grab power, execute a political enemy, whatever—you can always think up some high-toned reason to do so."

Laura's eyes flashed and for a moment he was afraid he was about to see another example of her temper. Then she controlled herself and placed a hand on his bare knee.

"That's not fair," she complained. "What we want is a better and more just world. In order to gain that world, we are some-times forced to take actions we'd rather not take. It isn't as if we went around doing things for our own selfish ends."

Phil grunted noncommittally. He was beginning to feel stupid. He had already broken his rule against arguing politics with a beautiful woman—and when they were both naked at that. It was time for him to shut his trap.

"Why don't you come to a few of our meetings," Laura offered. "If you could listen to our discussions—involve yourself in them, even—you might understand more about what we're trying to do."

"Maybe so."

"We're having an executive meeting this coming Sunday night. It's not open to the public of course, but I'll be happy to get you in."

"I'll tell you what," he said. "If you'll come with me on Saturday night, I'll be at the meeting on Sunday."

"Where would we go?"

"Someplace special," Phil said proudly. "My kid brother—he's fifteen now—will be fighting in a teenage boxing exhibition being put on at the Y."

"I don't know. . . ." It was Laura's turn to look thoughtful. "I've never been to a boxing match."

"Well, that'll just make us even," Phil said. "I've never been to any of your meetings."

"You win," Laura said with a laugh. "Give me the address and I'll meet you there."

"Why don't you let me pick you up?"

"That's sweet of you, but I'll be busy all day. Thanks for the thought, though."

Laura kissed him and sat on the edge of the cot. "Want to wash up now?" she asked.

But his hand was around her waist and cupping her full breast. He kissed her ear.

"Let's postpone it," he whispered.

Her eyes focused on his crotch where his penis was standing up perkily.

"My God," Laura said. "There's life in the old boy yet."

"You bet," said Phil as he pushed her back down on the cot.

Suddenly there was a knock on the room door and a female voice: "Can I come in?"

"Can't you read signs?" Laura said.

"Sorry..."

When the sound of retreating footsteps had died away, Phil plunged into her. She was moist and ready for him.

Her hand went beneath his thighs and she cradled his balls as he thrust. He grew inside her—grew and grew until he was ready. Then she squeezed gently and he came.

22

When Phil agreed to attend the meeting of the Y.A.S.D., it was a cynical move to satisfy Laura. He wanted to keep her happy, in other words, so that she would do the same for him. To his own surprise, however, he found himself looking forward to the experience.

In the first place, he was curious to learn how the members behaved to each other when they had their private doctrinal disputes. In public—when arguing with outsiders—they were spikey and defensive about their theories, refusing to admit that there was the slightest chance of being wrong. Were they that way in private, too?

But there was a far more important reason for him to be happy about the upcoming meeting. He felt that becoming accepted by a group like the Y.A.S.D. could be profitable for him.

He had been wrong, he believed now, to have left their cultivation entirely to Sid Frankel. Although he thought of Sid as a straight enough guy and trusted him as much as he trusted any of his assistants, he felt that Sid had to have been tempted to find a syndicate connection of his own to whom he could deliver such clients as the Y.A.S.D.

Phil was honest enough with himself to admit that he himself would have been tempted. And that he probably would not have resisted the temptation.

What he had been before was lazy, Phil reflected. He had not even taken the trouble to introduce himself to the Y.A.S.D. Until he'd made that delivery to the group's headquarters, no one there had known what he looked like. They were all Sid's people, not his.

So far he had been lucky. Sid had not tried to pull anything. But there was no percentage in depending on luck forever.

Phil had an intuition about the Y.A.S.D. If he played his cards right the group would be important to his future. He didn't know how yet or in what way. But the feeling was too strong to be ignored.

On the evening that Laura met him in front of the Y, therefore, Phil had two things to be excited about. The meeting that he would attend on the following night, and his brother's boxing match which was the fifth fight on the card.

He was anxious for Bob to win his contest. He felt guilty that he did not encourage the kid to spend more time sharpening his ring skills and even enter the Golden Gloves. Tonight was Bob's chance to box against a boy with roughly equivalent skills and perhaps learn what the joy of victory was all about.

The Y was charging a quarter per seat for admission—all money to benefit the athletic program. A sizeable crowd was on hand, made up of friends and relatives of the fighters and partisans of both schools.

Standing in front of the entrance, waiting for Laura to show up, Phil saw that a large number of Negroes were entering the building. He was surprised until he recalled that the rival school was in a mixed neighborhood.

Even though Lew Bocca had promised to hold two seats for

him, Phil was starting to become impatient. He wanted to be sure that there was enough time for him to go back to the locker room and wish Bob luck before the fights began.

Then he heard Laura call his name. He took her by the arm and hustled her inside the building.

"Come on," he said, taking her to the gym where a portable ring had been set up. He looked over the rows of metal folding chairs.

"Where are we sitting?" Laura asked.

"Wherever Lew managed to find some seats. They're not reserved."

"Aren't we sitting with your parents?"

"They're not here. Mama doesn't approve of boxing and Papa almost never leaves the apartment any more."

"Your mother and I have something in common," Laura said. "I don't really approve of boxing matches either."

"Yeah?" Phil felt unsure of himself. "Well, maybe you'll like this one."

"I hope so. In any case, I hope your brother wins."

"Thanks... hey, there's Lew down front." Phil grinned. "Ringside seats. I should've known he'd managed to get the best seats in the house."

He led Laura down the aisle and proudly introduced her to his friend.

Lew indicated his own companion, a flashily dressed girl with large breasts and a narrow smile.

"Meet Marge Brandt," he said.

Phil made sure that Laura was settled in her seat, then excused himself to hunt for Bob.

"I'll only be a few minutes," he promised.

He made his way to the locker room and waited unobtrusively while Bob and his teammates received a pep-talk from their coach. The talk was primarily a lecture on sportsmanship and fair play—how all the boys should follow the rules and how winning or losing was not as important as fighting on the square.

All bullshit, Phil believed. He hoped that Bob would not be taken in by it. Maybe it was okay in school—Phil wasn't sure about that—but it had no relationship to the real world.

He wished Bob luck and asked him if he'd found out yet who he was boxing.

"Guy by the name of Bill Keegan," Bob replied. "A black guy. Nice kid."

"A black guy?" Phil cursed mildly. "Watch out he doesn't foul you when the ref isn't looking."

"Oh, hell," Bob said in some disgust. "You think every Negro cheats. This guy from Detroit, Joe Louis . . . you know, that amateur champ of the light heavyweight division who just turned pro? Well, everyone says he's got the greatest potential of any young fighter around. And I can guarantee you he doesn't win his fights by punching below the belt."

Phil was surprised by his brother's vehemence—and also a bit ashamed of himself. "So this guy Keegan is all right?"

"Sure. Like I say. I mean he's a rough fighter, all right, but a clean one."

"Okay," Phil said. "Take care of yourself."

When Phil returned to his seat, Lew asked about the young man his brother was going to fight.

Phil told him. "He's a Negro. Name of Bill Keegan."

"Christ," Lew said. "I hope he doesn't low-blow the kid."

Laura looked furious. But Phil replied before she had a chance to say anything. "Just because a guy's Negro," he said, echoing his brother's words to him, "that doesn't mean he fights dirty."

Lew shrugged comfortably. "Maybe not always. But most of the time."

"Lew knows about these things," his girl, Marge, put in.

Once again, Phil could see that combative look in Laura's eyes. He placed a finger on her knee and shook his head discretely. Fortunately she got the message and held herself in.

The people in the hall, meanwhile, had grown tired of waiting for the fights to start. They began to stamp their feet and chant in unison.

After four or five minutes of this, the director of the event came out and stood in the center of the ring. He welcomed everyone and said that there would be eleven fights of three rounds each.

"Let's get on with it!" somebody called in a semi-drunken voice.

But the director was not going to be stopped. He held up his hand for silence and then went on about how much good their admission charges would do.

"Next year," he concluded, "our sports program will be even better than it was this year—thanks to you and to these fine boys who are going to entertain us this evening with an exhibition of amateur pugilism."

"So shut up an' let 'em fight!" cried the same voice that had called out before.

"Yeah!" several other voices agreed.

"All right," said the director, holding up his hand again. He introduced the referee to a chorus of boos and the first two fighters to a chorus of cheers.

"What are they wearing on their heads?" Marge asked curiously.

"That's their protective headgear," Lew told her. "All amateur fighters wear it. It protects their brains from being scrambled, but still lets them get hit in the jaw and the face."

"Can they be knocked out still?" Marge asked as the bell sounded for the first round.

"Yeah, sure."

Even as Lew spoke, one of the boys—the one from Bob's school—went down in a heap. The referee stood over him, counting to ten.

"What—what happened?" Marge asked.

"Your question was just answered, dear," said Laura. "He got knocked out."

"But—but I didn't see him get hit."

"Then you couldn't have been looking. I saw it. He was hit right smack in the jaw."

Marge looked at Laura as though she didn't know whether or not to believe her. But Lew and Phil both assured her that it had indeed been a knockout.

"Well," Marge said. "I do hope that the next fight isn't over so quickly."

"Or at least won't be so one-sided," Phil said.

But it was just as one-sided, though this time—at least in Phil's opinion—it was the right side that won. For the short, stocky white boy from Bob's school went after his Negro opponent with stomach punches until he was forced to lower his guard. Then, while the black fighter clutched at his middle, the white boy took him out with two clean shots to the jaw.

Some of the Negroes in the audience began protesting. They felt that their boy had been hit low and put out of action while he was trying to recover from a dirty shot.

A group of whites began to taunt them.

"Stop your crying!" one of them said. "He was hit in the

belly. You niggers can't never take it in the belly!"

"Oh, yeah!" said a black. "You want to come outside and see who can take it? You dumb white shit!"

"Who's calling me a dumb white shit, you black—"

"Gentlemen, gentlemen!" the director interrupted by talking into the microphone. He had entered the ring on the run and was red-faced and puffing. "The fighting is supposed to . . . ah . . . take place in the ring, ha, ha."

"Then tell *them* to shut up," the white voice said angrily.

"You tell *them* to," said a black voice.

"Stop it! Everyone!" the director said through the public address system. "There are ladies present, after all. If there are any more disturbances, I will ask for these events to be canceled."

The crowd—though still restless—did not take up the challenge. Everyone settled back in his seat.

After a brief pause, two more boys stepped into the ring to have their names announced. Once more it was a white meeting a black, and once more the white boy won. This time, however, the victory was so swift and so complete that there could be no disputing it.

Since fight number four found both schools being represented by whites, the tension inside the gym was reduced. It was a well-fought battle, though a contest between boxers rather than sluggers. When it was called a draw, there was a general applause.

Marge seemed puzzled.

"Why is everyone so happy?" she wondered. "Those boys hardly hit each other. I always thought a good fight was when they really had at it."

Lew regarded her fondly. "This was a demonstration of skill, babe. But don't worry about it. You can hardly expect to know all the finer points."

Phil was concerned that Laura might feel left out of the conversation. He asked her what she thought about the match.

"I guess I'm like Marge," she said. "I don't understand the finer points either. But I did like one thing about it. Both fellows were still on their feet when it was over."

Marge nodded sagely. "That's true, hon," she said.

Bob climbed into the ring along with Bill Keegan.

Marge favored Phil with a smile. Her long black hair was arranged in bangs, and she made a sensuous gesture of brushing them away from her eyes.

"I really do hope your brother wins," she said softly.

Phil smiled his thanks to her, then swung back to focus his attention on the ring.

He would have liked to be in Bob's corner as his second or coach. But the school only permitted its own personnel to attend the fighters so that Phil had to call advice and encouragement from his seat.

As the bell sounded, he did not even notice Laura clutch at his arm. He was totally involved with the two youths who met at the center of the ring to feint and jab and test each other out.

They seemed equally matched. Though both of them landed some solid punches as the round progressed, Phil could see that neither was able to gain any real advantage. When the round came to an end, there was cheering from all sections of the gym.

"Just keep doing what you're doing, Bob!" Phil shouted. "You'll take him out next round."

"Hey, Bob!" Lew Bocca shouted. He seemed as involved in the fight as Phil. "Murder the black bum! Show 'im what a white man can do!"

There were angry reactions and hostile mutterings from black spectators scattered about the gym. But they did not bother Phil nearly as much as did the stiff, furious looks Lew was receiving from Laura.

He knew what Laura must be thinking of Lew and, in a way, he couldn't blame her. The racist language was bothering him, also.

He reminded himself that Lew was Lew—a good friend who had done one hell of a lot for him. He was going to have to remember that. *And* he was going to have to make Laura see it as well.

Then the bell rang for the second round. The more vicious remarks of the spectators were suspended for a while so they could concentrate once more on the fight.

The second round started as a continuation of the first, with neither fighter able to make much of a dent in the other's defenses.

Then—without warning—Bob landed a stinging left uppercut to Bill Keegan's jaw.

The black youth was staggered. His knees buckled, his eyes glazed, and his head fell forward so that his chin was against his chest. He lurched toward Bob and wrapped his arms about him, holding on for dear life.

The referee moved quickly to break up the clinch. When

he did so, however, the audience gave a collective gasp. Bob was bleeding severely from a nasty cut just below his right eye.

"Jesus Christ!" Phil said as the referee signaled a halt to the proceedings in order to summon a doctor into the ring. "The son-of-a-bitch butted him."

"What'd I tell you," Lew muttered darkly. "About the way they fight."

Fortunately, he had kept his voice low enough so that none of the blacks in the hall heard him. The atmosphere was dangerous enough as it was. The whites, who wanted Bob to be awarded the fight on a foul, were complaining to each other in angry snarls, while the blacks glared at them defiantly.

By now the doctor had finished examining Bob's eye. He said something to the referee who started speaking earnestly to the fighters and to officials of both schools.

"Maybe we'd better get out of here," Laura said. "I know this sort of scene. It can turn ugly."

"You go ahead," Phil replied. "I'm waiting for Bob."

"What about us?" Marge asked Lew. If Laura had sounded concerned, she sounded terrified.

"You head for the entrance with Laura," Lew replied. "Phil and I will meet you both back there."

"But suppose you can't find us?"

"Yeah, you're right," Lew conceded. "Maybe you and Laura better go on to my place, then. We'll see you there."

"Go on," Phil urged Laura.

As the two started back, Phil saw that they were not the only females who were getting out while they still could. The potential for uncontrolled violence was growing.

Finally, the director stepped into the ring and signaled that he was going to make an announcement.

"Ladies and gentlemen," he said over the P.A. system. "Both fighters agree that the butting was accidental. Therefore—and after consultation with the officials of the respective high-schools—the referee is declaring the contest a draw!"

There was a roar of disapproval from the whites in the gym.

"Accidental my ass!" cried a male voice in the unmistakably harsh accents of lower-class Manhattan.

"You wanna fight?" challenged a black voice.

The director had remained in the ring and was complaining into the microphone that he would be forced to send for the police if order weren't restored at once. Both sides were ignoring him, however, and the situation was rapidly growing worse. On the far side of the gym, a couple of middle-aged men, one white, one Negro, were trading clumsy punches with each other. Closer by, two teen-aged girls were doing their best to tear out each other's hair.

Phil nudged Lew. "I'm getting Bob out of here, right now!"

"I'm with you, buddy," responded loyal Lew.

They were only a couple of rows away from the ring, where the fighters were standing next to the director who was still pleading impotently over the public address system. Phil and Lew reached the side of the apron without much trouble.

"Bob!" Phil shouted to make himself heard over the noise of the mob. *"Down here. Come on. Let's go!"*

Bob turned to see where his brother's voice was coming from. His gloves were off now, his rubber mouthpiece was out of his mouth, and he was pressing the bandage which the doctor had given him against his wound.

The doctor himself was nowhere to be seen. Phil thought that he must have run for shelter along with the referee—and wondered if he could really blame him

"Come on, goddamn it!" Phil cried, as he could sense the mob start to reach a point of no return.

"Yeah!" Lew shouted. "Let's go!"

"What about Bill?" Bob yelled down from the ring. "Everyone's gone nuts in here! If we don't get him away fast, the whites'll tear him to pieces!"

"Shit!" Lew screamed. He sounded disgusted. "We're worried about you! Let his own people watch out for him!"

"Forget it!" the black youth called. "I can watch out for myself!"

But Phil understood his brother well enough to realize that he'd never permit himself to be rescued from danger unless the youth who had just been his ring opponent was rescued also.

"For Christ's sake stop the bullshit!" he yelled. "The both of you—come on!"

23

It was Phil and Lew's knowledge of street-fighting that got them out of the hall. That and the fact that they had no desire to take part in the general melee.

They led their two charges up the aisle—not bothering anyone, avoiding all contact when they could. It was only when somebody tried to block their path and interfere with their escape that they aimed a foot, knee, elbow or thumb against a groin, kidney, Adams apple or eye. Then, with the obstacle removed, they headed once more for the nearest exit.

They reached the street to be greeted by the sound of screeching brakes and wailing sirens. Police tumbled from their prowl cars, nightsticks and guns at the ready.

A couple of them closed in on Phil and his friends.

"Holy Hell!" one of them exclaimed as he saw Bob's bloody bandage pressed against his cheek. "That happen in the ring? Or did someone beat you with a club on the outside?"

"It was in the fight," Bob said.

"You were probably fighting this one," said the other cop. He indicated Bill Keegan. "Was there something funny with his glove? Did he have a roll of coins inside it? Or a brass knuck? Tell me if he did, and I'll—"

"Hey..." Bill began.

But quick-thinking Lew Bocca, who wanted no trouble, interrupted him: "Nothing like that, officer. He's a good boy."

"Oh. If you say so."

"But I'll tell you," Lew continued. "My friend here would like to get the white boy to the hospital. Do you think you could help him out?"

"Well...I don't know...."

Lew Bocca was looking around at the other policeman at the scene. He saw someone he knew. He grinned.

"Hey, there's Lieutenant Sullivan. Lieutenant!"

The large, impressive man in uniform who was directing incoming police traffic turned to Lew and waved.

"Mr. Bocca! I'll be with you as soon as I'm free."

The officers standing near Phil and his brother exchanged knowing looks.

"Why didn't you say you were a friend of the Lieutenant's?" the first cop asked.

"My partner and me'll take the lad to a hospital in our squad car," the second offered.

"Thanks. We'd sure appreciate that. If you'll let me have your names, I'll mention them to the Lieutenant."

"Officers Boyle and Cohn, sir. But you needn't trouble yourself about us."

"No trouble at all, fellows. It'll be a pleasure."

The two officers began helping Bob toward the police car. Phil and the others followed them.

Lew took Phil by the arm. "I guess you'll go with Bob to the hospital. Right, buddy?"

Phil answered in the affirmative. He was still worried—not only about his brother, but about how his mother would react when she learned what had happened.

"I'm going straight home," Lew said. "The girls should be there by now and I want to check that they're all right. Want me to have Laura wait there for you?"

"Yeah, that would be great."

"Okay. Then why don't you bring Bob over when the docs are done with him? We can take him home from there."

"I'll do that. Thanks." Phil gripped Lew's hand and squeezed. "Thanks for everything."

"Shit. Forget it," Lew said. He turned to leave while Phil followed his brother into the rear of the squad car.

"Hey, Mr. Aronson," Bill Keegan called. "Mind if I come with you? I want to see he's okay."

Phil shrugged. He felt a certain natural resentment at the boy who'd injured his brother—a resentment which was doubtlessly aggravated by the fact that the youth was black. On the other hand, it was Bob himself who insisted that the butting was accidental. And Keegan did seem sincerely concerned. . . .

"Get in the car," Phil said gruffly.

The gash near Bob's eye was less serious than it appeared to be. After the doctors at the hospital emergency room had finished dealing with it, they said that Bob could return in a week to have the stitches taken out and the bandage removed. He'd have a small scar, they said, but it would fade with time.

Phil felt as though a weight had been lifted from his chest. "That's terrific," he said with a wide grin. "Really great!"

Bill Keegan grinned, too. If anything, he appeared even more relieved than the Aronson brothers.

"Jeez, I'm glad it's nothing too bad," he said. "I'll swear on anything you want, I didn't mean to butt you!"

"Hell," Bob said. "That's what I've been telling everyone."

Phil regarded the two youths for a moment. "I don't want to break this up. But, Bob, you and I have things to do. Lew Bocca's expecting us at his place."

"Hey, listen," Bob said. "Would Lew get real mad, do you think, if I didn't go with you?"

"No, I don't see why he should. But why don't you want to come along?"

"Well, for one thing I feel all pooped out. All I want to do now is to go home, take a shower, and climb into bed. You know."

Phil nodded. He knew he was being foolish, but he could not help but feel hurt at the refusal.

"You only have to stay for a few minutes," he said. "Then I could run you home in a cab."

"Look, if you really want me to come..."

"It's up to you," Phil said stiffly.

"In that case, I'll take a rain check," Bob said. He paused briefly.

"I really don't feel like going anywhere with my boxing gear on. Though I suppose I should be grateful that the referee had time to take off our gloves before he ran away to find a hidey-hole."

Bill Keegan chuckled. "Oh, man. You can say that again."

"And I must smell pretty bad, too," Bob continued. "I don't think the women would be able to stand me!"

"Okay," Phil said. "You've made your point. I'll drop you off at home on my way to Lew's. Or would you like me to come upstairs with you and explain things to Mama? Maybe I'd better. She's bound to be upset at what happened."

"Don't worry about that, Phil. You spent enough time already. I can talk to Mama myself."

"You sure?" Phil sounded dubious.

"Yeah. You go find out what happened to Laura. I can reassure Mama that I'm fine. If she doesn't believe me, I'll give her the name of the doctor who fixed me up here."

"Okay," Phil said. He turned to Bill Keegan. "What about you? I'll be getting a cab anyway, so I might as well drop you where you want to go."

"Why don't you come home with me for a while?" Bob suggested.

Phil did not believe that would be such a good idea. For one thing, he was worried about his mother's reaction to the boy who had injured her son. And the fact that the boy was Negro wouldn't help any either, he thought.

He was spared the necessity of saying anything by Bill Keegan himself.

"Thanks a lot," Bill told Bob. "But I think I'd better get back uptown."

"Should I let you off at a subway station, then?" Phil asked.

"That would be fine, Mr. Aronson. Any IRT."

When Phil entered Lew Bocca's apartment, he could see that the atmosphere was strained. Lew and Marge were not bothering to hide their hostility toward Laura who, in turn, was treating them with barely veiled contempt.

He sensed that he and Laura should leave as quickly as possible. He started to refuse Lew's offer of a drink, but his friend surprised him by insisting.

"Come into the kitchen with me while I make it," he said.

Phil followed him in and Lew shut the door.

"I wanted to talk to you."

"Yeah?" Phil said.

"About your girlfriend in there. If she doesn't start minding her tongue, she's liable to get her ass kicked!"

"What do you mean?" Phil was worried. He recalled Laura's temper and wondered what she had done.

"She started in on Marge as soon as they left the Y," Lew said. "You know what she told her? That *I* was exploiting her. *Me!* Who gave her the clothes she's wearing. The fucking jewels she's got on!"

"Yeah, well . . ." Phil began.

"But it's not my fault," Lew continued as though Phil had not tried to interrupt. "It's the fault of the system. The capitalistic system.

"You know something, Phil. She's a commie. A Red fucking Bolshie!"

"I wouldn't go that far," Phil replied. "I know she's left

wing as all hell, but she does speak out against Russia."

"Does she?" Lew sounded skeptical. "You sure couldn't prove that by me. All I can say is that she doesn't believe in good old American free enterprise. To her, that's a curse word. She thinks it's responsible for all our troubles. Even that riot tonight."

"Come again?"

"Really. According to your lady friend, the riot never would have started if it weren't for the capitalistic system.

"You see," he went on sarcastically, "the white people in the Y only thought they saw that nigger kid butt your brother. Or, if they did see it, they should have also seen that it was an accidental butt. And why didn't they? Prejudice, of course. And what caused the prejudice? You guessed it, the capitalistic system."

"Oh? . . ."

"Yeah. Capitalism makes us all into slaves. But we like to kid ourselves into thinking we're free. So we choose someone to look down on—the niggers, say, who used to be slaves— and then think at least we're freer than they are. Get it now?"

"No."

"Who could, buddy. Who in hell could?"

Phil shook his head.

"But it goes on from there," Lew said. "Did I tell you that she told Marge I was exploiting her?"

Phil nodded. "Yes."

"So get this. When Marge tried to defend me by saying how I always help out with the rent and like to buy her lots of nice things, your girlfriend said that I was treating her like she was a member of the demimonde. How do you like them apples? The demi-fucking-monde!"

"Jesus. What did Marge say to that?"

"She didn't say anything. She wasn't absolutely certain what the word meant. Which is kind of lucky for that cutie-pie of yours. 'Cause if Marge had known she'd just been called a whore, Laura would've wound up flat on her ass."

Phil was devoutly grateful for Marge's uncertainty. Not that he was fearful about Laura's safety with Marge. It was just the reverse. If she'd turned around and knocked Marge on her ass, it would have really loused him up with Lew.

"I'll tell Laura to be more careful about what she says from now on," he promised earnestly.

146

He wouldn't just tell her either, he thought. Once he got her alone, he'd really let her have it.

Lew regarded him cynically. "Listen, buddy," he said. "Maybe it's none of my business, but you'd better watch yourself pretty good when you're around that one. A dame like her—a broad who thinks the way she does—can be dangerous to a man."

On the other hand, though, Laura was a woman. And Phil believed that the right man could handle any woman. Even an independent one like her.

"I'll give it some thought," he said.

Lew finished his drink and poured himself another. He asked Phil if he wanted one more, too.

"I don't think I'd better," Phil said, placing his glass on the kitchen counter. "Maybe we'd better get back to the girls."

"Yeah. And see what in hell's been going on in the living room. It can't be too bad, though. At least we didn't hear any shots or screams or falling bodies."

When they returned to the living room, Laura seemed to look right through Lew and greeted Phil coldly.

"You took your time," she said as he sat down nervously beside her.

"Sorry. Lew and I . . . uh . . . we had some business to talk over."

"Oh? It must have been important."

"It was."

Then there was silence. Not just between Laura and himself, but between Lew and Marge as well.

Phil longed for some small talk. Anything—the weather, his brother's skill as an amateur boxer, even Marge's opinions of the latest fashions. Anything.

Almost in desperation, he asked Lew who he thought would win the National League pennant that year.

"St. Louis," Lew replied.

"You don't think the Giants can repeat?"

"St. Louis."

End of conversation.

Phil knew that he should get Laura out of there. Fast. Before anything else bad happened. But nobody seemed interested in helping him make a graceful exit.

All right, he thought. So they'd make an awkward exit. It would be better than no exit at all.

He looked conspicuously at his watch. "We'd better start moving," he said. "It's getting late and I have to take Laura downtown."

24

"What she is," Laura was saying in the restaurant the following night, "is a stupid cow."

"Hey, wait a minute," Phil said. "How can you say that about a dame you hardly know."

"Oh, I know her. Enough, anyway. I know she's got a good ass and a nice pair of big tits. And that she trades them for favors like a goddamn whore!"

"Like a what?" Phil sneered. "With her you came on like a real lady! What did you say then? A member of the *demi-monde?*"

"I didn't think you'd understand the word!" Laura shot back, trading taunt for taunt.

The two glared furiously at each other. They had been going on that way since they had sat down at the table, and the food they'd ordered was mostly turning cold on their plates.

Phil swallowed some water and took a bite of veal cutlet. It went down with difficulty and lay heavily in his stomach.

He'd been a damn fool to call her today, he thought. He should have let it end last night.

Their parting had been a dour one without even a perfunctory kiss. She had not wanted to go anywhere with him, not join him for a drink, not even permit him to see her home. She wanted to go home in the subway, but when he refused to accept that, she agreed to let him hail a taxi and give the driver enough money to take her home.

If he'd been smart, he'd have let it stay that way. But not him! He had to phone her this morning to ask if she still wanted him to come to that Y.A.S.D. meeting tonight. If so, he suggested, maybe she'd have dinner with him first.

Which was why they were here, now—in this stupid down-town restaurant near Y.A.S.D. headquarters.

Laura surprised Phil by breaking into sudden giggles.

"What's so funny?"

"I just remembered," she said. "The reason that I used that word to Marge. I started to say that your fine friend was treating her like a whore. Then I realized that would only make her p.o.'d at me. So I switched to demimonde at the last minute.

"See," she went on. "I wasn't showing off, after all."

Phil smiled in return. When Laura widened her eyes and wrinkled her nose in a grin, it completely melted him.

"As long as we're being honest," he said, "the only reason I did recognize the word was that my kid brother's a whiz at French."

Laura's leg touched his under the table. It stayed there, moving slowly back and forth in a teasingly erotic gesture. It was as though they had never quarreled at all; and for several long minutes it was hard to believe that they had.

At the same time though, deep within him, he knew that they were going to quarrel again. And again.

There were times when Phil thought about Laura and wondered how he could have become so seriously involved with her. She was very different from the other girls he'd been drawn to. She was more temperamental, more intellectual, more strong-willed.

The girls he had been serious about before Laura were not like that at all. Rita Crane, for instance—although she'd been older than he and more experienced—deferred to his wishes in almost everything. And while Kay talked tougher than Rita and seemed more self-reliant, she never really challenged him in any way except while they were in bed.

If any of Phil's former females had challenged him the way Laura did—if she'd put down his friends and his way of life, for example, or questioned his political beliefs as naïve and selfish—he would have given her a good hard kick in the rump and then walked out of her life.

But not with Laura. With Laura, Phil kept coming back for more.

And why? It was not merely her talent in bed. She was great there, all right, but so were other women—so was Kay. Nor was it just her looks—the way she smiled or carried herself or moved her hips when she walked.

All that counted, naturally. But there was a lot more.

A good part of it was the challenge itself. There was almost a sensual novelty in watching the soft, pettable creature, whose breasts he had kissed and whose sweet female parts he had just explored, turn into a keenly probing verbal warrior who refused to either give or ask for quarter simply because her opposition was also her friend and lover.

For they were friends. (Which may have been why their fights could grow so bitter.) They could enjoy each other as people, not only as objects of each other's passion.

This had never happened to Phil before. In his experience, males were for friendship, females for sex. One did not confuse the two. Or at least not until now.

Laura also took an interest in Phil's family.

She would ask how his brother was, for example, and wondered how his parents were reacting to Bob's continued interest in boxing. She encouraged Phil in his insistence that Bob stay in school. Like him, she felt it would be a serious mistake if Bob did not complete his education.

They talked about his parents. Laura tried to make Phil see that his mother was not the only one deserving of his sympathy.

"Your father's whole world went topsy-turvy on him," she said once, "leaving him no base on which to stand. It was the system that did him in," she continued. "The system. That's what you should be angry at. Not your father. He is only the victim."

"You like to blame the system for everything," Phil told her. "Don't you think an individual has any responsibility for himself?"

"Sometimes," Laura said in the tone she used when she was trying to win someone over through sweet reason. "If a person is ideologically aware, for example, it's his responsibility to try and change the system. But your father was never educated into ideological awareness."

Phil grunted so that he wouldn't swear. This was the kind of circular argument nobody could ever win.

At any rate, he didn't really want to discuss his father any more. For though he could not accept Laura's pat explanation of his father's behavior, he was not sure that his earlier accusations were right, either. The subject frustrated him—and whenever he thought about it too long he became angry.

• • •

Laura also tried to bring Phil and his sister closer together. She liked Naomi, and thought that she was bright and entertaining. She often suggested that he bring the girl along when they went out during the day.

Phil marveled at Laura's patience with his sister. As she neared her twelfth year, Naomi had become addicted to movie fan magazines, and could talk for hours about her favorite Hollywood stars. As Phil well knew, Laura really believed that the movies were a kind of drug which the ruling classes employed to take people's minds away from their real problems. She was able to put aside that point of view, however, and answer seriously when Naomi would ask her opinion of Clark Gable, for instance, or the romantic British film star Leslie Howard. The two talked about female stars, also. Who did Laura think was more beautiful, Naomi might ask for example, Norma Shearer or Joan Crawford?

On the twenty-eighth of May of that year, the well-publicized simultaneous birth of five baby girls to a French-Canadian farm family named Dionne gave Naomi something else to discuss with Laura. But Phil soon became more bored with the subject of the miraculous quintuplets than he was with the subject of Hollywood.

If he managed to put on mental earplugs and sit through a good many of these conversations without objection, it was primarily because he thought that Laura was right: he should spend more time with his kid sister. And the easiest way for him to do that was to have Laura there as an interested but neutral third party.

As for Laura, she not only tried to change Phil's attitude toward Naomi, she worked on the girl's attitude toward Phil.

He first realized this one day when the three of them had taken the BMT subway for a Sunday afternoon's outing at Coney Island. He had left them in order to visit a men's room at Steeplechase Park. When he came back, they were so wrapped up in their conversation that they didn't notice his approach.

He was about to make himself known when he realized that Laura was talking about *him.*

"Your brother really does love you very much," she was telling Naomi. "I know you think he's too rough on you sometimes, but that's only because he wants to teach you things now so that you'll grow up to have a happy future. Even when he's wrong, Naomi—and I believe he is once in a while, he's *trying* to do the best for you."

151

"But why is he so *mean* to me?" Naomi complained. "And he teases so. . . ."

"I know. And I tell him he shouldn't. But what he's doing is hard on him—taking on the responsibility of his whole family when he's so young himself. You should try to understand him more, sweetie, and maybe even forgive him."

"Young?" Naomi gasped incredulously.

"I know he's older than you." Laura grinned. "But he really is very young. Especially when you think of what he's doing."

Phil retreated silently, nervous that he might be seen to be a spy. He didn't return until he felt the discussion would be over.

What Laura had been saying was what he himself would have liked to tell his sister. But he could never seem to find the words.

Despite all the nice things they had together, though, the fundamental contradictions between Phil and Laura would not go away. They had two totally different views of the world. At the deepest level, their viewpoints were so opposed that what might represent good to one of them might be nothing less than evil to the other.

If Phil believed in anything, it was in a Darwinian universe where the survival of the fittest was not merely a physical law of existence, but a basic moral law as well. It was the duty of a man to fight, to struggle. Once he stopped fighting, Phil thought, he might as well die—since he was all but dead already. And if he refused to stop at nothing in order to win his struggle, that merely proved he had no manhood.

It was from this violent struggle between human beings, Phil thought, that all progress came.

He had no more read Adam Smith's masterwork, *The Wealth of Nations*, than he had read Charles Darwin's *Origin of Species* or *Descent of Man*. But many of the concepts derived from the work of the eighteenth-century economic philosopher had penetrated his mind along with those derived from the nineteenth-century naturalist. Basically, Phil felt that a laissez-faire economy which encouraged every citizen to accumulate wealth by working in his own self-interest would do more for the public good than all the New Deals, welfare programs, and government controls that ever existed.

What Laura believed was precisely the opposite. She was sure that too much reliance on capitalism and laissez-faire had brought America to the depressed state it was currently in. And if Roosevelt's New Deal was guilty of anything, it was in not controlling the marketplace and the economy strictly enough.

If someone had pointed out to Phil that his current beliefs were the same ones his father had followed before his own fall, he would probably have retorted that his father hadn't been willing to keep on fighting when the struggle got too tough. Any fight would have losers as well as winners. His father had been one of the losers.

Also, if someone had pointed out that the same laissez-faire philosophy would be used as an excuse for the underworld— for the less savory activities of the Boccas, for example—Phil might have said that many of the services they supplied, such as gambling and prostitution, could and perhaps should be legalized and made freely available in the marketplace. Just as liquor sales were legalized and strong drink made available with the end of Prohibition.

If, on the other hand, someone had reminded Laura that too much government control had *invariably* led to dictatorship (whether of the right or the left), and that controlling a person's money and work place was a good way to control the person, one of the things she would have said was that *pure* socialism had never been tried.

Laura might also have pointed out that the principle danger then lay in another direction. Though certainly no admirer of Stalin's Russia, and not even very comfortable with some of what Trotsky had done (his call for forced labor batallions in 1920, for example, and his crushing of the Kronshtadt sailors in 1921), she would still have preferred a mild dose of Leninism to free enterprise run wild.

So both Phil and Laura had their closed systems of beliefs. And while Laura was more verbal about hers, and had a far firmer intellectual grounding in it, Phil was every bit as convinced that his system was right.

It was obvious that if they could not change each other's beliefs, they were going to have to make some sort of effort to adjust to them. They could keep their differences—just as long as they didn't keep harping on them.

Phil knew very well what Laura thought about bookmaking, to take just one example. She did not have to keep reminding him of her belief that professional gamblers too often exploited those least able to defend themselves; that they would tempt the poor and the weak to play the numbers game, and to place very small baseball bets at very poor odds.

Phil did get her to admit that she wasn't against gambling per se. Mature, intelligent, politically aware people, like herself or Jed Symmonds or other Y.A.S.D. members, could gamble. They knew what they were doing and would even win bets from time to time. And it was surely no sin for a bookmaker to take as much money as he could from the rich.

But what Laura thought of as the undereducated and socially immature poor were different. They used gambling the way a heroin addict used his drugs, to gain some brief relief from the dull, gray world the system foisted on them. They wanted the quick fix, the stunning rush to the brain, and the happy glow that came with the feeling of future (always future!) riches.

What Laura did was make a separation in her mind between her friend, Phil, and bookmakers in general. It was bookmakers in general—or even "certain" bookmakers—who played their tricks on the poor.

If Phil did that, she would not have been able to rationalize it away. It was best not to know, therefore, and to assume that he took only from the rich.

As for Phil, he could never take Y.A.S.D. ideals too seriously. He kept going to the meetings, however, helped the group out financially from time to time, and learned not to poke fun at the members. Especially not in Laura's presence.

At one July meeting, it took all his willpower not to break his promise to himself and burst out laughing. That was when there was a serious discussion of whether or not to protest the killing of the bank robber John Dillinger by FBI agents in Chicago.

Several of the members—including Karl Grannet, Jed Symmonds and Glenda Krakaur—wanted to get in touch with other leftist outfits and call for a general strike.

"In strictly objective terms," Jed pointed out, "Dillinger was one of us. He terrified members of the ruling class by going after their strongholds, the banks. That's why they and their lackies in the press are gloating now that he's dead.

"It's up to us. We've got to prove to the rich and the powerful that they can't get away with ordering the FBI to murder everyone who gets in their way!"

Phil did not say a word. He even managed to keep a straight face.

Later that night, however, when he was alone with Laura,

he told her that he was glad she hadn't supported the plan.

"With you behind it," he said, "that harebrained motion might have passed!"

"Maybe it should have," Laura replied with a shrug. "Maybe it deserved to pass."

"Jesus!" Phil stared at her as though in shock. "Do you really believe that John Dillinger was 'one of us?' Do you think he robbed banks in order to back up the revolt against the vested interests of the ruling class?"

"I have no idea," Laura replied evenly. "It doesn't matter what his motive was. A person can be an objective socialist without knowing it himself. Just as he can be an objective fascist without knowing it himself."

"Huh?"

"If a person works against the interests of the people, then he's a fascist. Whether he knows it or not. Whether he wants to be or not. Or whether he's considered to be a real nice fellow by his family or not. That's simply the way it is."

"It must be great to know more about what a person really is than either he or his family," Phil muttered. "But give me a for instance."

"Okay." Laura smiled. She was waiting to be asked. "Let's take a judge in Hitler's Germany. Since he carries out the orders of a fascist government, he must be a fascist. That's an objective fact. It doesn't matter that he may have lived his entire life as a nice, upstanding guy and only wants to spend one more year on the bench so he can reach the age of retirement. He's still a fascist.

"And in the same way," she went on earnestly, "a person who promotes the interests of the people is a socialist. Now Dillinger was probably not aware that he was serving the people by attacking the banks. But that's what he was doing. Therefore—and whether he himself would have admitted the fact or not—he is a socialist. Understand?"

Phil sighed. He wondered if she realized how weird she sounded. She was logical enough. He had to give her that. But as his kid brother had said a few weeks ago in another connection, logic doesn't mean shit if your premises are all fucked up.

That was one thought Phil did not express to Laura. He had learned to control himself to that extent at least.

"If you really feel that way," was what he did say, "why didn't you speak up for Jed and the others?"

"I don't know," she said. "Yes, I do: Though *I* believe what I just told you, most people do not. The idea would never have caught on. All the Y.A.S.D. would've gotten out of it was bad publicity."

Phil could not help feeling personally proud of her last statement. He might have been fooling himself, but he liked to think that knowing him had given her a new sense of realism.

And so, although they continued to fight and fight hard, they made a great effort to keep aiming their punches well above the belt line. That way they managed to stay together.

It was at least partly because he realized that they *were* going to stay together that Phil moved into his own place that June. It wasn't very much—a small, studio apartment which he filled with poorly made, secondhand furniture. But it was his own.

Phil's mother was hurt by the decision. She took it as a personal affront when he explained that he wanted a bit more privacy.

"You have plenty of privacy here," she said. "Plenty. You have everything you want here. Here, you're the boss!"

"What he wants," his father rasped meanly, "is a place to bring his women. Isn't that so, Phil?"

Phil locked eyes with the old man. He kept staring until his father lowered his.

It was an effort for Phil not to give vent to his disgust. The elder Aronson was still in his robe and pajamas. And though it was past two on a Sunday afternoon, he had not yet shaved.

He wanted to tell his father that of course he'd be bringing his women there. Why the hell shouldn't he? He was a young guy with lead in his pencil, for Christ's sake! Why shouldn't he have some fun.

He did not say anything, however. He knew what a statement like that could do to his mother.

And his father had already upset her. She was giving Phil a troubled look.

"Was he right about that, Phil?" she asked nervously. "Would you really do what he said. Bring women up there?"

"No, Mama. Of course not." If his mother wanted to believe he was still a virgin, then God bless her. "I just need a place where I can be by myself and think. It can get a little noisy here. With Nommie. With Bob and his friends."

"So I'll tell them to be more quiet," Sophie said. But Phil

could see she was accepting his denial. "That's no reason for you to have to run off and leave home."

"Who's running off, Mama?" Phil smiled. It was the same smile with which he used to charm her when he was a little boy. "I'm only moving a few blocks away. To Columbus Avenue. I'll be here all the time."

"You will?" His mother was reluctantly coming to accept the inevitable. "Are you sure?"

"Of course, I'm sure. And anyway—I'll have to come here to eat."

"I suppose you'd starve to death if you didn't," Sophie replied with the faint beginnings of a smile on her lips.

Phil's father sighed deeply.

Phil was happy, now. Things were turning his way. Though still less than twenty years old, he was making more money than he would have believed possible just a couple of years ago. To top that, he had a terrific woman—and his own place in which to entertain her!

He'd been needing that privacy for a long time. He had not lied to his mother—he did need a place where he could sit back and think. But the fact that he and Laura had a terrible time being alone together (the place she shared seem always to be filled with other people and she was not very comfortable going with him to a hotel) only convinced Phil to do sooner what he would have done later anyway.

In the meantime, he was using the apartment to do a lot of quiet thinking about his future. His problem remained the same: he wanted to get away from the underworld—from the Boccas—without giving up any income when he did so.

There had to be a way, he kept telling himself as he sat alone in his room. There had to be a way if only he could find it.

25

Though he could not have said how, Phil was somehow sure that the answer to his problem was involved with the Y.A.S.D.

As he became better acquainted with its members, he came to realize that the Young Americans for Social Democracy was only one of a wide network of left-wing groups, each of which was involved to some degree with all the others. Those who belonged to any one of the organizations were members of a kind of extended family. Some were as close as brothers and sisters; others were more like distant cousins, many, many times removed. But they were all connected.

They also had certain things in common, like the ideology that led them to use the same language and respond to the same code-words and gestures. Also, the members were mainly young, enthusiastic, and very sincere.

Phil often thought of them as a market—a great, untapped market which it was up to him to tap!

He realized most businessmen would laugh at that notion. There's little point in locating a market, they might insist, if there's not enough money in it to buy whatever it is you're selling. Leftist organizations were notoriously made up of penniless malcontents.

Phil understood that point of view. He had believed in it himself. But the more he observed, the more he thought it was in error.

Of course he realized that many youthful leftists were flat broke. He would have had to be blind not to see this. But he also saw that a surprisingly large number came from well-to-do families. Phil had looked on while several of them had fought winning battles with their consciences over whether or not to accept the money that was sent from home each month.

But even without the regular influx of family money, the collective membership would not have starved. Some members had part-time jobs. Others worked for different government relief projects, such as the WPA. Still others begged on the streets, while a few even stole.

All of these facts added together made up a certain amount of purchasing power.

But how was Phil going to exploit it? That was the question. What was it that the membership of the Y.A.S.D. either needed or wanted—or could be induced to need or want—that Phil Aronson could supply?

For a brief time, he thought of trying to publish a left-wing periodical. A weekly newspaper, perhaps. Laura and her friends seemed to devour every left-wing scandal sheet they could lay their hands on.

But Phil knew very little about the publishing business. And from what he could observe, even those who did know something about it often went broke.

No. That wouldn't do. But what would? He was not satisfied with merely seducing the membership of the Y.A.S.D. into gambling for larger amounts.

He wished that there were someone to discuss the situation with.

Lew Bocca was prejudiced against the Y.A.S.D. in general and Laura Vaile in particular. He would automatically be against any scheme involving either of them.

Who else was there? His father? His brother?

His father was just barely possible, Phil admitted to himself. The old man did know what business was about, and the very fact that he no longer had his own business might make him more objective. But after everything that had happened—after the way their positions had been reversed and their reactions to each other had grown so abrasive—how could he now go to him for advice?

Bob, on the other hand, was not yet experienced or mature enough to give business advice. It would not be too terribly long, Phil believed, before he could turn to his younger brother. But that time had not yet come.

Then there was Laura herself. He knew very well how she'd react if he told her the story. She would be outraged. She'd accuse him of trying to use her to help him exploit the organization she loved.

So it was plain that he would have to work things out for himself. But try as he might, he was not yet able to come up with a plan.

• • •

By early fall, Phil had another problem to contend with. Mr. Lubbuck wanted to sell out and retire from the store.

"I've been working all my life," he told Phil. "I'm tired. And my Sarah . . ." Mr. Lubbuck sighed deeply. "Her health is not what it should be.

"I want to take her away from here. Out of the city. I want to move someplace where life is easier and my Sarah and I can enjoy our last years together."

Phil nodded silently. He reminded himself to be careful about how he responded to Adolph Lubbuck's pleas for sympathy. He was pleading for sympathy when Phil first met him.

When was that? Two and a half years ago? At that time he'd been praying for a miracle to save his store from bankruptcy and himself from being tossed out on the street. He'd been frightened that he and his wife might be forced to throw themselves on the mercies of his married daughter and her husband.

It had been Phil who'd provided that miracle; Phil who'd saved him from that fate.

He wondered now if Lubbuck remembered.

Mr. Lubbuck must have sensed something of what was in Phil's mind.

"I realize that the success of this store was due to your efforts more than my own," he said heavily. "I know that. I tell myself every day that it's because of Phil Aronson that the name of Adolph Lubbuck once again stands for some of the finest food in the city. It's true you also use this store for other purposes. . . ."

Phil glared at him coldly.

The older man shivered. "I know—it's none of my business . . . sorry. . . . But truthfully," he went on, "I wonder why I'm needed here at all. Wouldn't you rather buy me out?"

Ah, Phil thought. Here it comes. How much?

Mr. Lubbuck waited for Phil to answer his question. When he did not, he looked more troubled than ever. Any sale—any business deal—Phil believed, was a war of nerves. And Phil didn't want to lose this one.

"I was thinking," Mr. Lubbuck said then. "You already have twenty percent of the store. Now what would you say the whole thing was worth? Altogether? Good will, merchandise, fixtures, everything?"

Phil shrugged. He was damned if he was going to name a

figure or make an offer. Let Lubbuck tell *him* what he had in mind.

The older man sighed. He knew when he was being out-foxed, but he could not remain silent. He was too old and it was too much against his basic nature.

He named a sum. "Does that sound fair Philip? I'm asking you. Tell me what you think."

"Probably," Phil said, responding at last. "Yes. But only because of what *I've* done."

"Would I say different?" Mr. Lubbuck sounded hurt. "You saved my life. You think I don't know that?"

"If you do," Phil suggested slyly, "maybe you should lower the price of the store."

"Lower? By how much?"

"I don't know." Phil grinned. "How much are lives going for these days?"

"Phil . . . Phil . . ." Mr. Lubbuck stroked his cheeks and the loose folds of skin which hung from his throat. "You wouldn't be taking advantage of an an old man, would you?"

"Which old man?" Phil snorted. "You? You're sharper now than I'll ever be. That's what I'm bothered about. I think you're taking advantage of me."

Adolph Lubbuck beamed happily. This was just the sort of compliment he most enjoyed. One that was poorly disguised as an insult.

"You, I couldn't take advantage of," Mr. Lubbuck said. His accent was growing increasingly strong. "You're a—what do they say? A shrewd young cookie."

Phil smiled to himself. He had learned a long time ago that Lubbuck used his accent as a defensive wall—something to think and plot behind.

As they talked, however, Phil found himself getting used to the idea of buying the store. It might even be a good thing for him.

It was true that he was the one most responsible for the store's renaissance. It was he who had brought in the new customers—who mostly started out as his gambling customers—and won back the old. It was Phil or people he hired who made the deliveries and arranged the shelves. And he did not merely take care of the physical labor. In the past year, Mr. Lubbuck had deferred to Phil's ideas on what foods to carry and what to discontinue.

If Phil did not consider himself exploited—which he didn't—it was not only that he'd grown genuinely fond of Lubbuck—which he had. He had thought of the store as a sideline and cover for his real work. Whatever he'd done for it was with that in mind; and the reason he'd worked so hard to make the store into a quality operation was that he wanted it to contribute to an overall perception of himself as someone associated with quality—the sort of man a high-rolling gambler might feel comfortable with.

Of course Phil saw the balance sheets every month and knew very well how much money the store was making. But he did not connect those rising profits with himself and his future.

For, while Phil liked Lubbuck, he did not want to imitate him. The life of a small retailer—even a superior small retailer—was not for him. That was one lesson he had learned from what had happened to his father. Phil dreamed of the day that he would be too big, himself, to be crushed by the big boys.

If he did buy the store from Lubbuck, on the other hand, that fact need not type-cast him forever. What it would do would be to add to his income and keep providing the sort of cover which came in handy whenever New York's "Little Flower" prodded the police into one of their periodic crackdowns on gambling.

The idea was to make the best deal possible, and to pay as little as he could in cash.

He had expected Lubbuck to object to this—he would have, himself—and was both pleased and surprised when he didn't.

"Who needs a lot of cash all at once?" Lubbuck asked rhetorically. "If you'll pay me so much a year, I'll be like a wealthy man living on an annuity."

"How wealthy a man do you have to be?" Phil retorted, and they were back to haggling again.

Finally it was done. Hands were shaken, papers were signed, the deal was made.

Phil was now a storeowner.

At the time, he did not take it all that seriously. It did not solve his major problem. He was as deeply enmeshed in the world of the Boccas as ever.

It was only later that he was able to see it for what it was: another step towards a goal which—though now unseen—he would come to recognize as immutable and fated.

26

Phil's studio apartment was only a couple of blocks from the walk-up flat where he had once slept with Rita Crane and Kay Lentz.

The building was located on a side street, however, between Columbus and Central Park West. Nor was it a walk-up. It had a small, slow automatic elevator which, while horribly uncomfortable holding more than two riders, still gave the place a certain status—or at least Phil thought so.

Laura helped him to select the furniture.

She insisted on shopping at one of those nonprofit, secondhand stores that are set up to help the poor. Even considering where they got the stuff, though, Phil thought he could have done better on his own. He was convinced that his taste was a good deal better than Laura's.

He did not want to hurt her feelings, however. Certainly not over a matter which made so little difference to him.

Even at the beginning, Phil's hope was to leave that apartment just as soon as he could afford a better one. What he really wanted was more space in a plush building located in a far better neighborhood.

But getting there would take time.

The furniture he purchased for this place included an old double bed (but with a *new* mattress; that was one good item Phil did insist upon), a dresser, a small table, an armchair, two folding chairs and a worn shag rug. Kitchen utensils were also kept to a minimum: a stove-top coffee maker, a double boiler, a toaster, and a couple of pans.

Laura wondered if that was enough.

"Maybe too much," Phil said. "The only cooking I plan to do here is toast and coffee for breakfast."

"You'll be eating all your dinners with your family?"

"When I'm not eating out. Or unless you're in the mood to come over here and cook for me."

"You make it sound so exciting," Laura said caustically.

"Yeah. That's what I thought."

So, all in all, Phil realized the apartment would be a pretty spartan place. But it also served the purposes for which he had obtained it.

On the morning Phil conceived his great idea, he woke up in the apartment with Laura beside him in the bed.

It was fall, by then, and there was a snap in the air. He had accidentally pulled the blanket from Laura and she cuddled against him for warmth. The nearness of him gave her sexy dreams and she reached between his legs while she was still asleep.

Phil was having a dream of his own. It had begun as a nightmare—he had somehow lost all his clothes and was running naked down the street pursued by an angry mob. The dream became pleasurable when the mob turned into a group of beautiful girls who were stroking his genitals tenderly.

As he woke up, the girls became a single girl, and the single girl turned out to be Laura.

He moved toward her, kissing the perfection of her lower belly, parting her nether lips with his tongue.

Her own tongue curled happily around the tip of his rigid cock.

They came together—in a mutual climax of separate dreams.

"And that's how I like to wake up," Laura sighed a moment or two later.

"Mmnnn . . ." Phil murmured.

He watched her as she left the bed and headed for the bathroom. The way her ass and breasts swayed when she walked—it was damned near miraculous.

He waited a few more moments—still regaining his strength—and followed her into the john. She had finished urinating by then and was standing in the tub, adjusting the shower curtain.

"Want to shower with me?" she asked.

"Sure. Just let me take my own pee, first."

By the time he stepped in, she had the hot water turned on. It felt steamy and sensuous. Like Laura herself, he thought.

"Want me to scrub your back?" he asked.

"Please."

He took a cloth and swept it down the curve of her spine

while she cooed a little at the sensation. He soaped the cloth once more and ran it over her buttocks. Then he dropped the cloth and reached under and between.

"Oh, hey . . ." she said as he found her. "Oh, God!"

"Like this . . . ?"

"Mmnnn . . ."

She spread her legs wider and almost slipped in the tub. Phil let go of what he was holding and grabbed her waist to keep her upright.

Laura turned to face him.

"This is dangerous," she said.

"What's a little danger between friends?"

He reached for her thick brown bush that had darkened almost to black in the water. "Want a shampoo?"

Laura giggled. "Why? Are you a hairdresser?"

"Depends on the hair."

Laura cupped his balls and soaped his cock.

"Looks like your best friend is crowing for more," she said. "I thought I wore him out before."

"He never knows when to give up," Phil told her.

"I don't want him to give up. I just like it when he gets up."

Phil placed his hands on her shoulders and kissed her on the lips.

Laura dropped the soap, placed her arms about him, and kissed back. As their wet bodies came together, her thigh moved gently against his hard penis. That was when Phil's foot slipped on the bar of soap and they fell together into the tub.

Phil landed on the bottom. He lifted her shoulders up and asked if she was all right.

"Yes. Fine. I had you to cushion my fall." She pulled herself off him. "What about you, though?"

"I think I'm okay," Phil said. "But it was a close thing. You damn near nutted me on the way down."

Laura giggled and placed herself at the foot of the tub where she folded her legs beneath her and sat under the shower spray. She ignored the spray and reached for Phil's genitals.

"I'm glad it was only a nearly," she said as she played with his penis. "Even though Oscar here does act like a filthy capitalist at times."

"Like a what?" Phil had never heard that one before.

"A capitalist." Laura repeated. "When he gets all bloated up with his own power and wants to screw the world. But I have just the thing to shrink him down to human proportions."

"Are you talking about Mary Jane?" Phil asked with mock indignation. He touched the tip of Laura's groin. "She could never unbloat my capitalist."

"Oh yeah? Wanna bet?"

"Sure," Phil said. "I've never run away from a bet in my life."

Laura shrieked with delight. "Where do you want to do it?"

"Why not right here? As long as the shower's going, we can have a nice clean fuck."

Laura straightened her legs cautiously and arranged them on either side of Phil. He knelt above her and kissed her glistening nipples.

"Are you sure you're not taking water in your nose," he said. "I don't want you to drown."

"Don't worry about it," she told him impatiently. "Just put your pecker in where in belongs."

Phil grinned and did what she asked while the shower splashed its obligato upon their bare bodies, the curtain, and the tub.

Later—after they had risen painfully to their feet, turned off the water, and dried themselves—Laura reminded Phil that he had an early appointment at the store.

"You said last night that it's with some food wholesaler," she told him.

"Right," Phil growled as he looked at his watch. "And I'm not going to be able to make it. Shit!"

"That's what you get for playing with me," Laura said teasingly. "Now that you're a great big businessman, you'll probably find sex a waste of time."

"The hell I will," Phil said. "What I shouldn't have done was buy that goddamn store. Being there all the time is a waste of time."

Laura was surprised at the note of bitterness in his voice.

"I thought you told me it was starting to do well for you. Making money."

"A little money," Phil corrected. "And most of that I send to Lubbuck."

He cursed again.

"It's a trap," he said. "That the real trouble. It's a goddman trap. It takes all my time and effort and gives back practically nothing in return.

"There are times when I think that old man Lubbuck really set me up."

"You didn't used to talk that way." Laura frowned.

"Yeah. When I worked there. But that was different. I didn't have any responsibility, you see. It was just a headquarters for my bookmaking act. But now I own the joint."

Laura laughed at him. "You know what your trouble is? You think the store's too small for you. What you'd really like is to own a big corporation. Then you could have things your own way and tell little store owners to go stick it."

"Damn right," Phil admitted.

"You'd make a great robber baron, darling. You have all the instincts of one."

Phil nodded. He knew he was being gotten at. But he also realized that there was a certain amount of truth in what she was saying.

"What you ought to do," Laura said, "is to run a food wholesale operation. Then you'd really have things your own way."

And that was it! Phil thought. Suddenly—amazingly— everything snapped into proper place! That was goddamned it!

Laura was watching him nervously. The play of different expressions that passed over his face seemed to frighten her.

"What is it?" she asked. "What's wrong?"

"Nothing's wrong. Just the opposite. You came up with the most brilliant idea of the decade!"

"I did?"

"I should be a big shot! I should have my own wholesale food operation! That's exactly what I should do!"

Laura didn't hesitate to tell Phil she thought he had lost all contact with reality.

"What makes you think you can do something like that?" she demanded furiously. "You don't have the money. You don't have the contacts. You don't know anything about dealing with farmers or ranchers. Oh, sure it would be nice. But that's like me saying it'd be nice to be—be Jean Harlow, for Christ's sake!"

Phil grinned at her.

"I think you're sexier than Harlow," he said. "And I'll bet you're a lot better in bed."

"Be serious, will you."

"I'm very serious. I'll bet you are better in bed."

"Oh . . . damn you!"

Laura picked up a book from the floor and pretended that she was going to hit him over the head with it.

"Okay, okay," Phil laughed. He covered his head and retreated. "I promise to be serious. But first I want you to do something for me."

"What?" Laura sounded suspicious.

"Call this number and ask for Mr. Framer," he said. "Tell him that I'm not feeling too well and won't be able to come to the shop until much later—if at all. If he's not there, you can leave the message with his secretary so that she can get in touch with him."

Laura hesitated. She did not like to lie—not even over the telephone and not even to people she didn't know.

Phil smiled. He knew the girl well enough to understand what was bothering her.

"It's not really lying," he assured her. "It's business. It's done all the time."

"That's one of the things I hate most about business," Laura muttered. But she did make the phone call.

"Mr. Framer hopes you'll be feeling better soon," she said dryly as she replaced the receiver. "Now let's talk about this idea of yours."

"Ours," said Phil.

"Whatever. It's going to take money, isn't it?"

"Yes. Though maybe a lot less than you suppose."

"So where are you going to get the money?"

"I haven't thought out that part yet," Phil replied evenly. "But give me time. We only came up with the idea this morning."

Laura nodded patiently. "What part have you thought out? Only that you'd like to do it?"

"No. I've thought about the important part. The reason behind it."

"I thought that was so you could become a robber baron," Laura said.

"And I thought we were being serious."

"Sorry."

"Okay, then. I don't want to organize just another food company. There are enough of them already. The kind of outfit I have in mind can help solve a situation that you're always complaining about at the Y.A.S.D. The fact that people are literally starving here while farmers can't sell what they grow."

"But that's because of the system," Laura insisted hotly. "It's the nature of capitalism. The workers are either thrown out of work by the Depression or made to labor for such low wages that most of them can't afford to pay reasonable prices for their food. Do farmers lower their prices—and keep lowering them until they reach the point that it costs as much to produce eggs or wheat, for example, as they'd make by selling them? That's the point where they start destroying their products while people are dying for lack of food.

"Of course, the great President Roosevelt," she went on caustically, "has discovered a way to improve all that: Simply pay farmers not to farm. People may still starve, but they have the illusion that something is being done for them. And as long as they have that, they won't work to really change the system."

"Yeah," said Phil. "Well my idea won't change the system either. But it may help some of the people who live under it. Are you interested in that?"

"Go on," Laura replied.

"Okay," Phil said. "You do know, don't you, that there are some people making money out of agriculture?"

"Who?" Laura responded without thinking. If she had thought, she would not have had to ask.

"I want you to think of a chain of people," Phil suggested, "with the farmers and livestock raisers constituting the first link. The second link are the middlemen who process the raw material they purchase from the farmers and livestock raisers. They, in turn, sell to the grocers and meat markets which sell to the general public.

"Now, I can promise you one thing: That the average small grocer has one foot in bankruptcy court. I know I'm doing a hell of a lot better than most; and that's nothing to shout about.

"So if the farmer doesn't make much," Phil concluded, "and the retail markets don't make much, and the public isn't getting a bargain, who does walk off with the profits? It's the middleman, of course. The goddamned middleman!"

Laura had been listening to him with a growing feeling of disgust. Now it exploded out of her.

"You bastard," she said. "That's what you'd like to be, isn't it? The guy who gobbles up all the money. Like I said before, you have all the instincts of a robber baron."

"Will you let me finish?" Phil said coldly. "Before you condemn me?"

"You mean there's more?"

"Sure, there's more. I want to change all that—not just take advantage of it."

"Go ahead then," Laura said grudgingly. She was always suspicious of Phil when he started saying too many of the things he knew would please her.

"Remember that political party you told me about the other day?" Phil said. "The one that didn't make it in the East, but is still going strong in Minnesota?"

"The Farmer-Labor Party."

"That's the one. Supposing we had a farmer-labor food processing company? A corporation controlled by workers on the one hand and farmers on the other. It could treat the small store owner fairly so that he could compete with the big chain markets. It could pay its workers a union wage. And it wouldn't grab so much of the farmers' profits. And it could do all that while giving the general public a decent break."

Phil grinned. "So, what do you think?"

"Why it's—it's terrific!" Laura's grin slowly answered his. "You know something? If labor could really get together with the farmers on something like this, it would start a whole new era of cooperation. It could mean a nationwide movement— farmers and workers together, running this country the way it should be run!"

Phil had his doubts about that. But he knew enough not to express them to Laura. Certainly not then, when he just about had her hooked.

"But what about the money?" she asked with a sudden frown. "I know you said you hadn't thought about that yet. But—"

"All right," Phil said. "Part of it would come from the farmers who want to work with us. Another part will come from labor—and from groups like the Y.A.S.D.

"And don't say you couldn't contribute anything," Phil added before Laura had time to frame a protest. He grinned wolfishly. "I've seen you people go out and raise money for your different causes. You've damn well tapped me for enough dough! And if you're going to help run this co-op, you're going to have to put up some of the loot as well."

All of which sounded fair to Laura—but she still didn't like it.

She tried another approach:

"Let me ask you a question," she said slowly. "Suppose

everyone did pitch in the way you'd like—farmers, labor, groups like us..."

"Yes?"

"Would you have enough money even then? I mean, you'd need to find a factory, wouldn't you? You'd want workers, salesmen—all that takes money. And we are in the midst of a depression."

"So I'd heard," Phil countered. "Which is probably why there are so many abandoned factories around which can be picked up for peanuts."

"Canning factories? Grain processing plants? Are there any of them?"

"Probably," Phil said. "But what the hell difference does it make if there are or not? A building's a building, isn't it?

"Listen," he went on. "If we promise workers that we're going to have jobs for them—if we show them that they'll be sharing in the profits—don't you think they'll accept low wages for a while in order to help us get the factory in shape?"

"Yes... probably. But we'll have to keep those promises."

Phil smiled inwardly. It was "we" now.

"Don't you think I know we will?" he asked.

Laura nodded.

"But even with all that," she persisted. "We still might not have enough money to get started."

"Then we'll just have to find some more."

"But where? You don't know where we can find it."

"I will," Phil promised. "When the time comes."

27

Phil Aronson was impatient by nature. He hated to wait. When he wanted something—a meal, a suit of clothes, a woman—he wanted it now and not later.

On the other hand, he knew that the world didn't always work that way. There were times when one had to have patience. As his mother used to tell him when he was a child, "Rome wasn't built in a day."

Which was what Phil kept telling himself when he saw that it was taking a good deal longer than he wanted to get his plan moving.

His main problem wasn't money—at least not yet. It was getting people to listen to him with an open mind.

The farm groups were the worst. Phil used whatever time he could find to travel about the Northeast, visiting farmers' associations in New York State, New Jersey, West Virginia, eastern Ohio and several of the New England states. But no matter where he went, he found himself being treated as some sort of street kid who was both too young and too urban to be taken seriously.

To correct part of this impression, he grew a mustache. It came in thick and bushy, and gave him a rather sinister appearance. It did mature him, though. And at least the farm people stopped calling him "Sonny."

But he could not do anything about his main trouble—his New York mannerisms. New York City was too much a part of Phil to be disguised.

And the truth of the matter was that the farmers did not trust New Yorkers. He could explain what he had in mind over and over again. They would listen to his ideas politely enough, but behind their polite masks they believed him to be another city slicker trying to pull a fast one.

He was able to get a bit further with the union people. They spoke a similar language and many of them had an urban background like he.

With the unionists, however, Phil had another problem. They thought of him as management—the boss. He assured them that this was not so, that the only "boss" would be the collective will of the workers and farmers who belonged to the enterprise. But even though he came with good recommendations from people known to be sympathetic to labor, he was not believed.

The situation was driving him wild. He felt it was vital to have organized labor on his side. Only with union cooperation would he be able to keep his operating costs low enough to compete with the wealthy and powerful food giants, such as Swift and Armour.

And organized labor would also be able to give him the sort of publicity he'd need. It would be some time before he could afford the expense of enormous advertising campaigns. In the meantime, sympathetic write-ups in union papers and periodicals could help get his food products accepted by working people.

But though Phil did everthing he could think of to impress union officials, he could not seem to get anywhere with them.

Perhaps the worst thing about what was happening—or rather what was *not* happening—was that his frustration was distracting him from his store and his bookmaking business. Profits were beginning to fall off.

He kept telling himself that he was acting stupidly. He was neglecting businesses that were bringing in money in order to keep chasing an elusive pot of gold. He'd have been better off, he thought, if he spent his time at the race track!

And yet he kept on with what he was doing.

Christmas passed that way. Then New Year's. Then January and February of 1935.

Phil was becoming more and more irritable. People were starting to get on his nerves. He and Laura went through long periods of not speaking to each other. Even his brother—even his mother!—were beginning to grate on his nerves.

He had made a great effort to understand his father's problems. He had listened to his mother on the subject. He had listened to his brother. He had listened to Laura. He knew by heart all the reasons they gave for the old man's attitude. There were times, indeed, when he could sympathize with those reasons. But that didn't make watching his father go through his routine any less aggravating.

Phil knew that it bothered his mother as well. He could see that in her eyes . . .

If only his father would try, he thought. He might be able to find some sort of work with one of those alphabetical bureaus that Roosevelt's brain trust had set up: The PWA, perhaps, or the new one, the WPA.

Even one of those make-work jobs would be better for the old man than doing nothing at all.

But his father did not agree. When Phil mentioned it to him, one evening, he literally turned pale with fury.

"How dare you!" he spluttered. "You young—how dare you even talk to me that way! To think that *I*—Philip Aronson, Jr.—would consider joining a project set up by the government to feed bums and loafers!"

Phil bit back the snarling remark he wanted to make—something about how his father would rather live off him.

"It's still a job," he said. "You would be working."

"With what? A pick and shovel?"

His mother interjected herself then. She looked thoughtfully at the man she had married.

"He's talking for your own good, darling," she said softly. "It's important that you work. For your own self-respect."

"You know I want to." The elder Aronson had the nervous air of an animal cornered and at bay. "But this..."

"Like the boy said. It's a job."

"Yes, but for me? For..."

He broke off, looking more cornered than ever.

"Look, Sophie, I didn't want to say anything about this before, but I've been in touch with a few of my former customers. There's a chance of resurrecting my old store. Of bringing back Philip Aronson and Son!"

It took Sophie Aronson several moments to digest this. Then she began to beam even while tears were forming in the corners of her eyes. It was as if she did not know whether to laugh or cry.

"But that's wonderful, wonderful..." She took out a handkerchief and patted it over her face.

"Isn't that wonderful, Phil?" she asked her son.

"Yes," Phil replied cautiously. "If it works out."

He turned to his father. "Who are the former customers, Papa?"

"It's a whole group. You wouldn't know their names."

"Probably not," Phil had to admit. "But I'd like to try."

His father looked flustered for a moment. "Have you ever heard of Mr. Adolph West?"

Phil shook his head. "No."

"There. You see."

"I'm surprised I haven't heard of him." his wife said reflectively. "Remember how you always liked to discuss your important customers with me?"

"Not always, Sophie. Not all of them. And anyway...he's not the principal person I've been dealing with."

"Who is the principal person?" Phil asked.

"Mr. Sidney Kerson. Remember him? He's seriously considering forming a syndicate in order to back me."

Sophie was impressed. "Mr. Kerson is a very important man."

"Was very important," Phil corrected.

"What do you mean?"

"He's made some bad investments over the past year or two. Now he has trouble paying his bills."

"How do you know that?" his father demanded.

"He used to be a customer of mine. I had to shut off his credit."

"Is this true?" Sophie looked from son to husband and back to son again. "He couldn't do anything to help your father?" she asked incredulously. "Couldn't form a syndicate?"

"Mama," Phil said softly. "Right now, Sidney Kerson can't even help himself."

Phil watched his mother sadly as the hope drained out of her.

"It's all talk, isn't it?" she said to her husband. "There's no possibility of your reopening the store."

"You never can tell," he insisted. But though he was trying his best to sound confident, he had lost the knack of doing so. "A big man like Sid Kerson can't stay down forever. And when he does come back he plans to take me with him. He told me so himself."

"He won't come back," Phil said wearily. "I don't know what he told you, Papa. But there's no way he can make it again."

The elder Aronson looked cornered. He turned in panic to his wife. "You believe him?" he whined. "You think he knows more about the world than I do? He's a boy! Where's his experience?"

It was such a pathetic echo of his former tirades that it made Phil sad to hear it. He did not reply. He did not feel angry. He almost wanted to weep.

Sophie did not want to say anything either. How could she answer him without hurting him more than he already was hurt? Could she tell him that of course their son must know more about the world than he did? For it was their son who was managing to support them?

So she too tried to take refuge in silence. But her husband wouldn't permit it.

"Tell me," he insisted. "Tell me what you think"

"What I think," she said at last, "is that you should stop fooling yourself. For your own sake, if for no one else's. You must know by now that Phil is right—that you're not going to open the store again. For a moment I thought it was possible . . . but now . . ."

"Now?"

"Now, I know it isn't. And I think maybe you should do what Phil wants."

"Apply to the WPA?" her husband asked incredulously.

"It might be for the best. Yes."

The elder Aronson looked as though he had been struck. "I couldn't. . . . It would go against everything . . ."

"Then there is nothing more to be said."

There was resignation in Sophie's tone and a sort of regretful indifference that Phil found hard to digest. He remembered too vividly when his mother had been in awe of his father. When she had all but worshiped him. Now she was regarding him as she might regard the pieces of a shattered idol or the broken image of a deposed king.

Phil supposed that he should be feeling a sense of triumph at this moment. It was what he used to dream about, wasn't it? To see his father brought low and himself raised high in his place. But now that it was happening, he felt vaguely ill-at-ease.

"Papa," he said, his voice oddly gentle. "You really *should* try to get *some* kind of job. Even working for the WPA would make you feel better."

But his father turned on him with the bewildered rage of a wounded beast of prey: "You're telling *me* what I should do? How I should feel? I'm your father. A son doesn't tell his father. A father tells his son!"

As the elder Aronson paused for breath, his wife and son exchanged ironic glances.

"The WPA," the older man went on. "You want me to work for the WPA. But that's for laborers. *Laborers,* you understand! Not for people like me."

He paused for a moment, as though daring his son to reply. When Phil didn't, he took another breath and went on:

"Loafers work for the government. No-goods. People who can't be hired elsewhere. Do you know why Roosevelt started all those bureaus that hire people? Do you?"

"To try and fight the Depression," Phil said as he realized that his father would keep pressing until he said something.

"That's what you think? Of course. That's what you're supposed to think. The real reason was to make all the loafers in America feel grateful to him. Later on, maybe they'll help him start a communist state and make him dictator."

"My God, Philip," his wife said. She looked shocked, as

though she could not believe her ears. "Do you really believe that?"

"Who knows? He's trying to kill off private enterprise, isn't he? That's what the communists want."

"Private enterprise is doing its best to commit suicide," Phil interjected. Feeling he could not stay quiet any longer, he was repeating something Laura had said to him. "It was private enterprise gone insane that got us into this condition in the first place."

But his father was shaking his head. "That's what they like to tell you. But what really put us in the soup, my fine son with your new mustache, was the foolishness of people in government. I was only reading about it the other day in one of my magazines. If the people who ran the Federal Reserve System had done what they should after the stock market collapsed, maybe they wouldn't have stopped the Depression altogether, but they would have stopped it from being as bad as it is."

"What should they have done?" Phil asked.

"They should have pumped more extra cash into the economy by buying more U.S. Treasury bonds. Then more business could have repaid their loans and avoided bankruptcy. Banks, too, could have avoided going under...

"You know something," he went on. "If all that had happened, maybe the Greystock Bank would still be in business. And maybe my store..."

He broke off sadly, lost in his vision of what might have been, but never would be.

And Phil had to wonder if what his father had said could possibly have been true. He himself didn't know enough about the subject to say.

On the other hand, though, did it really matter? Now?

"The thing is," Phil said carefully, "the Depression did get as bad as it is. The banks did fail. And rightly or wrongly, one way President Roosevelt is trying to fight it is by funding public works programs."

"For laborers," his father put in, making his bitter point once more.

This time Phil refused to let him get away with it. "No. Not just for laborers. They're hiring white collar people, too. Like clerks and other office workers. I understand they are even starting projects for artists and actors."

"There you are," Sophie said, trying to interject a bit of lightness. "You can apply as an actor. Maybe you'd end up as a movie star and Naomi could read about you in her movie magazines."

Phil laughed a little too loudly, but his father turned his head away. He got to his feet then and sighed heavily as he walked back to his room.

As Phil watched his father leave, he felt like swearing aloud. He had tried this time. He really had.

His mother sensed what he was feeling.

"You mustn't blame yourself," she said. "You did your best."

"I'm not blaming myself."

"You're not? Good."

They sat quietly for a minute or two, then Phil asked his mother how her job was going.

Her face brightened and she looked almost youthful again. "I like it very much," she said. "It's good to be needed. You know, Leonard's business is picking up steadily. He says that a lot of that is due to my work."

"Leonard, hey," Phil teased. "Are you sure it's only the job you like?"

"Phil!" his mother protested in pretended outrage. "I'm a respectable, married woman. And Leonard Abel is married to one of my oldest friends."

Phil laughed comfortably, then checked his watch. It was almost ten o'clock.

"It's getting late," he said as he stood up to stretch. "If I want to talk to Bob tonight, I'd better do it pretty soon."

He walked back and knocked on the door of the room he used to share with his brother, then entered at Bob's call.

Bob was sitting at the desk with an open book before him.

"What are you studying?" he asked.

"A story by de Maupassant."

"In French?"

Bob nodded.

"Have you thought any more about college?" Phil asked.

"I'm not going," Bob said. "I told you that already."

"Shit you're not, " Phil said angrily.

The brothers scowled at each other. This was a constant battle now, and threatened to become a bitter one. Bob was sixteen and due to graduate from high school that June. Some sort of final decision would have to be made soon.

"Even Laura thinks you're a jerk," Phil said.

Bob flushed. "Because I want to get a job?"

"Because you want to get a jerk job—instead of preparing yourself for a good one."

"Look, I'm sick and tired of going to school. I want to be on my own. Like you."

"Yeah," Phil said. "I know how you feel. But I'm just another uneducated slob trying to scratch out a living. If you keep on with your schooling, you'll be a hell of a lot more than that.

"And anyway," Phil went on. "Your quitting now wouldn't be fair to me."

"What the hell does that mean?"

"You know that big deal I told you about?"

"Yeah."

"Sooner or later it will be too big a deal for me to handle by myself. That's when I'll need you—with an education."

"But it'll take years for me to get through college."

"And it may take years for this deal to really get going."

Phil laughed and dropped the subject. A few minutes later he said goodnight and left Bob's room.

He walked through the kitchen, then, to say goodnight to Naomi. She didn't answer his light rap on the door. Asleep, probably.

He went back into the living room, kissed his mother, and left the apartment.

28

When Phil received the phone call from Lew Bocca summoning him to the offices of the Southwood Investment Corporation on the following afternoon, he was certain he knew what the problem was.

Lew's uncle must have been going over Phil's latest bookmaking receipts. Instead of continuing to grow, as they had steadily since his last little talk with the Boccas, they had recently been sliding downhill

The important question was what Phil could say in his own defense. He surely did not want to admit that he was taking time from Bocca interests in order to try and promote his own independent future. That, to put it mildly, would make Al Bocca very angry.

Perhaps he should blame the situation on current conditions; explain that the still deepening Depression was hitting his customers harder and harder. That was not only a plausible statement, it had the advantage of being true.

But would it get him off the hook? Phil doubted it. Al Bocca was not a man to be impressed by an excuse—be it good or bad, true or untrue. What he wanted was results.

All right, Phil thought. So he would promise Al results.

And *mean* that promise.

No matter what happened with the Boccas, Phil had decided not to work on his plan any more—at least for a while. He would follow his mother's advice—follow his own instincts—and wait. He was sorry he hadn't made that decision a month ago.

But what if Al wanted something more than a promise? If he wanted Phil to do something to prove he was really back on the old money-making track?

There was something he could do: he could say he'd been wrong before when he refused to run some hookers as well as taking bets. He'd run them now, he'd say.

Not that he wanted to be a pimp. He still had all his old objections to pimping and, if pressed, could doubtless think of some new ones. But if it would help keep Lew and Al off his back, he'd do what he had to do.

There were times when a man had to bite the bullet, Phil believed. Or else risk having it come at him from the muzzle of a gun.

The Southwood offices were still in the same building in the West Eighties. But they had changed somewhat from the time Phil had first visited them. There was an outer office now with a glass partition and a switchboard. Seated at the switchboard was Dolly, a tall brunette with slim hips and large breasts.

Phil winked at Dolly as he walked in, then started to go around the partition to the inner office.

Dolly jumped up from her seat.

"No," she said, "Phil! . . ."

"What's wrong?"

"You can't go in there yet. I mean you'll have to wait out here until they're ready."

Phil was annoyed. "But I always go straight inside."

"I know you do, Phil." Dolly flashed a smile at him. "But this time, Mr. Al was most emphatic. He said that he and Mr. Lew would be talking over some private business and that you'd have to wait out here until they're through."

Phil sank into one of the three chrome chairs in the outer office. He tried not to show how nervous he was. He wondered if that was why he was told to wait out here—to make him nervous.

"Can I get you a magazine?" Dolly asked. "We've got *Life, Time, Liberty, Esquire, The New Yorker*. Whatever you want. It's Mr. Al's idea. He said, if we're going to have a reception room, we ought to have magazines in it."

"Let me see an *Esquire*," Lew said.

Dolly stepped around the partition and brought the magazine out to him. She thrust out her breasts as she walked and smiled seductively.

"You like those girls in there?" she asked. "Those 'Petty girls'?"

"Sure."

"I got a figure like that." She wriggled her shoulders. "Really."

"Hey," Phil said. "Maybe you'll pose for me, then."

"I didn't know you was an artist."

"I'm not. I'd just like you to pose for me."

Dolly giggled. "Oh, Phil! You're always putting me on."

Phil grinned. There were a lot of other things he'd rather do with Dolly than kid with her. But he knew that he never would. He had no idea if she was actually making it with either of the Boccas, but he did believe that she was their property.

What was taking so long? he wondered. Why was Al Bocca making him wait so long?

Dolly noticed that he had put his magazine down. "Want another one?" she asked.

Phil shook his head. "No thanks."

What he really wanted was for her to check with the inner office. To find out if they were finished with whatever they were doing and ask could he come in please.

But he wouldn't ask her to do it. If he did, he'd have as little respect for himself as the Boccas would have for him.

He sat waiting.

Finally the door to the inner office opened and Al's man, Sal, stepped out. Not Al himself. Not even Lew. Sal.

"He wants you," he told Phil in a flat, expressionless voice.

Phil nodded wordlessly. He followed Sal into the inner office.

He had planned to begin the meeting by confessing before he was accused. He would cry *mea culpa*, insist on his guilt, and hope that Al Bocca would let him off more easily than if he tried to defend himself.

Now he kept silent. He wouldn't crawl. Not after having been kept waiting outside as if he were a beggar.

He sat down in the chair Lew indicated, said hello to everyone in the room, and smiled.

"Sorry you had to wait," Al Bocca said softly. He had not changed at all. He was as slender and neat as ever, and his eyes were as cold and gray. "We had some business to talk over."

"So Dolly told me."

"Dolly?" Al laughed. "She's a great looking kid, isn't she? Terrific tits, huh?"

Phil nodded. "Yeah."

"How'd you like to feel those things in your hands? Give them a little squeeze? That'd be pretty good, wouldn't it?"

Phil started to blush. "I guess . . . I mean, sure . . ."

"Damn right it would." Al Bocca winked slyly. "A young man like you—if you didn't want to grab hold of a pair like that, there'd be something wrong with you."

Al turned to the other men in the room. In addition to Lew and Sal, they included Billy and a thug named Mike who had a battered face and the build of an overweight boxer.

"Am I right?" Al asked them.

They all agreed that he was right.

"So tell me, Phil," Al went on. "Have you ever done that? Have you ever given her a little squeeze?"

"No, I haven't," Phil said.

"Why not?"

Phil did not know what to say now. He wondered what in hell Al Bocca was getting at. He glanced at Lew for some hint as to what was happening, but found only a stony stare.

"I don't know," Phil replied at last.

"Don't you?" Al Bocca smiled. "I think I do. I think it's because you got brains.

"You don't know whose woman she is, right? She could be mine. She could be Lew's. She could be Mike's. She could belong to anyone in the organization. Right?"

Phil nodded. "Right."

"And you got brains enough to know that if you start messing around with the property of the wrong guy, you're liable to end up with your pecker shot off."

Still smiling genially, Al made a "gun" out of his thumb and forefinger. He pointed it at Phil's groin and pulled the "trigger."

"Bang," he said. "Bang, bang."

"Nothing's worth that. Am I right, Phil? The greatest lay in the world isn't worth having your pecker shot off afterward."

Phil nodded. He was feeling more ill-at-ease with every passing moment.

"You see," Al Bocca said. He was addressing the other men in the room now. "Didn't I tell you he was smart?"

"You did, Uncle Al."

"You did, Al."

"But there are times when a young man can be very smart in certain areas, but real stupid in others.

"Do you know that, Phil? Can you guess what someone like that might do?" Even as he talked, Al Bocca's voice grew less friendly and more frigid. Now it was dripping with ice: "He'd be oh so careful to keep his hands off of some stupid cunt, but not so careful as to try and start up his own food distribution racket without telling his good friend and benefactor, Al Bocca.

"Does that show brains, Phil. You tell me: What does it show?"

Phil shook his head silently. He couldn't speak. His tongue was too thick and his throat too dry. He had no recollection of his early determination not to crawl, not to be a beggar.

Al Bocca was looking at him curiously—as though he were some rare species of insect.

"You don't want to answer that question," he said. "All right. You'll answer another: If a young man can get his pecker shot off for squeezing the wrong pair of tits, what do you think can happen to him for trying to pull a fast one on *me?*"

"But—but I wasn't pulling . . ."

"Just answer the question."

"Answer it," the man called Sal said.

"I—I don't know. I don't know what would happen."

"But it wouldn't be anything very nice, would it?" Al Bocca

asked gently. It was almost as though he were sincerely interested in Phil's thought processes.

"No," Phil replied faintly. "It wouldn't."

"In fact it would be something so nasty that it might better be left undescribed.

"After all," he went on with a little smile. "Here in this room we are all gentlemen. And there are certain subjects that gentlemen don't need to get too deeply into."

He looked at the others: "What do you think? Am I right?"

"Yes, Al."

"Of course, Al."

"But I'll tell you one thing, Phil. And in all sincerity, as your friend. I can think of situations in which a man would beg to have his pecker shot off.

"Can you believe this?"

Phil nodded. He could.

"I am very glad," Al Bocca said. "Because I want you to understand what the consequences are of my withdrawing my protection and friendship. And in order for me to remain your friend, you must convince me that you were not being disloyal when you went around to different unions and farm organizations to ask their help in organizing a food cooperative without including me in the deal.

"Now, tell me: How are you going to do that?"

Phil felt as if he were sinking into a swamp. He could find no foothold, no firm ground on which to stand.

Why in God's name hadn't he gone to the Boccas first? Before he had talked to anyone else? How could he possibly convince Al after the fact?

"You'd better say something, old buddy," Lew Bocca told him.

Lew sounded a bit nervous himself. Was he in trouble too, now? Because of what his uncle thought Phil had done?

"I really was going to talk to you, Al," Phil said desperately. "I just wanted to get everything set up first. I swear!"

"You swear? Anyone would swear if they were in your shoes. But how do I know that what you're swearing to is the truth? Did you tell anyone? Or was this some secret plan locked away in your head?"

"But it's the truth!"

"So prove it."

"Al," Sal interjected. "I think we're wasting time."

"Maybe . . ."

"No, wait!" Phil pleaded. "Listen. Please. How do you think I planned to get the money."

"What difference does that . . ." Al Bocca began. Then he saw what Phil was getting at.

"From me?" he said. "You were going to try and get it from me?"

"Not all of it," Phil said honestly. "But a big part. Probably even most. Where else could I go? I have no other sources."

"So why didn't you talk to me. If you wanted me in this deal . . ."

"Because I didn't think you'd take me seriously," Phil said. He could sense that he was starting to make headway, now. That Al was really listening. "I thought that you'd think I was too young to set up the kind of operation I had in mind. But if I came to you with everything already set up, you'd let me go ahead."

"I'm hurt," Al Bocca said seriously. "I take all my friends seriously. I told you when you first came here that I consider you a man. I'm hurt you didn't remember that."

"I'm sorry."

"Are you buying this story, Al?" Sal wanted to know.

"I think I am," Al Bocca said thoughtfully. "Why? Aren't you?"

"I don't know. The son-of-a-bitch is shifty. He could be lying."

"If he is," Al Bocca said pleasantly, "I doubt if he'll put himself in a position where he'll have to lie again."

"I'm not lying," Phil said.

He wondered what Sal had against him. Did he want to take over his—Phil's—bookmaking business? Did he simply dislike him because he was Jewish while Sal was Italian? What?

He would have to do something about Sal, he knew. But that would take time. In the meantime he would have to be on his guard against him.

But Al Bocca was talking to him, lecturing him on his mistakes.

"Did you really think you could talk to all those people without my finding out about it?" Al asked wonderingly. "Let's see . . . you spoke to your first union rep last November, right? His name was Johnny Wokausky."

Phil nodded.

"Do you want me to tell you about your meeting?" Al Bocca asked. "Wokausky sounded very interested in your deal. He said you had a good idea. He wouldn't commit himself then and there, however. He said he'd have to think it over and then get back to you.

"But he never did get back to you. And when you tried to get in touch with him again, he was always out."

Phil was starting to sweat again. Did Al Bocca know everything? Was he connected everywhere?

Phil had been given Wokausky's name by Abner Dent, a former Wobbly and old time union organizer. Dent, whom Phil had met through Y.A.S.D. contacts, had served time with Wokausky right after the War when they had both been arrested for subversive activity. Dent had called Wokausky one of the few honest men he knew.

And yet this man—this honest man—had reported to Al Bocca? Phil found that hard to believe.

"Do you know Wokausky well?" Phil asked.

"I don't know him at all," Al replied blandly. "But a good friend of mine does.

"This friend is someone who Wokausky can go to for advice from time to time. Or for help. There are times when certain managements try to abuse Wokausky's union. They use strike-breakers, for instance. My good friend helps the union people to fight fire with fire—if you know what I mean."

Phil did.

"So Wokausky would never think of finalizing an important proposition, such as the one you brought to him, without first taking the advice of my friend."

"I understand," Phil said.

"Then, when my friend happened to remember that you and I are associated, he phoned me as a courtesy. He wanted to know if I had any preference in this matter. Did I want him to go ahead with this deal—which he said was a pretty good one. Or would I rather that he call Wokausky and have it killed.

"'I won't ask you to kill it outright,' I told him. 'But I would like a delay for a while—in order to have more time to think it over.'

"You see," he explained to Phil, "I did not want my friend to think that you were going around the country trying to set up deals without telling me about them. That would not have been good for my reputation as a serious man. It would show that my own people did not respect me."

"I'm sorry . . . I didn't mean . . ." Phil's eyes dropped to the carpet. "I do respect you, Al."

"I believe that. If I didn't..." Al Bocca shrugged expressively.

"From then on, he continued, "I made certain that I knew where you were going and who you were seeing. It took a little doing, but in each instance I managed to put the kibosh on you. It was for your own sake, Phil. I want you to know that." Al looked regretful. "I thought that if you had no success you would come to me. We could talk man to man."

"I'm sorry," Phil said. "I should have come to you."

"Very well. As long as you understand that. We will let bygones be bygones."

Al Bocca's fine, handsome features relaxed into a benign expression, the atmosphere in the room—which had been improving even since Al had accepted Phil's explanation for not telling him about his plan—improved still further. Lew seemed his old self again. He was grinning at Phil as if in encouragement. Sal and Bill and Mike were more relaxed also. They no longer had the look of trained watchdogs ready to spring.

"So now,"Al Bocca said. "We have to decide what to do next."

"Next?"

"What are you looking worried again for? I told you we were letting bygones be bygones, didn't I? And when I say something like that I mean it.

"Tell him, Lew. Isn't that right?"

"It sure is, Uncle Al. Phil, buddy, you can relax now."

"Thanks," Phil said. But he wondered if he'd ever totally relax again.

"We have to discuss that idea of yours. I think that a farmer-labor food distribution company would be a fine idea. And it would be a very valuable thing to have a friend of mine in charge.

"That is, as long as he *remembers* he's my friend."

Al Bocca smiled and waited for Phil to say something.

"Your friendship is very valuable to me," Phil said stiffly. "I could never forget that I'm your friend."

"Good. That's nice to hear. Isn't it nice to hear, boys?"

"Yes, Al."

"Yes, Uncle Al."

"All right, then. Now let me suggest what you should do next: go back to your unions and farm organizations. Only this time, follow my advice about the ones you should visit first and the people you should see."

"Yes," said Phil, "I'll do that."

"You see, there are certain organizations which I think will be more likely to sign up with you without an argument. Once you have them in your pocket, other unions and farm groups will be more likely to jump aboard your bandwagon.

"Once that's done we can see how much money you have and how much more you'll need. Okay?"

"Yes," Phil said. "Thank you. But what about groups like the Y.A.S.D.?"

"What about them?"

"I had planned to have a number of them on the board of directors."

"So?" Al shrugged. "Do it."

"Are you sure, Uncle Al?" Lew frowned. "I don't know if I'd trust any of those people."

"Trust?" Al Bocca looked amused—as though his nephew were teasing. "We never trust outsiders, Lew. You know that."

"Yeah, but they'd be on the board of directors. They could make trouble."

"That's possible. But not for very long."

Al Bocca smiled sweetly at his nephew.

"Who do you think is going to set up this corporation, Lew? Who do you think will draw up the papers? Don't you trust me to provide Phil with an outstanding attorney who knows his business inside out? Now I'm no lawyer myself, but I'd be very surprised if Phil didn't end up with the legal right to kick any and all troublemakers off the board and out of the company—whenever it seems wise to do so."

29

"You are one hell of a lucky bastard," Lew Bocca said after he and Phil had left the offices of the Southwood Investment Company and walked together in silence for a couple of blocks. "Do you know what you just did? You jumped into a tub of shit and came out covered with gold dust!"

"Yeah," Phil said seriously. "I guess maybe I did."

"Well, I'll tell you one thing," Lew went on. "I wouldn't try that again if I were you. The next time you jump into a tub of shit you're liable to stay there. Find yourself buried there—if you know what I mean."

Phil knew only too well what he meant. He felt as if he'd been thoroughly beaten up and wondered if he would ever regain his old aggressive self-confidence.

"My Uncle Al," Lew said then, "is one of the sweetest guys in the whole fucking world. Really. He took me in after my folks died and brought me up like I was his own son. Then when I asked him to take a chance on you, he didn't stall, he didn't argue, he just did it. All of my say-so. Remember?"

"Yeah."

"But, listen. The one thing you don't want to do with Uncle Al is make him think you're doublecrossing him. That's one thing he won't put up with. If Uncle Al thinks that someone he's trusted has stabbed him in the back, the guy's as good as dead."

Phil nodded solemnly. He knew that every word was true.

"You know I'd never try to pull anything funny on your uncle," he said earnestly.

"Yeah, I know it. But the important thing is that Uncle Al knows it too, now. I mean that's important not just for you, but for me too."

"You?"

"Are you forgetting, buddy? I'm the one who brought you in. If he thinks you're cheating on him, he might think that I'm cheating also. That we're in it together."

"Jesus!"

"Yeah. So what I'm getting at is this: be extra careful, now. Like Uncle Al says, remember who your friends are. Remember who's helping you get started."

"Yeah, I will. I swear."

"You're going to be a big man some day, Phil. Uncle Al thinks so. Why do you think he's helping you to get this deal of yours underway?"

"And I'm grateful for what he's doing."

"But remember this: no matter how big a man gets, he's always going to need friends. And it isn't too smart of him to forget who his real friends are. That's what Uncle Al always says. It's a rule he lives by himself."

"And he's absolutely right," Phil replied with conviction. What else could he say?

It was with the help of his friend, Al Bocca, that Phil began to make headway on his project. The same men who had avoided him before were actually pleased to see him now. Farmer representatives and union people who had stalled his requests for appointments were now asking to talk with him.

By spring he was well on his way. By midsummer his newfound popularity had brought him all the farm and labor organizations he could handle.

Al had also kept his promise to find Phil an attorney.

The man was Sidney Walters—sly, rotund, and the master of involved documents.

Some of the legal papers, however, seemed so simple that even Phil felt he could understand them. Among those was one promising certain left-wing groups—including the Y.A.S.D.— a perpetual voice in formulating company policy.

Phil didn't like that.

"Won't it tie my hands forever?" he asked.

"It doesn't matter." Sid Walters smiled cherubically. "You're not twenty-one yet. Which legally makes you still an infant."

Phil frowned. "I don't get it."

"What's to get? They'll read those papers and think you're giving them everything they want and more. They'll feel good about dealing with such an honest, dedicated man. They'll love you. They'll work hard for you. Which is just what we want— for now.

"Then, later on when you don't need them any more, we'll apply to the court for relief. Once we explain to the judge how you were a naïve youth—a legal infant—when you signed the papers, you're Red friends will be out on their collective asses."

"You really are something," Phil said.

"What's wrong?" Sid arched an eyebrow. "Are you starting to learn you have a conscience?"

"Let's just say I don't enjoy making plans to kick my friends in the balls."

Sid's expression became almost sympathetic. "You can't have it both ways, my young friend. You can't be an idealist *and* turn yourself into a wealthy captain of industry.

"Or is Mr. Bocca mistaken about your ambitions?"

Phil shook his head slowly from side to side. "No. He isn't mistaken."

"Good. But in that case, you're going to have to wait a while to develop scruples. First be a tycoon and make yourself a few million. Then become a civic leader and turn yourself into a famous philanthropist. That'll buy you all the scruples you can use. While you're getting there, however, the way is to protect your own crotch while you try to kick the other fellow's."

"Yeah," Phil said dourly. "I know."

"It's settled then?" the lawyer asked. "We'll handle your Y.A.S.D. friends according to my suggestions?"

"Sure." Phil paused. "I'll tell you one thing, though. I'm glad you're on *my* side."

"You should be. I happen to be an extremely creative lawyer. And right now, I'm using all my creativity on your behalf."

"I know. Don't think I'm not grateful?"

"Be grateful to Mr. Bocca," Sid told him. "He asked me to help you as a very special favor. And I never refuse to do a favor for Mr. Al Bocca."

Phil nodded. This was something he could understand.

The more Phil saw of Sid Walters, the more he thought about how wonderful it must be to have someone like him always on tap—the way Al Bocca did. He began to think that his brother might some day perform the same task for him.

The more he thought about it, the more he wanted Bob to go to law school. He was bright enough, certainly. There was no reason why he couldn't transform himself into a legal magician like Sid Walters.

Phil hadn't said anything to Bob. One thing at a time, he thought. It had been rough enough convincing him to go on to college. But he had made up his own mind at last. His brother was going to become an attorney.

Sid Walters noticed the abstracted expression on the younger man's face.

"Something wrong?" he asked.

"No. Nothing's wrong. I was just thinking."

Phil paused to adjust the extra wide knot of his necktie.

"I was thinking about my brother, as a matter of fact. He's someone who ought to be a lawyer."

"Your brother? How old is he?"

"He's still young," Phil admitted. "Just sixteen. But he's going to start college this fall."

"And you say he wants to be a lawyer some day?"

"No," Phil snapped. "I didn't say that at all. I said he ought to be one."

"You mean that you want him to be a lawyer."

"You could put it that way," Phil agreed. "Now, tell me. How many years do you have to have of college before you can get into law school. The full four with a diploma?"

"There's no set number," Walters replied. "I even know lawyers who never went to college at all. They went straight to law school from high school. Though that's not done very much any more, and I don't think it's too good an idea.

"Now you tell me something: How long do you think it will take to convince your brother that he really wanted to be an attorney all along?"

Phil let out a snort of laughter. "Yeah. I see what you mean. I don't know how long that'll take."

"Two, three years?"

"I guess so. If I can do it at all. Bob can be stubborn as hell sometimes. I had one bitch of a time getting him to agree to go to college even. And then he'd only say yes if I agreed to City. I wanted him to go to N.Y.U. or Columbia where he could have had partial scholarships. But he wouldn't let me spend any money at all on tuition."

"He sounds like a decent kid," Walters said. "And, incidentally, you shouldn't run down City College. You must know how high the admission standards are. There's not a kid there who didn't have to fight his way in on his own merits. And once he gets in there's the struggle to survive.

"Some of the fancier schools produce pussy cats. City produces tigers."

"You sound like you went there yourself," Phil said.

"No, Princeton. But sometimes I think my parents didn't do me as big a favor as they thought they did by sending me there.

"Figure on transferring your brother to law school at the end of his third year," Walters went on thoughtfully. "That is if you can convince him it's the thing to do."

"Okay. Thanks."

"And once he *is* convinced, bring him around to see me. Maybe I can help get him a scholarship."

"Really?" Phil was surprised.

"Why not? I have a number of friends who became law professors. I might have gone that route myself if I hadn't liked money as much as I do."

"Well, thanks." Phil didn't know what he should say. "I mean really! Thanks. That would be great!"

"Forget it." Walters waved his pudgy fingers in the air. "What I don't understand is why you don't want your brother to join you when he gets out of college. I have a feeling that this business of yours is going to get very big. Very important. I'd have thought you'd want to bring your brother into it."

"Maybe he will come in," Phil replied. "Who knows? But if he's a lawyer, he'll be able to support himself even if my business flops. While if he does join me, it'll be a hell of a lot better if he knows the law."

"So he can tell you what you can and can't get away with?"

"I'd rather have him be able to tell me how to legally get away with what everyone else thinks is illegal."

Sid Walter's smooth, round face broke into a smile. "You mean, like what I've been doing for you?"

"Sure. Why not?" Phil grinned back boldly. "Al Bocca says that you're the best. That's what I want my brother to be— the best."

"You don't think very small, do you?"

"Should I?" Phil shrugged. "That's another thing Al told me: any man who thinks small is going to stay small. Well, I'm not going to stay small. And neither is my brother Bob."

"Okay, I'm convinced," the lawyer said. "If your brother's anything like you—"

"He's one hell of a lot brainier than me!" Phil broke in to insist. "He may not have as much *chutzpah*, if you know what I mean. But Bob's the brain of the family."

"I'm relieved to hear about the *chutzpah* part," Walters said. "Knowing one brother with your *chutzpah* is enough."

Phil heard the touch of acid underlying the humorous tone and wondered if he'd gone too far, taken too much advantage. But apparently not.

"Don't forget to bring your brother to see me, though," Walters was saying now. "I really do want to help him select his law school. And if he's only one half as bright as you claim, I'll be interested to meet him."

"You will," Phil said.

"But in the meantime," Walters said somewhat regretfully, "we'd better get back to work. I have to start earning some of that not inconsiderable fee I'm charging Mr. Bocca on your behalf."

Sid Walters did earn his fee. He set up a corporate structure which was so involved and so complex that nobody but he could really understand all of it.

"What are you calling this operation again?" he asked Phil when they were working together one evening. "Are you still insisting on Farmer-Labor Food Products?"

"Something like that. It'll keep everyone happy and feeling good. Why? Do you have a better name?"

"We could call it Proteus." The lawyer grinned slyly. "After the Greek myth."

"What Greek myth?" Phil asked warily. He did not enoy it when Walters—or anyone—waxed erudite, but he knew the lawyer well enough by now to realize there was no way of stopping him.

"Proteus," Walters explained, "was The Old Man of the Sea. He had the ability to change his shape into anything he chose. That is what this corporation will do. It will be able to change its shape into anything it chooses."

"It's not going to change its shape on me, is it?" Phil demanded. "Some day when I'm not watching?"

"No, because I'm going to tell you the secret of Proteus. According to the myth, anyone who overpowers Proteus and can keep a tight grip on him despite the shape-changing will be able to force Proteus to do whatever he wants him to do. And that's the position you'll be in."

"I'll be in control, huh?"

"When we finish putting the business together, my boy, I will personally guarantee that you'll have Proteus by the nuts."

30

Perhaps the greatest service that Sid Walters did for Phil was to find his first factory for him.

When Sid told Phil about it, he was filled with enthusiasm—

something very rare for the lawyer. But after listening to him, Phil could understand why.

"It's just the sort of place you've been looking for," Sid said. "A good solid building which could easily be converted into a food processing plant."

"How much will it cost?" Phil asked cautiously. He was thinking "first things first." No sense in talking further if the price was out of reach.

But Sid shrugged off the question.

"A hell of a lot less than it's worth," he replied. "It's owned by a bankrupt corporation that wants to liquidate its assets. A friend of mine—an attorney who owes me a few favors—was just hired to do the liquidating."

"I get it," Phil said. He was starting to become enthusiastic himself. "And where is this place?"

"In New York State near the Pennsylvania border. About a hundred and fifty miles from here by car."

"Jesus." Phil whistled. "Really out in the sticks, huh."

"It's known as farming country, my friend." The lawyer was disapproving. "And if you're going to be dealing with these people . . ."

"Yeah, I know," Phil said impatiently. "I'll be careful when I'm around them. But where is this great building located? I mean, is it out in a field someplace, or in a town, or—"

"It's in Hermit, New York. A very nice town."

"Hermit? What kind of name is that for a town?"

"How the hell do I know?" Walters snapped. "They probably had a hermit living nearby at one time."

"Yeah, probably . . ." Phil said slowly. He was thinking as he talked. Trying not to get too enthusiastic. Looking for a catch.

"What about transportation?" he asked. "Is there a rail line?"

"A spur line goes right into the plant. And if you're interested in roads, Hermit is on a good, all-weather highway."

"It sounds good," Phil said. "It does sound good."

"Why don't you go up and take a look for yourself?" Sid Walters suggested. "You can take a day train up from Jersey tomorrow. I'll arrange for you to stay the night and have people there to show you around."

But Phil hesitated. He did not want to go too fast. He particularly did not want Al Bocca to think he was moving so fast that he was planning to leave him out. Phil still shuddered when he recalled what had happened the last time he'd done that.

"Maybe I should talk to Al about this," he said thoughtfully. "Get the benefit of his advice."

"I've already spoken to him," the lawyer said blandly.

"And . . . ?"

"And he said it's up to you. If you like the place and we can pick it up for the right price, then it's fine with him."

After a comfortable ride in a parlor car, Phil was met at the closest main line station and driven to Hermit by the mayor himself, Oliver J. Chesley.

Since the crash of 1929, Mayor Chesley had seen his town shrink around him with alarming speed. With the factory closed down, Hermit's major source of income had dried up. Most of its citizens who were able to, left in order to look for work elsewhere. Stores closed down, one after the other. Of the town's three banks, two failed and the remaining one was teetering on the edge of collapse. The town doctor left for greener pastures and if you wanted to make out a will you had to travel fifteen miles to find an attorney.

Phil Aronson represented the mayor's last hope—someone who might be able to get the factory started up again and bring jobs and people back to his town. He questioned Phil avidly on the ride back to Hermit, hoping against hope that the longed for miracle really would take place.

"Let me get this straight, Mr. Aronson," the mayor said as he drove his Buick along the blacktop highway. "Or may I call you Phil?"

"Sure," Phil replied. "Why not? Like they say, it's my father who's Mr. Aronson."

The mayor glanced sideways at the young man seated beside him. Phil was the only chance they had.

"You must call me Oliver," the mayor said.

"All right," Phil said. "Sure."

He was no more impressed by Hermit's mayor than the older man was impressed by him. With his paunch, his wide-brim hat and his steel-rim eyeglasses, he looked like a hayseed who was letting himself go to seed.

"Now, Phil," the mayor repeated. "Let me get this straight: I understand you're planning to buy the factory in order to turn it into a food processing plant. Is that right?"

"Not exactly planning," Phil said.

"Oh?"

"I mean, nothing's settled yet. First I have to see how I like it. If it's suitable. And the town, too, if you know what I mean."

The mayor winced inwardly.

"Oh, you'll like the factory," he said, forcing himself to sound friendly and enthusiastic once more. "The factory building's in marvelous shape. And as for the town—we're right in the center of great farm country, you know."

"That's what I keep hearing." Phil growled.

He wished that Oliver J. would stop trying so hard. He sounded as desperate, Phil thought, as a faded whore with an angry landlord.

"And we have a really fine labor pool nearby," the mayor was insisting. "Not so much in Hermit, itself—I'm being completely honest with you, now—not too many able-bodied people live in Hermit these days. But there's a fine supply of labor in nearby towns. And just wait till word gets out about what's happening—I'll bet a lot of our own former citizens start coming back . . ."

The mayor sighed deeply at his own vision. Then he went back to selling.

"And you won't find much of this union nonsense around here, either," he said. "I can promise you that. Folks in these parts don't even know what a sit-down strike means! We grow honest God-fearing people around here who aren't too proud or lazy to sell their labor for realistic wages!"

"I'd only be using union people," Phil announced—partly, at least, to wipe the smug look from the mayor's face.

Mayor Chesley gulped audibly. He glanced sideways at Phil, then brought his eyes back to the road.

"What?" he said.

"I said that I'd be using only union people. That is, if I buy the factory at all."

When the mayor gulped again, Phil decided that it was up to him to start explaining some of the more important facts of life.

"When Mr. Walters talked to you," he said, "did he happen to mention the name of my company?"

"Huh . . . ? Why, yes, he did. It's Farmer-Labor Food Products, Inc. Right?"

"You got it, Oliver. And with a name like that, you could probably figure that we're going to try to sell to liberals in general and union people in particular. As a matter of fact, we're not only going to be advertising our line in union papers, we will probably take out ads in publications that some people think of as Red."

Phil smiled thinly and waited for Chesley's reaction. There was none.

"Now," he went on, "do you really believe we could keep on pitching our products to union people if we were paying low wages to scab labor? Do you suppose we could hide what we're doing? Or do you suppose it's more likely that some muckraker would dig up the facts and rub our noses in them?"

"I—I guess you're right." The mayor blushed. "I guess I didn't think."

Phil was disgusted. He didn't believe that Oliver J. *ever* thought. He wished briefly that he was Al Bocca. Then he'd know how to really rake him over the coals.

He sneaked a look at the mayor. The man looked almost as though he were about to cry. Perhaps he'd done enough—or even too much— raking over the coals himself.

And he was here on business. He did expect to use this town. It wouldn't do him much good to leave the mayor feeling too crushed and forlorn.

"I must say you're right about this country, though," he said in an admiring tone of voice. "It really is beautiful farming land."

"It surely is," the mayor said, recovering immediately. "We can grow almost anything you want. Apples, pears, grapes, vegetables. We have some of the best dairy farms in the Northeast. And if we don't raise beef cattle, it's because the land is just too valuable."

Phil quickly stopped paying attention and let the mayor drone on. He knew nothing about farming and cared less. His own forte was buying, selling, managing men. He could and would deal with farmers. But how they ran their farms was their own affair.

So he sat back, relaxed, and gazed out at the passing scene. He listened just closely enough to be able to say "yes" or "you're right," when such statements seemed called for.

They reached Hermit just in time to save Phil from running out of patience altogether.

There was hardly any warning before they arrived in town. No outskirts—unless a few boarded-up houses alongside the highway could be called that. One moment they were driving through the countryside with a farm on one side of the highway and apple trees on the other, and the next moment they were in the middle of town.

It was desolate, even worse than Phil had imagined. He had not believed that there would be so many houses and shops in need of paint and repair.

There were no people visible, either. Theirs was the only automobile in motion, and there were only a few parked at the curbs. Incongruously enough, one of the parked cars was a black and white police car that was standing in front of the bank. The mayor parked his own car behind it.

"Let's go into the bank first," he suggested. "There are some people I'd like you to meet.

Phil nodded silently. He might as well go along with the gag.

He followed Chesley into the bank. There were no customers inside and the only teller was a man so old and decrepit that he looked as bad as the town itself.

"Let's go in back," the mayor said, leading the way to an inner office.

There were three people waiting for them. One was a heavy-set man dressed in a resplendent uniform. He was introduced as Chief Aaron Mason of the Hermit Police Force. Next to the chief was Arnold Jefferson, the head of the bank. Mrs. Jefferson, who was currently acting as the bank's vice president, stood next to the banker.

Chief Mason asked Phil what he thought of their fair city. He was making a determined effort to be friendly, Phil saw, like a large grizzly bear begging for a piece of meat.

Mrs. Jefferson turned on the chief to save Phil the embarrassment of trying to answer the question. She was in her mid to late thirties, Phil thought. She was still attractive, however, and if she'd been wearing more fashionable clothes might even have been beautiful.

"Mr. Aronson has just gotten here," she reminded Mason. "You can hardly expect him to have formed an opinion so quickly."

"Oh. Sure. I see what you mean, Alice. But I just thought . . . you know . . . first impressions."

He turned to Phil

"My wife—she's dead now, God rest her—but she used to swear by first impressions."

Phil nodded and smiled. He wasn't sure what he was expected to say.

"It is a good town," Alice Jefferson said.

"A fine town," her husband agreed. "Times are hard here right now, but it is a good town with fine people."

"And this is one place where you won't have any labor problems," Chief Mason said assertively. "Not in my town. I don't care who they put in the White House, when I see a union organizer coming down the road, I ride him out of town on a rail!"

The mayor went pale. "Mr. Aronson will be employing only union men," he said.

The banker tried to suppress a grin while his wife looked at Phil with interest.

Chief Mason had the grace to act embarrassed.

"Oh," he said. "I guess that's different."

"I hope so," Phil said. "I explained my reasons to Mayor Chesley. I expect he can make it clear to you, Chief. It's not only important to me personally, but to the success of my company."

"I'm sure we'll all cooperate," Jefferson said, meaningfully.

"Yeah, sure," said the chief.

"And now maybe I can take a look at the factory," Phil suggested. He smiled to take the sting from his word. "That's why I'm here, after all. You can tell me about the town after I've seen the plant."

They were all anxious to please, Phil thought. Good.

31

The mayor led a procession of three cars out to the plant. The mayor's Buick, in which Phil was still a passenger, was in the lead, the four-year-old Packard convertible belonging to the Jeffersons was in second place, and Chief Mason's police car brought up the rear.

It must be a traffic jam, Phil thought cynically. This many vehicles moving through the streets of Hermit.

The mayor pulled into a big lot behind the factory and the

car bounced toward the big building. The surface here, Phil realized, had once been smoothed and blacktopped. Now it was cracked and overgrown with weeds.

"This used to be the parking lot," the mayor said sadly. "Now it's—it's . . ."

"It's nothing," Phil finished. Chesley brought out the brutality in him, he decided. But then any man who could wax sentimental over a parking lot deserved it.

The mayor stopped the car and Phil got out to walk over to the building.

"It's big, isn't it?" Mayor Chesley said. He was standing at Phil's right.

Phil didn't bother to reply. He waited for the Jeffersons to join him with the chief of police.

He wondered about Mrs. Jefferson. The vice-president of the bank, they said. Strange.

Chief Mason, meanwhile, was banging on the door to the factory.

"Carl!" he cried. "Get the hell out here, Carl. We got visitors."

"The owners still keep a watchman," Jefferson told Phil. "Not that there's any need for one."

Phil nodded. He glanced again at the banker's wife. Here in the warm sunlight of midsummer, her face appeared more lined than it had inside the bank. She looked more tired now too, with a hint of weary desperation in her eyes.

"It was Mrs. Jefferson who saved the bank," Jefferson said.

"We never would have been able to reopen after the bank holiday if she hadn't put some of her own money into it."

"I see," Phil said—though he wasn't sure that he did.

"She is really a fine woman."

"She must be."

At that point the factory door was opened by a large, unkempt Negro dressed in blue striped overalls.

"Where've you been hiding?" the police chief complained. "You are the laziest man I know! You had better get yourself on the ball, Carl, and fast. If you don't want that job of yours, there are lots of folks in this town who do."

Carl lowered his head respectfully. "Sorry, boss. I was workin' at the other end of the factory. Doin' some cleaning."

"Hell," Chief Mason said. He was openly scornful. "You working? Tell me another. The only thing you'd work on is a jug of Dago red."

"That's enough, Chief," Alice Jefferson interjected sharply. "Mr. Aronson is anxious to go through the factory."

"Yes, ma'am," the police officer said.

Phil thought that the chief was as resentful of Mrs. Jefferson as Carl was of him. And as frightened to challenge him. Big fish eat little fish, Phil thought ironically. And bigger fish eat big fish.

"Carl used to work for Mrs. Jefferson and myself," Arnold Jefferson explained to Phil. "That's how he got the job as caretaker here."

"He was a fine, honest worker," his wife put in. "I was sick when we had to let him go."

"I wasn't happy about that either, dear. But I can also understand the chief. Too many people close to him are without jobs these days. Remember that bank guard we couldn't afford to keep on? That was his cousin."

"Carl worked for us in our home," Alice Jefferson said with finality. "We have a personal responsibility."

The banker nodded and resigned the argument.

It was becoming clear to Phil where the real power in the town lay—with the Jefferson family, the bankers.

And who was the power in the Jefferson family? Mrs. J., obviously. The neat and attractive Alice.

Phil dropped back a pace to walk alongside her.

"Why doesn't Chief Mason like Carl?" he asked innocently. "Because he's Negro?"

The woman winced. "Yes," she said tightly.

Then she shook her head and favored Phil with a smile. "Maybe I'm not being fair to the chief. He doesn't have an easy job."

"Oh? A lot of crime?" Phil could not believe this.

"Of course not. That's just the problem. There's nothing in Hermit right now but desolation.

"Chief Mason used to head up a nice little police force for a town this size. He had eleven men under him. He had to start firing them once the factory closed. Now there are only two left. He's a proud man. I suppose he's bitter."

Phil nodded. "Is *he* the one who placed that sign just outside town?"

"What sign is that?" Mrs. Jefferson parried.

"The one that orders the unemployed to keep out of Hermit, that says there are no jobs here and that the town has trouble feeding its own."

"I don't know who put it up. But it was done on the mayor's authority."

"Oh," Phil said. He knew damn well who the authority was *behind* the Mayor—the Jeffersons, and especially Mrs.

"What else could we have done?" Alice Jefferson's voice was harsh and defensive. "The town's broke. That sign only tells the truth."

Phil shrugged. Maybe she was right. Anyway, it was not up to him to make judgements. Survival was the important thing. To ensure it, people did what they had to do.

All such musings left him as they walked into the great factory building. For here, in the dim light provided by a few cracked and shattered windows, he could see that his dream was actually capable of becoming reality.

The factory, as Phil remembered, had been originally designed to make farm implements. But that was in the past. All the old equipment had either been carted off to be sold or left behind to rust.

Soon this place would be busy, humming. There would be new activity here.

He could close his eyes and see the great vats where vegetables would be washed as a first step in the canning process. He could see the different assembly lines for the preparation of his meats and vegetables. This, he knew, would be the place where he would make his start!

"What do you think?" It was the mayor, and his voice sounded nervous.

Phil's features did not hint at the annoyance he felt at being dragged out of his reverie. Nor did they hint at what that reverie might have contained.

"I don't know," he said. "I haven't decided."

"Oh, I—"

"I really have to think about it some more," Phil said. "You have to understand my position. The place looks pretty good. Very good even. But there are a lot of places that look good. I've got to find the best."

Phil looked over the glum faces and wondered why he was doing this to them. He had already decided. He could have told them that—make them grin instead of scowl.

Why hadn't he done it?

One reason was pure business. If he had said how much he liked the plant—if he had told them how he could see his future factory laid out inside this bare building—they'd have had information to sell. And Phil would have laid odds that one of them—probably the Chief of Police, he thought cynically, but maybe the banker—would have called up the owners of the building to say that they had a live one here.

And then the price would have gone up. That was only logical. When you have something that nobody wants, you put the price down. But if you learn that somebody wants it all of a sudden—*really* wants it—the price goes back up.

Phil preferred to let them belive that he didn't care, that he still had to be hooked. That way if there *was* a spy in this group, he might be convinced to urge the owners to actually lower the price.

So why did he feel like a son-of-a-bitch when he saw how sad everyone was.

It didn't matter, he told himself. He would simply be a son-of-a-bitch.

He realized with a start that the mayor had been talking for sometime. The mayor was still talking. Still selling for all he was worth.

". . . and you couldn't find a finer town," he was saying. "More quiet. More crime free."

"This is not like New York City," the chief chimed in proudly. "Here in Hermit, if we find a troublemaker, we take him to the town line and tell him to keep walking. Where he goes is his business—as long as it's not back to Hermit."

"What happens if he does come back?" Phil wondered.

"He's not thrown out so nice the second time."

"I'll bet," Phil said with a small grin.

He looked about the place to see if anyone else wanted to speak. There was only silence. It was his turn, but he had nothing he could tell them.

"I'm sorry," he said. "But I really will need some more time to think things over."

He turned to the mayor who was staring down at the factory floor. "Maybe you could drive me to my hotel. It's been a long day and I'd like to wash up."

"Oh, we wouldn't let you stay at a hotel," Alice Jefferson put in. There was a note of determined cheer in her voice, as though she were forcing herself to sound bright at all costs. "You're staying with Arnold and myself!"

"We insist upon it," her husband added. "We'd really enjoy the company. And out house is so big that it would be downright sinful not to have you—especially since there's not a decent hotel in this whole area. The only one we had closed when the factory did."

Phil tried to decline politely. The truth was he didn't want to stay with anyone in Hermit. He wanted to be by himself; even in a shoddy hotel room.

"We'll hear no more about it," Alice Jefferson trilled. "You are staying with us and that is that."

"I'll put Phil's suitcase in your car, Arnold," Mayor Chesley offered.

"Lovely," said Alice Jefferson.

"You can give me a hand, Aaron," the mayor said to his Chief of Police. "We'll be meeting them all later at the club."

"Fine, fine," Mason said.

Phil didn't see any purpose in saying anything. It seemed that everything had already been decided.

32

Arnold Jefferson had been understating the case when he'd described his home as big. To Phil, at least, it was enormous. The house itself had more rooms than he wanted to imagine. And, as if this were not enough, it was set in the middle of a one hundred and ten acre wooded estate about a mile or so out of Hermit, proper.

Phil was impressed. He had never seen anything quite like it. But even while he marveled, he could see that the place—like the town itself—had fallen upon hard times.

The estate had obviously been designed with servants in mind. At the time of its construction, indeed, it must have been assumed that there would always be servants for the Jefferson place. It was in the nature of things that the Jeffersons would have a chauffeur to drive their car and gardeners to keep their lawn trimmed, their shrubs clipped, and their formal gardens impeccable.

A whole different set of servants had worked inside. They

kept the rooms and halls spotlessly clean, washed the linens, and made the beds. Others had prepared and served the meals—elaborate dinners in the formal dining room, picnics on the lawns, breakfasts in the breakfast room.

Of all those former servants, the Jeffersons were now left with two—a female servant and a general handyman.

Thus the lawns were not mowed as regularly as they once were, the shrubbery was hardly ever clipped, and all but one of the formal gardens stood dying and neglected. The meals were no longer elaborate, and the great, formal parlor—where cocktails and caviar had once been passed by liveried servants while hired musicians played the latest waltzes of Kern and Romberg and Youmans—was locked up along with the formal dining room and one entire wing of bedrooms.

This must have been a big comedown for the Jeffersons, Phil thought as he realized what had happened to them. A very big comedown indeed. Though not nearly as big as the one his own family had suffered.

The Jeffersons were still clinging to their estate. As long as they did that, they could always have the hope that one day everything might be once more as it was.

For the Aronson family, on the other hand, nothing could be what it once had been.

Of course Phil Aronson II had never been as high and mighty as Arnold Jefferson, but what Aronson did have he lost. Jefferson kept his bank; Aronson lost his business! The Jeffersons had never hit bottom (this lifestyle was surely not bottom!) while Phil's father had fallen so low he'd forgotten what it was like to be up.

Arnold Jefferson showed Phil to a comfortable room with an adjoining bath where he was able to wash, shave, and change for dinner before coming back downstairs.

Neither of the Jeffersons had come down, yet, and Phil was heading for the study when he heard a commotion coming from the kitchen. He found his way there through curiosity and saw that the disturbance was being caused by two boys who were chasing each other noisily about the room.

"Whoa!" Phil said, holding his hand up like a traffic policeman.

The boys stopped what they were doing and grinned uncertainly at him.

Phil grinned back. They were unbelievably filthy from the outdoors, but under all the dirt appeared to be quite handsome. The elder of the two was about eleven or twelve years old, the other perhaps one or two years his junior.

"What are your names?" Phil asked.

"Eddie," said the older boy. "Eddie Jefferson. My brother's name is Frank."

"What's your name?" the younger boy demanded.

"Phil Aronson."

"How do you do, Mr. Aronson." Eddie, the older boy, was oddly formal. "We'd like to shake hands, but we're too dirty."

"So I see," Phil said dryly. "I'm surprised your mother lets you play in the kitchen when you're this dirty. My mother never would."

"Neither would ours," Frank admitted with a small giggle. "If she knew."

"Ah," Phil said wisely. "That means that if you wash yourself clean in a hurry, she may never have to know."

The boys were about to act on this when a wiry, middle-aged woman walked into the kitchen. It was Estelle, the Jefferson's maid.

When she saw the boys, her eyes almost popped out of her head.

"Edward!" she hissed. "Frank! Look at you! You are both disgraceful! Go up to your room immediately, take your showers, change your clothes. And be sure to use the back stairs when you go up. I just cleaned the good carpet."

The two boys left looking subdued.

Estelle turned her disapproving gaze toward Phil.

"If you would come to the study, sir," she said, "I would be pleased to serve hors d'oeuvres."

Phil nodded and obeyed. He had barely selected an over-stuffed leather armchair to sit in when Arnold Jefferson entered the room.

There was something about his host now that bothered Phil—that reminded him of someone. Phil thought hard about it, but could not decide what it was.

"May I fix you a drink?" Jefferson asked.

"Thanks. Do you have any Bourbon?"

"Yes. How do you like it? Straight? With branch water?"

"Ginger ale. And lots of ice."

Jefferson prepared the drink, then made a Scotch and soda

for himself. They raised their glasses in a silent toast and drank.

Jefferson set his glass down on a coaster and sighed reflectively. "This place was very different once."

Phil nodded. Having reached that conclusion as they'd passed through the main gate he was slightly amused now. As if he could not recognize a state of decline when he saw one. He had almost as much experience doing that as he had in recognizing a note of self-pity—like the one beginning to sound through Jefferson's voice.

"I'm sorry you couldn't have been here then," Jefferson went on musingly. "It was very grand. Very beautiful."

"It must have been," Phil replied. Thinking: And you wouldn't have let me in your front door in those days, never mind have given me any of your goddamn liquor to drink! "A lot of people might call it grand and beautiful today," he added.

"Yes. I imagine they would. They'd probably tell me that I'm lucky to have saved as much as I have. And they'd probably be right."

"And don't forget those two kids of yours. They look pretty healthy and husky. That's saying a lot these days."

"When did you meet them?" Jefferson asked in surprise.

"Just now. When I came downstairs. They were roughhousing in the kitchen and driving your maid nuts."

Jefferson chuckled. "Estelle's a good person. It's not easy for a woman her age to help with two growing boys. Especially with Mrs. Jefferson away at the bank so much."

The two halted their conversation while Estelle brought in a plate of hors d'oeuvres which she placed carefully on the coffee table.

Phil sampled one. It was made of cheese and was not very good.

"Did you tell me that it was your wife who saved the bank?" he asked.

"Yes. Alice—Mrs. Jefferson— has money of her own. Sometimes—when the bank is overextended—she has loaned me her personal money to cover a discrepancy. On a couple of those occasions the bank would have failed without her."

Again Phil was tempted to change his mind and tell Jefferson that he had already made the decision to purchase. Why not take a chance and remove the burden from his back? Tell him that he and his wife were about to be saved?

But then he forgot about this as he realized what it was about his host that had bothered him before: Jefferson was wearing one of Phil's father's suits! He must have been a client of Aronson and Co.!

Phil was about to say something when he checked himself. What was the point of digging up the past. It was the present that mattered.

"Is something wrong?" Jefferson frowned.

"Not a thing," Phil assured him. Then because he could not resist: "That's a nice suit you have on."

"Thank you." Jefferson patted the fine, dark worsted fabric. "It's seen good service. I bought it in New York several years ago. Just before the Depression."

"Do you remember where you bought it?"

"I know it was at a fine men's store, downtown someplace." Jefferson frowned in concentration. "Wait a minute . . . it's coming back . . . Aronson and Company. That's it, Aronson and Company."

"Like my name?" Phil asked.

"My word, yes," said Jefferson. "What an amazing coincidence." He stared at Phil. "I suppose it is a coincidence?"

"Yeah. Strange, isn't it."

"Oh, I don't know," Jefferson mused. "Aronson isn't such an uncommon name. There must be a great many Aronsons in New York."

"Lots and lots," Phil told him, enjoying the joke all the more because it was a secret one.

It was right after this that Alice Jefferson came downstairs to accept a glass of sherry while the men had their second drink. Then all three got into the car and drove to the Oak Tree Country Club which was located in the nearby town of Kenston.

Though only twelve miles from Hermit, Kenston had not been so badly damaged by the Depression. Its streets were kept up better, far fewer stores were shuttered, and the faces of its people seemed less depressed and downtrodden.

Just driving through Kenston lifted Phil's spirits.

When the Jefferson party reached the club, they found Mayor Chesley and Chief Mason already there. The two looked less pressured and grim-faced than they had during the day. It was as if getting away from Hermit for a while had cheered them up, also.

This was supposed to be a social affair and, as if to prove that it would be, the two had brought their ladies with them. The mayor had his plump, blond wife, while the chief of police was accompanied by a startlingly attractive woman who turned out to be the young widow of a state trooper.

The dinner was a good deal more enjoyable than Phil had expected. It was not just the food; what Phil really liked was the fact that no one brought up the subject of the factory.

A small orchestra consisting of seven string instruments plus a piano was playing old fashioned dance music. Though Phil protested because of his clumsiness, the three women insisted that he go around the floor with each of them. He danced with the mayor's wife to the strains of *For Me and My Gal,* and with the chief's date to a 1913 Victor Herbert tune called *Sweethearts.* The most modern song of the evening was the one they played when he danced with Alice Jefferson, the one-year-old *Beer Barrel Polka.*

All in all, it was a surprisingly pleasant evening. And one of the nicest things about it for Phil was that he felt no pressure concerning the factory until the meal was over and they were walking back to the cars. It came when the mayor took him slightly aside to ask if he'd given the matter any more consideration.

"Yes," Phil said. "I did."

"And have you reached a conclusion?"

"Not yet, Oliver. I have to go back to New York first. I'll let you know my decision from there."

"Can you give me some indication of which way you're leaning?" the mayor asked. He was beginning to sound desperate. "Hermit is a lovely town. I know it must seem sad to you now, but you should have seen it before..."

"Yes," Phil interrupted. "I really will let you know just as soon as I can."

He increased his pace as they headed towards the Jefferson's car. Alice Jefferson—sensing what was going on—dashed over to rescue him.

"Oliver!" she said warningly.

The mayor stuttered, excused himself, and returned to his wife.

"I'm sorry about that," Alice Jefferson said when she and her husband were driving Phil back to their house. "There are times when I believe that Oliver is hopeless."

"He's not as bad as all that," Jefferson protested mildly. "Once in a while he just gets carried away."

"Once in a while?"

"Don't upset yourself," Phil said. "He didn't bother me at all."

"You're being sweet," Alice Jefferson told him. "But I am very annoyed. It was decided by all of us, you see, not to spoil the evening by talking business."

"But the evening wasn't spoiled. I really enjoyed it very much."

"And he did make an effort, at least," Arnold Jefferson pointed out wryly. "You have to give him credit for that. He held out for a whole lot longer than I thought he would."

When they reached the house, Phil had a final drink with his hosts.

"It really was a good evening," he said as he refused a second one. "But this rich country air is making me groggy. I'm going to sleep well tonight."

"And I gather you still plan to catch the eleven-thirty train to Hoboken tomorrow morning," Jefferson said.

"That's right. I'll phone you my final decision from New York."

"I understand," the banker said. "Oliver'll pick you up about twenty minutes to eleven. I'll tell him not to pester you about the factory." Jefferson chuckled softly. "But I can make no guarantees."

His wife started to say something to him, then changed her mind and turned away.

"Will I see you two at breakfast?" Phil asked.

"I'm afraid not," Jefferson said with a grin. "No bankers hours for us. We'll be out of the house by a quarter to eight."

"I'll tell Estelle to serve your breakfast whenever you come downstairs," Alice said.

"Well, let me say goodbye to you now," Phil said. He shook hands with each of them and went up to his room.

He changed into pajamas, got into bed, and turned out the light.

He had been telling the truth about the country air making him groggy. He closed his eyes and was immediately asleep.

He was startled wideawake again by the sound of a door being opened.

It was still pitch dark and, for a long moment, he was sure that he was in his own room in New York City with a sneak thief creeping in to rob him. Then, slowly, he began to realize he was somewhere else—a place where the weirdly unfamiliar sounds of whirring insect wings had replaced the reassuring traffic noises he knew so well.

But *where* was he? And *why?*

Hermit, he realized suddenly. The Jeffersons.

A shadowy form approached the bed and whispered to him. "Are you awake?"

"Yes, but who—?"

"Shh . . .!"

The form slipped into the bed next to Phil. It was soft and female.

"Who . . .?" he whispered again. "Alice? Mrs. Jefferson?"

There was a small giggle. "Alice. You don't have to be formal now."

"But—what time is it?"

"Sometime after midnight. Who cares?"

Alice sat up and shrugged off her robe. She moved toward him and he could tell that she was naked. One of her hands unbuttoned the fly of his pajamas and curled sweetly around his penis.

Phil was bothered by her initiative. He pushed the hand away. "What the hell?" he said.

"Are you going to toss me out of bed, Phil?" the woman hissed dangerously. "I didn't think you were the sort to throw any woman out of bed as long as she knew how to fuck and still had a decent figure. And, believe me, I qualify on both counts."

"But—"

The whole thing was crazy, Phil thought. The sophisticated Alice Jefferson talking like that? Using that language?

"But we're in your home," he said. "You husband's sleeping only a few doors down the hall."

"Don't worry about that. Arnold's a sound sleeper." There was a note of bitterness in her voice which was growing more intense. "Even if he did wake up, he probably wouldn't care."

"What does that mean?"

"Don't you know what your factory could do for this town? For the bank? Arnold would sell you his own body if he thought it would do any good."

"So you came instead?" Phil wondered if he sounded as disbelieving as he felt.

"No." Alice seemed angry. As though Phil was being deliberately stupid and insulting. "What do you think I am?"

Phil shrugged. There was an obvious reply to that, but he saw no reason to make it.

"I'm here because I want to be here," Alice said.

"I see," said Phil, who didn't.

"I want to tell you something about my husband." Alice said then. "He's too nice to be a banker."

"Oh?"

"He has an old-fashioned sense of what's right. He still believes a bank should lend money on the basis of character."

Phil nodded. He wondered what all this was leading up to.

"In the old days," Alice continued earnestly, "before the start of the Depression, that is, he was actually able to get away with it. He saved a number of farms and businesses here from collapse. And though some loans weren't repaid, enough were so that he could write off the ones which went bad and still make money for the bank.

"Then came the stock market crash and the Depression. Everyone had problems then, the bank too—we were facing ruin ourselves. But Arnold wouldn't change. He kept making loans to anyone who he thought deserved it. There's no trick to lending money when times are good, he used to say. A real bank helps out when times are bad."

Phil grinned inwardly. His father could have used a bank like that instead of the Greystock.

"What he was doing was madness," Alice was saying now. "Sheer insanity. He kept his nutty loans and threw his own money into the bank in order to cover them until prosperity returned and our whole area was rich and happy again. He really did believe that good times were just around the corner."

"What happened then?" Phil asked.

"Just what you'd think: he ran out of his money and asked if he could start using mine."

"And you said yes." Phil remembered what her husband had told him.

"Not at first," Alice insisted. "That would have made me as crazy as Arnold. Father left me a rather large inheritance. But if left to his own devices, my husband could have run through it in less than a year. So when I did agree to help, I insisted on two conditions: one, that all loans start being handled on a businesslike basis and two, that I be placed in charge of them."

"I don't blame you," Phil said. "Though, from all you tell me about him, I'm surprised your husband agreed."

"He didn't want to. He even said he'd rather see the bank go under if that meant he could make a few more loans his way. But I didn't give him a real choice."

"How's that?"

"I told him that if he said no, he'd lose more than the bank. I'd leave and take the children with me. I was sorry for him, I said, but that was the way it was going to be."

"So he accepted the deal?"

"He had to," Alice said simply. "I don't know how much he loves me anymore. But I know what he thinks of his children."

"It must have been rough on him," Phil said. "As serious as he was about his style of banking."

"Quite rough. It cost him his—his manhood."

"His pride, you mean?"

"No, not just his pride. His manhood. He hasn't been a husband to me since."

"He hasn't been a—"

"He hasn't been able to get a hard-on," she said. "Is that clear enough for you? We haven't fucked!"

"And you think that's because of what happened at the bank?"

"What else? When it first happened. I asked my husband to see a psychiatrist. He wouldn't, so I talked to one myself— to try and understand. He said that my husband had withdrawn from that aspect of life. I had metaphorically castrated him, you see, so he could no longer have sex."

"Jesus," said Phil. He wondered if there was anything in what Alice had said. Personally, he thought it was crap. Phil believed that there were only two reasons for a man not being able to get it up for a good-looking woman. Either he was physically damaged or he was getting so much on the side that he was exhausted.

Maybe the latter was Arnold's trouble. Maybe he was getting too much on the side.

But Alice was speaking again. And as she talked, the note of self-flagellation which had been in her voice from the beginning grew more intense. "So now you know why I'm here— not for the bank, not for my husband. But for me! I had an idea you could give me what I've been missing.

"All right," she went on after the briefest of pauses. "So the idea was a lousy one. You're going to toss me out of your bed after all."

214

She started to leave, but Phil took hold of her arms. "Wait a minute..."

Alice tried to jerk her hand away. "What do you want? Are you going to do me a big favor and stick your thing in me?"

She kept struggling, but to Phil it was less of a fight than a personal challenge—her struggles had aroused him and he wanted her to be aroused as well. He held her flat on the bed while he kissed her face and breasts and belly. When his lips worked their way past the thick hair of her bush, she stopped struggling and reached for his penis.

"You win," she breathed. "Do it. Now. Get those damn pajamas off!"

Naked now, Phil moved on top and reached beneath her buttocks. Her ass was thicker than Laura's, but it was surprisingly firm.

Not that that mattered anymore. As it didn't matter if she were too old for him or if her breasts were slightly flabby. Right then—at that moment—he wanted her.

And she wanted him, he reminded himself. For she probably needed this more than he did.

He was doing her a favor, he told himself. If he were a religious Jew, he might even have called it a *mitzvah!*

33

Phil swiveled his parlor car seat toward the window so that he could watch the north Pennsylvania countryside as the train ran through it with increasing speed.

He was grateful for the seat for its size and luxury. It gave him a chance to rest his body.

His body needed rest desperately. Every part of him was sore and exhausted: His arms, his legs, his torso, his back. And of course his pecker. That part had been so tender when he'd gotten up this morning it had hurt him to pull on his undershorts.

Christ, he thought. That Alice Jefferson was some woman!

They had made it five times, last night. Five times! He still couldn't get over it.

Who could have guessed she'd have that much staying power at her age. She had damn near ruined him! He was the one who'd had to call it quits.

But only after five times, he reminded himself. Which was pretty damn good.

The first time, he recalled now, had been too easy. They had both come too fast and it was over almost before it had begun.

Then, just a few moments later, she had started playing with his tool again.

He'd pushed her hand away. He wasn't ready yet and anyway aggressive females annoyed him.

She began to taunt him with pooping out so quickly, and he immediately got it up again. Probably the challenge, he thought now.

They started in again and she took him in her mouth. He buried his face in her muff and they came together. It was one hell of a double explosion.

Phil lay back on the pillow and fell asleep. That was it, he was sure.

But he did not yet know the banker's wife. Twenty minutes later he was dreaming that his penis was being stroked. He woke up to learn that the dream was for real.

He did not protest this time or try to push her hand away. He was already hard when he awakened and was feeling a strong sexual urge. Perhaps he had gotten his second wind— if such a thing ever happens during sex.

That was when she took some petroleum jelly and lubricated her anus.

"Stick it in there," she demanded.

"Won't I hurt you?" Phil had never done it that way before and was a bit ill at ease over the prospect.

"Just stick it in," Alice said impatiently.

It was wild. Strange. Different than any sex he had had before. When they were finished, Phil's penis was tender and he was exhausted.

He collapsed back into sleep—only to awaken a half hour later with his penis in Alice's mouth. He automatically moved towards her crotch.

Though Alice worked diligently on Phil, using a plethora of oral techniques, it took her a while to bring him off. She, on the other hand, came twice with no trouble at all.

When Phil was awakened for the fifth time, the night sky was starting to change into a predawn gray.

He did not want to have sex again. He was too tired for one thing. For another, getting an erection was becoming physically painful.

But Alice was persistent. And Alice had her ways. He managed to come for the last time just as the dawn was breaking.

The next time Phil opened his eyes it was to bright sunlight. He was alone in the bed and someone was rapping on his door.

It was Estelle, calling through the door that it was nine-thirty already and asking what he wanted for breakfast.

Phil shaved and dressed as quickly as his aching body would permit him to and staggered downstairs for his scrambled eggs and coffee.

The Jeffersons had left for the bank at their normal time, Estelle told him in answer to his questions. They had both asked her to bid him goodbye.

Phil had not seen the lady of the house leave his bed to go back to her room. But he imagined it must have happened right after their final time. He wondered how she had felt when she got up this morning. She couldn't have had more than two or three hours sleep. He'd had more sleep than that, yet was feeling like death warmed over.

When Oliver appeared to drive him to the train station, Phil was too tired and abstracted to pay attention to the mayor's nagging hints. He said he'd be in touch one way or the other, and hardly spoke at all during the rest of the car ride.

Now that he was on the train, however, he could decide about the future.

He would buy the factory, of course—that decision was firm. And with Sid Walters handling negotiations, he did not think it would take too long or prove too difficult. The deal would be made and he would phone Hermit to tell Jefferson and Chesley.

He wondered if Alice was going to prove difficult. Although last night had been one hell of an adventure, the next time they made it would be on his terms, not hers. He was certainly not going to risk his relationship with Laura for a married broad with a couple of kids, one of whom was as old as his sister! Nor was he going to stand ready to remove his trousers every time his being in Hermit happened to coincide with her getting a sex urge!

217

No. If they went on, they would do so with him as the boss. If she had any questions about that, he would simply set her straight.

Phil needn't have worried. The next time he visited the town—it was for the official ceremonies honoring the signing of his contract to purchase the facotory—Alice Jefferson was friendly but highly proper. She behaved precisely the way a loving wife might have been expected to behave around a much younger male associate of her husband.

Alice stuck to this behavior on all of Phil's subsequent visits. She was gracious but impersonal, and somehow arranged to never see him alone. It was as though the night they'd spent together had never taken place.

Though his first inclination was to grow angry (Who did Alice think she was? He was supposed to give her the brush-off, not the other way around.), Phil managed to be pretty smooth himself. The more he thought about it, in fact, the more the situation amused him. He had to admit that the lady was handling things well and, when he left Hermit again, he was probably more fond of her than he'd been after they slept together.

There was so damn much to do. New machinery had to be ordered, a new interior had to be designed, workers and contractors had to be found. And it all had to be done as quickly as possible. Even with Al Bocca's help, Phil hardly had time to breathe.

But little by little the work got done. By mid-October one small assembly line was in place. Phil hired workers to run it even while the rest of the equipment was being installed.

He had already signed up farmers, of course. But now he was taking on the far more difficult task of trying to get his products into food stores and factory cafeterias. Al Bocca helped him and advised him on who to see and how to talk to them. But it was up to Phil to do the actual selling. His success as a one-man sales force surprised even himself. For by the summer of 1936, Farmer-Labor Food Products was starting to operate in the black.

Success took its toll. It drained Phil of energy and interfered with everything from his relationship to his family to his sex life.

Laura noticed it first. Her lover—the man whom she had

thought of as having a perpetual hard-on—was now hardly interested.

Once she even accused him of seeing other women.

"I don't really mind if you sleep with a girl once in a while," she said wryly. "But if there's nothing left over for me . . ."

Phil winced. The last other woman he'd slept with had been Alice Jefferson. And that had been four months before.

Well, he wasn't going to tell her that.

"I'm sorry," he said. "I've been working my ass off. I don't seem to have any energy."

"Then get some. I'm a healthy young woman. I need a healthy young man."

Phil looked as if he had just been punched in the stomach. Had it been as bad as all that? Maybe it had.

And, Christ, but she was sexy. Her long legs, her honey-blond hair, her hips, her thrusting breasts—all were at least as lovely as when he first saw her.

He drew her to him and it was like it had been in those first days. They literally tore their clothing off in their rush to mutual nakedness and their coming together was ferocious.

Their sex life became much better for a while. But then Phil's long out-of-town selling trips and his preoccupation with business when he was in New York started interfering once more. By March, they were nearing another crisis.

This time, though, Phil realized what was happening to him. He apologized to Laura for it.

"You'll see," he told her. "Everything will be much better once I know that the business is solid enough not to go under. I don't only have a responsibility to myself and my workers, you know. I'm doing this for labor in general—for the farmers, for the unions, for the Y.A.S.D."

"I know," Laura breathed with a slight laugh that could have been mistaken for a sigh. "The things I have to give up for the cause . . ."

Phil took her in his arms and kissed her. Then—as if to prove that her complaint was not completely justified—they made love. It was while they were resting afterward that she asked when he thought the business might become less hectic.

Phil hesitated before he replied. Although he did have a date in mind, he had always been reluctant to tell anyone else about it. It was superstition, really. As though by mentioning the date aloud, he might challenge fate to prevent him from making it.

But now Laura was growing more insistent. He gave a mental shrug and gave in.

"July," he told her. "By mid-July everything should be in place."

Which, of course, was how it worked out.

It was not only his relations with Laura which were interfered with that year, but also his relations with his family.

He was so busy now that he hardly knew what was going on in his parents' apartment. He hardly knew what his family was saying and doing.

He was aware of some things that were going on. But those were the things that hadn't—and, as far as Phil could see would never—change.

His father, for instance. He was still spending most of his time in bed—or at least in his room. Most of his time was taken up with reading magazines, critizing Phil, and complaining about his lot in life.

Phil's mother was still working. She was looking more drawn and exhausted than Phil could remember and he begged her to give up the job. But Sophie wouldn't hear of it.

His brother was doing fine at college. Phil did take the time to throw out a few hints about how great a future law career might be, and Bob appeared to take the suggestion seriously. That, Phil thought, was a definite plus.

Then there was the minus—Naomi. Her attitude and behavior hadn't changed, but she was starting to change physically. She was beginning to grow breasts.

When Phil first noticed the phenomenon he could hardly believe it. It seemed crazy to him. She was only twelve, for God's sake—a baby. And she behaved like a baby much of the time, still going into a shitfit if he dared call her Nommie, for instance.

But there was no doubt about it. She was beginning to mature. And that was causing him problems.

The trouble was that her personality hadn't developed along with her glands. She was still a tomboy. She still scorned pretty dresses and girls' parties for boys' sports. She liked to play baseball and football with the boys, even wrestle and fight with them.

He knew what that meant. He used to love to have tomboys in his games when he was twelve or thirteen. It was fun. Play touch football with a girl and cop a free feel on every play.

Only that had been with somebody else's sister. Not his!

He wished he had the time to check up on her himself. But he didn't. Not with everything that was going on. And no one else that he was willing to trust had the time either.

His mother was working at that job of hers, Bob was too busy with college, and he didn't trust his father.

He tried to talk to Naomi about the situation, to explain the facts of life, and tell her what she was risking. But it didn't do any good. Even before he finished his argument—as soon as she got the gist of it, that is—she pointed her nose toward the ceiling, told Phil he was disgusting, and flounced off.

And nobody else regarded the matter seriously enough, Phil thought. Not even his mother.

"She's feeling certain urges, Phil," his mother said. "It's only natural at that age. You went through that, remember?"

"But she's a girl."

"So, she'll have to control her urges more than you did. But she's a good girl who's had a decent upbringing. Don't worry. She'll be fine."

Phil sighed. He hoped his mother was right, but he wasn't so sure. Naomi was too independent for a girl, too feisty. He foresaw a great deal of trouble with her.

But there was nothing he could do about it now. Now he had to concentrate on his business.

34

In July of 1936, two events took place which were to seriously affect Phil's life. One event was a private matter. That was when his business passed over the hump of uncertainty and showed that it was going to be a success. The other event occurred halfway around the world in Spain and in Morocco. For it was in that month that General Francisco Franco led the revolt of the Spanish Army in Morocco and took those forces back to their mother country.

At that time, Phil was much too busy with his own affairs

to pay attention to the start of the Spanish Civil War. When he did hear about it, he automatically assumed that Laura and the Y.A.S.D. would be on the rebels' side.

When the horrified Laura started to berate Phil for his assumtion, he was frankly puzzled.

"But I thought you were always for the revolutionaries," he said with a frown. "I don't think I've ever heard you defend an established government before."

"We are for people's revolutions," Laura explained. "This is a very different matter. We're talking about a situation in which the real revolutionaries are the leaders of the established government. Franco and his pack of tame hyenas are counter-revolutionaries.

"Do you understand, now?"

"I'm not sure that I do," Phil admitted.

"My God," Laura said. "For a bright man, you're amazingly naïve about international politics and political idiology. I'm glad you said what you did to me and not to Jed or Karl."

"Yeah?" Phil was feeling resentful. "Maybe if either of them was trying to set up a farmer-labor co-op the way I am, he wouldn't have so much time to study politics."

"Perhaps you're right," Laura said after a moment or so. "I guess I am being unfair. You may be doing more for the cause than any of us."

Phil looked embarrassed. "I didn't mean to say that. Only that I'm up to my ass in work."

"I know you are. Would you like me to tell you something about Spain? What the background is?"

"Sure. If you would."

"Well, about five years ago the people of Spain decided that they didn't want a king any more. They kicked good King Alphonso out on his rear and founded a republic on socialist lines.

"Then, in 1933, they held a new election. This time it was the right wing that gained a majority. The left then formed a 'Popular Front' composed of liberals, socialists, and communists, in order to try and win power in the next election which was to be held this year."

"And did they win power?"

"They certainly did. But, unlike the leftists, the right wing refuses to accept the will of the people. They are fighting a counterrevolution instead."

"Ah," Phil said. "Now I get it. But I do have one question."

"Go ahead."

"If the people are basically behind the government, how could a counterrevolution succeed? I thought revolutions can only be successful when they carry out the will of the people."

"Spain is a special case," Laura said.

"How so?"

"Because, while the people may be for the government, most of the army is against it. As is the nobility, the wealthy class, and the clergy. For all practical purposes the government has no army—only volunteers. Nor does it have enough money to pay for weapons or food."

"Jesus," Phil said. "I see what you mean."

"Then there's something else," Laura went on. "I don't think there's any question but that the fascist states—Italy and Germany—will help out the rightists in Spain. But who will help the Republicans? The Soviet Union? Maybe. The U.S., France, England? I doubt that very much."

"So the fascists are going to win?" Phil asked.

"If they do," Laura stated, her eyes flasing as fiercely as they did when she addressed a protest meeting, "it won't be without a battle! Just because the U.S. government is as craven as those in England and France, that doesn't mean there aren't individuals who understand what's happening and are trying to do something about it! And not just here, mind you, but in other parts of the globe as well."

"But what can they do? From what you tell me, the games's already been fixed."

"It's not a game, Phil." Laura was angry. "That's your problem. You think of everything as a game."

"Sorry," Phil said. He did not want to get into a fight with her. "Just tell me: What are you going to try and do?"

"It's too early to tell yet," Laura said more calmly. "There are a great many people working on plans. There's even talk of sending a brigade to Spain to fight for the Republic."

"Maybe I should volunteer." Phil grinned.

"You bastard." But Laura was grinning also. "Perhaps you really should. It might do you some good."

"Yeah, but it would hurt you to have me so far away."

As Laura protested, he took her in his arms.

"Right now I want to do us both some good," he said.

• • •

It wasn't too long before Phil was admitting to himself that his first reaction to the Spanish Civil War had been a foolish one.

Perhaps because the war *was* Spanish, he had not taken it very seriously. He'd thought of it as a kind of comic opera affair. He knew that it was important to those who took part in it, but for everyone else it could be played for laughs.

Nor was he impressed very much by the fact that groups like the Y.A.S.D. were so involved with the situation. They would knock themselves out for any cause, he believed, as long as it was radical enough.

But when his brother Bob spoke about Spain in much the same terms that Laura did, Phil started to reassess his feelings.

Bob himself was not a radical. For his age and the time in which he lived, indeed, he was rather conservative. And yet he was every bit as concerned with the Spanish situation as was Laura.

"Hitler and Mussolini are using Spain as a training ground," he said. "They try out their new weapons there, experiment with new techniques and tactics. Franco will win for them in Spain. They can't afford to let him lose. And once that little war is over, they'll use the lessons they've learned against the fat and happy people of England, France, and the rest of Europe."

"You think it's that serious?" Phil asked.

"Yes. The problem is that we can't afford to lose in Spain either. But where our side doesn't realize that, the fascists do."

"What about the commies?" Phil demanded. "I've heard the Russians are helping the Republic in the same way that the fascists are behind the rebels."

"What's your point?" Bob asked.

"Then why does it matter so much who wins. I mean, with the Russians on one side and the Nazis on the other, maybe they should both lose."

But Bob was shaking his head.

"Maybe someday Russia will be as great a danger to the world as Germany," he said. "Who knows? But someday isn't now. And right now, Hitler wants the whole pie—the entire world. No one can argue with that; he said so himself. And what he's learning in Spain—how to combine modern weapons and strategy in a new kind of warfare which will place a country's civilians in as much danger as its army—will help him to do it."

If anyone other than his brother had made that statement, Phil might have found it hard to believe. But he knew Bob too well to think that he was speaking only out of emotion. Even at his present age, Bob was too clearheaded to permit that.

The next time Laura spoke to him about Spain, therefore, Phil listened more carefully. It wasn't that he thought Bob so much brighter than she; but he was a good deal less likely to be blinded by politics.

One of the projects that the Y.A.S.D. was becoming involved in was the collection of food and clothing for the Spanish Republic. Laura herself had little to do with the clothing project. But, possibly because of her closeness to Phil, she was asked to chair the committee in charge of food.

"The situation is starting to get bad," she explained when she told him about the project. They were in his apartment and he had just returned from a two-week sales trip.

"Yes?" he said sleepily.

"Really, Phil. It's urgent. Republican cities like Barcelona and even Madrid are already suffering. And from everything I hear, it can only get worse."

Phil nodded: "How are you going to handle this? Are you going to try to collect money with which to buy food? Or are you going after the food itself?"

"Either. Both." Laura shrugged. "How much will Farmer-Labor Food Products contribute?"

"We'll do everything we possibly can," Phil promised without hesitating. He had been expecting that question. "The only problem is that I don't know how much that will be."

Laura frowned. "What do you mean?"

"Look," Phil said. "Thanks to you and Bob, I know how important Spain is. What happens there affects us all. But it's also important the Farmer-Labor Products, Inc. stay in business."

"Are you comparing the two things?" Laura demanded. She sounded incredulous.

"In a way, maybe I am," Phil said, allowing his voice to become just the slightest bit querulous. "I know my company doesn't concern as many people as the fate of Spain does. But it does concern a whole lot of plain, decent American workers and farmers!

"If we went out of business . . . okay, it would delight the giant canners and packers and food chains. But it would sure screw up the lives of a great many little people."

"You're right," Laura said, lowering her gaze to the floor. "And I'm sorry. I know you'll do whatever you can."

"I'll tell you one thing I will do," Phil said.

"What's that?"

"We won't make a profit on you. Whatever food you buy from us in order to ship to the Republic, you can have at our cost. In other words, I will charge you for the raw materials, the labor, the cost of operating the plant. That sort of thing. But I'll deduct our normal profit mark-up.

"Does that sound fair?"

"More than fair," Laura admitted. "You make me feel bad for what I said before."

"Don't feel bad." Phil grinned. "Whatever you said, I probably deserve. If not now, then in the past. Or if not in the past, in the future."

Laura giggled. "I'll bet that I think you're nicer than you think you are."

"I know that I think *you're* nice," he replied as he turned to kiss her.

Phil was surprised when Al Bocca did not greet his plan with more enthusiasm.

"Al," he said, "I don't think you understand. I know I promised we wouldn't take a profit. But—"

"But you'll still be making money," Al Bocca said, finishing his sentence for him. "What made you believe I wouldn't understand a simple thing like that. I knew that when you were a baby—before you were a baby—when *I* was a baby: Money is money—whether you call it profits or cost overruns or whatever. It's still money.

"Is that what you're saying?"

"Uh . . . yes."

Al turned to Sal and Mike who were with him in the Southwood offices.

"Did you hear him? He thinks Al Bocca wouldn't know a simple thing like that. Make you laugh, huh?"

The two laughed dutifully.

"But I don't understand," Phil said. He sounded as confused as he actually was. "If we'd be making money . . ."

"Maybe money isn't everything," Al told him almost defensively. "Maybe I think we'd be helping the wrong side."

"But the Republicans . . ."

226

"Republicans?" Al fairly spat his contempt. "They're commies, is what they are! Atheists! You know what your Republicans do in Spain? They shoot down priests, that's what! They murder them!

"Imagine being so against religion you murder priests. A terrible thing . . ."

"Terrible," Lew echoed.

"Terrible," said Mike.

"But—"

"But what, Phil?" Al Bocca asked softly. "Don't be so nervous, my friend. What were you going to say?"

"Just that Franco's not all that good either. He's supported by Hitler, isn't he?"

"So I understand. And that bothers me. But it also bothers me that Mussolini is a friend of Hitler's. And yet Mussolini's done a lot for Italy. Certainly no one could deny that."

Phil did not think it necessary to say that he personally knew a great number of people who would have no trouble at all denying it.

"I don't know," Al Bocca went on after a long silence. "I realize that not everything I do is perfect. But a man must have limits. Should a company I'm interested in help atheists who murder priests? Just to make money?"

Al Bocca shook his head in perplexity.

"What do you say, Phil? I understand you're not a Catholic. But you do believe in God, don't you?"

"Yes, of course," Phil said quickly—though he did not know what he believed in.

What he did not believe was that this was happening to him—that he was having this conversation about religion and morality with Al Bocca.

"So tell me," Al went on. "Doesn't it bother you to do business with priest-killers and atheists?"

"It would," Phil said slowly, "*if* I thought the stories were true."

"So you think the stories are lies?" Al Bocca asked coldly.

Phil felt the hostility in the room as a palpable thing. He wondered if Al had heard the stories from his own priest. . . .

"I think maybe a few people went crazy," he said carefully. "It sometimes happens in war. But, to me, that's not the important thing."

"What is, then? What is this important thing?"

"That women and children may starve to death in places

227

like Barcelona and Madrid. They are innocent certainly—the young mothers who need food so that their breasts won't dry up and their babes won't starve for lack of milk."

Al Bocca brooded silently behing his enormous blond desk.

Phil was growing more optimistic. He was sure he had struck home, hit the rich vein of sentimentality which was a part of Al's complex and contradictory personality.

"I can't see where there'd be anything so terribly wrong in helping those mothers and their little ones," Phil suggested in a soft, almost insinuating, tone.

"And in picking up some extra dough while doing it," Al retorted.

Phil recognized another side of Al's makeup. The shrewd, streetwise "I won't be conned" side. He decided to meet it head-on.

"That too," he said. "Why not? If we can make some money by doing good for people, we'll have it both ways. Isn't that what everyone wants?"

Al began to grin. It was an admiring grin, and the tension in the room which rose and fell like a barometer of his moods became almost nonexistent.

"For a kid," Al said, "you're a pretty clever son-of-a-bitch."

Phil smiled his pleasure at the compliment. He knew there was no sense in his saying anything. He'd pushed his views as hard as he dared. Whatever decision Al reached now, he would reach without help.

"All right," Al said then. "You talked me into it. I may disappoint one or two people, but it won't be anything I can't handle."

"Thanks, Al."

"For what?" This time, Al's smile was sharply laced with irony. "It's your company, isn't it? You're the boss. You can come to me for advice—I think that's wise on your part—but you're the one who's responsible for the decisions."

Phil nodded. He was under no illusions as to what that final statement meant.

"Thanks anyway," he said equably. "For the advice."

"Forget it. "Just make sure you're right about this—that we do make money from the deal."

35

The company did make money on the deal. A lot of money. And, though Phil did have one or two attacks of conscience, he basically felt good about himself.

What the hell, he thought. It was the way of the world, how things got done.

He really did agree with what he'd said to Al Bocca. With Spain's economy left in ruins by the still raging war, there was no guessing how many innocent people would have starved to death if it weren't for him. It was only fair for him to skim something off the top. He was entitled to it.

He did realize that there were a great many people who would disagree with him on that. People like Laura, for example. But, so what? He simply wouldn't tell Laura. What she didn't know wouldn't hurt her.

When he thought about it—which was not very often— Phil realized that there were a good many things about Farmer-Labor Food Products, Inc. that Laura would not understand.

She would not understand, for instance, how he could stand to look the other way when the company's employees had to pay so-called union dues which were really kickbacks to those who got them their jobs. Nor would she understand the need for strong-arm methods to get his products into certain stores or the deals he had to make to get them into the employee cafeterias. Or even why certain union newspapers lauded his products and his policies toward his workers, while other— much smaller—papers seemed to despise him.

Oh, he knew she heard rumors about him. Everyone in the movement heard rumors about him. But there were rumors about almost everyone. And Laura was too loyal to take them seriously unless she was shown proof.

In the meantime things kept going Phil's way. Unlike many factories, his plant ran smoothly—with no labor disputes and with increasing productivity. It was running so smoothly, in fact, that by the end of the year Phil was seriously negotiating to buy a second plant which would allow him to increase his line of products.

As he kept telling himself, he was doing all right.

During the first two months of 1937, Phil was becoming more concerned about his sister.

Naomi was thirteen-and-a-half then, and was rapidly gaining the appearance of a woman. In the past year, her breasts had developed astonishingly, and she had nearly reached her full height. Only the narrowness of her hips and a certain "baby" look to her face helped reveal how young she really was.

That she was attracting boys was only natural. What upset Phil was the type of boy she attracted.

On more than one afternoon, walking toward his parents' apartment building, he saw Naomi surrounded by a whole mob of overeager boys. And though he didn't know any of their names, he did know what they were—junior wiseguys of fifteen and sixteen, too old for their years and trying to get cheap thrills from a younger girl they thought of as "easy."

Phil knew all about guys like that. He'd been one of them when he was that age. And he didn't want them to con and take advantage of his sister the way he used to con young but well-developed girls. The very thought that they might do this to her sent him into a rage.

Was he being a hypocrite? Applying a double standard? The question did not occur to him. He was interested in his sister, not in abstract ethical theory.

He did wish his mother had taken him more seriously when they had discussed Naomi the previous year. She had said then that the girl was going through a stage.

"Some stage," Phil thought.

That February, he invited his mother out to dinner. He chose a small restaurant a couple of blocks from Leonard Abel's office in the garment district. They were drinking their after-dinner coffee when he brought up the subject of Naomi.

Sophie listened while her son said what he'd come to say.

"What do you think should be done?" she asked when he was through.

"I think she needs you at home, Mama. She needs you to guide her. Papa refuses to correct her, and she resents it when I try to. Maybe she'll listen to you."

Sophie thought for a moment, then looked directly at Phil. "What you want is for me to give up my job."

Phil played with his coffee spoon. He found it hard to meet his mother's gaze.

"It's not as if you have to work." he said at last. "If you ever did."

"Did I ever say so?" his mother challenged gently. "I enjoy working, Phil. It makes me feel good about myself."

Phil did not reply. His mother had changed a great deal in the past years, he was thinking. She no longer had the sweet, vulnerable look of a beautiful girl. Her waist had thickened, and there were lines in her face where there had been none four years ago.

She was still handsome. And she had a newfound air of strength and confidence which—in one sense—made her even more attractive than she had been before: Made her more of a woman.

"You're asking a lot," she said after a while.

"I know."

He wondered if it was too much. Did working make all those changes in her? If so, what would happen to her when she gave it up?

And for what? That was the question he had to ask himself: For what?

Was he only asking her to do it for his sister's sake? Or even primarily for his sister's sake?

He did think it would be good for Naomi to have her mother there when she came home from school in the afternoon and when she stayed away from school on various holidays. But he could not honestly pretend—not to himself, at least—that this was the only reason he wanted their mother to quit working. He was bothered about it. It did embarrass him to have people like the Boccas know. (Al had once remarked to him that important men took care of their mothers. And even Lew had said something about Phil's mother's small-time furrier boss.)

"Do you think it's *essential* for Naomi that I stay home?" Sophie Aronson was asking her son. "Do you think it's *essential* for her?"

Phil shrugged. He suddenly remembered having teased his mother about a possible relationship with Leonard Abel. She had parried that question—laughed with him over it—and, of course, he himself had only been having a little mild fun.

But now he wondered if he'd accidentally struck deeper

than he had guessed. Perhaps she really was having an affair with Abel! Could it be *that* which was making such a difference in her?

A wave of self-disgust swept over Phil. What was he thinking? About his mother? He told himself to wash it out of his mind.

But even so. She was a human being, after all. And Phil could not believe that she was having any sort of love life with his father these days.

Just because he personally didn't like Abel, that didn't mean his mother couldn't be drawn to the man. . . .

Well, he'd never tease his mother about that subject again. Next time she might tell him what he'd prefer not to know.

But now Phil's mother—no mind-reader, thank God—was coming to a decision about working.

"All right," she told her son. "I'll try staying home for a while and we'll see if it makes a difference to Naomi. If it helps, it will be worth it. If it doesn't, I can always try to go back to work again."

"For the Abel Fur Corporation?" Phil could not resist asking.

"Maybe." his mother replied blandly. "Or, who knows, maybe I'll try to find another job."

Phil was feeling a mixture of emotions when he kissed his mother goodnight and left the apartment. Mainly, however, he felt satisfaction. For no matter what his motives were, he was positive he'd done a good deed for his sister.

And his mother? Had he done a good deed for her too? He didn't know.

He did wonder if she would be happy not working and frankly hoped she would. It would solve a great many problems, not the least of which was that her having a job lowered him in the eyes of people like the Boccas who disapproved of him for allowing it.

Perhaps, Phil thought, that reaction was unfair. And perhaps some day the world would change enough so that even the Boccas would not criticize a man for permitting his mother to work. But Phil did not expect to live long enough to see it.

As he returned to his own place, his one regret was that he couldn't phone Laura and ask her to meet him there. He wanted to be with her.

But Laura was not available. She was off in Chicago talking to some group or other about the war in Spain.

She was doing a lot of that lately—traveling around the country, making speeches, inspiring young idealists to go off to Spain and fight.

On second thought, Phil decided, it might be fortunate for him that they couldn't get together this evening. He probably would have admitted his relief at his mother's decision to leave her job. And Laura would not have attempted to hide her disappointment in him.

It seemed to Phil that she'd been showing a lot of disappointment in him lately. She did not approve of many of his opinions, and she liked it less when he deferred to the opinions of the Boccas. While Phil had never claimed to be a great idealist, Laura felt that he really was one deep down and was doing his best to smother the fact. This was what troubled her most.

She had said something to that effect on the night before she left for Chicago. It had precipitated a serious fight.

"I'm me!" he had snarled at one point. "And I'm goddamned sick and tired of your trying to make me into someone else!"

Laura had been hurt. "If you're so sick and tired, maybe we should call this thing off."

"Any way you want it, sugar pie."

They had made it up, of course, in their usual way—in bed with their limbs wrapped about each other. But it had left a bad taste in their mouths.

Though Phil kept meaning to move into new, more luxurious quarters—after all, he felt he'd earned it—he hadn't yet found the time to look for a new apartment. So it was to his old, somewhat seedy studio that he returned after leaving his mother.

He poured himself a drink and considered making some phone calls. What he wanted was a woman. Nobody complicated, just a well-made lady he could sleep with. The thought of a well-formed female body was almost more than he could deal with.

Almost—but not quite. For though it would have been comparatively easy for Phil to make a contact and find a lady for the night, he fought with his conscience and decided not to do it. Tonight he would stay faithful to Laura. It was a fairly close thing, however. If Laura didn't get back to New York soon, there'd be another battle which his conscience might well lose.

Though Phil preferred being true to Laura, he was not a

fanatic about it. He was a man, after all. And he didn't think it was possible for a real man to keep away from sex for too long a time without risking his health or sanity—possibly both.

If Phil expected Laura's behavior to be ruled by a stricter code than his own, this was due less to conscious hypocrisy than it was to his mid-1930's, masculine way of regarding male and female anatomy. It was obvious, he felt, that a man's exposed and external sex was more difficult to control than a woman's internal one. Which meant that *his* needs were more urgent than hers.

Lew Bocca, one night, had put it another way.

"A man has a cock, right?" Lew asked rhetorically. "And if you don't let a cock crow, he's just liable to turn into a capon!"

Phil still grinned at that. When Lew got tight, he could come up with some good ones.

He was thinking about Lew when he heard a loud rap at the front door. He opened it to see Lew standing there.

Phil couldn't help gawking at his friend. The coincidence of seeing him put him momentarily off balance.

"Hey, buddy," Lew said, then paused at the muddled expression on Phil's face. "What's wrong?" he winked. "You got someone in there you don't want us to know about?"

A tinkle of female laughter came from the dimly lit hall behind him, and Phil realized that there were a couple of women with him. Knowing Lew, that could only mean one thing.

For the briefest of instants, Phil thought of making up some excuse and sending them all away. He could find some music on the radio, pick up a magazine he'd been planning to read, and remain faithful to the resolution he had so recently made.

Then he gave a mental shrug. It was fate, and you couldn't argue with fate. Not even Laura herself could claim that his intentions hadn't been good.

He stepped back from the doorway.

"No, no," he smiled. "I'm all alone. I was just caught up in thinking about something. Some business, you know . . ."

"To hell with business," Lew said happily. "You think too damn much about business. We've come to concentrate your mind on other matters. Right, ladies?"

The two girls giggled again and stepped into the apartment. They were both tall—about five foot seven, Phil judged—and

234

were dressed in identical gray coats and smart, fur-trimmed gray hats.

Lew shut the door behind them and took the large package he was carrying into the kitchenette. Then he came back to join Phil in helping the women off with their coats.

"This one is Lita," Lew said as the girls laughed and rubbed their hands together in an effort to warm up. "The other is Rita. They're identical twins."

"So I see," Phil said.

They did look exactly alike. They had lovely slender bodies with nice bosoms and identically flawless skins. To complicate things even more, they were wearing identical red gowns.

"How do you tell them apart?" Phil asked Lew. "Or don't you?"

"Oh, I do."

"How?"

"They're ticklish in different places," Lew cried triumphantly. "See!"

He goosed Lita and caught Rita under the ribs. They both let out whoops of laughter.

As the women gradually stopped laughing, Lew went over to his friend.

"I was telling them about you," he said quietly. "And they wanted to come over. So I said I'd bring along some champagne and caviar, too, and we could have a party."

"Where'd you get the champagne and caviar?"

"The same place where I got the ladies. The Imperial Palace. The owner owes a few favors to my uncle and me. So when I asked him if these two lovely creatures could miss the one A.M. show, tonight, he agreed."

"He wasn't happy about it," Lew added with a grin. "But he did agree."

Phil nodded. He'd bet the owner wasn't happy to have two great-looking chorus girls out of his Saturday night show. That must be some set of favors he owed the Boccas!

Phil had heard of The Imperial Palace, of course. Who in New York hadn't? It was a rare day that the former speakeasy was not trumpeted in one of the newspaper columns. Only a few days before, Walter Winchell had plugged the entire chorus line in the *Daily Mirror*.

"I read that Winchell piece." Phil grinned. "If your friends here are fair examples, that line is even better than he said."

The girls giggled with pleasure.

"I wouldn't say they're fair examples," Lew replied judiciously. "The other broads are good, all right. But these two are better than good. They're great!"

Rita and Lita preened themselves some more. They pulled back their shoulders to thrust their breasts out.

Phil was watching them shrewdly.

"Okay, ladies," he said. "That's enough compliments for a while. Time to start in on the champagne and caviar."

A half hour later, they were licking the last of the caviar from their fingers while they worked on their second bottle of champagne. Lita was sitting on the edge of the bed with Phil, while Rita was sharing the armchair with Lew Bocca.

Lita took a sip and let out a small, ladylike burp.

"'Scuse me," she said, placing a hand to her lips. She was starting to slur her words now. Phil thought that she was a bit more affected by the liquor than was her sister.

Phil grinned at her. "It's okay."

She leaned over to kiss his earlobe.

"I'm glad we came here," she said. "You're nice. Lew was right about you."

"What'd he say?"

"That you're nice." She giggled again. "But that you work too hard. You need more fun and excitement."

"Do I need more fun and excitement, buddy?" he asked Lew.

"I don't know, buddy," Lew said abstractedly. One hand was inside Rita's blouse, now, while the other was resting on her thigh. "But Uncle Al thinks you do. And that's good enough for me."

"Your uncle?"

"Sure. He worries about you. Thinks you take life too serious. Says you'll burn yourself out if you don't play more. And I don't know anyone better to play with than Rita and Lita.

"Ain't that right, Reet?" he asked as he did something with the fingers that were inside her blouse.

"Oooh!" Rita gasped. "You get me all weak when you do that."

"I'll do it again, then. I'm strong enough for the both of us."

Lita leaned over on the bed again. She blew some breath into Phil's ear and reached inside his shirt. She felt the hair beneath his undershirt and tugged gently at it through the cloth.

"Mmnnn . . ." she said. "I like a hairy man."

"And I like hairy girls," Phil said, poker-faced. "Ones with all sorts of hair on their chests."

Lita made a face.

"Wouldn't that be awful," she said. "Oh, I'd hate to have hair on my chest!"

"You mean you don't?" Phil asked. He pretended to be shocked.

Lita began to laugh uncontrollably.

"Bastard," she said after she'd gotten her breath back. "Now you're putting me on."

"Would I do a thing like that?"

"Boy, wouldn't you!"

Phil placed his lips against Lita's. Their jaws unlocked and their tongues met.

Phil pulled away and ran his fingers up between her thighs.

"I'll bet I know where girls do have hair," he said.

"Oh, yeah?" Lita said between laughs. "Then you tell me something: Why is it that guys have great big pencils in their pants whenever they kiss me?"

"To write you love letters, of course."

"Then start writing," Lita snorted.

Lew and Rita—having started a little earlier and having known each other a little longer—were further along along than Phil and Lita. But they were also having more trouble. Lew was seated in the armchair while Rita was straddling him. But though they were both doing their best, it was all but impossible for them to get proper leverage.

"The goddamn cushion's too soft!" Lew swore with frustration. "There's nothing to push against."

"Let's get on the bed, Rita suggested.

"You mean, with them?"

"Why not? Lita won't mind. You don't think Phil will mind, do you?"

"Hell, no," Lew said. He heaved Rita off him so that she almost fell on the floor.

"Mind if we get on the bed with you?" he called to Phil. "This chair's too soft and the rug's too scratchy."

"Be my guest," Phil said.

Rita got on the bed first. Her long, slender torso was indistinguishable from that of her sister. Then Phil noticed Lew with his erect member.

He turned away automatically from the sight of another hardon. Which was why he happened to be staring at the apartment door when it clicked open to admit Laura.

She stood there for a moment, her face pale with repressed fury.

Phil stared at her, going limp so quickly that Lita thought he might have injured himself somehow.

He was waiting for Laura to scream at him, to curse him. He almost wished she would—and get it over with.

But when she did speak it was in a quiet, mocking tone which was somehow more terrifying than all her curses would have been.

"Holy shit," she said sweetly. "Is this a private orgy? Or can anyone join in?"

36

It was as though the hot, steamy atmosphere inside the room was invaded by a sudden blast of arctic air. Pleasure-moans ceased as bodies separated. Faces froze and hands fumbled to protect private parts.

Phil pressured to break the long silence that followed. It was his duty to break it, he thought. It was *his* apartment, after all, and Laura was *his* girl. It was up to him to do something.

But do what? Say what?

"Laura, I—"

"Don't apologize, you son-of-a-bitch." Laura's voice was as cold and deadly as that of a snow maiden. "Whatever else you do, don't you dare apologize!"

"Look, honey," Lita said. She smiled nervously while her arms tried to cover her crotch and breasts. "I'm just a stranger in the night—you know what I mean? Gee, I didn't think that he might belong to someone!"

"Don't fret about it, he doesn't. Not any more, he doesn't."

"Oh, hey," Lita protested in a quavering voice. "It only happened this once. I swear. There's no guy in the world who won't let you down once. You can't break off with him for that."

"Horseshit," Laura spat out scornfully. "That old chestnut again: just because a man has a dong, he has a perfect right to stick it into any open cunt, right?"

"Hey. If you're trying to call me names—"

"Just shut up, dear. Do yourself a favor and shut the hell up before I start getting mad at you!"

Rita spoke quietly to her sister: "Better do what the lady says, sweetie. I hate violence."

Lew, who had managed to get his undershorts on, gave Rita a reasuring pat on her bare ass. He did not say anything, though. He kept watching the scene as though he were trying to decide what he should say or do if this or that happened.

Phil tried to speak again: "Laura—"

"You can shut up, too," Laura snapped. "Just listen to me for a change."

Phil's lips worked angrily. His earlier nervousness had turned first to shame and now to resentment.

To hell with her, he thought. So he'd cheated on her. Too bad. But who told her to come barging into his apartment without so much as a phone call first?

"All right," he said. "Go ahead."

"The first thing I'm going to tell you is that we're through. Did you catch that, Phil? *Through*. If I never see you again, it'll be too soon."

"Wait a minute. Don't I get a chance to explain?"

"No. No chances and no explanations. I don't want to hear you go through one of your routines. You're a great salesman, Phil. But I'm not buying."

"But—"

"Anyway," Laura said dismissively. "What I saw here to-night isn't all that important. We were finished before I stepped through your door."

"I don't get it."

"You don't?" Laura smiled. "Well, let me remind you of a few things. The first is that nice little deal you gave us at my Spanish food project. You were selling us food at cost, weren't you? No profit—only at cost. Right?"

"Yeah, well . . ."

So she'd found out, Phil thought. What was he supposed to say now?

"I did have expenses," he went on lamely. "I told you I'd have expenses."

"Those expenses really must have been something. Your great idealistic company which was founded by a combination of farmers and labor in an effort to stop profiteering at their expense charged more by *not* taking a profit than most other companies I checked charged *with* a profit!

"What do you say to that, lover?"

"Well . . . maybe you should have checked around first."

"Maybe you're right. But the thing is, I *trusted* you." Tears of rage began to fill Laura's eyes. "How could I have been such a fool? I actually trusted you!"

Phil turned away from her, embarrassed by the outburst of emotion. He reached covertly for his shorts and sneaked a quick look back toward Laura to see if she was watching.

Laura interpreted the look.

"Go ahead," she said. "Put them on. Please. I don't want to see your pecker any more—even by accident. It disgusts me."

Phil showed her his back while he pulled up his underwear. When he moved to face her again, his face was still crimson.

"Fucking bitch," he growled.

Laura laughed. "And what do you think you are? A fucking pig?"

"Just take it easy," Phil said, showing her his fist in a threatening gesture. "Or I'll—"

"You'll what? Hit me?" Laura's tone was scornful. "Go ahead. Show everyone what a hero you are."

Phil grimmaced in frustration. It would have been bad enough if they'd been alone. But to shame him this way while the others were looking on . . .

"Want to know the second thing that made me decide that we were finished?" Laura went on tauntingly. "What I found out *after* I found out what you were pulling with Spanish relief."

Phil shook his head. "Do we have to talk about it in front of everyone? I mean . . . can't we just go someplace and talk about it ourselves?"

"Yeah, why don't you do that?" Lita said eagerly. "Rita and I don't want to know things that are none of our business. Do we, Rita?"

"Of course not."

Lew still hadn't said anything. His eyes were cool, calculating, like his uncle's.

Laura was paying no attention to him. Her eyes were focused brightly on Lita.

"Don't run away dear," she said. "I think you should learn something more about the man you just let screw you."

"Hey, just a minute—"

"But why don't you put on some more clothes. You have a very nice body, but I'm just not interested."

Lita began to flush now, as did her sister. Both girls began to throw things on hastily.

"In Chicago," Laura went on, I learned how Farmer-Labor Products forces its way into stores, into factory cafeterias. How labor unions are forced to endorse Farmer-Labor Products even while the members despise everything that company stands for!"

"That's not true," Phil said hopelessly. "We give people better deals than the giants give them."

"Better deals? Like you gave Spanish relief a better deal?"

"Lets not go into that again," Phil said. "We just talked about that."

"All right, we'll talk about what made your great success—your underworld connections."

"Just a minute—"

"That's the truth, Phil, isn't it? You have a nice, friendly backer from the underworld. He's the one who makes certain that your products get in everywhere. People have to accept your stuff, don't they? It's either that or get shot. Right?"

"I never heard of anything so wrong in my life!"

Laura merely grinned at him. "And who is this mysterious backer who made it possible for you to start a successful business at a time when established businessmen are afraid to? Who is he? . . ."

As Laura paused dramatically, Phil felt a cold fish in the pit of his stomach. What was she going to say next? And how much did she actually know?

"Laura," he said, pouring as much emotion into his voice as he possibly could. "Laura, be careful."

If Laura understood what he was trying to do, she gave no sign of it. She was in full cry now and would not be stopped.

"Mr. Al Bocca," she hissed. "Mr. Al Bocca is the man. Of course you like to deal with his number-one boy, don't you Phil? Mr. Al Bocca's charming nephew, Lew."

After she had said those words, Laura looked nervous—like a reluctant believer who blasphemed near a church or synagogue. Then—as she realized just how nervous she was—she looked defiant.

Lita and Rita did not bother to hide how they felt.

"We better get out of here," Lita said.

"Yes," Rita agreed. "Don't worry about us. We can find our own way home."

"What for?" Lew Bocca asked. (Those were the first words he had spoken since Laura had entered the room.) "Phil and me'll take you home."

"But—"

"I said we'll do it," Lew told them.

Phil stared at Lew, who was straightening his tie. He wondered how he had dressed so swiftly without anyone even noticing him.

Lew smiled calmly at Phil, then turned his grin on Laura.

"That information you think you have," he said reasonably. "It's nothing. It's all lies."

"It's the truth," Laura said. "And what's more, you know it's the truth."

"You don't have proof—of anything. You were mad at Phil because you think he overcharged you on that Spanish food deal. So you were ready to listen to the first creep to crawl out of the woodwork.

"Who was it? Who told you all those lies about me and my uncle? We're respectable businessmen. We don't like being slandered."

Laura shook her head impassively.

"All right," Lew said. "So you won't tell me who it was. But he didn't give you any proof, did he? If he did, you'd have gone to the cops."

Laura's eyes blazed: "I don't run to the cops. Your friend Phil knows that much about me. I don't trust the cops—I haven't trusted them since I was a little girl—and I never go to them when I'm in trouble."

"It's true, Lew," Phil said. "She wouldn't tell the cops."

Laura looked at him disdainfully. "I'll tell you who I *will* go to—my own people. I'll tell everyone I know in the movement about you, Phil. And, believe me, I know a lot of people. I'll have you investigated by the socialist press. There'll be stories about you in left-wing and radical publications all over this country!"

Phil's frustration was making him furious. He wanted to punch some sense into Laura, but was helpless to do it.

But why in hell didn't she stop? She was not stupid. Couldn't she understand what was at stake here? Couldn't she see that he—Phil Aronson—was not the issue any more, that the issue now was Al Bocca and what his nephew was going to tell him?

Even Rita and Lita understood that. They might not have Laura's intellect, but they were shrewd enough to understand that they were in danger simply because they happened to be here while Laura was making her little speech.

Phil glanced over at them. They had moved off the bed and were huddled quietly together in a corner.

He forced his anger under control and spoke calmly to Lew: "I don't think we have to take her too seriously. She's mad now, of course. But once she gets over her mad she'll calm down. She's not going to actually do anything."

"The hell I'm not," Laura broke in.

"All right," Phil conceded in disgust. "Maybe you *will* try to do something. But what? You still don't have proof. Your boyfriends will want proof before they publish anything."

"I have lots of proof about how you overcharged us when you supplied food for Spain. All I have to do is to compare your charges with those of other concerns. As for the rest of it—how you used the underworld and screwed the workers—my word will be enough. You can't sue the whole movement for libel!"

"The hell I can't," Phil said.

"You know what I think, Laura," Lew Bocca said suddenly. He had been watching the girl curiously and now his eyes were glinting with amusement. "I think you're kidding yourself."

"What does that mean?"

"You tell yourself that you want to stop Phil because he hurt your precious movement. You say you want to expose him so that no one will be fooled by him ever again. Right?"

"Sure. What about it?"

"I don't think that's your reason at all."

Lew grinned as he saw Laura about to frame a protest. He went on before she could.

"Oh, I'm sure that's part of the reason," he said. "I never said you weren't serious about what you believe. But the real reason—the deep down reason—is pure, old-fashioned jealousy. You're sore because you walked in here and found Phil laying another broad!"

"You egocentric male bastard!" Laura said. "Do you really think that a woman will only get angry over something physical? Over a lover betraying her? Don't you think that a woman can become as deeply involved with a cause as a man can—and want to protect that cause?"

"I don't see where it has anything to do with being a man or a woman," Lew replied reasonably. "I simply find it hard to believe that anyone—male or female—could get as furious as you did over some abstract cause."

He turned to Phil: "What do you think, buddy?"

The question took Phil off guard. He wondered how he should answer it. With the truth?

"I don't know," he said at last. "But I don't think *I* could get that mad over a cause."

"There you are, Laura," Lew said. "Neither could I."

"That's because neither one of you would ever commit yourself to anything," Laura came back in a low intense tone. "You are both too busy filling your pockets and your bellies."

"We commit ourselves to our friends," Lew countered. "That's one thing. We don't rat on them."

Laura did not reply.

"And what do you do that's so noble?" Lew continued. "You hide behind that cause of yours—use it as a shield—while you try to kick Phil in the balls."

"That's not fair!" Laura cried.

"No? Well, how fair is it for you to hurt innocent people just because you're mad at Phil?"

"What innocent people?" Laura asked suspiciously.

"Me, for instance. I know that you and I don't like each other very much, but I never hurt you. Did I?"

"Not—not personally, no."

"Yet if you give all that information to your journalist friends, you know I'll be dragged into it. You know I'll be hurt."

Laura was silent.

"And my Uncle Al," Lew continued after waiting a moment. "You plan to involve him as well. Why? Has he ever done anything to harm *you?*"

"But he . . . you . . . you're *gangsters!*"

"*We* consider ourselves businessmen," Lew told her easily. "Of course, everyone is entitled to his or her own opinion. There are lots of people, for instance, who'd consider you a stinking commie. But I imagine you would rather call yourself a fighter for democracy and social justice."

Laura flushed. "It's not the same."

Phil saw that she was wavering. He wanted to jump in the argument to confront her with logical points of his own. He didn't know though. He was afraid he might do more harm than good. Every time he had spoken, Laura grew more angry and stubborn.

He decided to chance a comment anyway. Gently, gently, he told himself.

"Be fair, Laura. Lew's got a point."

"No, he doesn't, Laura said.

She did not sound hostile, now, so much as she sounded sad. There was a catch in her voice and it seemed as if she were having to struggle to keep from crying.

"It's *not* the same," she repeated. "Maybe it sounds to you as though it *is* the same, but it's really not. . . .

"You see, *I*—no matter if I'm going about it the right way or not—am at least *trying* to help people. Oh, he can sneer about causes all he wants. But all that I'm doing—all that people like me are doing—is trying to give *everyone* a little more control over his own life.

"Can you say that about yourself, Phil? Can you say it about your friend here?"

"I don't know," Phil said helplessly. "I—"

"Now do you understand the difference between us?" Laura said brokenly. "Why it *is* fair for us to be judged by different standards?"

Phil could not meet her eyes. It struck him that this was the real moment of parting, this realization that the forces which had held them together were not as strong—nor could they ever again be as strong—as the forces which drew them apart.

"All right," he said now. "But can't you leave it at that? Can't we just go our separate ways and wish each other luck? Or do you have to have your revenge by exposing me?"

"I don't know!" Laura cried as she rushed from the room. "I don't know!"

Rita and Lita watched the door slam shut while still huddled together in a corner of the room. They looked nervously toward Lew, hoping for reassurance.

He understood their looks and grinned at them.

"Well, ladies," he said. "What did you think of that? Have you ever seen a broad get that pissed before?"

"Sometimes," Rita answered.

"But not very often," said Lita.

Phil watched as the fear and tension drained rapidly from the girls' features. They could not have known before how Lew would react to their being here tonight, to their seeing and hearing what they should not have seen and heard.

Now that Lew had spoken pleasantly to them, however, and had treated them to a sample of his usual banter, they felt they could relax. They were home free.

Phil wondered if they were right. He hoped so; he never thought the odds were with them. But he could not be sure. One of the special talents that Lew Bocca shared with his Uncle Al was that of masking his true feelings.

"That Laura is a crazy woman," Lita was complaning now. "I was really afraid she was going to hurt me!"

"You didn't have to worry, babes," Lew told her with a wink. "I wouldn't have let her damage your equipment. I promised your boss that you'd return to the Imperial Palace in the same gorgeous shape you were in when you left it."

The twins giggled happily. Any reference to their beauty made them happy.

Lita sat down beside Phil again. She placed a hand on his knee.

"You know something, honey," she said. "You're such a sweet guy. How'd you ever get mixed up with a girl who has a temper like that?"

Phil shrugged. The question angered and embarrassed him.

"She's got other things beside a temper," he muttered.

"Don't all girls?" Lita asked innocently.

"I didn't mean—"

"What my sister's trying to say," Rita interjected, "is that you didn't lose all that much when she walked out on you."

"That's right," said Lita. "And anyway, she's gonna be back. You're too good a catch for her not to be."

Phil wanted to change the subject. He turned to Lew.

"Don't you think we'd better be taking these ladies home?" he suggested.

"Yeah. Well look, buddy. On second thought, maybe you'd better take them home by yourself. You wouldn't mind doing that for me, would you?"

"Why? What's wrong?"

"Not a damned thing, buddy. Why should something be wrong?"

"Did we do something?" Rita put in before Phil could make his own reply.

"You?" Lew laughed. "All you two did tonight was look gorgeous and act willing. What could be wrong with that?"

"Hell, I wish I could take you home tonight. But I just remembered I promised I'd meet someone later on. The time's gone faster than I thought."

"Your going to meet someone?" Rita sounded hurt. "This late?"

"Sure, babes. But don't worry. It's a guy. Some entertainer I have to see on business. He doesn't get off work until late."

"Oh." Rita looked as though she were still puzzled, but did not want to press any more.

"So, what do you say, buddy?" Lew asked Phil. "You gonna do me that favor? Take the girls home?"

A sensation of helpless terror seemed to shoot through Phil's frame. He did not understand what caused it but it was as though he saw the floor begin to open wide and realized there was nothing he could do to stop it.

He must not allow himself to reveal his feelings, however. Revealing them might give shape and form to his now amorphous terror, might give life to what was merely a chimera.

So he put all the cheer and eagerness he could into his grin.

"Sure I'll take the girls home for you," he said. "I'd be a sucker not to."

37

Phil was home again within the hour.

This was not the girls' fault. They wanted him to spend the rest of the night playing with them and were hurt when he indicated that he had to leave.

"But you must stay." Lita insisted. "We know all sorts of games."

"We're twice as much fun when you take us together," Rita said with a giggle.

"I'm sure you are," Phil said. "But I'm too knocked out to be any fun myself."

"Are you sure?" Lita asked dubiously. "You didn't seem all that bushed before."

"That was before," Phil said. "This is now. And I'm going to have to get up early tomorrow."

"Well . . ." Rita pouted. "If you say so."

"Do you have our phone number?" Lita wanted to know.

"I'll get it from Lew first thing tomorrow," Phil promised. "I'll call you soon."

By the time Phil had undressed and gotten into his bed, he had forgotten all about the twins. This didn't mean that he wouldn't phone them. Sooner or later—depending on his mood—he very possibly would.

As far as Phil was concerned, Rita and Lita had but one thing to offer. But that was all right with him, too. There were times, he believed, when all any man needed was a fucking machine—a broad who could give him all the sensual enjoyment he would ask for without expecting to discuss anything more profound than the selection of her gown or hat.

But one of those times was not tonight. Tonight, he wanted what he couldn't have. He wanted Laura.

If only it were possible, he thought. If he could only spend the rest of the night with her. Just talking, if he had to. He had a great deal to talk about, and he needed someone sensitive and bright to talk to.

The situation was so complex now. He could not understand it. He could not even understand his own feelings.

He wondered what Laura would think about it, what her ideas would be about what might happen next.

But most of all, he though ironically, he wanted to discuss Laura with Laura. How much truth had there been in that terrible picture she had painted of him before? A lot? A little? Or was her fury just another name for jealousy. As his good friend, Lew Bocca, had claimed.

And maybe Lew was partly right, Phil thought. Laura was human; she could be as jealous as anyone else. But he knew that Lew's truth wasn't the whole truth. He refused to make himself feel better by pretending that it was.

He did not want to think about it any more, though. The jumble of thoughts was becoming too much for him. He closed his eyes and tried to empty his mind so that he could sleep.

But his mind would not stay empty. Laura moved in to fill every empty space.

He found himself visualizing her: he saw her walk toward him again from across the street. He could admire her long, easy stride and the lovely honey-colored hair which she had started to wear in a new, swept-back style.

And now she was here with him. In the room. Undressing.

He watched as she pulled off her blouse and stepped out of her skirt. He saw her slip come off and looked on as she reached behind her back to unhook her bra. Her breasts hung beautifully pendant as she bent forward to slide down her garter belt and stockings. She walked toward the bed dressed only in her panties. Then she took those off and crept in beside him.

She was *there*. In the bed—her body soft and supple and willing...

He came back to reality with a sudden jolt.

Jesus! he thought. He wanted her that badly. He had grown a hard-on from wanting her.

His self-conscious awareness of what had been happening withered his erection. But that did not help him to get to sleep. Though his mind had left sex, it went racing on to other things— like the possibility of convincing Laura to come back.

Was there a chance? Was there a single solitary chance for him to convince her?

The only sure thing about it, he realized, was that it wouldn't be easy. Hell; it would not even be easy to convince her to talk to him! He would phone in the morning. But when he did, she would probably send word that she was busy or out or simply not interested.

But he was not going to take no for an answer, he thought grimly. He would keep phoning—over and over again—and if that didn't work, he would try to see her in person. He'd damn well plant himself in front of the building in which she lived, stake out Y.A.S.D. headquarters, even follow her around the country if he had to!

All he'd ask for would be twenty or thirty minutes of her time. It wasn't much. Eventually she would have to break down and give it to him.

And when she did? What would he say to her then?

Here was the real puzzle—to find a way to convince her to trust him again.

Maybe honesty was the answer. Pure and simple honesty. It would be something different for him: No lies. No con jobs. Just the plain unvarnished truth.

He would do it. He'd tell her everything that he and the Boccas had done in order to get his company started and what the future was supposed to hold in store.(She didn't know the half of it, he thought grimly. She didn't know how the unions, the farmers, and the radical groups were due to be tossed out on their collective ears, for example, whenever it suited his purpose.) He would tell her everything—all the details—and throw himself on her mercy.

And would she have mercy? Perhaps she would. If only because he would promise faithfully to work his ass off in order to set things right, to undo the harm he had done.

And he would really mean it! he thought. A feeling of exhaltation ran through him. It was a task he would set himself, a war he would wage.

He wasn't kidding himself. It was going to be a war in more ways than one. The Boccas would consider him a turncoat, a traitor. Lew would reason with him. Al would call him in for a conference. And then the threats would begin.

Nor did Phil believe that it would end with threats. The Boccas' tame unions would start striking his factory. Mysterious accidents would threaten his machinery. His trucks would be overturned and his people hurt. His own life would be in serious jeopardy. It would be rough as hell.

It would be more than a battle. It would be an all-out war. And one he could easily lose.

He'd try his damndest not to lose, though. That much he would promise Laura. For once the wiseguy ex-bookie could bet against the odds!

It was about four-thirty or five that morning when Phil fell into a fitful sleep from which he awakened at a quarter to eight.

It took him a long time to get fully awake. For several minutes he remained in a mental fog, knowing that something important had happened—or was about to happen—but not being able to recall what it was.

It was only as he looked around the room that he remembered Lew Bocca bringing Rita and Lita the previous night. Then he remembered how Laura had shown up. And then he remembered what she had said.

He swore softly as the whole affair came back to him. Not

just all the words and actions, but those silent promises he had made in the small hours of the morning.

He staggered into the john and washed his hands and face. When he came out again, he brewed some coffee for himself and ate a sugar doughnut he found in the refrigerator.

He was feeling somewhat better when he dialed Laura's phone number. The phone hadn't been there for very long. One of the girls Laura shared her loft with had a friend who worked for the phone company. She'd talked him into splicing into the line of a nearby corporation and assigning them an unused number.

When Laura told him how she and her friends obtained their phone, Phil was delighted. They somehow managed to live a fairly comfortable life without having to pay for it.

He thought about all this as he dialed the phone. Then he settled back to decide what to say when someone answered it.

It seemed to take forever before someone did. But when the phone was finally picked up, Phil realized that something was terribly wrong.

The voice on the other end sounded familiar, but he could not make out what was being said. It was a woman's voice, and the woman was sobbing.

"Hello," he said. "Hello."

Perhaps he had reached the wrong number. He repeated the one he had dialed.

This was the right number, the voice managed to say.

"Hello," Phil said once more. "This is Phil Aronson. Who is this? Who am I speaking to?"

The woman said something that Phil could not understand. Then she handed the phone to someone else. Jed Symmonds.

"That was Glenda," Jed said. His own voice was shaking and Phil sensed that he was very near the breaking point. "I'm afraid she's not in good shape."

"So I heard," Phil said. "What is it? What in hell's going on?"

"You don't . . . know? I thought maybe someone had called you. It only happened twenty minutes ago . . ."

"What happened twenty minutes ago?" Phil demanded. There was panic in his own voice now.

"Laura . . . she's—she was hit by a car. She's gone off in an ambulance—"

"Wait!" Phil cried. He could not believe what he had heard. It had to be some weird practical joke that she was making Jed play on him to get even for what had happened last night. "Wait. did you say, hit by a car? How, for God's sake?"

"She was crossing the street... right in front of this building. It was a fucking hit and run driver.... Glenda happened to be looking out the window and saw the whole thing.

"That's how come she's so hysterical. Glenda, I mean. First she told us all about it, then she..."

"Yeah," Phil said shortly. He didn't want to hear about Glenda's hysterics. Not now. There was only room in his mind now for Laura.

Hit by a car? How could that happen. Laura had never been careless or inattentive. She was one of the most alert persons Phil had ever known.

Could it have been their argument that had made the difference in her? he asked himself suddenly. Had their fight been so much on her mind that she wasn't paying attention to what had been going on around her?

Phil felt the heavy weight of personal guilt. Had this whole thing been his fault?

"What happened?" he said into the telephone. "Was she crossing the street in a daze? Did she have anything on her mind?"

"According to the girls here, she did have something on her mind. Something she didn't want to talk about until after she had decided what to do about it."

"But, from what Glenda said, that had nothing to do with the fact that she was hit. I mean no one could have avoided that son-of-a-bitch. The fucking car swung around the corner, barreled down on her at fifty, sixty miles an hour and kept right on going after it hit her!"

"My God—"

"And no one even got the license plate."

"But listen. You say an ambulance came for her. Do you know where she was taken?"

Jed gave him the name of the hospital.

"And Phil," he added, his voice starting to shake again. "It's pretty bad. I think that fucking car busted up her insides. Maybe—maybe you'd better prepare yourself."

"Shit," Phil said bitterly. "How in hell do you do that?"

Jed had no answer to give.

Phil muttered something and hung up in order to dial the hospital. He spoke to an emergency room nurse who told him that Laura had died a few minutes before he called. She had never recovered consciousness, the nurse told him.

And she had been so alive! . . .

Phil was hardly aware that he was dressing to go out until all his clothing was actually on. And even when he was downstairs and on the street—walking purposefully with his overcoat buttoned high against the cold—he had no idea where he was going or what he was going to do when he got there.

Yet if his mind had no sense of his purpose, his body understood it. For his route to his destination was straight and direct, and his stride hardly varied until he was at the luxury apartment house in which Lew Bocca lived.

The doorman saluted Phil as he entered the lobby, then rang upstairs to let Lew know that he was on his way.

If Lew was puzzled about Phil's unexpected visit, nothing in his voice gave evidence of the fact. "Send him up."

Phil nodded to the elevator operator who greeted him by name. He had often visited Lew here and was well-known by the entire staff.

He waited until the elevator started down again before he rang the doorbell. He was in a semi-daze and still did not know why he was here. Only when Lew opened the door in his silken robe and pajamas did things become crystal clear in his mind.

"Hey, buddy—" Lew began. But before he could get any other words out Phil had hit him.

He hit him twice. The first was a short jab to the solar plexus—a sucker punch which left Lew doubled over and gasping for breath so that he was unable to defend himself against the second blow. That was solid right to the jaw.

Lew's eyes glazed and he collapsed on his own carpet. Phil stepped over him and shut the door.

Lew got to his hands and knees and shook his head slowly.

"What in hell did you do that for?" he moaned as he struggled the rest of the way to his feet. "Jesus Christ . . ."

Phil came at him again, puching him first in the kidney and then on the temple.

Lew dropped. He did not move for several moments, and when he did, his motions were feeble.

"Get up," Phil snarled. Those were the first words he had spoken since he had left his own apartment. "Get up."

But Lew didn't. He lay where he was, fighting the pain, and trying to gather his wits.

"Why? . . . ." he gasped. "Why? . . . ."

253

"You know why.....Bastard! Shit! You know why."

Lew looked up at him.

"Laura..." Phil said. The name came out reluctantly—as if it had been torn out of him.

"What about her?"

"She's dead, you fucking shit-heel!" Phil's voice broke. He brought himself back under control with an effort. "You ought to know. You set it up."

"I?... Set what up?..."

"It wasn't hard to do. You knew where Laura lives...lived. You've even been there a couple of times. With me..."

"What are you talking about?" Lew insisted. "What did I do?"

"Last night. After you left us. You headed straight for a phone, didn't you? You called someone—maybe your uncle, maybe someone else—and you arranged for a hit-and-run accident."

"You're out of your mind," Lew said flatly.

"You mean you deny it?" Phil sounded incredulous.

"Fucking aye, I do."

Lew shifted carefully on the carpet. He rubbed his sore kidney.

"But about Laura...What happened? You say it was some kind of hit-and-run accident?"

"That's what it's supposed to be—a car going fifty miles an hour turns the corner next to her place just as she happens to be crossing the street.

"But you wouldn't know about that, would you?"

Lew chose to ignore the sarcasm in Phil's voice. "No, I wouldn't. Where in hell do you get your ideas, anyway? Is it because of last night? Do you really think I'd murder her because of last night?"

"She was threatening to tell journalists everything she knew," Phil reminded him. "That could have hurt a lot of people besides me."

"I don't think it would have done too much damage," Lew said judiciously. "I'm not saying it would've helped anyone; but it wouldn't have hurt too much either.

"And anyway," he went on, "she wasn't going to actually *do* anything. She was just letting off a little steam. And I'd need a hell of a lot better reason than that before I'd kill a beautiful woman!"

"You never trusted her," Phil recalled. "Not from the be-

254

ginning. No matter what you say now, you can't deny that."

"I'm not sure what you mean by trust. If you're saying that we never saw eye to eye on most things, I'll admit it. But so what? If I killed off all the people I didn't agree with, there'd be one hell of a lot of corpses filling up the streets of New York."

Phil gazed thoughtfully at Lew's prone figure. Was he lying? He had every reason to: He was stretched out on the floor, helpless, at the mercy of a man who might literally kill him with his feet if he said the wrong thing. So why not lie?

Nor could Phil believe that Laura really had been killed by some unknown crazy with a car. It would have been too huge a coincidence for it to have happened in front of her own apartment on the morning after she had made some very dangerous threats.

But—and this was a very big but—Phil knew there wasn't a chance in hell of his actually proving anything.

Everything would be all covered up, now. The only way to get proof would be to make Lew talk. And Phil did not believe this could be done. Bullying—intimidation—would not work with Lew. He was human—he could be made to suffer just like anyone else—but even while he was suffering he would be protesting his innocence. He would *die* protesting his innocence!

Phil sighed. He was just starting to realize that something strange was happening to him: he was losing his rage. The pure, blind, unthinking fury that directed his movements since he'd learned about Laura's death, was growing less pure and less blind as thought took over from feeling.

It wasn't that he was any less affected by Laura's death, any less sickened by it. But he was thinking and reasoning now, rather than simply reacting.

Lew—who had been watching Phil closely—seemed to be reading his mind.

"Can I get up, now?" he asked.

"Huh?"

"Without your knocking me down again, I mean." Lew carefully touched his jaw and the sore places on his body. "You have one hell of a punch, buddy."

Phil backed off so that Lew could get to his feet and check himself for damages once more.

Phil watched as he leaned against a flocked wall. He was disgusted with himself. He should be taking vengeance now.

He should be stomping the prone, helpless body of his woman's killer! . . .

But suppose—just suppose—that Lew hadn't killed Laura. What if the "unbelievable" coincidence had really taken place and Lew was innocent?

Bullshit! Phil told himself.

But it was possible.

Bullshit! Phil thought again, as he made a conscious effort to regain his lost sense of fury.

Thoughts were spinning about in his brain now. He began to hold onto the wall for balance.

"What's wrong?" Lew asked. "You're all white. I thought I was the one who'd been knocked around."

Phil staggered over to Lew's modernistic white couch. He sat down on it and stayed there with his head in his hands.

Lew looked at him sharply, then went to his small bar in order to pour two drinks.

He offered one of them to Phil.

"Here, take it," he said. "It's a good straight brandy. I think we could both use some."

Phil took a sip. The liquid slid smoothly down his gullet and seemed to start a fire in his stomach.

Lew drank some himself, then sat down in an armchair across from the couch.

Phil frowned at him.

"How come you're not sore?" he asked. "If someone did to me what I did to you—worked me over without even giving me chance to get set—I'd want to kill the son-of-a-bitch! How come you don't?"

Lew seemed prepared for the question—as though he had been wondering about that himself and was now repeating a conclusion he had already rehearsed.

"Because I figure you went off your rocker when you heard about Laura," he explained. "That makes you not responsible."

Phil stared at him and Lew smiled tightly.

"If I though you were fully responsible for what you did, you'd have cause to worry. The only way you'd be able to stay alive, in fact, would be to knock me off first. And then you'd have Uncle Al to deal with."

Phil took another sip of brandy. The warmth had spread up to his head by now. It was pleasant and comforting.

It was a lucky thing that Lew hadn't figured out the truth, he thought sagely, that his berserk actions had been due to an excess of sanity, not craziness. Only now that he appeared to be sane was he out of his mind.

Lew was watching him carefully now. Wondering— or so Phil believed—whether he was completely under control or if he might still be subject to another fit of violence.

"You don't have to worry," he told Phil. "I understand what happened to you. It'll be okay as long as it doesn't happen again."

Lew's dry chuckle told Phil that he had just attempted some humor.

Phil placed his brandy glass on an end table. He stood up.

"I'd better be going," he said.

"Okay, buddy. Want me to get dressed and come with you?"

"No. I'll be all right."

"I never thought you wouldn't be. It's just that . . . maybe you shouldn't be alone now. You know—too much brooding and . . ."

"Don't worry about it."

"Okay. If you say so. But tell me something: What are you going to be doing for the next couple of weeks?"

"What'll I be doing? I don't know. What I did last week, I guess. Working."

"Maybe you should forget about work for the next couple of weeks. Take a vacation. Go down to Havana, say."

Phil stared at him. "Havana?"

"Uncle Al has great connections there. I'll come along with you, if you like. You'll love it. They got everything: All the gambling you could want and more sweet pussy than you ever saw before in your life!"

But Phil was already shaking his head gravely.

"I don't think so," he said. "I think I'll be better off staying in New York and working. The best thing for me right now would be to work my ass off."

Part Three

38

Phil followed his own advice. In the weeks and months after Laura's death, he involved himself in his work to such an extent that it was difficult to get him to think about anything else.

And he made money. By summer, he had three factories— two in full operation and one just starting up. He had a more complete food line, now, and his products were taking a larger and larger share of the market.

If his romantic life suffered during this period, Phil hardly seemed to notice. As far as he was concerned, there was more than enough romance to be found in business. The moves and countermoves of deal-making were every bit as intriguing to him as the moves and countermoves of love.

Sex was something else again. For that he employed some of the most beautiful prostitutes in the city. They would give him the physical release he needed while permitting him to save his emotional energies for more important things.

But that was it. He stuck to the professionals. They kept things neat and tidy, while amateurs were apt to complicate things by expecting too much from a man.

Which was why he arranged to be busy when Alice Jefferson came to New York in order to shop. He had not slept with that lady since their night in Hermit. Nor did he plan to sleep with her in the future.

And if an occasional affair was to be avoided, falling in love was to be avoided at all costs. Love was like a raging fire which consumed all rational thought. He had learned that much from Laura at least, that he could not afford to fall in love.

He did plan to marry some day. Marriage played an important role in his vision of the future. But his future bride was going to be a suitable young woman who had a proper background of wealth and influence.

And why shouldn't he choose a girl with a helpful family? He himself planned to bring a great deal to the marriage. It was only fair that she contribute something as well.

One thing he had decided about his future wife—she was not going to be any sort of an intellectual. Certainly not a left-wing intellectual. He didn't mind if she knew something about literature, say, or classical music. Such knowledge could even be a social advantage. But her political ideas were going to vaguely reflect his own.

That had been the basic problem between Laura and himself, the main reason they would surely have broken up even if she had not stumbled into his apartment on the terrible night. As strong as their love was, it was being ground to pieces by the two hard rocks of their opposing commitments: Laura's commitment to egalitarianism, Phil's to personal freedom; Laura's to state socialism, Phil's to free-enterprise capitalism.

While Phil was by no means a political philosopher (he liked to say that Bob was the deep thinker of the family), he did have firm ideas about the political scene. It was obvious to him that, though the New Deal might have been necessary in 1933, it had now gotten way out of hand. Roosevelt wanted it all. If it weren't for the Supreme Court—those "Nine Old Men" whom the New Dealer's kept bitching about—Washington would now be regulating how much profit a businessman could make, how much he could charge for his products and how much he had to pay his workers. It would have been a goddamn dictatorship!

Even as it was, Phil found that government was interfering one hell of a lot in what he considered to be his private business. Every time he turned around, there was another New Deal agency to get in his way. The only thing that Roosevelt and company were not doing these days was whipping the Depression.

Phil believed that the reason for this failure was that the New Deal, which had started by helping matters, had now gone so far that it was actually hurting them. Laura would have laid the blame on the New Deal not going far enough.

When Phil thought about this he would sometimes concede the possibility that he was wrong. Certainly Bob's viewpoint was closer to Laura's than it was to his own.

But that was beside the point. The vital thing was to never again become seriously involved with a woman who had deep convictions which were diametrically opposed to his own. He would not want a woman to serve as his loving and loyal opposition, but rather as his junior partner.

So when Phil married, it would only be to a girl who would look to him for guidance.

Not that she'd be mindless, of course. He could never be interested in some vacuous creature without a thought to call her own. He would want her to have her own opinions; and he planned to encourage her to speak up for them. But when all the talking and arguing was over, he would have to have the final word and she would have to prefer it that way.

One of the things which he accomplished during the months that followed Laura's death was a move to a new apartment.

His old studio apartment had grown too depressing. It was dark and dingy—the home of someone hanging on by his fingertips, not a young man on the rise. He would have moved earlier if Laura hadn't asked him not to. Now the place reminded him of her—and depressed him still further.

He found a one-bedroom apartment on an upper floor of a fairly new building located on Central Park West in the Seventies. The rooms were large and airy and he had a splendid view of the park.

When he left the studio, Phil sold all his old furniture in order to make a clean break with the past. He didn't care very much what he replaced the stuff with. All he demanded was that it be modern, sharp-looking, and suitable for his new station in life. He got the name of an interior decorator from Sid Walters, told the man how much he was willing to spend, and let him select the furniture. It was simpler that way.

It worked fairly well, though he did find that some of his new possessions—the sweepingly curved, overstuffed white leather sofa for instance, or the chrome and ebony bar—a trifle too modern.

Generally speaking, however, he was proud of his new apartment. He liked to entertain people there—his parents, his old friends, his business associates. But most of all, he liked to entertain his brother.

Bob was turning nineteen now and had become more of a good friend than a kid brother. Phil enjoyed talking things over with him, exchanging ideas with him. No matter how they argued—and they did argue a good deal—neither of them could hold a grudge against the other.

One subject that the two constantly argued about was the possibility of the United States getting into another foreign war.

Bob felt that there was a strong likelihood of it. Phil could not understand how his brilliant brother could believe anything so obviously ridiculous.

"Is that what those professors are teaching you in college?" he would ask. "I guess I was wrong—you should've gone into the business. At least you would have learned how to use your common sense."

"It's too late now, I'm afraid," Bob said with a laugh. "I've been infected by intellectuality."

"Up yours." Phil grinned.

"Anything you say, brother. But what I said to you just now was right. Before too many years go by, we are going to get involved in a war."

"But that's crazy. The world may not be perfect, but at least we're at peace. And people like it that way."

"It's a phony peace, Phil. The sort of peace which allowed Mussolini to occupy Ethiopia while the League of Nations stood by helplessly. Which permitted Japan to occupy Manchuria and now lets it threaten the rest of China. Which lets Hitler defy the Versailles Treaty and rebuild the German war machine."

"Hitler." Phil snorted. "I knew you were going to bring him into it. You're obsessed with the man."

"You'd better think about him too," Bob retorted. "A world under Hitler—"

"Shit! There's not going to be a world under Hitler." Phil shook his head slowly. "What's wrong with you, Bob? The man's a joke with his Charlie Chaplin mustache. I'll admit he can push around those little countries in Europe, but that's all."

"If he's a joke, Phil, he's a goddamned lousy one. Look at what he's gotten away with already: He's built up his armed forces, remilitarized the Rhineland and made an alliance with fascist Italy. Right now he's playing war games over the corpse of Spain.

"God knows where he's going to strike next; but I'll tell you one thing: he won't be satisfied until he's taken over all of Europe."

"Maybe so," said Phil. "But that makes him Europe's fucking problem. Know what I mean? If they won't take care of him over there, why should we have to bother?"

"Because we won't have any choice. If Europe is ruled by Germany, America will be isolated throughout the world. No nation will dare to have anything to do with us unless the Nazis give their permission. Uncle Sam will turn into Peter Rabbit and the American eagle will become Hitler's pet canary."

"Bullshit," Phil said uncomfortably.

"Oh? Do you think we're respected now? Like hell we are. According to the rest of the world, we're too fat, smug, and rich to take a stand on anything."

"What do they want us to take a stand on?" Phil countered. "Saving the precious asses of England and France? We did that once. When we went to war for them in 1916. According to the rest of the world we're too damned selfish and insular to take a stand."

"We're not going to rush into anything," Bob admitted patiently. "But sooner or later it's going to happen. Like I say, we won't have any choice."

At the end of that argument, both brothers held the same positions that they'd held in the beginning. Each was convinced that he was right. But after a series of similar disputes, Phil began to have some second thoughts.

It wasn't until December, however, that he was convinced that the United States was eventually going to change its attitude. That was on December 12, 1937—the day on which the U.S. gunboat *Panay* was sunk by aircraft under the command of the Japanese Navy.

The attack, which took place on the great Yangtze River in China, shocked Americans. The Stars and Stripes had been flying at the time and there was no way for the Japanese not to have known what nation the gunboat belonged to. It looked suspiciously like a deliberate provocation, and there was even some talk about teaching Japan a lesson by setting up a naval blocade of its coastline.

Then the Japanese made an abject public apology and dismissed the officer held responsible for the incident. Everything went back to normal. American anger and resentment died down as quickly as they had risen.

There had been at least two aspects of the incident, however, which made Phil stop and think.

The first was the briefly furious reaction of his fellow countrymen. He would not have believed that the national mood could have turned to outrage so swiftly. And what happened then, he reasoned, could just as easily happen again.

The second aspect was the clever way that the *Panay* incident was being used by those who wanted the country to rearm.

Under the headline NO MORE PANAYS!, for instance, one editorial writer called for making the U.S. Navy the mightiest in the world: "So strong, indeed, that no other country will ever again dare to challenge the smallest of its ships." Another, even more extreme, editorialist suggested that the time might have come for the nation to think seriously about a peacetime draft.

There were few who took the draft idea seriously. This was America, after all, not Germany or France. But Congress *was* debating a Naval Expansion Act.

While Phil still believed that the country was going to keep out of any major war, it did seem clear that America was starting to prepare for the possibility of being dragged into one. A new era was beginning, in other words. An era in which national preparedness was no longer a dirty phrase.

The more Phil considered all of this, the more the possibilities excited him. New eras were always exciting times in which to live, he thought. It was then that great fortunes could be made by those who were clever enough or lucky enough to read the signs.

39

It was Napoleon who was supposed to have said it first: *an army travels on its stomach.*

Phil didn't think that saying went far enough. For a navy had to travel on its stomach also. And so did an air force. And a corps of marines. For no matter where he went or what he did when he got there, first of all a man had to eat. And in a country like America, that meant another man could make money by feeding him.

That was what Phil wanted for himself. The chance to make money by feeding an expanded armed forces.

He saw this as a great opportunity, one whose like he had never seen before and probably would not see again. It was a chance for his corporation to expand along with the military until it was transformed from one of a group of lesser food companies into a competitor of the great giants like General Foods or Del Monte. Or he might even get into meats, he thought. That would be something—ready-to-eat canned meats which could be carried into battle!

These ideas obsessed him to such an extent that he couldn't understand why everyone he talked to didn't get as excited by them as he did. But others—his plant managers, for instance, or his top salesmen—were far more dubious. Where he felt he would make a fortune, they foresaw nothing but problems.

This opposition would not have bothered Phil very much if Al Bocca had not agreed with it. But, as Phil found out when he requested a meeting to discuss his new plans, Al was definitely on the "anti" side.

Al listened carefully to everything that Phil had to say before glancing first at his nephew and then at two of his men who were in the room.

"Tell me something, Phil," Al began mildly. "Why do you want to bring the government into business with us? I've always found it wise to keep the feds as far away from me as I could.

"What do you think, Lew? Am I right? Or have the feds suddenly become good news?"

"I'd say that the feds are definitely bad news, Uncle Al."

"But—" Phil was frustrated. "I don't want to bring the government into our business. I just want to be able to sell to the Army and the Navy."

"And you don't think that would be bringing them in?" Al Bocca smiled sadly. "You're a bright fellow, Phil. But sometimes I have to admit you act like a kid. Let me explain something to you. Whenever you make a sale to the government— and I mean any sale—you are taking on fifty to a hundred bureaucrats as your not-so-silent partners."

Phil did his best not to let it bother him when Al's men snickered happily at their boss's remark.

"But it still may be worth it," Phil pointed out. "I can always hire people to deal with the bureaucracy. And this is the best way I can think of to expand the company."

"That's the part I don't get, Phil. I'll be honest with you. You keep talking about expanding and growing big. But you admit that all the important money will have to wait until Roosevelt can maneuver his pet bills through a reluctant Congress. Am I right?"

Phil nodded. "Yes. But FDR'll do it."

"I hope so, my friend." Al grinned slyly. "Personally I never had that much faith in politicians."

Once again Phil heard the derisive sound of snickers from Al's men.

"It's not just a matter of trust," he protested. "The Naval Expansion Act is almost sure to pass. And there are other bills already in the hopper."

"Yes?" Al Bocca seemed to reach a conslusion. "In that case let me make a suggestion which you can follow or not as you please."

He paused to stare straight at Phil.

"I've always told you that you were the boss, haven't I?"

"Yes, Al. You always have."

"But if you want my advice—"

"You know I do."

"Then here it is: You'll wait until that Naval Expansion Act gets through Congress and is signed by the president. Then— if you still feel you want to go ahead with it—you can try to work out a deal with the Navy. Don't go too crazy with it, though. Wait'll you see how the first deal is working out before you get involved in any more. *Capish,* my friend?"

"Absolutely, Al. I'll play it just that way. And thanks."

The Naval Expansion Act was signed into law on Tuesday, the seventeenth of May, 1938. By Wednesday, Phil was in contact with the Navy Department and making appointments to see people in charge of food procurement. A week later, he was stepping off the *Congressional Limited* and taking a taxi to Washington's Mayflower Hotel where he had rented a room.

His welcome at the Navy Department was a warm one. This puzzled him at first, but then he began to understand the reason: he had very little competition.

Most food suppliers, as it turned out, were not very anxious to sell to the Navy, which was still somewhat strapped for funds. The average food merchant preferred to work with the much larger and usually more reliable civilian market.

Phil thought this attitude was amazingly short-sighted. How could anyone assume that conditions were going to remain the same? If he'd felt that way about it, he himself would have remained in New York.

As it was, he was extremely honest with the people who ran the procurement offices and even tried to give them the benefit of his own experience in the food industry. If he helped them then, he thought they might help him later. He wanted to be one of the men that the Navy felt it could count on.

The procurement officers did appear grateful.

"The Navy owes you a great deal," said one of them, Commander Richard Allen. "I hope you won't be disappointed in us."

"I'm sure I won't be," Phil replied with a satisfied laugh.

But as things turned out, he almost was.

After returning to New York, Phil waited to be notified about the success of all his efforts in the capital. In order to break the ice with the Navy—to be invited in—he had made several small bids at absurdly low figures. He was certain that most of them would be accepted.

He had been promised some sort of an answer within six weeks. When that date went by without his hearing anything, he tried writing letters and placing phone calls. His letters went answered, however, and the people he called never seemed to be in. It was as if some sort of impregnable shield had been set up between him and the U.S. Navy.

The whole business reminded Phil of what had happened when he first tried to form his corporation. But then it had been caused by Al Bocca trying to teach him a lesson. He could not imagine who or what was messing things up now.

One thing he did feel sure about—it was not Al Bocca this time. First of all, he did not believe that Al had any influence with the Navy. Secondly it would have made no sense.

But what did make sense? Phil did not have a clue.

Finally, through sheer dogged persistence, he managed to get Commander Allen to come to the phone. He pleaded with the man to tell him what was going on.

"I don't want you to do anything about it," Phil assured him. "Even if you wanted to use your influence on my behalf, I'd ask you not to. But I surely don't think I deserve to keep getting this silent treatment."

"No you don't," the commander agreed. "You were a great help to me in Washington. Some of your advice will save the Navy a hell of a lot of money. You do deserve better treatment than what you've been getting."

"Then you tell me," Phil said. "What's wrong? I don't think you've gotten too many bids a great deal lower than mine."

"We haven't. Most of the bids have come in a lot over yours

In the normal course of events you would have been awarded the contracts some time ago. But as it is, the Navy is sitting on them until some sort of decision can be reached."

"But—why? What in hell's the problem?"

"I don't know all of it," Allen admitted. "And I'm not really supposed to talk about what I do know." The commander chuckled. "If you want to get real technical about it, I wasn't even supposed to have told you what I did."

"So who wants to get technical," Phil responded with what he hoped was an easy laugh.

"Not me," the commander replied agreeably. "And as long as I already told you that part, you might as well hear the rest."

Phil waited.

"It seems that a number of admirals checked up on your company and were not very happy with what they learned," Allen told him. "From what I understand, it's not you yourself that they object to. It's some of your associates. They don't believe it would be good for the Navy to become involved with them."

"Jesus!" Phil moaned.

There was a sinking feeling in the pit of his stomach. It was the Boccas, obviously. The Boccas and their friends. The Navy did not want to get involved with the underworld.

Well, he couldn't do anything about it. You don't kick Al Bocca out of your life because you suddenly find that he's bad for business. Not if you want to keep on living that life!

But the commander was still talking.

"How'd you ever get mixed up with people like that?" he wanted to know.

"Well, I—I guess it just happened . . ."

"Yeah, I know how it is. Things happen and then they come back to haunt you. Right?"

Phil grunted something. He wanted to stop the conversation; hang up the phone. What good was it doing him?

"It is a shame, though," Commander Allen continued "I wish there was something I could do to help. If they were ordinary leftists—like New Dealers, say. After all, we do have a New Deal administration . . ."

"Wait a minute!" Phil broke in insistently. "Repeat that, would you? About ordinary leftists, I mean."

"Yeah, but they're *not* ordinary leftists. Not from what I hear, anyway. Those admirals believe that you're mixed up with a bunch of commies!"

270

Phil was struggling to clear his mind. It was not the Boccas, then. Not the Boccas at all. Either the admirals didn't know about them or didn't mind them that much.

"Slow, now," he said. "Let me get this straight. The only thing that's holding me up are those people your admirals believe are communists?"

"Yeah. You could sure put it that way." Allen paused. "Of course this is all unofficial, you understand. I don't know anything officially."

"Sure," said Phil. But tell me something. *Unofficially*— what would happen if I got rid of all those people?"

"You can do that?"

"I don't know," Phil responded. "But let's just suppose I could. And then went ahead and did it. Would that do anything to help?"

"Maybe. If everyone thought you were sincere. The people I'm talking about are still upset that the Palmer Raids had to end in 1921. They'd like to see every radical in this country put in a big box and shipped to Russia."

"Look," said Phil, "if they're that right wing, I don't know if they'd approve of me either."

"Maybe not," Allen said with still another chuckle. "But as long as you're not a dyed-in-the-wool Red I don't think it would really matter. As far as I know they don't approve of their current commander-in-chief either. Yet they manage to get along with the president."

"But I'm not the president," Phil pointed out.

"You know what I mean."

"Yes, I do. And I can promise that I'm not a dyed-in-the-wool Red either. As a matter of fact I don't even agree with most of what my associates do. Just how I got involved with them is really a long story which I may tell you someday. But right now, I think we're about to come to a parting of the ways."

Phil said goodbye to the commander, hung up the phone, and dialed Sid Walters.

It was time for him to see his lawyer.

He met Sid for lunch on the following day. It was a long, slow business lunch which gave him plenty of time to explain the entire situation.

Sid listened intently, interrupting only to ask an occasional question.

"I think you're right," he said when his client was finished. "As a matter of fact, Phil, I was going to advise you to get rid of all those characters pretty soon in any event."

"Really?"

"Sure. They're not doing you any good these days. They've already served their purpose. All they can do now is hurt you."

"And you think we can get rid of them?"

"There's no 'think' about it. I know." Sid Walters sounded offended. "Didn't I tell you that I arranged for this when I was setting up the corporation for you?"

"So you did," Phil conceded.

He was annoyed at himself for not having guarded his tongue. He was always forgetting just how touchy Sid's ego really was. Now he was going to have to stroke it.

"I guess I was frightened that the law might have been changed or something," he admitted. "I should have known that it wouldn't matter. You'd be prepared either way."

Sid beamed as the compliment did its work.

"Semper paratus," he said. "When it comes to the law, I'm always prepared."

"And I'm lucky you are," Phil replied, thinking that another bit of stroking could not do any harm.

"So at any rate, my boy," Sid told him then, "this particular problem should be solved within the next several weeks. Unless I seriously miss my guess, all those groups—the radicals, the farm people, the labor groups—will be out of your hair by then. Of course they could delay things for us by choosing to go to court. But I don't think they will."

"Why not?"

"In the first place, because they'd lose. That I can guarantee. Any lawsuit would only be a nuisance. And we'll be able to avoid a series of nuisance suits by employing the old, tried-and-true technique of the carrot and the stick."

"Oh?"

"The carrot will be in the form of a sum of money which you will offer to anyone who'll leave quietly. It will be full payment for whatever past services they think they performed."

"And the stick?"

"I'm hoping that we won't even need to use a stick," Sid said earnestly. "But if we should, I think we both know who can be counted on to provide it."

Phil nodded. He was no more anxious to go into details than was Sid Walters. Indeed, he thought, they were both in similar

272

positions: they took advantage of violence—benefited from its use—while trying to insulate themselves from its operation. If Sid was more successful at this task, perhaps that was because he'd been around longer and had had time to develop more and thicker layers of insulation. Phil was still learning.

"I have a couple of other suggestions," Sid said.

"What are they?"

"Well, as long as we're going to get rid of your unwanted associates for you, it may be time to change the name of the company. Farmer-Labor Food Products won't mean very much without farm and labor people being involved. But it does have a socialistic sound. Like the Farmer-Labor party. That in itself might be enough to hurt you in certain circles. There's no sense at all in your being political."

"Yeah," said Phil. "I guess you're right."

He felt a sad reluctance, however. He was severing one more connection with Laura, he thought. And there weren't that many connections left.

If the lawyer noticed Phil's brief change of mood, he gave no sign of it.

"About the new name," he said. "How would you feel about Aronson Foods, Inc.?"

Phil felt flustered. And absurdly flattered. Oh well, he thought, so Sid Walters wasn't the only one with an ego.

"That—that would be nice."

"Good. Then it's settled." Sid Walters smiled briefly.

"Is there anything else?" Phil wanted to know. He moved his chair back slightly from the restaurant table. "Because, if there isn't, I really should get back to work."

"There is one more thing," Sid told him. "I've been thinking about this for several months, but I've hesitated to push you before I thought you were ready. Now I believe you may be."

Phil settled back in his chair again. He signaled the waiter to bring more coffee.

"Go ahead," he said.

"How would you like to go public?" Sid asked.

Phil lifted his coffee cup to try and conceal his surprise. He had never even considered anything like that.

He tried to stall: "You mean offer stock to the general public?"

"Why not?"

"Well . . ." Phil hesitated, but could think of no more delicate way to phrase his question. "What would Al Bocca say?"

"Mr. Bocca and I have already discussed the idea at some length. He's in favor of it. Though he's willing to leave the timing up to you and me."

Phil was incredulous: "You say he's going to let strangers into the operation?"

Sid smiled thinly: "I wonder if you really understand Mr. Bocca's position."

"What's that supposed to mean?"

"Let me put it this way: when Mr. Bocca invests in someone, he himself prefers to keep in the background. He wouldn't have invested in the man in the first place unless he trusted him to do a decent job. He doesn't see the need, therefore, to be constantly interfering in the normal, day-to-day management of things.

"Let's take your own case, Phil. How often did he do this with you?"

"Never. But—"

"The only times he did insist on being consulted was when you were about to make important decisions which could have affected the totality of his investment. Am I correct?"

"Yes, of course you are. But what has that to do with what we were talking about?"

"It has to do with Mr. Bocca staying in the background."

"And in order to do that, he's willing to let people he doesn't know into the corporation?"

"As investors, Phil. Only as investors. They surely won't control it. Control will remain with you and Mr. Bocca. Just the way it is now."

"I don't get it."

"Then listen carefully." Sid's voice was sounding its first note of impatience. "Aronson Foods will be a publicly owned corporation with, say, half a million shares distributed to a large number of people in all sections of the country. The company will be able to use the proceeds from the sale of those shares to expand its facilities and to compete for new orders.

"Okay so far?"

Phil nodded.

"Now, if things go as I plan," Sid went on, "control of some twenty percent of the shares would be enough to give a person control of the company. You and Mr. Bocca will have twice the required percentage—forty percent between you.

"Half of that forty percent—or twenty percent of the total— will be reserved for you, Phil. The other half will be divided between Mr. Bocca and certain persons and dummy corporations under his control. Mr. Bocca will probably not have more than five percent of the total under his own name."

"He doesn't want to call attention to himself?"

"Exactly. He doesn't want jealous people in government, for example, to punish the corporation when they are frustrated at not being able to punish him. He feels that his investment would be safer if something like that couldn't happen."

"I think I get it," Phil said. "The more anonymous he is, the better off he'll be."

"That's one way to put it. Yes. Of course, he will still be a very big investor. Anonymous or not."

"I understand," said Phil. "And I naturally plan to keep consulting with him on all major decisions."

"That's something I would strongly advise," Sid said.

There was a brief silence.

"What do you say? Do you want me to go ahead with the plan? Would you like to go public?"

"Yes. Let's do it."

Sid smiled. "I'm glad. You're doing the right thing. This lunch is going to turn out so profitable for you, in fact, that I won't feel a single twinge of regret when I let you pick up the check."

40

As Phil grew ever more successful, it became important to him that his family reflect that success. It helped reinforce the changes in his own lifestyle to have them change their lifestyles as well.

And they did live better now. He saw to that. He moved them into a new apartment building near his own place on Central Park West. He hired a maid to help his mother and tipped the doormen and elevator operators to give his family good service.

He insisted that his parents start dressing well again. His father would buy one suit a year at Tripler or Brooks Brothers, while his mother would purchase all her things at Saks Fifth Avenue or B. Altman.

But though both his parents could now dress well, only his mother would accept Phil's invitations to dinner or to the theater. His father hardly wore his new clothing at all, and refused to go any place where wearing it would be appropriate.

Phil was hurt by this. He took it as more evidence of how his father resented his success.

"Your father today is living in a world of his own," his mother said with a little shrug. "He refuses to *comprehend* your success. So how could he resent it?"

"But, Mama—"

"You want to know when he *most* resented your success?" Phil's mother continued. "When you started making good with that food store. That sort of success he could understand. You were a merchant, like he used to be a merchant. But now that you've gotten so big, he simply refuses to believe it. He'd rather hide the facts from himself."

"What do you mean hide? He must know that I bring home money."

"Oh, yes. He knows that. But how much money you make or what you do or how important you are . . . that he doesn't want to know."

"And you say he doesn't resent me?"

"Not like he did." Sophie hesitated briefly. "He still resents God, of course. For destroying his business."

"Why won't he come out to dinner with us, then?"

"Why won't he take me out to dinner alone?" Sophie countered. "You give us enough money so that he can."

"You tell me, Mama. Why?"

"Because he'd rather stay in his room and read. The only times he'll go out at all, nowadays, is either to take a walk with Naomi or—once in a while—to visit an old friend who'll sit around with him and discuss world politics. That's all."

Though Phil was far from certain that Sophie was right about her husband's lack of resentment, he decided to let the subject drop. It was far too depressing.

At least his mother enjoyed it when he took her to dinner. He could be grateful for that. *And* for the fact that she no longer brought up the subject of going back to work for Leonard Abel.

He tried to help his brother and sister in different ways and with varying degrees of success.

The main thing he did for Bob, he believed, was accomplished during the preceding winter. That was when Phil convinced his brother to accept a scholarship he'd been offered to Harvard Law School.

Bob was in his junior year of college then, and was growing weary of student life. He had just about made up his mind to go through his senior year, take his B.A. degree, and go to work. If he didn't go into business with Phil, he said, he was sure he could get a job teaching French or German. If not that, he might even coach high-school boxing. The main thing was that he'd be earning his own keep and would no longer feel that he was being a drain on Phil.

But Phil would have none of this.

"You mean you'd be a drain on me if you went to law school?" Phil asked incredulously.

"Well, yes."

"But you'd be going on a scholarship."

"But that's just tuition and a few expenses, Phil. You know that. You're the one who'll feed me. Clothe me. Just like you've been doing for the past five years."

"I guess you're right at that," Phil shot back. "I have been feeding and clothing you for the past five years. And now you're trying to turn it into a waste!"

"Huh? What waste? What are you talking about?"

"You tell me: What do you think it would be if you went this far with your studies, and then quit before you went as far as you *could* go?"

"Hey, a B.A. isn't all that bad."

"A B.A.'s terrific, Bob. It's a lot more than I have. But you can do more. All you have to do is to stick with it for three more years instead of one and you'll have a Harvard fucking law degree!"

"Well, but—"

"That's 1941!" Phil persisted. "You hear that. In 1941 you can pass your bar exam and be on your own. Bob, I beg you: *Don't throw this chance away!*"

In the end, Phil's logic won the day. Bob was convinced. He was going to become a lawyer.

As for Phil, he was delighted. It was wild. His kid brother was going to have a law degree from Harvard!

Naomi was something else again. Naomi was a puzzle.

What Phil wished for his sister was what he wished for himself and for his brother—success. His experiences in the jungle-like world in which he found himself had convinced him that there was no easy choice: you either fought to carve out a place for yourself or you were brought down and destroyed by stronger beasts who were carving out their own places at your expense. Success in such a world meant first owning as much territory as possible, and then securing it from attack.

Which was one reason he was pushing Bob into law school. A Harvard law degree would be a potent weapon in the fight for survival.

But what should he do about Naomi? Should he try to convince her to prepare herself for a good profession?

If Phil dismissed that notion, it was not merely because she was female. He was well aware that—despite the Depression—increasing numbers of women were entering such male bastions as medicine, journalism, and the law. It had been Laura who'd made him aware of that. But Laura had also made him aware that a woman applicant to a law or medical school had to be a great deal better qualified than the men she was competing against.

Which seemed to let Naomi out. Even if she had the brains (and Phil thought that a sister of his—no matter how silly she acted—would have lots of brains), she didn't have the desire to do the extra work. She was bored by school and didn't mind saying so. She neglected homework in favor of boys; and when forced to stay home and study, she'd try to hide a film magazine in her textbook in order to read the latest gossip about Charles Boyer or Clark Gable or Ginger Rogers while listening to Glenn Miller's band on the radio.

So how could she achieve success? The only way, Phil believed, was the tried and true way of marrying the right man.

And why shouldn't she? She was already turning into a beautiful woman. That and the fact that she was Phil Aronson's sister, he thought immodestly, should give her a head start in any future marriage sweepstakes.

But though beauty was a great help in marrying the right man, it was not everything. The kind of man Phil wanted for his sister would not marry a slut—no matter how good-looking she was or how rich and powerful was her brother.

Of course, Naomi wasn't a slut. She was still a kid only fourteen years old. But she was heading down what her brother believed was a dangerous path. She was still hanging around with the wrong boys, for example. Even her mother couldn't put a stop to that. She was still playing touch football with them, still play-fighting with them, still—so Phil thought sourly—giving them cheap thrills.

That had to stop, he vowed. And quickly. His sister was not going to get the sort of reputation which—if it clung to her for the next several years—could destroy her chances to make the right sort of marriage.

But when he went into Naomi's room in order to talk to her about this subject, she grew indignant.

"Why don't you leave me alone?" she said. "I haven't done anything wrong. You're mean to think I have."

"I never said you did something wrong," Phil countered. He was trying to force himself to show patience. "But these boys you go with. Suppose one of them gets the wrong idea about you. And suppose when you tell him to stop, he gets sore and won't do it?"

"Oh, yeah?" Naomi's green eyes glinted nastily. "I'd like to see someone try. I know how to hurt a boy real bad. Any boy who gets physical with me will be sorry!"

Phil was torn between admiration of his sister's feistiness (how like his own) and concern over her implied knowledge of masculine anatomy (who in hell had taught her?). Anyway, he thought, she shouldn't be so sure of herself.

"That's not the point," he said gruffly. "I don't want you to get a lousy reputation."

"Why, brother dear?" Naomi simpered. "Are you afraid it'll hurt *your* reputation?"

Phil lost his temper at that, and began shouting at her. Naomi shouted back and Phil stormed out of the room wondering (again!) why his sister was the one person in this world he couldn't speak to for more than five minutes without ending up in a shouting match.

All of which did not change the fact that he felt he had to do something about her.

He considered the situation for several more days before coming up with an answer. When he did, however, it seemed such an obvious one that he wondered why he hadn't thought of it before.

If Naomi were musically inclined, he told himself, he would send her to a good music school. Since he expected her to make a good marriage, therefore, he should remove her from the New York City public high school she attended and send her to a place which would give her the sort of social training he wanted her to have—a first-rate girls' boarding academy, in other words, which would keep her uninhibited private life under strict control while she learned the skills needed to be a cultivated lady.

But if Phil regarded this as an ideal solution, his mother was not so sure. And Naomi herself was adamantly opposed.

"I won't go!" she cried when Phil first told her of the plan. They were sitting in his parents' living room with both his mother and father present.

"You will," Phil said.

"I won't. And if you make me, I'll run away. Or else I'll flunk out on purpose."

"And where do you think you'll go then?"

"I don't care. Maybe I'll go to work for a 'five and dime.'"

"It's not that easy to get a job in Woolworth's," Phil reminded her. "Or anywhere else, for that matter."

"Then I'll be a streetwalker!" Naomi announced, theatrically.

"Naomi!" her mother gasped.

"Don't worry, Mama," Phil said. "She doesn't mean it. She's trying to scare us."

"I do mean it!" Angry tears were starting to form in the corners of Naomi's eyes. "You'll see. You'll have it on your conscience."

"Why do you want to make her unhappy?" Phil's father interjected. He was speaking for the first time that afternoon. "Let her stay where she is."

Phil could feel the resentment build inside him. The old man was as bad as Naomi. They both refused to understand.

"I don't want to make her unhappy," he said tightly. "I want her to learn to be a lady."

"That's why you're going to send her off to a boarding school? So she'll learn to be a lady?"

"I thought I explained . . ."

"Your mother never went to a boarding school. Don't you think she's a lady?"

Realizing now that his father had been setting a sly rhetorical trap for him, Phil opened his mouth to explode.

But his mother managed to speak first. "Can't we compromise? Suppose Naomi was willing to go to a good private day-school here in the city? What would you say to that, Phil?"

"A *co-ed* school," Naomi put in fiercely.

"All girls," her brother snapped. "You're with boys all the

time when you're not in school. It wouldn't hurt you to spend *some* time away from them. Maybe that way you might even learn something."

Sophie called her daughter over to her.

"Did you ever meet the Weissmans, Phil?" she asked her son. "Shirley and Harry Weissman?"

Phil shook his head. He didn't know them.

"Harry Weissman is a stockbroker. An important man."

"I never liked him," her husband put in.

Sophie ignored the interruption.

"I met Shirley Weissman at the hairdresser's the other day," she told Phil. "And she said that her daughter, Maddie, is going to a very fine all-girls school."

Naomi wrinkled up her nose. "Maddie Weissman is a goop."

"She is a very sweet girl," her mother chided. "I only wish you had her manners."

"What school is she going to?" Phil asked.

"The Elvira Laddbourne Academy. It's very highly thought of."

Phil frowned. He had wanted to remove his sister from the local scene; tear her away from the crowd she hung around with. If she went to Laddbourne she would still be able to be with them—only after school.

"I still think a sleep-away school would be better," he said. "A finishing school."

"Oh, no—" Naomi began to wail. But her mother took her hand and she subsided.

"Try it this way for a while, Phil," Sophie said. "Please, I'm sure Naomi will try to do better."

"I will."

Phil knew that he was beaten. "All right," he agreed. "We'll try it."

It did not take long for Phil to decide he'd been wrong to have given in that day. Naomi didn't change. She still hung around with the same crowd, and her final grade average for the school year of 1937-38 was even worse than he had feared.

Phil felt that he'd been made a sucker of. It was for the last time though, he swore to himself. She could promise to do better until she was blue in the face and it wouldn't make any difference. He had already made an arrangement with a strict and proper finishing school. Naomi would positively be going there in the fall.

In the meantime, though, there was her summer vacation. And this was proving to be a strain on everyone. Naomi was free on weekdays, now, not merely on weekends. And she was growing more and more secretive about how she was spending her time.

As June came to a close, Phil began seeing some changes in his sister's way of life. She was not hanging around with her old crowd as much as she used to, and she had apparently given up such rough sports as touch football.

At first Phil was pleased by these changes. But then he began to wonder. Had Naomi given up playing with boys because she was starting to play with men? The more he observed her, the more he feared that his suspicions were right. She was too much at ease with herself these days. Too cool. She had the self-contained, highly amused look of a woman with a delicious secret.

But she was not a woman. She was still a kid. Not just his kid sister, but a *kid!* And if some man was sticking it into her, Phil would find him and have his ass!

But *how* would he find him? Or even find the proof that he was correct about what was going on? For Phil could not completely disregard the possibility that his suspicions of his sister were products of his own mind.

What he would have liked to do was to spy on her. Simply follow her at a safe distance until he had collected enough evidence to be sure one way or the other.

But that was far too impractical. Even if he were not afraid that Naomi might catch him at it—and she was not unobservant; in fact, she was pretty damn sharp!—he was simply too busy. He had a large organization to run.

So he made it a point to drop in at his parents' place a few times a week and talk to Naomi. He feared that she was too clever to reveal anything to him, but felt that there was no harm in trying.

"Where did you go today?" he might ask when he saw her come into the apartment in the evening.

"Coney Island," she might reply.

"Terrific. Who with?"

"Just some girls from school."

"Did you swim there?"

"Sure. The ocean was great. Then we changed in the dressing rooms and went over to Steeplechase Park to go on the rides. It was fun."

"I'll bet it was," said frustrated Phil.

"We had hot dogs at Nathan's for lunch," the girl said.

"Yeah. They're good there."

It all sounded so innocent. And maybe in this case it really was. But Phil was still certain there was a man involved with his kid sister. And he was more determined than ever to find the son-of-a-bitch and take care of him.

So he kept after Naomi—though without getting anywhere.

After a while, his own inability to learn the facts led him to consider hiring a private detective. But that would have to be a last resort. He had heard stories about private eyes, and what he'd heard he didn't like. He didn't want to trust one of them with his sister's reputation. Not if he could help it.

Then he had another idea.

41

Back in the fall of 1936, when Phil realized how much of his time was being taken up by the food corporation, he told Al Bocca that he could not keep supervising the bookmaking operation.

Al agreed with Phil—he had been thinking along similar lines himself. He even had a man who was anxious to take it over. The man's name was Artie Macchio.

Artie turned out to be a tough little hustler who was not too proud to ask Phil to show him some of his own more successful techniques. One of those techniques was to hire bright, ambitious kids who had dropped out of high school in order to make money.

Phil was thinking about those kids now. He felt sure that they could pick up some word on what was doing with his sister.

He called Artie and asked him to do him the favor of assigning some of his junior bookies to the task.

"It doesn't have to interfere with the work they're doing for you." he said. "And I'll be glad to give 'em a few bucks for nosing around."

Artie felt that he still owed Phil one for being so friendly when he took over. Now he didn't hesitate.

"Sure," he said. "Glad to help."

It did not take long. Artie phoned Phil in less than a week to say that he had some news.

"It's not very good news, though," he said. "I'm sorry."

"Go ahead. Let's hear it."

"She's been making out with a guy named Marty Opper who has a small place off Tenth Avenue in the Fifties." He gave Phil the address. "Opper's about thirty—thirty-five years old. He's a small-time drifter who runs a floating crap game."

"Jesus!" Phil said.

"Yeah. It stinks, don't it." Arite paused. "Listen. There's some more. The other stuff I got right away, but I thought you might want something about his background."

"Yeah. Thanks."

"I checked with other sources," Artie explained in his rough, gravelly voice, "and word is that he comes from Detroit. I understand he was married twice there. First wife left him with their kid—a girl. The second's in the jug. From what I hear, she's taking a rap for something Opper did."

"Jesus," Phil said again. "He sounds like a real prince, doesn't he?"

"Prince of the shithouse, maybe." Artie laughed. "Do you want some help with this?"

"I can handle it," Phil replied dismissively.

"Sure you can," Artie told him. "I know you can. I just thought it might save everyone some trouble if a couple of boys visited him and advised him to go back to Detroit. Know what I mean?"

Phil suddenly realized what must have happened.

"That was Al Bocca's idea, wasn't it?" he asked.

"Well . . . yes."

"When did you tell him about my sister?"

"When I started getting the lowdown on Opper and learned what kind of a geek he was. I had to phone Al, then. You know that's true."

"I do know it," Phil agreed. "You did the only thing you could."

"Thanks . . ."

"I think I know what's troubling Al," Phil went on. "He's

284

afraid I might do something too stupid about Opper. Get myself in trouble with the law. Right?"

"Yeah, Phil. You know what Al thinks of you. You're almost like a son to him. He doesn't want you to get hurt."

"I understand that," Phil said. "And I'm grateful."

Phil also understood that Al had a great deal of money invested in him now. He did not want to endanger that investment simply because Phil might be crazy enough to kill the bastard who was screwing his underage sister.

But that was one thought Phil was going to keep to himself. However skeptical Al might be about the motives of others, it made him furious to have anyone question his own.

"Don't worry, Artie," he said crisply over the phone. "I'll speak to Al myself. In the meantime, stay away from Opper."

"Well . . . are you sure it'll be all right? I thought maybe today—"

"It'll be fine, buddy. I give you my word."

"That's good enough for me."

Phil said goodby to Artie and hung up the phone. He sat behind his desk thinking for several minutes. Then he asked his secretary to place a call to Al Bocca.

When Al came on the phone, Phil told him about his conversation with Artie.

"It's a terrible thing about your sister," Al said with sonorous sympathy. "Young girls today have no respect for decency. They don't know what they're doing. They're still babies and they want to act like fallen women."

"You're right," Phil said.

"It's a terrible problem," Al went on. "And I don't know what to tell you to do. If you were of my faith, I'd advise placing the girl in a convent where the holy sisters could straighten her out. But this way, I don't know.

"There are no Jewish convents, are there?"

"None that I know of," Phil said.

"That's a shame. I know it's none of my business, but perhaps you people ought to start some."

"Hey, Al, that's not a bad idea. But in the meantime, I'm going to send Naomi off to a strict all-girls boarding school. Starting this fall."

"This fall, you say."

"Yes. So it's only the summer I have to worry about. This creep, Opper."

"You are right to call him a creep, Phil. A man like that shouldn't be walking the streets. Imagine, a man in his thirties taking advantage of a—"

Al broke off suddenly.

"How old is your sister again?" he asked.

"Not quite fifteen."

"Taking advantage of a fourteen-year old girl," Al Bocca continued. "In the old days, we would have known how to deal with him. We would've taken him someplace quiet and cut off his balls. That's what you do with creeps like that. Fix 'em so they won't go after young girls ever again."

"Yes, Al. You're right."

"But unfortunately, my friend, times have changed." Al's deep sigh came through the receiver. "We don't teach the old harsh lessons in the old harsh way any more. Today we make do with warnings."

"Warnings?"

"I'll have a couple of my soldiers pay a call on him, Phil. They'll explain to him what could happen if he keeps seeing your sister and advise him to go back home to Detroit. I don't think he will ignore the warning. But if he does . . . then we can speak of punishments.

"And so my friend. Do you agree?"

Phil wasn't sure how he should proceed. He wished he were in the room with Al, now—looking at him.

It was his own fault, too. He had deliberately chosen to talk to Al on the telephone instead of asking to see him in person. He had wanted to avoid the steady, searching glare of Al's cold, gray eyes and the chorus-like effect of Al's men constantly saying he was right.

Now though, he thought he'd been wrong. He needed to see Al in order to judge how he himself was coming across.

"It's great of you to make the offer," he responded carefully. "I really do appreciate it. The only thing is, I'd rather handle it myself."

"That could be foolish, my friend. That could be very foolish indeed. You could get yourself into serious trouble. There are too many people who know about this person and your sister. If he should be killed—even in an accident—you're the logical person for the cops to question."

"I know that, Al," Phil replied. "And I hope you don't think that I'm stupid enough to kill him. But if there is to be a warning, I'd rather deliver it myself. By hand."

Al chuckled. But when he spoke, his tone was serious.

"Think, now," he said. "Is this what you really want?"

Phil had a flash of insight. He knew how to phrase his appeal now, how to couch it in such a way that Al wouldn't be able to turn it down.

"Al," he said intensely, "Naomi is my sister. She is flesh of my flesh. How could I call myself a man if I let anyone— even someone as close to me as Lew or yourself—take care of this business for me. Don't you understand, Al? This is something I have to do personally."

"Yes," Al Bocca said heavily. "Sure, I understand. When it comes to family, a man has to do what he has to do. Go ahead. I won't interfere with you."

"Thanks, Al."

"Sure. But be careful, *mio figliòccio*. You hear me? Be careful."

42

By six-thirty the following morning, careful Phil, Al Bocca's honorary godson, was standing outside the building in which Marty Opper lived. He wanted to get the feel of the place before he entered it. He wanted to see if it was really as rundown and unprotected as he'd thought it would be when he learned the address.

Phil was planning a surprise for Opper—and he was making certain that it was a surprise. He did not want Opper to have any time at all to think about fighting back.

The building was precisely as Phil had imagined it. It was old, with a faded brick exterior and hallways so filthy that one could not even make a good guess as to what color it had been painted all those years ago.

He thought of his sister coming here—actually entering this slimy hangout of bums and winos, pimps and whores—and his fury mounted.

The stupid little bitch—visiting a dump like this to see an

asshole like Opper. No matter how young she was, she should have been smarter than that. Some people were born with the smarts, Phil thought. Naomi was born with the dumbs!

He smiled grimly to himself. As lousy as this hole was, it suited this morning's purpose fine. People here would be apt to mind their own business and ignore strange noises from other apartments. Like Opper's apartment!

He tried to ignore the disgusting odors of mold and garbage and overripe humanity as he climbed the three flights of stairs to the floor on which Opper lived.

He thought suddenly of Laura's building and how different that had been. The former factory might have been older than this and was certainly less sound structurally. But Laura and her friends had kept it scrupulously clean.

When Phil reached the fourth floor, he saw that the hall was not lighted. This would help also. It meant that even if Opper had a peephole, he could not peer out and see who was there or how he was dressed.

He used matches to find apartment "D" and pressed his finger against the doorbell.

He had no idea whether the bell was going to work or not. He hoped that it did. For though he did not believe that banging on Opper's door would stimulate the curiosity of the other dwellers here, he did not want to make noise unless he was forced to.

At last he heard a voice from within the apartment. It sounded confused—like a man who'd had too rough a night to be roused this early from bed. That was one of the things Phil had hoped for.

"All right," the voice grumbled truculently. "You can stop the fucking ringing now. What do you want?"

"Western Union, sir." Phil said politely. "I have a telegram for a Mr. Opper."

"Yeah, that's me. Shove it under the door and get lost."

"I'm sorry, sir. Company regulations. You'll have to sign for it."

"Yeah, yeah . . . okay."

Phil could hear the locks being turned. He grinned in anticipation.

He was surprised that Opper was falling so easily for such an ancient trick. He had thought he might have to do some fast talking in order to gain entry. But Opper was probably not at his best this early, nor could he have had any idea he was in jeopardy.

The door began to open outward. Had it been one of those which swung inward, Phil would have placed his shoulder against it as soon as he saw it move. This way, Opper had an extra second or so of comparatively pain-free existence before the opening was wide enough for Phil to step through and paralyze his Adam's apple with his thumb.

Opper's eyes widened in shock and pain and sickness. He clutched at his throat and collapsed soundlessly while Phil carefully shut and bolted the door.

Phil turned to look down at him. He was wearing a yellow silk robe which billowed about him as he lay there gasping for breath and trying to nurse his crippled throat.

Opper tried to say something. But though his lips moved, he could not manage an intelligible whisper.

Phil assumed that Opper wanted to ask him who he was and what he was doing there.

"I'm Naomi Aronson's brother," he said. He grinned nastily. "You know Naomi Aronson, don't you? She's that piece of fourteen-year-old jailbait you've been fucking."

Opper's eyes grew still sicker. He produced some croaking sounds which Phil could not decipher.

"Are you trying to say that you don't know my sister?" Phil asked.

Opper shook his head.

"Good. I wouldn't like it if you tried to lie to me."

Phil looked him over appraisingly. He was a tall man with a dark complexion and straight black hair. Some strands of black chest hair showed through where his robe was parted below the throat. He might have been a handsome man a moment or so before Phil had entered his apartment.

"Get up," Phil said now. "I want to talk to you. Sit in that chair."

Opper got to his hands and knees and crawled over to the chair Phil had indicated. He tried to pull himself up and shook his head to show that he couldn't make it.

Phil prodded his buttocks with his foot.

"Try again," he said.

Opper pulled himself into the chair and sat there. His hands went again to his throat.

Phil smiled his approval.

He turned his eyes away from Opper in order to briefly explore the living-room. It was simply and inexpensively furnished. In contrast to the building itself, however, everything here was clean and in good repair.

Phil wondered if that was his sister's doing—if, in addition to using her in bed, Opper was also using her to clean up the goddamn apartment.

He was about to turn again—to ask the bitter question— when he heard some soft noises from the rear. He glanced toward the hall which apparently led from the bedroom.

"Hey, honey," a female voice called. "What in hell's going on out there?"

It was not Naomi. That was the first thing which registered with Phil. It was not his sister who had spent last night here with Marty Opper.

It was an older, blonde woman who came sleepily out of the hallway, a hand over her mouth to stifle a yawn. She was on the short side, Phil saw, her hair was frizzled and unkempt, her face pale and somewhat blotchy. She gave a start as she noticed Phil and pulled her robe tighter.

"Who are you?" she demanded. "Where's Marty?"

"I'm someone who dropped in for a visit," Phil replied evenly. "But what are you doing here? Are you a regular? Or are you just a one-night stand?"

The blond drew herself up and stuck out her chest until she reminded Phil of a pouter pigeon.

"You've got one hell of a nerve!" she huffed indignantly. "Who do you think you're talking to?"

She kept looking about for a protector.

"Marty? . . ." she went on to call. "Who is this jerk? Where are you, honey?"

"Marty's right over there." Phil pointed toward the armchair. "He's not in such good shape, though."

The blonde rushed over to Opper. She reached down to touch him, but his hoarse croaks made her shudder and withdraw. When she turned back to Phil, all the indignation had fled from her face and fear had taken its place.

"What—what did you do to him?"

"He'll live," Phil said flatly. "What's important now is who the hell are you?"

"Sadie . . ." the blonde replied in a quavering voice. "Sadie Trevor. I'm nobody, really. Nobody. I don't count."

"That's what I want to find out," Phil said. "How much you do count.

"Are you one of his regular women?"

Sadie shrugged, then shook her head from side to side. "No. I mean, I been here twice before, but that's not regular, is it?"

"How long've you known him?"

"A month, maybe. I met him in a bar. My old man's away, you know what I mean, and—"

"In jail?"

"Yeah. And—with him being away, you know how it is. A girl gets horny..."

Phil nodded slowly. He was sure she was telling the truth, now. And would continue to do so. She was far too frightened of him to make up lies.

"And you've only been here three times altogether?"

"Yeah, three times." Tears were starting to form in her eyes. "That's all—I swear."

"Who else comes up here?"

"Huh?"

"His other women? Do you know any of them?"

"Well, no..." She saw Phil begin to get angry again and amended her statement. "I mean, I've seen a couple. But I don't know any of them."

"The ones you've seen," Phil went on inexorably. "Tell me about them."

"Well...there's one. She's real young, you know. Almost like she's in her teens."

"Go on," Phil prodded gently as Sadie came to a halt. "What does she look like."

"Well, I only saw her once up close. That was when Marty happened to bring her into a coffee joint and I was there, too. But she had a real cute figure. Know what I mean? And black hair. And—and her eyes were green."

Phil swallowed. So much rage was burning inside him now that he felt as if he were going to explode.

"Do you know her name?" he asked.

"No...but I know what he called her."

"What's that?"

"'Jailbait.' Kind of cute, huh? It's like a pet name. I think he likes her best of anyone."

"So how come you stayed here last night instead of her?" Phil asked tightly. "If he likes her so much?"

"It's her family." Sadie was still pathetically anxious to tell

291

everything. "Marty says she's scared to stay here. Her brother's some kind of big shot who'd maybe have her killed or beat up if he knew about them."

"Or maybe have him killed?" Phil suggested between clenched teeth. "Or maybe even kill him, himself?"

"Jesus..." A slowly growing comprehension spread over the blonde's face. "Are you?...Jesus!"

Phil turned his back on her in order to face Marty who was still hunched over in the armchair.

"What do you say, Marty. Is that what I should do? Or would you rather I killed 'Jailbait' and let you go?"

Opper's face was a mask of fear and sickness. He clutched feverishly at his throat as he made some more gagging sounds. He motioned for Phil to come closer.

"Jesus!" Sadie was repeating from behind him. "Jesus...don't kill him!"

As Phil responded to Opper's gesture, Opper slowly drew back his knees. He gauged the distance carefully. Then—with and explosive outpouring of patiently husbanded strength—he aimed his unshod feet precisely at Phil's groin.

And missed as Phil swiveled and sidestepped as gracefully as a matador avoiding the charge of a bull.

Phil laughed now and grabbed Opper's extended legs. He'd been expecting some kind of dirty trick and was pleased to have been proved right. It made it so much easier for him to do what he was doing.

He jerked Opper from the chair and twisted his legs around so that he lay face down on the floor. He knelt on top of the man—his knees pressing into Opper's back—then leaned over and hooked his powerful hands under Opper's chin.

Opper's head and shoulders came up off the floor. His back arched unnaturally. He let out a terrible lost and croaking scream.

"I could snap your spine now," Phil told him. "Just like that. It would be fucking easy."

Sadie cried out from somewhere in the room.

"You'll kill him!" she shrieked. "Don't kill him!"

Phil sensed, rather than saw, a movement from behind him. He released Opper, rolled to one side and scrambled to his feet even as Sadie was struggling with the heavy lamp she was trying to swing at his head.

He took the lamp from her and backhanded her hard across the face so that she stumbled back and fell against a wall. Her robe opened up and she burst into tears.

292

"That was fucking stupid," Phil said.

"You were going to kill him," she wailed.

"Shit. If I'm going to kill him, I'm going to kill him. You wouldn't stop me."

The blonde cringed at the words and pulled the robe closed again to cover her large, pendulous breasts.

Phil gave her a glance of disgust—and wondered what he was going to do.

He was not going to kill Opper. That much he knew already. Killing the man who lay belly down on the floor—too frightened and weak to move, unable to speak—would not only be a mistake, it would almost be redundant. For all practical purposes, the son-of-a-bitch was dead already—at least here in New York.

"Get up," Phil said.

There was no movement. A muffled sob came from the man on the floor.

"Better do what I say," Phil advised. "If I kick your ass this time, I won't stop there."

Opper struggled to his hands and knees. He reached behind him with one hand in order to touch himself where he hurt.

"My back," he said in a broken whisper. "I—I think it's broken. . . ."

"Bullshit," Phil said harshly. He grabbed the hand, gave it a twist and jerked Opper to his feet.

Opper's face turned white. He half gagged with the pain and his eyes watered.

"It may be a little sprained," Phil conceded with a nasty grin. "But that's all. When you think about it, Opper, you're a lucky guy. I could've done something vicious to you. Like putting your nuts in a nutcracker."

"Oh, my God," Opper croaked.

Phil laughed. "So you can see what a nice guy I am for not doing it."

He turned to the woman who was still cringing against the wall. She seemed nearly as frightened as Marty Opper.

"Your clothes are in the bedroom?" he asked.

"Yes, I—"

"Go back there and get dressed."

Sadie shot Phil a look of gratitude and retreated to the rear of the apartment.

"But keep the door open," he called after her. "I want to know just where you are."

He regarded Opper who was still nursing his back and his throat. "I want you to write a note to my sister. Where do you keep your paper and a pen?"

"I think I left some . . . in the kitchen. On the counter . . ."

Phil found some five-and-dime stationary there along with a cheap fountain pen. He brought them into the living room and placed them on a low table.

"Here's what you're going to say," Phil told Opper. "And I want this word for word. Understand?"

Marty nodded fearfully.

"What do you call her again?" Phil growled. "'Jailbait'?"

"I—"

"Okay. So that's how you'll begin: 'Dear Jailbait.'" He waited for Opper to pick up the fountain pen and start to write. "'Dear Jailbait, by the time you get this note I'll be on my way out of New York City. I am not giving you my new address, or even telling you what city or state I will be living in. I ask you not to try and find me. I plan to be living with a woman there, and it would be embarrassing if you showed up.'"

Phil waited for Marty to finish. Then he grabbed the note-paper, blew on it until the ink was dry, and read it through.

"I guess that covers everything," he said. "Sign your name at the bottom and I'll stick it in an envelope."

Marty did as he was told.

"About . . . leaving town," he said sickly as he handed the paper back. "Do you really . . . ?"

"Yeah," Phil said. "I really. Take a last look around. When you leave this place with me this morning, you're not coming back."

"But I—I . . ."

"This is what I'm going to do," Phil told him. "I am going to buy everything in this goddamned dump for one hundred and fifty bucks. It may not be worth that much, or it may be worth more. I don't give a shit. One-fifty is what you're going to get."

"I—"

"Point number two," Phil went on. "I'm giving you an extra fifty to buy yourself a ticket out of town. I don't care where you go, understand, as long as you don't come back here. Ever."

"But—I can't just . . ."

"You'll do what you're told," Phil said dangerously. "I know all about you, asshole. I know you run a little, tinhorn floating crap game. I know you've been married twice. I even know you have a daughter from your first marriage who must be about the same age as my sister. Right?"

Marty looked steadily at the floor.

"So if I ever hear of your setting foot inside the boundaries of New York City after this morning, I'm going to turn you over to some people who aren't nearly as squeamish as I am. They actually enjoy cutting off a man's pecker and stuffing it into his mouth! And that's before they kill him."

A bit of saliva ran down Opper's mouth and he began to shake with fear. Phil found it more difficult to keep on hating him. He was almost too spineless and disgusting to hate.

"Another thing," Phil said. "You're never going to brag to anyone that you made out with my sister. In fact, you're not even going to speak her name again. Because I'm just liable to hear about that, too."

Opper moaned and nodded. He was not just moaning in pain any more, but in submission.

Phil stood up and peered down the hallway that led to the bedroom. "Aren't you dressed yet?" he called to Sadie.

"I'm coming out now. I was just putting on some makeup."

Sadie appeared wearing a green skirt and sweater combination that was slightly too small for her. She had too much rouge and lipstick on, and her eyelids looked blue from mascara.

"Can I go now?" she asked Phil. She was still wary of him, though a bit less terrified than she'd been before she'd put on her clothing.

"Sit down. We'll wait for lover-boy to get dressed and all leave together."

"Well, I . . . All right."

Marty Opper got shakily but obediently to his feet. "Are we . . . coming back here . . . ?"

"No," said Phil.

Sadie looked puzzled, but did not ask either of the men for an explanation.

"Should I pack, then?" Opper asked.

Phil checked his wristwatch. He was feeling impatient and was anxious to get going. "Do you have any suitcases back there?"

"Well . . . yes."

"You get dressed. Sadie and I'll stuff everything we can in one of them. In your condition," he added sardonically, "you shouldn't carry any more than one suitcase."

43

It was about twenty minutes later when Phil placed Marty and Sadie in a taxicab. He gave the driver a generous two dollars and told him to take the woman wherever she wanted to go, but to leave Marty off at the Greyhound bus terminal in the West Fifties.

When Opper entered the cab, he was still moaning and complaining. He had Sadie carry his suitcase for him, groaned that his back hurt too much for him to take a bus trip, and whined—probably untruthfully—that his furniture had cost a good deal more than what Phil was paying for it.

Phil did not sympathize. He handed Opper four crisp fifty dollar bills, told him he was lucky to get anything, and reminded him of what would happen if he showed up again in New York.

Phil watched the taxi pull away and stared after it for a moment. He didn't know or care where Opper was going, though he suspected it might be Detroit. He wondered briefly if Sadie would be leaving with him. She'd be a goddamn fool if she did, Phil thought, even though it wouldn't surprise him. Her old man was in the clink and Opper had the kind of looks that women went for. It could be a case of any port in a storm.

But Sadie Trevor's problems were no more his business now than Opper's were. He was concerned about his sister.

He looked for another taxi, didn't see one, and began to walk. He found himself fingering Opper's letter to Naomi, which he had placed in his jacket pocket. He wondered if it had been such a good idea, after all. If it would, in fact, do the trick.

There had been a point in Opper's apartment when he'd considered phoning Naomi and forcing Opper to talk to her. That way he would actually tell her he was leaving for parts unknown and not just put it down on a piece of paper. It could have been more convincing.

On the other hand, Phil had thought then, the sound of his sick, croaking voice would have aroused her sympathy. So he'd decided on the letter, after all.

And he was going to give it to her in person. They would discuss the situation face to face, rather than from the opposite ends of a telephone wire.

But what was he going to say to her?

Phil still had no idea. He didn't even know how he was going to react when he saw her. When he thought about what she had done, rage nearly overcame him. But then he remembered that she was only a kid and that Opper was a smooth-talking son-of-a-bitch with a clever line of talk that could hook females with far greater experience in life than Naomi.

So he began to feel sorry for her. Until he recalled that she was his—Phil Aronson's—sister; and that if she didn't have the equipment to deal with Opper on her own, she should have had the sense to come to him.

Which was when he grew angry all over again.

He was thinking in circles, he realized. And the circles were getting tighter and tighter, while his thoughts flew faster.

To hell with it, he thought.

Suddenly he spied an empty taxi. He summoned it and got in.

Phil still kept a key to his parents' apartment. He used it now to let himself in. He hadn't wanted to ring the doorbell in case his mother was asleep. Not that there was much chance of that—she was the earliest riser in the family.

As he had expected, he found her in the kitchen making herself a cup of coffee.

She was surprised to see him, however. "Phil? What are you doing here? And so early in the morning."

Phil went to the cupboard and took out a cup and saucer. It *was* early. A quarter to eight. So much had happened in such a short time.

"Pour me some too, Mama," he said, referring to the coffee. "Is Naomi up yet?"

"No. Why should she be up? It's her summer vacation."

Phil nodded. He added cream and sugar to the steaming black liquid and sipped cautiously. "Would you mind getting her up, Mama? I'd like to talk to her."

"Is that why you're here this early? To talk to Naomi?"

Phil nodded again. "Yes."

"What is it? Has she done something?"

"Yes, you could say that," Phil replied carefully. "You certainly could say that she's done something."

His mother looked at him. Her face was still largely unlined and her eyes were calm and shrewd. She was clad in a fashionably modest summer-weight robe she had recently purchased at Saks Fifth Avenue.

"What is it?" she asked. "Maybe you should discuss it with me first. Before you see her."

But Phil shook his head. He feared that if he started talking about the situation with his mother he might work himself up into an uncontrollable rage. He wanted to at least start out calmly with Naomi.

"All right." Sophie Aronson sighed. "If you think it would be best."

His mother walked back to Naomi's bedroom. She knocked briefly, then opened the door. The two talked for several moments. And though he could not make out his sister's words, her sulky-sleepy tone of voice told Phil that she was protesting.

"She'll be right out," his mother said as she walked back into the kitchen. "She wants to brush her teeth first and make herself presentable."

"Fine."

When Naomi did enter, she had her lips set in a defiant pout of resentment. Phil could almost read her mind: why should she have to drag herself out of bed to see him? What did he want with her this time?

Sophie Aronson smiled blandly at her daughter—as though she were determined to hold on to everyday normality. "Would you like some orange juice, dear? And some scrambled eggs?"

"No eggs, Mama. Just a little dry toast."

"And cocoa?"

"Make it tea. With no sugar."

"Your sister's on a diet," Sophie said dryly.

"So I see."

Phil hesitated. Now that it was time—now that he was here and his sister was facing him—he was reluctant to do what he'd come here to do.

"Good morning," he said to Naomi.

"Good—good morning."

Then he took the plunge: "I have a message for you from Marty Opper," he said flatly.

Naomi turned pale. Her eyes darted about the room as though she were looking for a place to hide in.

"Who is Marty Opper?" Sophie Aronson asked.

"Ask your daughter," Phil told her. "She knows who I'm talking about. Don't you?" he said to Naomi.

Naomi cringed and remained silent. She was waiting for another blow to fall.

Phil was beginning to feel sorry for her. He told himself not to get soft. "Don't you want to read the letter?"

Naomi still refused to speak. She held out her hand and took the envelope.

She took out the note and appeared to read it at a single glance. She gasped and flung it onto the table.

"He didn't write that!" she said desperately as she tried to stop herself from crying. "Marty would never write anything like that!"

"It is his handwriting, isn't it?"

"I don't care!" Naomi insisted. "You made him write it, Phil. You! Whatever he said in that note, you forced him to say!"

Phil shrugged. There was no sense in denying it.

"Who is this Marty?" their mother pressed, her tone more urgent than it had been before.

When there was still no answer, she reached for the note and read it herself. Bafflement spread across her face. Then anger. Then sadness.

"He's your lover? . . . " she said at last. "Your age, and you have a lover?"

Phil looked at his mother. His own anger rose once more at her sadness. "He's her thirty-five-year-old lover."

"He's only twenty-five," Naomi protested, as if the fact of Marty's age were something vital to her.

"Thirty-five," Phil repeated wearily. "Not that it matters a damn. But he's thirty-five, he's been married twice, and he has a daughter as old as you are."

"My God . . . " Sophie Aronson said softly. "What have you done to yourself? To us? . . . "

Naomi clenched her fists tightly so that her fingernails dug into the palms of her hands. She gnawed at her lower lip and tears streamed freely down her cheeks.

"The point is, Mama, it's all over," Phil said. "He won't be seeing her any more. You read his note. He's leaving town and he's not coming back."

"You—you made him say that," Naomi wept. Her tears were resentful now, and her misery was overwhelmed by bitterness. "What did you do to him? How did you threaten? . . . "

Phil shrugged. He bit back the words of fury that boiled inside him.

"But he'll come back to me, anyway!" Naomi cried. "No matter what you did! He loves me!"

And now Phil could not stop himself from speaking. "Good God, Naomi! That tinhorn bum doesn't love anyone except himself! He was using you. Don't you get it? Know what he did when he left you last night? Found another dame and took her up to his place! How is that for love?" Phil could not stop himself from adding.

Naomi let out a long shriek. "I don't believe you! You're lying!"

Rage brought Phil to his feet. "One more crack like that . . ."

Suddenly he realized what he was about to do. He turned away from his sister and took a deep breath. Then—calmed somewhat—he turned to confront her again.

"I don't have to lie," he said. "The woman's name is Sadie Trevor. And if you'd like proof, I can arrange that you meet her."

Sophie Aronson was shaking her head sadly at her daughter. "Your brother doesn't lie to us. You should know that by now."

"No, he only does worse things," Naomi sobbed. "Like spying and . . ."

"Spying!" the outraged Phil put in. "Jesus Christ. How the hell else was I going to find out what you were up to?"

"Phil," his mother warned. "Whatever he did was for your own good," she said to her daughter.

Naomi glared furiously at her brother.

Phil sensed the unverbalized violence in his sister's soul (it was Aronson violence, after all, very much akin to what was in his own soul) and held back the savage response which was instinctive to him.

His mother took his hand, felt his tension.

Phil smiled at her. "I guess it's good that we're sending her to sleep-away school next season."

His mother did not respond directly. "Maybe I'd better take her to a doctor," she said instead.

"A doctor?"

"If she's been with a man . . ."

"Good God," Phil breathed. Could his sister be pregnant? He hadn't thought about that. . . .

And what would he do if she were? Force her to have an

abortion? Start asking around until he came up with the name of a hungry and willing doctor?

But who would he ask? Not Al Bocca. Al didn't approve of abortions. It would have to be someone else.

Maybe it wouldn't be necessary, however. Maybe he was getting upset over nothing.

"Do you think? . . ." he asked his mother. "Do you believe she's really . . ."

"No," his mother said. "It's not that easy to have a baby. And who knows: Maybe this—this person took precautions. But she should be examined."

"Yes," Phil agreed. "You're right."

His sister, meanwhile, kept wailing. If she understood that she was being discussed, she had no notion of what was being said about her.

Then Phil's father came into the kitchen.

"What's going on here?" he said. "Everyone's yelling. You woke me up."

His gaze suddenly fixed on Naomi. He didn't care that no one had answered him. He was sure he knew what had happened.

"What are you doing to her?" he demanded as he sat down next to his favorite child. "Why is she crying?"

He tried to cradle her in his arms, but she hunched away from him. Not even her beloved father could comfort her now.

"What is it, my darling?" the elder Aronson said in the sort of crooning voice one would use with a very small child. "My sweet baby girl . . ."

His father's tone grated nastily against Phil's nerves. He felt like telling the old man to shut up. Naomi was not a baby.

"What did you do to her?" his father complained. "The two of you—you and your mother. What did you do?"

"Ask Naomi," Phil said.

"I'm asking you."

Phil and his mother exchanged ironic glances. Neither of them replied to the question.

"Look how you've made her cry," the old man sighed after another few moments. "The poor baby . . ."

At the sound of her father's voice, Naomi sobbed harder. She couldn't look at him. Her moist, reddened eyes were focused desperately on Phil as though to beg him not to tell their father about Marty Opper.

Perhaps they should, though, Phil thought savagely. Maybe he should learn what his "baby" had done.

But what for? It would have been useless. The old man couldn't cope with Naomi. He could hardly cope with anything these days. So let him keep his lousy illusions.

Phil got up from the table. He wasn't sure what he'd accomplished by coming here this morning except to make himself feel bad.

He was glad that his brother was off at law school. At least he hadn't had to witness this scene.

"I'm going," he said abruptly. "I have work to do."

44

Meanwhile, the world was going mad.

It was a madness of confidence as much as anything else. The world's leaders were acting like overconfident auto drivers, sure of their God-given ability to negotiate hairpin mountain curves at breakneck speeds. As for their passengers—the ordinary people—they snoozed on happily in the sublime faith that everything would come out all right in the end and that they would reach their destinations intact and with a minimum of inconvenience.

In Germany, the people cheered their leader, Adolph Hitler, as he won a series of bloodless victories which seemed destined to go on forever. In 1935, the Saar Basin was taken back from France. In 1936, the Rhineland was occupied. In March of 1938, it was Austria's turn to be annexed. In September of that year, a nice hunk of Czechoslovakia was bitten off.

And all of that without bloodshed. All of it without war.

It was true that many Germans were unhappy with the direction their leader was taking. They did not approve of the way political dissidents kept vanishing mysteriously into concentrations camps, for example, nor of the brutal treatment of Jews and other non-Aryan types. But what was the present discomfiture of a comparative few as compared to the future glory of a new German Empire which their leader promised would last for a thousand years?

In Italy, the people cheered their leader, Benito Mussolini, as he tried to recapture the glorious days of Ancient Rome. In 1935, he took a step toward a new, expanded overseas Roman Empire by attacking Ethiopia. In 1936, he joined Hitler in sending troops to help Franco in Spain. In May of 1939, he guided Italy into a formal pact with Germany and invaded Albania the following month.

Here, too, the future looked assured. Mussolini was a genius who would turn the Mediterranean Sea into a Roman lake. And while many Italians were displeased with their leader's love affair with Hitler and tried to subvert the new anti-Semitic policies which Hitler pressured him into starting, most agreed that this was not too great a price to pay for such a marvelous future.

In the U.S.S.R., the people cheered their leader, Joseph Stalin, as he consolidated the Revolution and purged all possible enemies of the party and the state. Eventually, the leader promised, the state would wither away. But in the meantime, the people had to trust Stalin, the "Wisest of the Wise."

They trusted him in 1936 when he ordered that aid be sent to the loyalist goverment in Spain. And they trusted him equally in 1939 when he signed his nonaggression pact with Nazi Germany.

In Japan there was no single leader to cheer. Certainly not the Emperor. The Emperor was a semi-divine, almost mythical figure—too godlike to be a human leader. There were emerging *leaders,* though. These were the heads of the country's military party who—in cooperation with the *zaibatsu,* the great banking and industrial combines—were taking control of the government.

In 1931, Japanese armies invaded the Chinese province of Manchuria and turned it into the puppet state of Manchukuo. In 1937, these armies invaded the rest of China.

Eventually, the military party would make Japan ruler of all Asia. Its Emperor would fulfill his divine destiny to rule half the world. Now that was something to cheer about.

In England, the people cheered their Prime Minister, Neville Chamberlain, who went to Munich to sign a pact with Hitler and Mussolini agreeing to the dismemberment of Czechoslovakia. He came home boasting that he had won "peace in our time."

Not all of Chamberlain's countrymen approved of the pact. There were those who thought that it was a dishonorable sellout of an ally and that it would eventually cost a great deal more than standing up to Hitler would have. They were sure that the long policy of appeasement had not prevented war, but merely postponed it. And that, when it did come, the war would be even more dreadful.

But these people—the Edens, for instance, and the Churchills—were not cheered by their people. They would be eventually, but not then.

In France, the people cheered their premier, Edouard Daladier, who traveled to Munich with Chamberlain and also signed the agreement there.

There was evidence that Daladier had his doubts about the Munich Pact. But Chamberlain was insistent, and France would not attempt to defend Czechoslovakia from Germany all by itself. And anyway, all those cheers were nice to hear.

From the vantage point of a still insular United States, Phil Aronson observed what was happening. To him, the implications were clear: politicians could swear as often as they liked that America would never again become involved with Europe's problems; but the world would be too much for the resolve of politicians.

Unlike his brother, Phil was not sure that the United States would involve itself in fighting another World War. But like it or not, he did believe that the nation was going to have to prepare itself to fight one. Which would mean more and more men in the armed forces, more and more men who would have to be fed. And Phil was determined to be the one who fed them.

In keeping with his earlier resolve, he pulled every string he could find to help get military contracts for Aronson Foods. He did not even insist on making his normal profit. If he broke even with this end of the business, he was happy. And at times, he was willing to take a loss.

Though Phil was sure he knew what he was doing—that in the long run it was bound to pay off—many of his associates had strong reservations. By March of 1939, Al Bocca had joined these nay-sayers by reverting to his original skeptical attitude. He believed that the experiment had lost enough money by now. It was time for Phil to admit he'd made a mistake and call a halt.

If it had been a year ago, and Al had felt that strongly about a situation, there wouldn't have been any real argument. Al would have summoned Phil to his office and given him his orders. Phil might have discussed the matter with him—tried to convince Al that he was right—but if he failed to convince him, he would have followed the orders. And no one would have had to spell out what the penalty might have been for refusing.

But now things were different. The very fact that Aronson Foods had grown into a successful, publicly owned corporation meant that it was being scrutinized by sharp, governmental eyes. Though Al could still give Phil his orders and know that they would be obeyed, he was a bit more reluctant to do so— at least before he used up his other options.

One of those options was to work quietly through the board of directors and through stockholders' committees. He was not at all reluctant to do that—but he did know it would take time. So, before he did any thing else, he decided to send emissaries to talk some sense to Phil.

The first emissary was his nephew, Lew. Who turned out to be a poor choice.

Although Lew could no more grasp Phil's theories than his Uncle Al could, he did have an almost magical faith in his friend's ability to make money. When Phil pleaded for more time, therefore, Lew tried to convince Al to give it to him.

"After all," he pointed out, "The company's making enough from its other departments to go on taking small losses on its military business. Phil's naver failed us before. Why don't we give him the time he needs to turn it around."

Al looked puzzled for a moment, then furious, then amused.

"He's been talking to you, hasn't he?" Al snorted. "I sent you over to talk to him—but he's the one who talked to you! He's got a real tongue on him, that Phil. I wonder if his brother'll turn out to be that good a talker when he's a lawyer."

"I don't know about that Uncle Al," Lew replied. "But the thing is that Phil's got a point."

"Sure he has, my nephew. But so do I. And *my* point is that there's no sense in throwing good money after bad—even if you can afford to do it."

Al smiled to show he wasn't angry any more. "I know it was Phil's good judgement and hard work which made that corporation what it is today. That's why I went against my better judgement and let him try this military crap. But he's had his chance with it. He should cut his losses and quit. No one can be right all the time. Not even Phil."

Lew sighed. He'd made his pitch—and failed with it. He knew better than to keep pushing.

"What are you going to do, Uncle Al?" he asked.

"Send someone else to talk to him. Someone who won't be talked around to the other side."

Lew Bocca lowered his eyes. "Sorry, Uncle Al."

"Don't be. You're my nephew. You can say anything you want to me as long as you're sincere. But Sid, I think, sincerely agrees with me. And in this case, that might be better."

Sid really did agree with Al. And though he would have made a good emissary in any event—he had trained himself never to allow his own inner doubts or convictions to interfere with the presentation of a client's case—his beliefs might have enabled him to speak somewhat more frankly and say what he himself believed: that Phil was permitting an idea, a notion, an experiment to turn into an obsession.

"It's time to stop kicking a dead horse," he told Phil. "The United States isn't going to build a massive army and navy. We'll let all of Europe—and all of Asia, too—go down the drain first."

"You didn't feel that way about it last year," Phil reminded him gently.

"Last year you managed to convince me. But that was before Munich." Sid shook his head. "Nobody wants to fight a war, Phil. No one!"

"But they will fight," Phil said. "Or else they'll go under. Which would be the same thing as far as an American arms build-up is concerned."

"America? America?" Sid was becoming angry at Phil's obtuseness. "Do you think America wants to prepare for war? Bullshit it does! Do you want to know what really convinced me you're wrong, Phil?"

"What's that?"

"Sometime after Munich, the Gallup organization took a poll to find out what Americans thought about that sad affair. Can you guess how the poll turned out?"

"Most people approved, didn't they?"

"Damn right. When it comes to appeasement, my friend, this nation has very little to learn from Britain or France!"

"But that's now!" Phil replied just as vehemently. "We're going to change, Sid, all of us. We're going to be forced to change. Do you think that England and France will appease Hitler forever? Well, we won't be doing that either."

Sid Walters sighed, settled back in his seat, and tried to think of a different argument.

He gazed absently about the office. It was a lovely plush office—the New York office of the president of Aronson Foods—and Phil was sitting behind a massive, presidential desk. The boy had come so far, Sid thought. So far, so fast. It would be a shame if he lost it all through stubbornness....

"Phil," he said carefully, "Even if you're right—which I don't believe for a minute—don't you think what you're planning to do is...I hate to use the word, but...well, kind of immoral?"

"Pardon?"

"You are betting on a war, after all. That means, if you do make money it will be over the dead and mutilated bodies of your fellow human beings."

"Please don't give me that crap!" Phil said angrily. "I'm not going to start a war. I'm not Hitler or Franco or the Japanese general staff. But if the war does get any closer, this country is going to expand its military forces—which means that somebody is going to make a lot of money feeding soldiers, sailors, and marines. Is it so goddamn immoral to hope that that someone will be me? And even if it is, buddy—this is the first time I ever heard you worry about it."

Sid sighed again.

"I suppose you're right," he conceded. "And if I agreed with you on what's going to happen, I might even be on your side. But I don't agree."

"And neither does Al Bocca," Phil said with a half smile.

"Yes. You're right a second time. That's the important thing—not the fact that Sid Walters disagrees with you, but that Mr. Bocca does."

"What's going to happen, Sid?" Phil asked quietly.

"That depends. If you're smart, you'll give up this whole thing. You'll stop taking military contracts at less than cost. You'll stop spending money trying to develop a processed canned meat which only the army and navy could love. You'll get back into the civilian market and make lots of money for everybody. If you do that, nothing will happen except a fattening of your personal bank account and lots of nice praise from everyone on your board of directors—including Mr. Bocca."

"And if I keep doing what I've been doing?"

"I was afraid you were going to ask that question," Sid said. He had the grace to look embarrassed. "If you keep doing what you've been doing, you will lose the company."

"I'll—"

"It'll all be quite legal," Sid continued. "I give you my word as a lawyer on that. It will simply be pointed out to the other stockholders how much money your ideas have been costing the corporation. I don't think there's too much doubt that you'll be voted out of office.

"Oh, you won't be penniless," Sid went on. "You'll still have your stock—which I'm sure the corporation will make a generous offer for. And maybe you can take that money and start a new, noncompetitive business. But as far as Aronson Foods is concerned, you'll be through."

"Jesus," Phil said. "You play rough, don't you?"

"You're not in a kiddie's game, my friend. You should know that."

Phil brushed some hair from his eyes. He got up from behind the great oaken desk which he had purchased for this office when he had come here six months before.

"Give me some time," he said, wheeling suddenly to face the lawyer.

"How much time do you want?"

"I don't know. Two months...one. Maybe I can make some kind of a deal in a month that will change Al's mind."

But Sid Walters was shaking his head sadly.

"No," he said. "It's too late for that. A deal wouldn't change any minds."

"Christ," Phil said. "You mean it's shape up or ship out? Love it or leave it?"

"It's not my decison," Sid reminded him. "If it was...hell, if it was, I'd give you the extra month or two."

"I thank you for that," Phil said, meaning it.

"His pride was hurt," Sid suggested softly.

Phil looked sharply at the lawyer and waited for him to go on. It was the first time he had heard him attempt to explain Al Bocca's motives.

"You went against his advice," he said, "and then refused to quit when you knew he wanted you to. You even convinced his nephew that he might be wrong. If he wants to rub your nose in it now...well, you know how he is."

Phil nodded stiffly. He knew.

"How about a week? Would he let me have a week?"

"Christ," Sid said. He regarded Phil with a mixture of annoyance and admiration. "You're as stubborn as he is. Don't you ever give up?"

Phil remained silent.

"Why?" Sid pressed. "What do you need a week for?"

"To make up my mind. He likes to tell me that it's my company; that I'm the boss. Now I see that isn't true. Perhaps the best thing would be for me to sell out."

Sid thought for several monents before replying.

"He's not going to back down," he reminded Phil. "You must know that much about him. No matter how much he thinks of you—no matter how much money you've made for him in the past—he's not going to do anything which could possibly be conceived of as crawling. I don't think he'd crawl to God if it meant the difference between going to heaven or hell."

"You're right," Phil snapped. "I do know that much about him."

"Then you're serious? You really may give up—" Sid gestured. "—all this?"

"I'd like to think about it, at least."

"Okay, then." Sid sighed in resignation. "You'll have your week. I'll fix it with Mr. Bocca. I just hope you make the right decision."

"So do I," Phil said.

Alone again in his private office, seated behind his great desk, Phil wondered just how serious he really was.

It would not be easy to give up what Sid had referred to as "all this." He had worked too hard for it—for the carpet on the floor, the panelled walls, the massive desk, the secretary who sat in the outer room. It was all his. He was Aronson Foods.

But was he really? That was what he had to get straightened out in his own mind. If Al Bocca could get rid of him like that—with a snap of his fingers—wasn't he just a trained dog who was allowed to give his name to the company if he would jump through hoops on his master's orders?

And it would never change. Al Bocca would always be the real boss—the man behind the scenes who called the shots.

But supposing he did sell out. What then?

Phil knew that he would get a fair price for his stock. By his own standards, at least, Al was a fair man. But the money would not be enough for him to do anything big.

Perhaps he could purchase another small quality food store like the one he had worked in and finally bought from old man Lubbuck. It might even be fun to improve such a store and make it the best of its kind in the city. It would bring him a nice income—nothing like the money that the president of Aronson Foods could expect, but nothing to sneeze at either. And . . . he would be his own master.

But could he do it? Could he give up not just the income but the glory of being even a figurehead president of Aronson Foods in order to be the proprietor of a single store?

He didn't know. His only certainty was that he had one short week in which to decide.

45

Phil had been mistaken. What he'd thought of as a certainty never came to pass. He did not have to decide anything within the week. For within that week, Al Bocca was dead.

It was not a knife in the dark or a rain of bullets from an unfriendly gun that did Al in. It was a small clump of his own bodily substance—a bit of a tough, elastic protein called fibrin which is formed during the coagulation of blood.

There is no telling how long the bit of fibrin stayed fastened to the inner wall of one of Al's arteries. Nor does it matter. It did not become an instrument of death until it broke off from the wall and became the nucleus of an embolus—a clot of blood.

The embolus began bouncing through Al's arterial system like a log floating down a rushing stream. But it reached an artery that was a just a little too small for it, and got stuck there forming a kind of dam which prevented the blood behind it from reaching its destination.

Approximately seventy-five hours after Sid Walters had convinced Al to give Phil the extra week he'd requested, an embolus lodged itself in one of the arteries leading to Al's brain.

Al was in a nightclub at the time, sitting at a table with an exceptionally attractive young woman. When the embolism occurred, he frowned at his companion as though he had something of vital importance to say to her. Then his eyes glazed over and he slid almost casually from his chair.

According to a doctor who happened to be in the nightclub at the time, he was dead before he hit the floor.

Phil got the news a few hours later when Lew Bocca woke him up from a sound sleep.

"There may be trouble," Lew said. "Word is out that a lot of what Uncle Al controlled may be up for grabs. Or at least that's what some assholes think. I don't plan to let them grab it."

Phil was trying to clear his mind and come to grips with what had happened. Al Bocca dead? He couldn't accept it. Al was a force of nature—not simply a human being.

"What—what do you want me to do?"

"Make yourself scarce for the next few days," Lew replied without hesitation. "Take a trip someplace. It's not going to be very safe around here for my friends."

"You think I'll run away?" Phil asked. He felt insulted. A man didn't run out on his friends. Not if he was a man.

"What I think is you'll use your head!" Lew snapped. "The only guys I need around me now are specialists in the art of knocking people off. You know, gunsels...soldiers. Shit, Phil, when was the last time you handled a gun for real?"

"I could learn," Phil muttered.

"Don't talk like a fucking asshole! What do you think I'm running here—a school for would-be heros?"

"Listen," Lew went on. "There are a couple of so-called bigshots in this town who think I've been knocked so flat by Uncle Al's death that I won't be able to hold onto what's mine. Shit—maybe I feel like rolling over and playing dead. But if I did, my uncle would climb out of his coffin and kick me in the ass! That's not his style. So, first I'll take care of these shits by hitting them first the way he would have. Then I'll mourn for him."

He really was taking over, Phil thought. Even over the phone, the change in him was fantastic. The king was dead; long live the king!

But Lew was saying something else.

"And meanwhile," he explained to Phil, "I don't want to have to worry about you. If you did stay in town, buddy, those bastards would probably put the snatch on you. Just to try and put more pressure on me, if you know what I mean."

"Yeah," Phil said. "You made your point. Is there anywhere special you'd like me to go?"

"No. Just get lost. And give me a ring in three or four days. One way or another, this should all be over by then."

Phil spent the next three days holed up in a modest and unpretentious hotel a block and a half from the beach in Atlantic City, New Jersey.

They were restful days with no women, no business deals, and very little liquor. What he did was to get up early each morning to swim in the ocean, take long afternoon walks on the boardwalk, eat simple dinners followed by some salt water taffy and go to bed early each night.

It was a healthy little interlude, in other words, during which the world of New York City only intruded when Phil read the *News* and the *Mirror* at breakfast. He read those papers avidly, however, searching through them for any and all stories on crime.

The fourth morning of his stay in Atlantic City was the first in which he did not see a story about another underworld assassination. He decided to phone Lew and see if it was safe for him to go home.

Phil reached the city at about ten-thirty that morning. He went straight to his apartment to change into more appropriate clothes and then went to the West Side funeral home where the body of Al Bocca was lying in state.

Phil stood before the casket for several minutes, gazing down at the serene features of the man who had been so great an influence on his life. There was very little of that man here, however. This was more like a wax effigy—a reclining statue in a wax museum.

He walked over to where Lew was sitting placidly between

315

a pair of elderly women whom he introduced as his aunts. The women were in veils and all three were wearing mourning black.

"Thanks for coming so soon," Lew said, rising to his feet and leading Phil a short distance away where they could talk without being overheard. "You must have just gotten back."

"I should never have gone away," Phil said. He was feeling guilty. "I should have stayed here with you."

"Let's not start that again. You did the right thing."

"Did everything work out the way you wanted?"

"Yeah. Perfect. He—" Lew nodded in the direction of the ornate, open bronze casket. "He would have been proud of me."

"I'm glad," Phil said.

He looked back toward the casket himself.

"It's strange. Until I saw him lying there just now I couldn't really believe he was dead. It was like some hoax—a con he was setting up for his own personal reasons."

"I understand what you mean," Lew replied. "I know he's dead and it's hard for me to believe it."

"He was something," Phil said. "He'll be remembered."

"He surely will."

Both men nodded slowly. They were lost in their own private thoughts about the late Al Bocca.

"The funeral's tomorrow at eleven?" Phil said at last. He felt he had to say something.

"Yeah." Lew reminded Phil of the name of the church. "You'll be coming out to the cemetery, too, won't you?"

"Of course."

"Good. It's arranged for you and Sid Walters to share the third limousine in the procession. I'll be in the first one with Aunt Flora and Aunt Adina. A couple of the boys will be in the second car—just in case." Lew smiled sardonically. "My bodyguards. Uncle Al had plenty of bodyguards. A lot of good they did him, huh?"

Phil looked uncomfortable. What could he say to that?

"Anyway," Lew went on. "You and Sid can change places with my aunts on the way back to the city. We can all talk then."

"Fine," Phil said.

46

Phil and Sid rode to the cemetery in the rear seat of a black, twelve-cylinder Packard limousine which had been supplied by the funeral parlor.

Despite the fact that the partition window had been raised for privacy, they hardly spoke to each other at all. Once or twice, when the silence between them had become too strained, they awkwardly praised the dead. But after a few heavy words about Al Bocca's shrewdness, for example, or his modesty, they fell silent again.

The truth was that they were embarrassed by each other's company. Each was nervous that the other might bring up the subject of business. And that was something they were both anxious to avoid.

It had been little more than a week since Sid Walters relayed the message from Al which had faced Phil with one of the hardest choices of his life. And if Phil had decided the wrong way, it would have been Sid's job to remove him from the corporation which bore his name.

But now everything was changed. The king was dead. Lew—his heir—was the new king.

Neither of the two men in the rear seat of the Packard knew what Lew was going to do. Would the respect he held for his dead uncle lead him to follow the wishes of the late Al Bocca? Or would he strike out on a new path of his own?

Only Lew himself knew the answer to that. And he wouldn't be talking until after the burial.

So Phil and Sid rode in awkward and uncomfortable silence all the way to the cemetery where they stood back from the crowd to watch the unfamiliar graveside ceremony.

Then it was over. Loose earth was shoveled atop the coffin while Lew's aunts sobbed inconsolably. The impressive figure of a black-garbed priest chanted in Latin and a stern-faced Lew made the proper responses.

"It was a beautiful ceremony," Sid said as he walked with Lew and Phil to the limousine which Lew had inherited from his uncle. "Extremely impressive."

"Yes," Lew agreed. There was a hint of a smile on his face. "The church does give you a good send-off. Maybe that's why so many of us stay in."

"The Jews could learn from you. We like to bury a person fast. Get everything over with."

"I don't know. I've been to a couple of your funerals. They were pretty impressive, too."

Lew opened the rear door of the great, sixteen-cylinder Cadillac his uncle had purchased the year before. It was a very special automobile. Not only was it larger and far more luxurious than the fine Packard which had brought them to the cemetery, it had another more important advantage: Underneath the shiny black exterior paint was thick armored steel, and every window was made of bullet-resistant glass.

Lew motioned Phil and Sid into the most comfortable seats. Then he said a few words to the driver, pulled down a jumpseat and got in himself.

As the limousine started off, Phil noted that a second auto was following behind them. There were two men in it. The bodyguards.

If Lew was attacked while inside the car, the car itself would protect him while the bodyguards were destroying the attackers. Or at least that was the theory.

"I'm still not used to all this," Lew said pensively. "Uncle Al worked out the alterations in this car himself."

"And many's the drive I've taken in it with him," Sid said.

Phil had the impression that the lawyer was working overtime to score points with Lew. Perhaps that's what he—Phil—should have been doing.

"I still find it hard to accept that he's gone," Sid was saying now. "It's as though I could shut my eyes and open them again to find him with us—giving us the benefit of his wisdom."

"I know what you mean," Lew said. "But it's not true. He won't be back with us. We're going to have to work things out without him. Do our own thinking."

Phil looked at his friend. He saw a new strength there. A new toughness.

Sid seemed to think so, too.

"You're taking this better than I could," he said.

"I had to," Lew told him. "When Uncle Al died, I had to make a choice: either start fighting right away and keep what he wanted me to have, or mope around feeling sorry for myself and lose everything. I decided to fight."

"I know," Phil said. "I was only sorry that you made me leave town."

"You, too?" Sid asked. It was one of the few times Phil had seen him surprised.

"I asked you both to leave," Lew reminded them, "because you couldn't have helped me and you might have been used against me. In the few days you were out of town, I managed to fix things up. How—what I did—you're better off not knowing."

Both men nodded.

"Now I don't have anything more to say on that subject," Lew told them. "Do either of you?"

"I don't," Phil said.

"Nor I," Sid added.

"Good." Lew nodded with satisfaction. "So let's talk about where we go from here."

"All right," said Phil.

He glanced out the window. The car was going along Northern Boulevard in the direction of the Queensboro Bridge. Behind them, the second car was still in its designated place.

"The first thing," Lew said, "is Aronson Foods. Phil, I know that you and Uncle Al were arguing about whether or not to keep on with your attempts to sell to the Army and Navy, or to stick with the tried and true civilian business."

Phil was trying not to squirm under Lew's steady gaze. It was hard, though. It was almost as if it were Al Bocca himself looking at him from behind Lew's gray eyes.

"Then Uncle Al sent me to talk to you. But when you convinced me that you might possibly be right, he got mad and sent Sid with an either or proposition—you would either do things the way Uncle Al wanted, or he'd pull the rug out from under you, force you out of your own company.

"Am I right so far? Is that what happened?"

"Yes," Phil said. This was making him uncomfortable.

"I gave him the message," said Sid.

"Uncle Al expected you to fold, Phil. But from what he

was told, you didn't. You were even considering selling out."

"I told Sid I'd need a week to think it over," Phil explained. "He said he could get it for me."

"Which I did," Sid put in.

"You know, Uncle Al admired you for that. He really did. 'The son-of-a-bitch won't let himself be pushed around,' he told me. 'Not even by me.'"

Lew smiled at the memory while Sid and Phil exchanged glances. They were both wondering what Lew Bocca was really thinking about.

"But he would have let you go," Lew said suddenly. "No matter how much he liked and admired you, no matter how much he wanted you in the company—he still would have let you go unless you agreed to his terms."

"I know that," Phil said.

"He would have had to, Phil. First of all, he was sure you were wrong. He really felt you were lousing up the corporation and refusing to make more money out of sheer stubbornness. And secondly, there was his pride."

"Those make up two powerful reasons, Phil. Feeling in the right and having your pride hurt."

"You're right." Phil smiled. "They do."

"But what would you have done? Would you have left Aronson Foods? Or would you have swallowed your own pride at the last minute?"

"I don't know," Phil replied honestly. "I don't know what I would've done."

"Yeah." Lew nodded. "I don't know what you would have done, either. I don't know what *I* would have done. But the real point is you didn't have to do anything. Uncle Al died before your week was up."

Phil nodded. He wished Lew would get to the meat of the situation.

"So now it's up to me," Lew said. "I've got to decide what to do. Should I follow my own views and take the chance that you know what you're doing? Or should I do what I know Uncle Al would have wanted me to do?

"I thought about this long and hard. On the one hand, I wanted to be respectful to my dead uncle. On the other, I knew that I was going to have to start making my own decisions. So this is how I decided, buddy: I'm going to give you your head. What the hell, you've done pretty damn good for me so far."

"Thank you," Phil said.

It was as though an enormous, crushing weight had been removed from his chest or a vise about his head had been loosened.

"I think you're doing the smart thing," Sid said.

"I hope you're right," Lew told him. "But anyway, let me tell you the way I have it figured out."

"Go ahead."

"Number one, Phil here knows a hell of a lot more about his own corporation than I do. Uncle Al might have found someone to replace him. I don't know as I can.

"Number two, I like the fact that I'm a big stockholder in the corporation. It's a good, legitimate place for me to invest my money."

"Your uncle felt the same way," Sid said.

"I know. But let me get to number three. Which is that, even though I'm now an important stockholder in Aronson Foods, it's still Phil Aronson's company. His name is on it. It was his dream that started it. And he didn't go into this military thing to be a wise guy, but because he was sure we'd all make good money from it in the long run.

"Now my feeling is that we should give him the longest possible chance to prove himself right or wrong. If he's wrong enough so that he's running a risk of really wrecking the corporation, then let's kick his ass out. But even Uncle Al thought he was a long way from that."

"I agree," Sid said.

"What do you say, buddy?" Lew asked Phil.

"That you'll never be sorry," Phil told him. "Aronson Foods is going to make you a very wealthy man."

47

Events in Europe were taking place now with devastating swiftness. The complex set of carefully derived values which made up the fabric of Western civilization were being pushed aside. In Yeats's fearful image, mere anarchy was being loosed upon the world.

In March of 1939—at about the same time that Al Bocca was deciding that Phil's faith in American rearmament was a blindly foolish one—Germany was grabbing what was left of the truncated country of Czechoslovakia. A month later, Mussolini's Italy sent its armies into Albania and took it over.

Hitler was now eying Poland with hungry eyes. If he hesitated, it was only because he knew that Russia was seriously considering the possibility of military agreement with Britain and France. The negotiations broke down in early August. In late August—the twenty-third, to be exact—Russia signed a nonagression treaty with Germany.

This gave Hitler the chance he'd been waiting for. His forces entered Poland on the first of September, and World War II was officially launched.

Though Britain and France did honor their agreement with Poland by declaring war on Germany, that did not do the Poles any good. In a terrifying demonstration of a new brand of mechanized warfare they termed *"blitzkrieg"*—or "lightning war"—the Germans rolled through most of Poland just seventeen days before stopping voluntarily so that the Soviet Union could grab the rest of the country.

The United States was still officially neutral. With the start of the war against Germany, indeed, many prominent citizens were urging the government to an ever stricter interpretation of the Neutrality Act. Unofficially, however, many people high up in the government were trying to prepare for the conflict which they believed would have to eventually come.

Both the isolationists and those who believed that America had to get ready to join the war were shocked at the ease and speed with which Germany overran Poland.

The two sides derived different lessons from the event, however. To the isolationists it proved that the Germans were invincible. There was no point in trying to oppose them. The United States had better decide to leave Europe to its fate and try to get along somehow with the Nazi masters.

The interventionists saw something else: no one was invincible; it was the other side that was unprepared. America had to help strengthen Britain and France, therefore, and prepare its own forces in case those measures did not turn out to be enough.

In the meantime the war itself had settled into what a number of newspapers liked to call a "phony war"—a period in which the major opponents were not actually fighting each other.

A good many people began to relax during this period. Perhaps the war would simply grind to a halt, they thought, with neither side harming the other. France would be saved by its impregnable Maginot Line—a series of fortresses along the Franco-German border that would stop any enemy from advancing further. England would be defended by its undoubted mastery of the sea. Germany—whose great army could defend it from any invasion—would have to give up all thoughts of future conquests and be satisfied with what it already had.

A nice dream—which vanished when Germany launched a series of new *blitzkrieg* attacks in the spring of 1940.

The first of these came against Denmark and Norway on the ninth of April. Then, with Denmark completely taken and Norway crumbling fast, the Germans struck to the south— against Luxembourg, Belgium, and The Netherlands.

That invasion was started on the tenth of May. By the thirteenth, the Maginot Line had been outflanked. It simply stood there—as impregnable as ever—while German tank units raced around it to the sea in order to try and cut off the French and British forces.

The British Army was rescued—at Dunkirk. Its men would live to fight again. But on the twenty-second of June, a defeated France was forced to sign an armistice.

In America, meanwhile, the debate over neutrality was becoming angrier and fiercer than ever.

It could have been even worse, though. President Roosevelt was running for an unprecedented third term of office. If his opponent had been a convinced isolationist, their arguments might have torn the country apart.

But Wendell Willkie was not an isolationist. His arguments with the president had to do with domestic policy—not foreign.

In December of 1940, the President of the United States called upon the nation to become the "great arsenal of democracy" in the fight against Nazism. It was Franklin Roosevelt who made that speech. But if the election had gone the other way, it might well have been Wendell Willkie. There was nothing in it he could quarrel with.

By the time FDR made that December speech, Aronson Foods, Inc. had become an important supplier of food—not just for the U.S. military, but for a beleaguered Britain as well.

Money was always available to the company now. If Phil wanted to start a new product line or build another plant, he had hardly to ask before the funds appeared—and at very good interests rates. And if some of this money came from British-owned banks or from banks owned by close connections to important figures in the United States government, Phil was delighted. He was having the best of both worlds. He was considered a patriot, and was getting well paid for it.

No one in Washington asked any embarrassing questions about his background these days. If anyone knew of his former connections with the Y.A.S.D., they were careful not to say anything about it. And with Al Bocca dead and Lew keeping well out of the limelight, nobody questioned Phil's current associates.

And why should they? He was the young, dynamic founder of what was turning into a great corporate empire that was already serving the nation well. It would not only be foolish to question such a man too closely, it might be considered un-American.

As successful as Phil was in his business life, however—as rich and powerful as he was becoming—it bothered him that his personal life did not give him more satisfaction.

His relationship with his sister was what bothered him most.

That never had been very good. Now it was worse than ever.

He was able to recognize now that there were times when he'd been too rough on Naomi. In his anxiety to fight and scrounge and make money, he had given his sister short shrift. But now that he wanted to make amends, she wouldn't let him.

The worst of it was that she seemed least resentful about those things he was most willing to apologize for—the way he'd treated her when she was little, for instance, how he'd teased and bullied her and called her Nommie. What she resented most fiercely, on the other hand, were two actions he was not sorry for having taken—forcing Marty Opper out of her life and sending her to a fine all-girls school in Massachusetts.

Phil had tried to discuss the Opper situation with her on several occasions. He wanted his sister to understand why he had to act as he did. What other choice was there? he had demanded. What would she have done if she'd been in his shoes?

Every time he broached the subject, however, he was met by a wall of angry silence. She would look at him with defiant eyes and refuse to answer.

Phil kept asking himself why. Why was she so angry at him? Why couldn't she at least try to understand?

He refused to believe that she was still in love with Marty Opper—or the memory of Marty Opper. Certainly, he'd been her lover. But that only meant that he'd swept an immature girl off her feet. Naomi herself had to have realized that by now.

"I don't get her," he said to his mother, once. "Is she simply stupid? Or—"

"She isn't stupid," Sophie Aronson responded quickly. "She must feel terribly humiliated by the entire episode. First of all, the way she'd been fooled by that awful man, and then the way you intruded into her private life—"

"But I had to," Phil interjected.

"And that would make it even more humiliating to a sensitive young girl. The fact that you had to."

Phil looked baffled. "It seems like you just can't win."

"Not in everything," his mother replied shrewdly. "Sometimes, Phil, it's enough if you don't lose too badly."

Phil smiled ruefully at her. Inside, however, he was still frustrated.

When it came to the battle of Naomi's school, Phil did lose badly.

Her grades were terrible from the beginning. That was nothing new, though. What did bother him were letters the school kept sending his mother—letters complaining about Naomi's deportment.

She was not respectful enough to her instructors one such letter said. She didn't have the proper school spirit, according to another, and the girls she chose to be her friends all had similar attitudes.

The grand finale came when Naomi was expelled for sneaking a fifth of rum into her dormitory room and throwing a rum-and-cola party there.

When she arrived home she was plainly unrepentant. Indeed, as far as Phil could make out, she was happy about what had occurred.

"But why?" he moaned. "Do you have to defy *everyone?* Can't you even follow a few simple rule"

"A *few* simple rules?" Naomi repeated incredulously. "Rules were all they had in that place. Rules for making your bed the right way and wearing the school uniform and curtsying properly and acting like a lady and saying 'yes, ma'am' to the teachers and—"

"Enough," her mother murmured. "We understand what you mean."

"It was like a girls' reform school!" Naomi continued breathlessly. "A woman's prison!"

Phil rolled his eyes in anguish. "A reform school? A woman's prison? It's one of the finest schools in the country!"

His father muttered something to himself which Phil was just as happy he couldn't understand.

"I suppose it doesn't matter to you that you cost me a half-year's tuition," Phil said to Naomi. "I had to pay the entire year in advance."

"And you mean they won't return the unused portion?" his mother said.

His father snorted. "That's the sort of business to be in. The private school business . . ."

Phil felt as if he were going to explode.

"Well," he insisted to Naomi. "What do you have to say about it?"

His sister shrugged. "I told you not to send me there."

Phil turned so that he couldn't see the expression on her face. If he hadn't done something like that, he might have hit the girl.

"What do you think we should do now?" he asked his mother.

"How about sending me back to my public high-school," Naomi said.

"Not a chance," Phil replied without turning around.

"If she's going to go away again," Sophie Aronson suggested, "perhaps it should be to a girls' school that's a little less strict."

"But she needs strictness. She needs to be taught right from wrong. And if she isn't forced to study, she'll refuse to do it. A free and easy school—like that private school here in the city—would be the worst thing for her."

"Maybe so," Sophie admitted. "But I think a school can be too strict, also."

"And therefore?"

"Therefore, we find a happy medium. One that's neither too strict nor too lenient."

"I have a strange suspicion that you have something in mind," Phil said slyly.

His mother smiled. "As a matter of fact, I have a friend whose niece is an assistant to the headmistress of the Margaret Creighton School for Girls."

"A happy medium school?"

"A very good school," his mother responded seriously. "It specializes in sensitive and intelligent young ladies who may have had problems in other schools."

Phil nodded thoughtfully.

"It would be a very healthy environment," Sophie went on. "It's located in the Adirondack Mountains where there are a lot of winter sports. Naomi and I have already discussed it, and—"

"What do you say, Naomi?" Phil interrupted to ask.

"I suppose it would be all right."

"You'll have to do better than that," Phil told her evenly. "If I'm going to spend my money to send you to this place, it has to mean more to you than just all right."

"Okay," Naomi agreed sullenly. "I really do want to go there."

"Sounds like a pretty good place, huh?" Phil pressed. "Even if it *is* all girls? Lots of sports and not as strict as the last school?"

Naomi nodded.

"Do you think you can make decent grades there and stick to whatever rules they do have?"

"I think so. Sure."

"Good. You'd better. This is positively your last chance."

His sister gave him a puzzled frown. She wondered what he was getting at.

"I heard about a place the other day," Phil went on, "which actually is like a girls' reform school—complete with locks on all the doors and escape proof windows. Mess up one more time, sister dear, and that's where you'll be going."

Sophie gave her son a startled look, while Naomi appeared frightened.

Phil didn't mind. If the thought of such a horror school could keep his sister in line, it had served its purpose. Even if he himself had no idea whether one really existed.

The Creighton School, on the other hand, really did exist. And when Phil visited the place with his mother, he found that it exceeded his expectations.

He was so impressed, indeed, that he decided to take out an "insurance policy" for his sister. Without his mother's knowledge, he guaranteed funds which would allow Creighton to complete its unfinished indoor swiming pool.

His sister didn't know about the gift either, or course. Part of the deal was that no outsiders were to know who put up the money. But the powers-that-be of the school knew. And that— or so Phil hoped—would put them under an unspoken obligation not to kick Naomi out of Creighton short of murder or sleeping with the headmistress's husband!

Phil did not resent handing over the money. He had never been stingy when it came to his family. And if this school could help Naomi solve her problems, it would be worth it.

Naomi herself would resent it, however. Phil knew that much about his sister. She would accuse him of trying to bribe people.

In her feelings about this sort of thing, Naomi was very

close to Bob. They both disapproved of the merchant mentality. They disliked trading and bargaining and felt that bribery was a sin. They were not altogether unrealistic—unlike some socialists Phil had known, for instance, they could recognize that the profit motive exists. They merely thought it one of the more shameful sides of human nature.

Phil had to smile when he thought of how closely they agreed about that. For in most everything else, their natures were opposed.

It was not just that Bob was a top student while Naomi was . . . Naomi. Bob seemed warm and sympathetic by nature. He could understand what Phil had gone through in his efforts to hold their family together. Naomi, on the other hand, seemed determined to see everything he did in the worst possible light.

There were times when Phil thought Naomi actually hated him!

On the other hand, he kept telling himself, his sister was still young and immature. Perhaps as she grew older she would begin to understand what he had done for the family—including herself. She might even start to appreciate it.

Or maybe not. Maybe she would imitate their father and continue to resent him.

Either way, there seemed to be little he could do about it.

But he shouldn't complain too much. He should be grateful for his mother's support, at least. And for his brother's.

Phil was very proud of Bob, who was due to graduate from law school in May of 1941. The only part which made him feel sad was that his brother had already decided not to join Aronson Foods.

It was too bad, Phil thought. He'd been looking forward to having his brother in the firm. He could understand how he felt, though. He himself had always valued independence; why wouldn't Bob feel the same way?

Still and all, Bob's decision had an impact on him. Until now, he had been working for his family—to keep them together. But Bob's decision signalled that the Aronson tribe was about to fragment.

Bob would go one way. Naomi would eventually leave home (hopefully to marry) and go hers. His parents trod their own path. And he—Phil Aronson—which way would he go, now?

His business was booming. It was growing bigger and more

successful every day. But, as grand as this was, it was not enough.

Phil (and he could not have admitted this to anyone else, now, and was only just beginning to admit it to himself) had dynastic leanings. He wanted to found a family of his own. He wanted a son who would rule the empire of Aronson Foods after his own death!

It was time to consider getting married.

48

Phil Aronson kept a picture in his mind of the woman who would be his future wife. It was a fantasy portrait of a girl who might never exist. But it had not changed since he'd first conceived it a month or two after Laura's death in 1937.

She would be slender, beautiful, aristocratic. She would be witty, of course, and have a first-rate mind. But her foremost quality would be loyalty to her man.

There would be more: she would have to come from a well-established family—one which would give her the status to complement his own self-made condition in the same way that her necessary knowledge of the social graces would soften his own harshness.

She would not only be a good wife to him, but a good addition to the Aronson family. Her connections might be able to help Bob, for example. And—who could say—having her as an example might even do his sister Naomi some good.

Where was he going to find her, though? This paragon. This creature of fantasy.

In December 1940, he met a girl at a Christmas party who filled the bill.

• • •

Her name was Eve Goodman. She was raven-haired, nineteen, and the daughter of a judge on the New York State Court of Appeals. Phil took one look at her and managed to wrangle an introduction. He spent most of the evening talking with her and her resentful escort.

The girl reminded him that this was actually the second time they had met. The first was in the summer of 1939 when a mutual friend had introduced Phil to her father and herself at the New York Worlds Fair.

"How could I have forgotten that?" Phil asked in mock horror.

"I was kind of bratty then," she said with a pert smile. "And a 'Plain Jane.'"

"You?" Phil shook his head. "Impossible."

"A year and a half ago? I definitely was. And anyway—you had more important things on your mind."

"I did?" Phil sounded incredulous. What could have been more important than meeting *her?*

"Daddy said so. He told me that your company was involved with military preparedness. He admired you very much."

"Well, thank you," Phil said. "I take it he believes we're going to get into the war."

"He's been saying we might get involved in one since before I can remember. Ever since Hitler came to power."

"I'm afraid I didn't have his foresight," Phil said with a laugh. "Back then I didn't know Hitler was alive.

"But your father . . . he must be a very remarkable man. I'm sorry I don't know him better."

"That could be arranged."

Phil nodded thoughtfully. He knew that if he weren't careful now, she might wind up thinking of him as her father's friend. That he did not want.

"Then let's arrange it," he said. "After we get to know each other better."

Eve flushed and Phil offered to get her another drink.

"A Tom Collins," she said. "My last for the evening."

Phil brought the drink back and they chatted some more.

He tried his best to include the escort—a young man named Harry something who was one year out of college and working in a bank. He did not want to look like he was pressing. That would be fatal with a girl like Eve.

But Harry was doing his best to sink his own ship. He was

furious at Phil's hanging around and not clever enough to disguise his feelings. Phil made a mental note of the fact that ill-tempered jealousy was something not to show in Eve's presence.

When the party showed signs of breaking up, he offered to give Harry and Eve a lift in his car.

"Oh, that would be lovely—" Eve started to say.

But Harry shook his head.

"We'll take a cab," he announced proudly.

"Okay." Phil grinned in his most easygoing manner—a man placating a boy. Then he stuck out his hand for Harry to shake. "Great meeting you."

Turning to Eve and standing in such a way that Harry could not see his face, he winked cheerfully. It was as if he were sharing some private and unarticulated joke with her.

"I surely enjoyed meeting *you*," he said, laughing.

Though Phil often liked to come on as carefree, at this stage of his life he was a very careful man. Before he phoned Eve to ask for a date, he spent a day or two quietly checking her background.

What he learned was what he wanted to hear. The Goodmans were wealthy, well-connected, and respectable. Not a hint of scandal had ever attached itself to the family name.

Eve's father, the judge, was widely respected. Though logic said he must be somewhat political (all judges had to be at least *somewhat* political, Phil considered, especially in New York where they were elected to office and needed the backing of a political party), Judge Goodman had never been known to sacrifice his principles for political expediency. Which might have been why—though he was a registered Democrat who never attempted to hide his admiration for Roosevelt's New Deal—he had run unopposed in his last two elections.

Phil himself was a subscriber to the theory that everyone had his price. He soon learned, however, that no one had yet discovered the judge's.

The reason for Judge Goodman's exaggerated sense of honor, Phil believed—or at least for his ability to indulge it—might well lie with his choice of wife. For Eve's mother was the former Lucille Glazer, one of the heirs to the Glazer Pills fortune.

Those tiny aids to digestion were no longer being manufactured. But there had been a time when they were used to medicate half the stomachs in America. The originator of Glazer Pills, Dr. Marvin Glazer, had become a multimillionaire. And it was his grandaughter who became Judge Goodman's wife.

A lot of people might have unbending moral codes, thought cynical Phil, if they had that much money behind them.

He himself did not need to marry money. If he did not already have as much as the Goodmans, he was confident that he soon would.

What Phil wanted was respectability. Social acceptance. And they were things that the Goodmans had in abundance.

So he would have gone after Eve Goodman even if he hadn't liked her very much. But the truth was that he did like her. She was everything that his reason and his instinct told him he needed in a woman.

Did he love her? Did his passions rise when she approached? Not really. But that, he hoped, would come with time.

Cautiously, carefully, Phil began to court Eve Goodman. He felt almost as if he were a fisherman trying to pull in some fabulous catch with a fine, silken line. If he pulled too hard, the line might break; not hard enough and the baited hook might slip from the creature's mouth. Either way, the fisherman would lose.

Eve posed a similar problem. She was drawn to him—that much was evident. But at the same time she was frightened by his air of controlled strength. It was as though she couldn't make up her mind whether he represented a threat or a promise—or perhaps both.

At that time, Eve was a serious student at Vassar College, where she was majoring in political science. After she graduated, she told him on one of their earlier dates, she planned to get a Master's degree and then go into government service.

"Is that your father's idea?" Phil asked.

"No. It's mine!" Eve blushed. "Of course, he's all for it. . . ."

"Of course," Phil said with a tolerant smile.

To avoid making her more nervous than he had to, Phil led into the subject of marriage by painstakingly slow degrees. At first they were just good friends. It was only after they had known each other for several months that he began to make oblique references to some sort of shared future.

Nor did he try very hard to get the girl into bed with him.

He was gentle with her—kissed her, stroked her—but that was all. Though he knew in his bones he could have had her if he tried, he would not take advantage.

Later—after they were officially engaged—Eve confessed to him that she had once had an affair.

"It was last summer," she said. "A boy I met at the country club. One night we both lost control. . . ."

"It doesn't matter," Phil stroked her long, silky black hair. "What matters is us. We mustn't do anything until it's right."

Eve turned her head to kiss him. She trusted him completely then. Her eyes held nothing but love and trust.

That conversation took place at the end of August—a week before the engagement was announced.

Phil was a bit nervous about what the judge's reaction might be when he told him that he wanted to marry his daughter. He knew the judge liked him—admired him—but he was also aware that he wanted very much for Eve to finish school.

What really frightened him was the possibility of the judge investigating his background. Despite Sid Walters's skill at covering traces, there was always a chance that Goodman might discover his connection to the Boccas.

Fortunately, however, the judge did not investigate. It would have smacked of spying—something that no honorable man wants anything to do with.

The matter of his daughter choosing not to finish college and having a career was something else again. This saddened both of Eve's parents.

But on the other hand, they would not stand in the way of her happiness.

"If this is what she really wants," the judge said sadly.

"Maybe it's for the best," said his wife.

She looked steadily at Phil.

"You *will* make her happy? . . ."

"I'll surely do my best," Phil said seriously. "I can promise you that."

The wedding was held on the sixth of December. It was a big, beautiful wedding—a society wedding—one of the great weddings of the season.

Afterward, the bride and groom were driven to Newark

Airport where they caught a DC3 to Miami Beach where they would honeymoon.

Phil would have perferred going to Bermuda or Cuba. But that was out, of course. The threat of U-boats had ruled out all ocean pleasure travel.

They would be there that very evening. They would take a moonlight swim as a brand-new married couple. . . .

Coda
December 7, 1941

49

Philip Aronson II—Papa, the Old Man, the lost leader of the
Aronson Clan—was reclining on his bed.

It was about two-thirty on a Sunday afternoon. Not that this
made much difference to Mr. Aronson. He did not get very
excited about the days of the week any more, or the hours of
the day.

His days went pretty much the same now—unless his
daughter happened to be at home, that is. He would get up in
the morning, exchange some words with his wife, and pick at
his breakfast of cooked white rice made with sugar and milk.
Afterward, he would go back into his room to rest until lunch—
which would be a bowl of soup, toast, and coffee. Then it was
back into bed until dinner. And so on.

When Naomi was there, he would vary his routine in order
to spend some time with her. Naomi was the only person, these
days, who could arouse a spark of interest in him. But today,
Naomi was not there.

What did he do with all those hours in bed? The ones
between breakfast and lunch, lunch and supper, supper and
breakfast. He dreamed, mostly. He did not necessarily sleep,
simply dreamed.

He dreamed of the past. He rearranged it, strengthened his
own role in it and dreamed of the past as it should have been.

Today he was dreaming of early 1933 again. One of his
favorite periods—when his wife was as loving as she was
beautiful, when his oldest son was only a rebellious teenager,
and when the fine men's clothing store of Aronson and Son
was still in business.

The day he was dreaming was an important one. And the
fact that it had never taken place outside his dreams made it
even more important.

He was in his office in the store now. He had a sudden
hunch—one of those brilliant hunches which a man has to

listen to. He picked up his telephone and called Thomas Leyland, his account executive at the Greystock Bank and Trust Company.

"No!" he said to Thomas Leyland. "I *won't* go to lunch with you to discuss those rumors! I have a strong hunch about this! I'm taking my money *out! I'm withdrawing all of it!*"

And this he did. And so the business was saved. And so he was saved. . . .

The radio was on in the living-room and the harsh tones of some announcer came faintly into his room. The announcer was saying something about Hawaii.

If the store did well, he would take his wife to Hawaii some day. He might even bring his two youngest children along—Bob and Naomi.

Not the older boy, though. Not his firstborn. Philip III had become stubborn and disobedient. Sometimes he even acted as if he thought he was the boss of the family—the bread-winner—instead of his father. . . .

Sophie Aronson, then, had her radio tuned to a station with soft background music—mindless music, really—which enabled her to direct her thoughts to other things. Right now, she was thinking about a fifty-eight-year-old widower named Myron Hoech who happened to be a cousin of one of Sophie's female friends.

He was a very nice man, Mr. Hoech. Tall and distinguished, with silver hair and a handsome face. And furthermore, Sophie was certain that he liked her.

And why shouldn't he like her? She was still a handsome woman. Her hips hadn't spread like those of most females her age. There was little excess flesh on her stomach. Her breasts looked like those of a woman ten—maybe even fifteen—years younger.

So if she should decide to have an affair with him, he would be a very lucky man

But they were still at the crossroads. He hadn't asked her, yet. And she hadn't decided whether to encourage him to ask.

She was trying to decide if Myron Hoech was looking for a wife and only for a wife. If so, it would be wiser not to start in with him.

Sophie Aronson had long since made up her mind to stay with her husband. And she would not leave him now—not for the most eligible of widowers. She had made a commitment when she married, and she meant to abide by that commitment.

Many of her friends thought she was foolish; and she herself had moments of doubt. She was only too well aware of how little in common the whining, self-indulgent, day-dreaming wreck in the bedroom had with the strong, young lover she'd married.

But that didn't matter. She would have stayed with her husband if he'd been incapacitated by a terrible illness. Couldn't his childlike behavior—his terrifying retreat into a world of make-believe—be considered an illness?

And so she would not leave him.

Lovers were something else again. She'd had several since 1933—decent men who filled lonely hours in her life as she helped to fill the loneliness in theirs. She was a woman, after all. She needed the comfort of a man. And she had not been comforted by her husband in more than eight and a half years.

But all the same, he was her husband.

Sophie decided to let the future take care of Myron Hoech. If he didn't insist on taking over her life it could be very nice with him. Otherwise?... She gave a mental shrug.

Her thoughts drifted to her son, Phil, and the girl he had married in that beautiful ceremony yesterday.

Sophie approved of Eve Goodman. She was bright, attractive, and had a mind of her own. Just the sort of girl Phil needed.

There was no doubt in Sophie's mind, however, that Phil would wear the pants in the family. He was strong, her son. Stronger that his father had been, even in the wild, strong days of his youth.

Suddenly, she was brought out of her reverie. The soft music on the radio had stopped and the announcer was saying something incredible about a place called Pearl Harbor—about a sneak attack on American forces there by planes of the Japanese Navy.

It was war, Sophie realized with a sinking feeling in the pit of her stomach. War...

And her sons? Phil... Bob... what was going to happen to them, now?...

When Bob Aronson heard the news he was in a one-room apartment in Washington, D.C. He had a job in that city with the War Department.

It was Judge Goodman who had found him the job—right

after Bob had passed his Bar examination. He hadn't wanted to accept anything from his brother's future father-in-law, but the judge had talked as if he were doing the War Department a favor.

"The government's going to need some very good people," the judge explained. "Most of the top law-school graduates are trying for clerkships with important judges, or knocking on the doors of the famous law firms. Not too many go with the forces—unless they happened to be inducted, that is."

The judge paused to chuckle.

"What's your draft status, by the way? You're not going to do your year right away, are you?"

"My number won't be called up for a while yet," Bob replied.

"Good." The judge emphasized his satisfaction with a nod. "Meanwhile, you can serve your country by working for the War Department."

So it was settled. Bob went to Washington.

Yesterday he had taken the train up to New York to attend his brother's wedding. But now he was back again—going over some work he had taken home Friday night.

As his mother did in New York City, Bob switched on his radio in order to play some background music which was interrupted by the news of the Japanese attack.

He felt as though he were in shock. Not only because of the attack, but at the extent of its success. It sounded as if the whole damn Pacific Fleet had been destroyed.

He made a phone call to a friend at the War Department, but nobody picked up the receiver at the other end.

He felt he couldn't stay cooped up any longer inside this room.

He went outside where he found a number of other men as angry and upset as he was. He became involved in a discussion about where to find a recruiting office.

Naomi Aronson was told about the bombing of Pearl Harbor by another girl at school.

She had been alone in her room, sulking over something she had just found out about. The swimming coach had let it slip that it was her brother, Phil, who'd put up the money for the school swimming pool. The fact that she loved to swim and was one of the stars of the team made her feel even more pissed off by the revelation.

Why wouldn't Phil just go away someplace and stay out of her life?

It was when she had worked herself up to a fine fury of frustration that Ruth Solby burst into her room.

"Hey, Solby," she said. "Don't you ever knock?"

"Up yours," the other girl said. "I thought you might want to hear about the Japs."

"What about them?"

"They bombed Pearl Harbor."

"Huh?"

"They bombed Pearl Harbor," Ruth Solby insisted. "In Hawaii. It's war!"

Ruth Solby spun on her heels and ran from the room. There were still other girls that she might be the first to tell.

Naomi stared at the half-closed door and let the facts slowly sink in to her mind. She thought about how they might affect herself and her family. She had a strange feeling that her brother Phil was going to make some money out of the situation.

Phil Aronson was resting on a reclining beach chair. His wife, Eve, was on the chair next to him.

Before they had made this first foray into the Miami Beach sun, Eve had insisted on smearing a heavy, protective lotion on all the exposed sections of their bodies. Phil normally didn't use the stuff. It felt uncomfortably greasy and he didn't like the smell. Furthermore, he didn't think he needed it. His skin was the sort that tanned without burning.

But when Eve insisted, that had been it. He allowed her to rub it into his back and shoulders, while he put it on his own hairy chest and legs and on the belly which was just starting to grow an embarrassing layer of fat. Eve had suggested putting a bit of the lotion on his bald spot as well. But Phil drew the line at that. It was still a fairly small spot—just slightly larger than a silver dollar—and he could protect it the same way he disguised it, by combing his hair over it.

Eve was something, though, he thought now. She was quite a woman, his new wife. He had found that out last night. While her single premarital affair had left her still awkward and inexperienced (Phil would have been upset if that had *not* been the case), she had a warmly passionate nature and was as anxious to learn as Phil was to teach.

They didn't fall asleep until after two last night. And when

Phil woke up at nine-thirty in the morning, it was with Eve's gentle fingers fluttering at his crotch.

He smiled happily. It was one terrific life. He was twenty-six years old, already a captain of industry, and had a beautiful woman who damned near worshipped him!

He wondered what the guys he grew up with thought about when they saw his name in the papers, now. Guys like Harry Engels who was still probably working with his old man in their neighborhood stationery store.

Engels probably thought he was lucky. That's what most people felt. That success was mostly a matter of luck.

Phil believed he knew better. Sure, luck came into it, but so did a lot of other things—like guts and shrewdness and a determination to make your own luck!

He smiled again. It was one terrific life, all right. And unless he missed his guess, his future was going to be brighter than his past.

He closed his eyes contentedly, and was beginning to doze off when a beach attendant came from the hotel with news of Pearl Harbor.

Even as he digested the announcement, Phil's mind began to churn.

War! . . . It was finally a reality. It would mean many conflicting things to many different people. To him—to the head of Aronson Foods—it would mean a challenge and an opportunity.

He turned to his wife to explain that their plans had changed. They were going to go back to New York on the next available flight.

Bestselling Books for Today's Reader

Bestsellers you've been hearing about—and want to read